PAPER DRAGONS

THE FIGHT FOR THE HIDDEN REALM

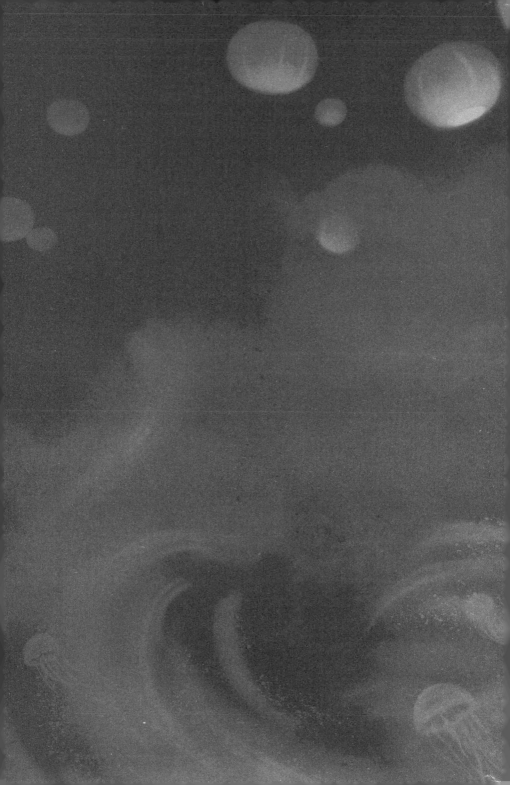

PAPER DRAGONS

THE FIGHT FOR THE HIDDEN REALM

SIOBHAN McDERMOTT

麥舒雲

DELACORTE PRESS

Text copyright © 2024 by Siobhan McDermott Ltd.
Jacket art copyright © 2024 by Vivienne To

GetUnderlined.com

Educators and librarians, for a variety of teaching tools, visit us at RHTeachersLibrarians.com

Library of Congress Cataloging-in-Publication Data is available upon request.
ISBN 978-0-593-70611-4 (trade) — ISBN 978-0-593-70612-1 (lib. bdg.) — ISBN 978-0-593-70613-8 (ebook) — ISBN 978-0-593-80926-6 (int'l ed.)

The text of this book is set in 11.5-point Calisto MT Pro.
Interior design by Michelle Crowe

Printed in the United States of America
10 9 8 7 6 5 4 3 2 1
First American Edition

For Blathnaid,
who patiently sat through, and improved,
every version of Zhi Ging's story

PROLOGUE

The figure paused and glanced again at the instructions scrawled across his palm, marveling at how small it looked now that his talons were gone. Apart from a pair of moths fluttering around the threadbare lantern, the street was deserted. He shifted the basket to his elbow, and his pale skin rippled, stretching to wrap his body in a heavy black cloak. A low hood dropped over his face before he slid the screen door open.

The village healer stood from her position by the hearth, a wizened hand pressed against the wall for support.

"Well, come in then. Or were you waiting for the moonlight to take the first step?" She chuckled, gesturing toward the table.

The man placed the basket on its scuffed surface while the healer ambled over with two cups, then pushed one toward him. He lifted the amber liquid to his nose, breathing in its heady jasmine scent, then lowered the cup back down, untouched.

She raised an eyebrow before sipping her own tea.

"That's fine, no need to drink it. But do I at least get a name? I assume you already know mine's Aapau, and it only seems fair to trade."

The figure shifted uncomfortably, then shook his head, tapping the basket.

"Suit yourself."

Aapau turned away, her hands focused on untangling a thin copper wire from the braid wrapped around her head. She twirled it between her fingers, then slid the wire into a thin crack in the side of the table. A wooden panel sprang open, and the healer lifted out a rectangular bundle wrapped in faded strips of silk. She unraveled the cloth to reveal a book made entirely of glass.

Aapau caught the man's eyes, her own sparkling as firelight glinted against the pages.

"Fei Chui is a village of Glassmiths. It took generations for us to learn how to harness dragons' lightning and turn sand into glass." She snapped a blank page out from the end of the book and leaned forward, her expression suddenly serious. "Before we start, I need to know you understand what you're risking. Once it's in the book, that's it. There's no way to break the contract. Are you sure you want to go ahead?"

He paused, glanced across at the basket, and breathed a silent *yes*. Before the word even had a chance to form, Aapau launched herself forward, snatching the air in front of him and then slamming it hard against the thin sheet of glass.

The man's eyes shot down, but instead of having broken into shards, the glass now had a smooth indent, roughly the size of a coin. Aapau snorted at his shocked expression before patting him reassuringly on the arm.

"Sorry about that. I didn't want to risk the agreement escaping and diffusing across the room. We couldn't have continued without it."

He gaped at her, wondering if she really was as old and frail as she seemed. Aapau peered at him out of the corner of her eye, as if reading his thoughts.

"Oh, I'm definitely as decrepit as I look. Age has just made me exceptionally good at what I do."

She held up the page and inspected it closely.

"Good to see you meant that 'yes' too—a lie would have shattered the glass. I've wasted far too many pages on half-truths. Glass doesn't forget," she continued. "It keeps a record of what's owed. If a year passes without payment, your page will start to flush red. At the same time, your hand will begin to prickle. That heat will keep rising until the payment is settled. Now, would you prefer to pay annually or . . ." Aapau trailed off as the figure dropped a heavy pouch on the table. In the flickering light, it looked like it was filled with hundreds of gleaming metallic fireflies. Aapau plucked out one of the coins, the soft gold warming between her fingers.

"Wah, impressive! This is more than enough to cover a lifetime."

She bent down and lowered the page into the hearth's smoldering embers. Golden flames roared up, encasing her hand and the glass in a crackling sphere. A warm yellow glow bloomed from the center of the glass. Just before it reached her fingertips, Aapau pulled the page out and the fire vanished back into the coals. She snatched up the copper ribbon and scrawled on the molten glass, words gliding across the shimmering surface. Aapau looked up, and her eyes darted around the room.

"Why are you suddenly skulking in the corner? You're needed for this part!"

The man inched forward, never taking his eyes off the embers. Aapau grabbed his left hand and pressed his thumb firmly into the glass indent. There was a faint hiss as his skin touched the surface. Once Aapau let go, he slipped his hand back into his cloak pocket. She peered at him and tutted.

"*Aiyah,* you're as white as a sheet—not that you had much color to start with. Make sure to drink that tea before you leave, it always helps. And don't worry about your thumb, it'll heal soon enough," Aapau continued cheerfully. She pressed the page into the book, expertly fusing it against the glass spine. Once the copper wire had been twisted back into her braid, she lifted the basket's blankets.

The baby was smaller than Aapau had expected, large brown eyes filling her face. Like everyone else in Fei Chui, she had thick black hair and warm sandy skin. Peering closer, Aapau realized the girl's eyes weren't just a deep shade of brown. They were the iridescent black of a starling's feather. The baby gurgled, chewing on a crumpled scrap of paper. Aapau eased it out of her hand, but the message had already run, purple ink seeping across the note's surface.

"What was on this? Does she already have a name?" Aapau demanded, waving the sodden note under the man's hood. He blinked sheepishly, then shrugged, unsure.

Aapau shook her head in exasperation, then lifted the baby up, dabbing at the stains around her mouth.

"You'll be a Yeung, of course. All babies brought to us from beneath the cloud sea are given that surname. Hmm, how about Zhi Ging? You don't hear that name much anymore, but I've always liked it." Aapau smiled down at her. "I can already tell you'll bring it back."

Zhi Ging wriggled cheerfully in Aapau's arms while the healer turned back toward the hooded figure.

"Is there anything you can tell me? They always ask questions when they're older. At least tell me which of the six provinces she's from."

He shook his head and backed awkwardly toward the door.

"Go on, then. There's no more need for you now anyway."

The figure nodded and slipped out the door without even a goodbye wave to Zhi Ging.

"What a strange man," Aapau murmured. "Silly thing didn't even drink his tea in the end."

Her hand stopped just before it closed around his untouched cup. The tea leaves swirled wildly, soaring and colliding beneath the surface. Aapau spun around and hurried out onto the street, but he had already vanished.

It was only when he reached the cliff bordering Fei Chui that the man eased his hand out of his pocket. The thumb Aapau had pressed into the glass had disappeared, long since crumbling to ash. He watched the smoldering line creep across his hand, transforming everything it touched to delicate wisps that floated away in the breeze.

The hypnotic glow flickered over the purple instructions on his palm, and he smiled. He'd carried out his purpose; there really was no need for him now.

Within seconds, the dawn sky began to glimmer through his cloak. The air filled with the crackle of burning paper, and what was left of the man fragmented into a thousand pieces. Through the flurry, there was a glimpse of scales, and the paper dragon's shadow stretched thin across the clouds as he swept back toward the horizon.

CHAPTER 1

Z hi Ging scowled up at the glass dragon blocking
her way. *Since when does the Lead Glassmith lock his
office door? Why is he making it so difficult to break in?*

The glass door had been designed to look like a coiling
dragon, and its body curled from ceiling to floor in a protective circle, its head snarling out at her from the center.

Zhi Ging flicked its snout in frustration, and a hollow
chime echoed across the Glassmiths' workshop. The dragon's long whiskers jangled together, and she flung her arms
around them to muffle the sound. Curled glass pressed uncomfortably against her sleeves, but Zhi Ging couldn't risk
moving until the noise stopped. The last thing she needed
was a curious Glassmith catching her before she had a
chance to find the letter.

The predawn haze was doing little to help, filtering
down the corridor like a spotlight on her break-in attempt.
She groaned and ran a hand along the dragon's overlapping

scales. Any one of them could be the switch needed to unlock the door.

Fei Chui, the village Zhi Ging had grown up in, was set to announce its new Silhouette at noon, but she couldn't wait until then. Not when she knew Iridill would be watching, ready to pounce if her name wasn't called. Visions of the Lead Glassmith's sneering daughter flashed across Zhi Ging's mind, and she shuddered. No, she wouldn't give Iridill the satisfaction. If she found out now that she hadn't been chosen, she could at least hide her disappointment later.

Zhi Ging frowned and shut her eyes, head pressed against the glass in concentration. The dragon's carved face was ice-cold beneath her forehead, and she grimaced. Training as a Silhouette was her only chance to escape Fei Chui. If someone else was picked, the Lead Glassmith would force her to spend the rest of her life trapped inside glass much colder than this. Now that Aapau was gone, no one would stop him from sending her into the post pipe, her chances of drowning creeping up with each minute she spent squeezed inside that narrow, water-filled space.

Zhi Ging straightened up and winced when she opened her eyes. A large smudge had appeared on the dragon's polished glass, marking the exact spot where her forehead had rested on its surface. *So much for a stealth break in!* The Lead Glassmith might not care about her, but he would definitely notice if there was anything different about his precious door. She tugged her sleeve over her palm, ready to wipe the smudge away, and froze. *If pressing my forehead against the glass left a mark, maybe . . .*

Zhi Ging took a deep, steadying breath and exhaled gently over the dragon's glass face. Her eyes darted between the soft pale clouds that bloomed across its surface.

There!

Faint fingerprints had appeared on one of the dragon's spiraling whiskers, revealing how the Lead Glassmith entered his office each morning.

"And you thought you could keep me out." She beamed, pulling the whisker down. The dragon jolted to life, and scales chimed against one another as it uncoiled around the doorframe. The faint clicks of whirling glass cogs rippled along the length of the dragon, and its long body stretched tight against the corridor wall.

Zhi Ging slipped inside. There was a faint rumble behind her, and the dragon curled back into its protective circle, plunging the office into an eerie gloom.

Centuries earlier, another Lead Glassmith had stumbled across a shed dragon skin and draped it around the ceiling beams. Over time, the scales had dried and faded to a milky opal until you could almost mistake them for fused shards of glass. But no glass would make a Glassmith's hair blaze with crackling white light. Only dragon scales could do that.

For Zhi Ging though, there wasn't even a hint of static along her braid. She puffed out her cheeks and tried to squash down the all-too-familiar pang of frustration. Why was she the only person in Fei Chui whose hair didn't glow near dragons or dragon scales?

The muffled sound of footsteps bustling past the door jolted her back to her mission. Zhi Ging hurried across the sand-covered floor, wincing in pain when her foot hit the Lead Glassmith's desk. Letters fluttered to the ground, and she scrambled after them, peering closely at each one before tossing it aside. Every faint sound on the other side of the door added to the nerves already bubbling in her stomach.

She yelped in excitement when she finally spotted an ornate envelope flecked with gold. Heart pounding, Zhi Ging pulled a glass hairpin out from the top of her braid. Her shoulders hunched in concentration while she eased the slim edge under the seal, tensed for the sound of wax snapping in half. Time slowed as the glass pushed forward, and there was a faint pop when the seal came loose in a single piece. Zhi Ging hugged the hairpin tight between her hands before sliding it back into her braid. It might not have been what Aapau intended when she'd gifted it, but Zhi Ging couldn't help feeling her old guardian would have been proud.

Despite the darkness, the letter seemed to glow, a narrow triangle of white shimmering up from the opened envelope. She wiped her hand against her loose green trousers, suddenly worried her fingers would mark the spotless paper. Whoever was picked as Silhouette would spend the next year training in Hok Woh, the Cyo B'Ahon's hidden realm, learning the skills needed to become immortal. If she passed her Silhouette year, not even the Lead Glassmith could force her back to Fei Chui and into the post pipe. Zhi Ging's eyes skimmed across the handwriting, both dreading and desperate to reach the chosen name.

The letter fell from her hands.

Behind her, the glass door chimed again and the room filled with a soft pearly light. The Lead Glassmith stepped inside, followed closely by a second man, but Zhi Ging barely noticed them. Her eyes were glued to the letter that now lay on the ground.

In the newly lit room, the name on the paper was impossible to miss. Nothing existed apart from that name. The person chosen as Silhouette, promised a chance at immortality, blazed up from the white page:

Iridill

CHAPTER 2

"Miss Yeung! What do you think you're doing?" The Lead Glassmith snatched the letter from the floor, brushing specks of sand from its surface.

Zhi Ging glanced past him in a daze and spotted Reishi, the Silhouette Scout, looking at her with concern. He was in the same official yellow robes he'd worn a week earlier on the day of her exam, and the long-necked crane embroidered across his chest seemed to stare accusingly at her. Zhi Ging looked away, still unused to seeing him look so formal. She had to force herself to remember that he was the same Reishi who had, on multiple visits, knocked entire bowls of congee over himself in his enthusiasm to tell Aapau about his latest discovery. *He looks much less intimidating when his knees are poking out through Aapau's spare robe.*

"Well, explain yourself. You better have a very good reason to be standing in my office," the Lead Glassmith snapped. "The upper levels of the jade mountain are sacred and reserved for Glassmiths. Aapau may have raised you but that doesn't mean you have the same privileges as the village healer."

"I know, I only wanted to find out if I'd—" Zhi Ging's eyes flickered toward the letter, and she bit her tongue.

The Lead Glassmith followed her gaze and snorted.

"I should have guessed." He lowered his voice to a snide whisper. "Honestly, just because Aapau was old friends with Reishi, did you really think *you* would be chosen as Fei Chui's Silhouette?"

Angry tears threatened to blur Zhi Ging's vision, but she held his gaze.

"Why not? I studied as hard as Iridill, she—"

"Is everything all right?" Reishi strode forward, frowning as he stepped between Zhi Ging and the Lead Glassmith. The two silk pouches that hung from his belt swished from side to side as he moved, the rustling sound reminding Zhi Ging of a bird's wings in flight.

The Lead Glassmith sprang back and ran a distracted hand through his wispy beard, sending sparks flying between his fingers. Not for the first time, Zhi Ging couldn't help but imagine a glowing dandelion attacking the lower half of his face.

"Absolutely fine. I do apologize for this *unexpected* interruption to our search. I assure you your jade stone will—"

"Please," Zhi Ging blurted out. She looked desperately at Reishi. "I want—I *need* to be picked as Silhouette so much more than Iridill. More than anyone in Fei Chui. Now that the Lead Glassmith's sent Aapau away for her Final Year, they're going to get rid of me too. He said I can't stay in her house by myself, but none of the Glassmiths will take me on as an apprentice, not when my hair doesn't glow. Aapau made him promise I'd be all right after she left, but he lied! They're going to send me into the post pipe, even though the last two post pipe scrubbers drowned in their first month."

"Utter nonsense! The child is simply upset she hasn't been chosen," the Lead Glassmith said, the glass beads that covered his robes jangling loudly as he waved away her claims. Reishi held up a hand and bent down until he was eye to eye with Zhi Ging.

"I'm sorry, Zhi Ging. Truly. I know from Aapau just how hard you studied, but there's nothing I can do once the final name has been chosen. Scouts have strict, thousand-year-old rules on Silhouette selection, and we can only invite one candidate from each town or village." He paused, trying to find a way to soften the blow. "Perhaps you could take the entrance exam again next year? I probably shouldn't say this, but if you hadn't run out of time for that final question, my Silhouette choice would have been much more difficult."

Zhi Ging sniffed and smiled weakly while the Lead Glassmith glared at her over Reishi's shoulder. *Will I even make it to next year once I'm in the post pipe?*

Reishi straightened up and turned to face the Lead

Glassmith, who quickly hid his scowl behind an unctuous smile.

"I hope you don't plan on punishing Zhi Ging for her enthusiasm. In fact, I'm pleased to see the chance to be trained by Cyo B'Ahon like myself still holds this much excitement in Fei Chui. It's refreshing. Now," he continued, a commanding tone sliding into his voice, "it's about time we met with the Glassmiths searching for my missing jade. It would be *such* a disappointment if I had to return to Hok Woh in the morning without it."

The Lead Glassmith paled.

"They're gathered by the lower terraces now," he croaked. "We'll find it ahead of your farewell feast. I guarantee tonight's celebrations won't begin until we do." The Lead Glassmith hurried toward the door and pressed against a glass scale, tapping his foot impatiently while the dragon unfurled. Reishi followed after him but paused at the entrance. He turned back to face Zhi Ging, the embroidered bird shimmering on his robe.

"I'll be back next year. I promise."

ZHI GING WAS TRUDGING BACK ALONG THE CORRI-dor when she spotted the figure smirking at her from the courtyard.

Iridill.

The girl's smile widened at Zhi Ging's swollen red eyes, and she strode forward, the colorful glass beads stitched across her clothes glinting in the light. Not for the first time, Zhi Ging felt a sharp twinge of jealousy. Her own robe had only a single clouded bead, gifted to her by Aapau on the healer's final day in Fei Chui.

"Well, NoGlow, aren't you going to congratulate me?" Iridill held a paper lantern in her hands, its surface covered in scrawling calligraphy. The unmistakable outline of her silhouette had been cut into one side, and she spun the lantern around to admire it. "Once Reishi lights this for me at noon, I'm leaving for Hok Woh. Maybe I'll visit you after I've graduated from Silhouette to full immortal Cyo B'Ahon." Iridill's eyebrows knit together in mock concern. "Although, you probably won't have much space to wave back from inside the post pipe. Those glass pipes get incredibly narrow, don't they?"

Zhi Ging's hands clenched into fists. Her nails pressed down, leaving angry half-moons across her palm while she forced back the insults raring to hurl themselves at Iridill. *It isn't worth it.*

Iridill glanced down at Zhi Ging's hands and smirked.

"Are you actually surprised you weren't picked? No one even wants you here in Fei Chui, NoGlow. So why would anyone want you in Hok Woh?"

Zhi Ging stepped forward, despite barely coming up to Iridill's shoulders.

"Just because your hair glows and mine doesn't, how does that make me any different to anyone living beneath the cloud sea. Even your brother—"

Iridill's mouth twisted into a furious snarl. "Don't you *dare* compare yourself to him," she hissed, cutting Zhi Ging off. "If you don't drown in the post pipe, I hope the Fui Gwai gets you." She leaned forward, pleased to see the sudden fear in Zhi Ging's eyes. "I heard the spirit has started preying on villages right beneath the cloud sea, turning even more people into mindless thralls. Once you're trapped in the post pipe, you'll be its easiest possession ever."

"What's going on here?"

The two girls spun around to see a senior Glassmith marching toward them.

"Murrine!" Iridill trilled, her bottom lip suddenly shaking in fake terror. "NoGl— Zhi Ging was threatening to summon the Fui Gwai to curse all Glassmiths. She's so jealous I was picked as Silhouette that she wants to punish the entire village!"

Zhi Ging drew in a sharp breath, stunned by the viciousness of Iridill's latest lie. Although Aapau had tried to shield her from the stories, whispers had spread between the Glassmiths of a prowling spirit, known only as the Fui Gwai, attacking villagers right across the glass province. While the spirit's existence was officially no more than a rumor, this was worse than if Iridill had accused her of plotting to burn down Fei Chui.

Zhi Ging opened her mouth to argue as Iridill sidled past the Glassmith, but one look at Murrine's pinched expression forced her to grit her teeth together in silence. She knew from bitter experience that no one in Fei Chui would ever believe her over the Lead Glassmith's daughter.

"Young lady, the Fui Gwai is no joke," Murrine barked. "Spirit summoning of any kind is forbidden in our province. Even *threats* of summoning must be reported to the Lead Glassmith. Come with me."

A flustered Glassmith came racing across the courtyard, his shoes sending sand flying around him.

"Murrine, didn't you get my message? All senior Glassmiths have been summoned to scour the glass terraces for Reishi's missing jade."

"How are we meant to find the right stone when our entire mountain's made from jade?" Murrine grumbled, Zhi Ging instantly forgotten as he hurried after the other Glassmith.

"Look for his Cyo B'Ahon seal on its surface," the flustered Glassmith urged, thrusting a crumpled scroll toward Murrine. The illustration's still-damp ink glinted in the light, and Zhi Ging caught a glimpse of Reishi's seal—two golden cranes circling one another in flight.

She stared after them, her mind whirring while the two men raced out toward the glass terraces. Maybe she had one last chance to make it as a Silhouette after all. If the stone really was that important to Reishi as the Silhouette Scout, maybe she could trade it for a place in Hok Woh.

All Zhi Ging had to do was find it before anyone else.

CHAPTER 3

Zhi Ging shivered and inched farther along the concealed mountain path. An icy fog had settled earlier that night, and the cold was seeping through the soles of her cloth shoes. She had spent the entire day searching the terraces and was beginning to worry. What if one of the Glassmiths had already found the jade stone? Had she missed her chance?

She turned and tried to spot the bright lights of the workshop below her, sighing with relief when all she could see was an unending soft dappled gray. Since Reishi had arrived a fortnight ago, there had been nightly feasts in the Lead Glassmith's private wing. Packed with Glassmiths hoping to speak with the Cyo B'Ahon, the entire place would glow, its iridescent glass walls twinkling like a jewel fused to the mountainside. No lights meant the Glassmiths were still searching.

Zhi Ging clambered farther up, careful not to step off the path and onto an empty terrace. The glass terraces were flat platforms cut into the upper half of the jade mountain, some several meters deep. Glassmiths would create complex designs by pouring different colored sands into the hollow terraces before luring dragons toward them, channeling their lightning through copper rods to transform the sand into shimmering panels of glass. When dawn caught against the newly fused glass, it would drape the mountain in a patchwork quilt of blazing light, fragments of sky captured in the jade.

There was a muffled grunt up ahead, and Zhi Ging froze, her heart pounding. What if it was a spirit? What if the Fui Gwai had finally reached Fei Chui? A solitary figure loomed out of the fog, and she clamped her hands over her eyes, knowing from ghost stories that eyes were always the Fui Gwai's first target.

"Zhi Ging? What are you doing up here?"

She peeked through a small gap between her fingers and spotted a bemused-looking Reishi walking toward her. She lowered her hands sheepishly, embarrassed by how quickly she'd panicked. Stupid really. After all, the only real danger this high up were dragons, and they never hunted in fog. Their eyesight wasn't strong enough for anything other than clear, cloudless nights.

"Uh, I'm . . . trying to find your jade stone," she admitted and, taking a deep breath, added, "and, I'd like to swap it for a place as a Silhouette."

Reishi's eyebrows shot up in amusement.

"Well, I think it's safe to say I've never met anyone as

determined to be a Silhouette as you, Zhi Ging. And this is coming from a Scout who's waded through seven centuries worth of intense, and often illegible, exam scrolls." His smile faded. "But I'm sorry, I really can't invite anyone else from Fei Chui for the next twelve months. Cyo B'Ahon have strict rules on equal invitations for a reason. We can't be seen to favor any village, town, or city across the six provinces."

"But I'm not really from Fei Chui," Zhi Ging cried. "You know I wasn't born here. What if I'm from somewhere that hasn't been visited by a Silhouette Scout yet?"

"Or you could just as easily be from one of the countless places that's already sent someone to Hok Woh this year." Reishi shook his head. "Go home before you get into any more trouble, Zhi Ging. There are four Glassmiths still searching these terraces for my stone, I'm sure one of them will find it soon."

"But they've been searching for hours now. What if I find it before them?"

"Even if you did, I still couldn't—" Reishi began, but Zhi Ging darted back into the fog before she could hear the rest of his answer.

AN HOUR LATER, ZHI GING REACHED THE JADE mountain's highest terrace and frowned down through the fog. The sunken space was filled with swirling shades of fine sand, with a few jade pebbles scattered across its surface. If Reishi's stone wasn't here, she'd have to restart her search. Zhi Ging sighed, heavy fog closing in above her as she stepped into the terrace and crouched to gather the pebbles. She flipped over one of the larger pieces of jade in her palm and yelped.

She'd found it!

A gold seal with two cranes circling an ornate *R* shimmered up at her.

"I knew I'd find you," she whispered, brushing grains of sand from its surface. "Iridill can say what she wants about my hair, but I can do anything a Glassmith can—" She broke off with a gasp, her left thumb pulsing with a sudden, sharp pain. Zhi Ging jerked back, the stone dropping to the terrace with a dull thud.

It had almost felt like a paper cut, but when she squeezed the tip of her thumb, there was no sign she'd been hurt.

Zhi Ging snatched the stone back up before anyone else reached the terrace and lifted it in triumph, sand cascading down her arm. There was a faint plink, and her glass hairpin slipped out of her braid and rolled into a corner of the terrace. Zhi Ging bent to pick it up, then froze, her shadow stretching out in front of her.

Her *shadow.*

How was there enough light to cast a shadow in this fog? The entire terrace was bathed in a bright glow, even her faint trail of footprints now visible in the sand. In a daze, Zhi Ging raised her free hand toward her head. Her fingers caught in a fizzing white light, static flickering over her hand when she touched her hair.

Her hair was glowing!

The brief burst of excitement curdled almost immediately and was replaced by a troubling thought. There was only ever one reason for someone's hair to glow: being near dragons or dragon scales. But there were no dragon scales in the terrace, which meant—

Zhi Ging spun around and found herself staring up into rows of gleaming teeth.

A dragon loomed over her, each scale on its scarred body larger than her face. Its heavy talons scratched against the terrace, sending sparks skittering across the sand. A piercing ball of white lightning crackled between its jaws, and the dragon coiled its wiry tail behind Zhi Ging, cutting off her escape route. Her entire body howled at her to run, but she couldn't move. The paralyzing fear coursing through her was so powerful she couldn't even open her mouth to scream.

The dragon leaned down, and its long whiskers sparked against her face. The jolt shocked Zhi Ging out of her frozen panic, and she leaped sideways, scrambling as fast as she could for the path. She dove behind a boulder and curled into a tight protective ball around Reishi's stone just as the dragon unleashed its lightning.

The heat was unimaginable. From her hiding spot, she watched in horror as her hairpin blazed white-hot, then shattered, her last birthday present from Aapau destroyed in an instant. Zhi Ging whimpered and burning air scalded her throat. Sand bubbled around her, forming shimmering pools of glass that threatened to spill over the terrace borders. An earsplitting crack boomed across the mountain, and the boulder, which had taken the full brunt of the lightning strike, crumbled. Fragments of molten rock hissed and spat while acrid steam surged over Zhi Ging. Panic ripped through her, and in her desperation to get away from what was left of the boulder, Zhi Ging slipped, plummeting backward into a lower terrace.

She screamed as she hit a layer of molten sand, the shock of the heat knocking every other thought from her mind. The sand washed over her, and a thin layer of dark glass began to fuse around her sleeve, trapping her left arm in place. She spluttered and fought to keep the rest of her body above the cooling glass. Not even a healer like Aapau could save someone with glass solidifying in their lungs.

The dragon snapped at the air, its tail swishing in frustration as it prowled toward her.

"Get away from me!" Zhi Ging hurled the jade at it in desperation, but the stone simply bounced against one of the dragon's horns to land back in the upper terrace. The air filled with crackling heat, and her vision blurred as more lightning swelled at the back of the dragon's throat.

Suddenly, a glowing white ribbon shot out from the darkness and wrapped itself around the dragon, wrenching it away from Zhi Ging. She blinked hard, strands of glass sticking to her still-glowing hair as she twisted to follow the ribbon. *Has the lightning already hit me? Is this what all Glassmiths see in the final seconds of a dragon attack?*

The dragon thrashed wildly and strands of light tore between its talons, but it couldn't escape the twisting ribbon. It roared as it was dragged away, mercury eyes locked on Zhi Ging, until the fog swept back across the mountain, obscuring her.

Zhi Ging could hear Reishi calling in the distance, but when she tried to cry out, her scorched voice came out as nothing more than a hoarse whimper. *What if the dragon comes back before he finds me?*

Her trapped hand began to prickle, and a pulsing light flashed beneath the warped glass. Sand spilled down from the upper terrace, and the jade stone tumbled toward her. The newly formed glass shattered beneath it like eggshell, and Zhi Ging hurried to pull herself free. Her sleeve tore against a shard of glass as she swung her arm back to the terrace, snatching up the stone and dropping it into her pocket.

"There you are!" An ashen-faced Reishi raced toward her, his silk robes swinging wildly as he stumbled along the charred path between the terraces.

"Are you all right? I saw it creeping toward you, but you couldn't hear me shout—"

"There she is! The spirit summoner!" Two Glassmiths were scrambling up the jade mountain toward them, beaded cloaks jangling as they jumped between the fractured terraces. Both had pulled their hoods low, only the lower halves of their faces visible beneath the dark glass beads.

"What are you talking about?" Zhi Ging croaked. "I was attacked by a dragon. Reishi, tell them."

"Liar!"

She flinched, recognizing Murrine's voice beneath the hood.

"I should have reported you immediately. You threatened to curse Fei Chui and now the Fui Gwai is here. Our hair did more than just glow like it does near dragons, that spirit's arrival seared a warning across all our scalps."

"We *saw* you release that cursed light, guiding it into our village!" the other Glassmith added.

"Cursed light?" asked Reishi, bewildered.

"You mean that white ribbon? I have no idea what that was, but it didn't have anything to do with me, I swear. How would I even do that?"

"Your hair was glowing. I saw it," Murrine spat, a copper rod clenched tight between his fists. "You have no Fei Chui ancestors. The only way your hair could do that is through spirit magic."

Two more Glassmiths appeared through the fog, hands gripped around their beaded hoods as they stalked toward Zhi Ging.

"Look at her arm! Let's see her try explaining *that* to the Lead Glassmith."

Zhi Ging glanced down and yelped in surprise. Her left sleeve hung loose, revealing an arm covered in delicate gold lines. The shining strands curled up from her palm, twisting past her elbow before coiling back on themselves.

"Everyone just needs to take a moment," Reishi cautioned, stepping in front of Zhi Ging to block her from the enraged Glassmiths. "We have a child here who just survived a dragon attack. Let's hold off on accusations until a healer has checked her for injuries, shall we?"

"And give her a chance to escape? What if she summons another spirit? Look at the damage she's already done to our jade mountain."

"I say we take her straight to the Lead Glassmith. Let him show the other provinces just how seriously Fei Chui takes the crime of spirit summoning."

"She should have been placed in the post pipe the second Aapau left," the closest Glassmith added, his voice thick with rage. "No one from outside Fei Chui can ever be trusted."

The others murmured in agreement, gnarled glass cracking beneath their feet as they closed in.

"Right, good to know there's no point trying to reason with you," Reishi sighed before turning back to Zhi Ging. "New plan," he whispered, looking pointedly above the Glassmiths toward a faint glowing point that seemed to grow brighter with each second. "Get ready to jump when I say so."

"What?" she hissed, her eyes never leaving the circling Glassmiths.

"Now!"

The ribbon burst back through the fog, and the Glassmiths scattered across the terraces, their copper rods sticking to the still-warm pools of liquid glass. Reishi leaped up, pulling Zhi Ging with him, and they grabbed on, fingers sinking between glowing threads of light.

Her breath caught in her throat as she was lifted off the ground, and Zhi Ging swiveled to stare open-mouthed at the mountain shrinking beneath her.

Their legs swung in the air as the ribbon twisted over the shouting Glassmiths and soared down toward the cloud sea on the edge of Fei Chui.

CHAPTER 4

When Zhi Ging was little, Aapau would bring her to play by the cloud sea's shore, careful never to let her sink beneath its soft, billowing surface.

Now, she and Reishi shot toward it, the white ribbon picking up speed as they sailed over rooftops and swooped toward the border. They released the ribbon and landed with a muffled thud at the brim of the cloud sea.

Zhi Ging staggered to her feet, clouds lapping against her ankles. Above her, the ribbon's light winked out, the glowing strands fading to black.

"Come on, they won't risk following us down." Reishi was already waist-deep in cloud, and she hurried to catch up with him. Just before the clouds reached her chin, Zhi Ging took one final breath of Fei Chui air and sank beneath the surface.

All movement slowed inside the cloud sea, and she was relieved to discover Aapau's old warnings had been greatly exaggerated. Although the cloud fizzed and tickled her lungs, breathing was no harder than anywhere else in Fei Chui. *I knew Aapau just didn't want me wading out too far!*

Reishi waved a languid hand, signaling the way through the clouds, and soft tendrils clung to his arm. Zhi Ging wriggled her own fingers, and small wisps puffed together like cotton in her palm. She blew the miniature clouds away, watching them bounce against one another, before following after Reishi.

All too soon, they emerged onto the cliff edge on the other side of the cloud sea. Zhi Ging felt her stomach lurch as she peered over the steep drop, her skin tingling after the chill of the clouds. This was, she realized numbly, the farthest she had ever traveled from Fei Chui. She had spent years dreaming about leaving the village but had never thought it would happen like this!

The dawn seemed more vivid here. Sunrise was always bleached by the time it reached Fei Chui, but now rich purples and crimsons filled the sky. Zhi Ging turned, watching the colors bloom across the clouds they had passed through.

"Are you sure they won't follow us?"

"Yes, the Glassmiths won't risk traveling past Fei Chui's protective border, especially if they think there's a chance of a spirit ambush on the other side." Reishi paused and crouched beside her. "More importantly, how's your arm?"

Zhi Ging bent it carefully, staring in awe at the thin gold lines, which glinted in the light. They were fainter now, as if they were sinking beneath her skin.

"I can still feel where the sand burned me, but these lines don't hurt at all. Did the dragon lightning do this?"

"No, dragon lightning is far too strong for that." Reishi shook his head, frowning at the gold. "If that had hit your arm, there would be nothing left but bone."

Zhi Ging shuddered, the dragon's white, crackling mouth flashing across her mind.

"Thanks for rescuing me," she murmured, tracing a finger across the lines. "If you hadn't released that ribbon . . ." She didn't even want to think about what punishment the Lead Glassmith would have had in store for a spirit summoner.

Reishi frowned. "That wasn't me. I had nothing to do with its appearance."

"Wait, what!?" she asked. "Then where did that thing come from?" She peered up at the sky, though the ribbon was long gone.

Reishi rubbed the back of his neck, lost in thought. "I wish I knew. It was a risk, grabbing on to it, but after it saved you from the dragon, I figured we'd rather take our chances with that than the Glassmiths." He glanced back toward the cloud sea swirling above them. "I have a feeling you won't be very welcome in Fei Chui right now. Let me speak with the Lead Glassmith, try to explain what really happened. In the meantime, I know someone who can look after you."

A burst of adrenaline shot through Zhi Ging, and she scrambled for the jade stone in her pocket.

This is it. My last chance.

"You don't need to talk to him. Right before *this*"—
Zhi Ging waved her gold-lined arm—"I found your stone.
So, just how valuable is it? I'll swap it for a place as a Sil-
houette."

Reishi's eyes widened and he thrust out his hand.

"Are you sure? Let's see its Cyo B'Ahon seal."

Her fingers closed around the jade, and a blistering
heat pulsed across its surface. Zhi Ging yelped, snatching
her hand out of her pocket. The stone caught against her
palm, and they watched in horror as it sailed over the cliff
edge. It glinted as it arced across the sky, but then, rather
than dropping, it spun and stopped to hover several feet
from the path.

"Impossible!" Reishi's jaw dropped open, and he hurried toward the cliff edge.

"I—I'm so sorry," Zhi Ging stammered. "I don't know
what happened. The stone suddenly—"

Reishi waved her apology aside and lifted a thick
branch from the path, swinging it toward the stone. It was
too short to reach, but his face lit up and Reishi gestured
for Zhi Ging to join him. Her stomach sank when she saw
what he was smiling at.

The post pipe.

Stretching down through the cloud sea to the rest of the
glass province, the post pipe had been created by a Lead
Glassmith decades earlier and was still considered one of
Fei Chui's most valuable inventions. Safer and faster than

any horse-drawn cart, the water-filled pipe carried letters and Glassmith commissions in waterproof mailbags. A bright dye would be added, transforming the glass pipe into a vibrant color-coded ribbon. Once the new color was spotted, people farther along the post pipe network would slide open various glass panels, allowing the mailbags to flow through the system until they reached their destination. It was all incredibly impressive.

Unless you were the one scrubbing it.

Those tasked with scrubbing every hint of dye from the glass between mailings never lasted long. The narrow, twisting pipes had led to countless drownings over the years.

Reishi, unaware of the sudden knots in Zhi Ging's stomach, smacked the side of the glass post pipe, watching the bubbles rise up through the water, back toward the cloud sea.

"I've got it. I'll hold on to this and stretch the branch out over the edge. I'll hold on to the post pipe for support, then raise this branch out over the edge. If you stand on the end of it and lean forward, we'll get the stone back in no time."

Zhi Ging gulped and eyed the post pipe warily. *At least I'm not trapped inside.*

"Fine, but *only* if you promise I can be a Silhouette after I get it." She narrowed her eyes, trying to imitate the steely expression Aapau had often used in arguments against the Lead Glassmith.

Reishi sighed and shook his head.

"Zhi Ging, it's not that simple. I tried to explain earlier before you ran off. Even if I take you to Hok Woh, the entrance won't open unless you have a Silhouette lantern." He held up a hand, predicting her next argument. "And no, a normal paper lantern won't work. These lanterns have to be created using Scout exam scrolls. They're made from an extremely rare kind of rice paper, using rice grown in the underwater terraces that surround Hok Woh. Just as the tide always returns to the sea, no matter how far it's traveled, Silhouette lanterns will always float back home. Without that rice paper, a lantern would just drift away. It wouldn't be able to guide someone across Wengyuen's six provinces to Hok Woh."

Zhi Ging scrunched up her nose, not seeing the problem. "Okay, then let's just use my exam scroll . . ." Her words trailed off as Reishi began to shake his head.

"Unfortunately, Fei Chui was my final stop as Silhouette Scout this month, and unsuccessful scrolls are burned after the last Silhouette has been chosen. I couldn't offer you a lantern even if I wanted to." He winced at her disappointed expression. "Be patient, Zhi Ging. If the Lead Glassmith refuses to listen to reason, I know someone who would happily take care of you for the next year. I can retest you then, the time will pass faster than you think."

"That's easy to say when you're immortal!" Zhi Ging cried, her cheeks flushing red. "I grew up listening to stories about Hok Woh and watching you test the Glassmiths' children but—" Her voice cracked. "You didn't even visit Fei Chui last year when I was finally old enough to take the entrance exam. How do I know you'll actually show up next time? I only have one more year before I'm too old to become a Silhouette."

Reishi's eyebrows shot up, and she immediately regretted her outburst. She didn't know anyone else beneath the cloud sea. *What if he refuses to speak to the Lead Glassmith for me now?*

"Forget it," she muttered, turning to face the cliff edge. "Let's just get your stone."

Reishi moved the branch into place, then wrapped one arm around the post pipe. Zhi Ging balanced herself on the branch, and he began to lift it over the cliff edge. He wobbled as she leaned forward, and Zhi Ging froze, her hand inches from the stone. Aapau's horrified face flashed across her mind, and she shut her eyes.

Why am I risking my life again for this piece of jade? It's not even going to get me to Hok Woh!

"You know what," Reishi gulped, the branch shaking in his arm. "Turns out I'm not as strong as I thought. Let's get you back."

Water roared through the post pipe, and the entire structure shook. Reishi's arm slipped from around its smooth surface and the branch jerked down. Reishi lurched forward, trying to catch Zhi Ging's sleeve, but she plummeted out of reach. She tumbled over the cliff edge, her terrified reflection warping along the post pipe's slick glass surface.

Zhi Ging screamed, arms flailing in the air, and her right hand clamped around the stone just before she dropped. She felt a sharp jerk as gravity tried to drag her down . . . and failed. Instead, she hung in the air, anchored by the floating stone. Zhi Ging glanced down and immediately shut her eyes. From this height, she could barely make out the bottom of the cliff.

"Hold on, I'm going to get you!" Reishi yelled, scrambling to find another branch.

With her eyes still clamped shut, Zhi Ging flung her other arm out to try to swing herself back to safety. The post pipe gurgled as more water rushed through, and she tightened her grip around the stone in furious determination.

The post pipe is not *going to claim me as its next victim this way.*

She swung her left hand higher, and it brushed against something that felt like a solid metal beam. Her eyes sprang open, and the beam evaporated as her hand fell back to her side.

"What are you doing?" Reishi shouted from the path. "Don't move, the stone could drop at any second."

"Well, I'm not going to wait for that to happen! I felt something just now, I think I can get back by myself."

Zhi Ging spun her left arm in a wide circle, but there was no trace of the beam anywhere. She shut her eyes in frustration and, immediately, hit against it. Zhi Ging inhaled sharply and forced herself not to peek.

Initially only her thumb could feel it, but slowly the idea of the beam trickled through the rest of her fingers and she gripped it tight.

There was a strangled gasp from the path, and she could hear Reishi starting to babble to himself.

"—incredible . . . centuries of research . . . is this what Gahyau sees?"

Zhi Ging faltered and almost lost her grip on the beam.

"Reishi," she muttered through clenched teeth, her knuckles white around the stone. "Please, stop talking. I *really* need to concentrate right now."

Zhi Ging inched herself along the invisible beam, her arm shaking from the strain of her body swaying beneath it. Her entire body prickled with sweat, but she couldn't risk wiping her hand. *What if I never find the beam again?*

Just as Zhi Ging was sure she would lose all feeling in her arm, Reishi's hands grabbed hold of her shoulders.

"I've got you! You can let go now."

Zhi Ging shuddered with relief, and her fingers slipped from around the invisible beam.

CHAPTER 5

Zhi Ging ran a shaking hand over her face, the jade stone still clutched tightly in her other palm. When she opened her eyes, Reishi was peering at her in concern, his outline blurred behind a thick wall of water.

Panic and confusion ripped through her. *Did I somehow land inside the post pipe?*

Suddenly, the air shimmered and the water pulled back, revealing itself to be a large bubble. A bright yellow jellyfish floated inside it and waved a tentacle shyly at her.

She jerked back, sand scattering beneath her feet.

"What is that?" she shrieked, pointing a finger at the jellyfish. It spun away and hid itself behind Reishi's ankles. The Silhouette Scout laughed and raised his leg to reveal the bubble.

"Zhi Ging meet Gahyau, Gahyau meet Zhi Ging. He travels with me everywhere in case I ever need to send an urgent message to Hok Woh. Although I usually keep him hidden inside the silk pouch. Mostly to avoid reactions like that."

"I had no idea jellyfish could do that," she murmured, watching in a daze as Gahyau swirled up to float above Reishi's shoulder.

"Oh, they normally can't, but Gahyau would like you to know he's special." Reishi rolled his eyes good-naturedly as the jellyfish shimmied two tentacles in a dramatic *ta-da!* "*This* is the other reason he usually travels inside my pouch, he's a terrible show-off!"

"Well, I like him." Zhi Ging grinned, watching Gahyau pirouette in the air.

"How did you do that?" Reishi asked.

"Do what? Keep hold of your stone? I think knowing I was dangling miles above the ground definitely helped."

"No, no, not that. How did you make the air rails appear? I've been researching them for centuries and what you just did"—Reishi began to pace in excitement while Gahyau bobbed behind him, tentacles mirroring his hand movements—"it shouldn't be possible. I can barely sense the rails even with hypersensitive equipment but you . . ." He stopped and stared at her in obvious wonder. "You, Zhi Ging, made them glow like they were made from *solid gold*."

Zhi Ging whipped her head around to stare back out over the cliff.

There was nothing.

No hint at all of the beam that had pulled her to safety.

Her thumb, on the other hand, looked like it had been dipped in gold, gilded threads unspooling across her palm to spill across her fingertips. *Has the air rail stained my hand?*

"I can't see anything." She crinkled her nose. "Do you still see the rails?"

"No, they vanished once you made it back over the cliff edge." Reishi gestured toward the jellyfish and pulled a crumpled piece of parchment from his silk pouch.

"I have to get back to Hok Woh immediately and record every detail while I still remember. This is the first case of air rails becoming visible to the human eye. Take this, my seal will let others know you're under Cyo B'Ahon protection. Gahyau will guide you to a friend of mine you can stay with. And don't worry, I'll be back tomorrow to speak with the Lead Glassmith for you."

Frustration bubbled inside her and Zhi Ging crouched down, clenching her free hand into the sandy path. *Why do people keep passing me around like this?* She hadn't had a choice when she'd been sent to Fei Chui as a baby, but she was old enough to push back now.

"No," she said. "Even if you burned my exam scroll, I worked too hard not to be Fei Chui's next Silhouette. *I should be the one with a lantern going to Hok Woh right now. The only reason I didn't have time for the last question was because the Lead Glass—"

"Zhi Ging, I'm not having this conversation again."

Suddenly, more scraps of parchment floated out of Reishi's pouch, as if enchanted by spirit magic. The piece in his hand rustled and broke free, then floated up to join the others. There was a loud crack behind Zhi Ging, and a branch splintered into fragments. Thin strips of bark shot through the air, binding the parchment together.

"What's happening?" Reishi breathed as the pieces came together. Although the makeshift structure was simple, its shape was unmistakable.

A lantern.

A sharp sliver of wood danced across one side, cutting through the parchment to create a new silhouette.

"That's me!" Zhi Ging leaped up, watching her long braid appear across the lantern's paper surface. Reishi inched forward and tapped a finger against it in wonder. He hesitated, then turned back toward Zhi Ging with a wary frown.

"No one in Wengyuen should be able to do this. Did you actually summon a spirit on the mountain?"

"What? No, I wouldn't even know how."

"But those were just ordinary scraps of parchment. A Silhouette lantern can only be made with Hok Woh rice paper. And even then, the Scout still has to stitch it together by hand." He shook his head in confusion. "This is closer to elemental magic, something only spirits can achieve."

"I promise I haven't . . ." Zhi Ging trailed off. A small flame had flickered to life in the center of the lantern, her outline shining down between their feet.

"What are you?" Reishi whispered, his eyebrows knitting together in confusion.

Zhi Ging glanced at the jade in her palm and pressed her spare hand around it. The Cyo B'Ahon seal now seemed pale compared to the gold that gleamed across her fingertips. She hesitated, then offered the stone back to Reishi, holding it between cupped hands.

"A Silhouette?" Zhi Ging risked, holding her breath for his reaction. Was she making a mistake? Once she handed the jade over, that was it; she'd have nothing else to bargain with.

In the silence, the post pipe shook and gurgled as more water rushed through.

"Keep it," Reishi croaked. "It can be your welcome gift."

"My welcome gift?" Zhi Ging pressed, her heartbeat threatening to drown out his answer. Reishi pulled the lantern out of the air, running a finger over the papercutting outline.

"As Hok Woh's first ever Second Silhouette."

Relief flooded through Zhi Ging, and she hugged the stone tight, her face almost sore from beaming.

The post pipe would never get her now.

Reishi pulled a blue vial from his silk pouch and pointed toward a tree. When Zhi Ging squinted, she could just barely make out a glass cart hidden beneath its branches.

"If we use that, we should reach Hok Woh by sunset. I'll send Gahyau ahead to notify Sintou, Head of the Cyo B'Ahon. She'll have final say on whether or not you can spend the next twelve months in Hok Woh as a

Silhouette—but between this lantern and the air rails . . ." Reishi rubbed the back of his neck in bewilderment. "I have a feeling it'll take much longer than your Silhouette year for us to work out what you just did."

Zhi Ging nodded furiously, happy for anything that would keep her away from Fei Chui. Reishi tucked the lantern under his arm and began marching toward the cart.

"Come on, you'll struggle to catch up from there once this starts going."

Zhi Ging clambered onto the cart while he tapped the front glass wheels. Two small hatches popped open, and he emptied the vial between them. "I knew I made the right decision leaving this cart beneath the cloud sea," Reishi muttered, half to Zhi Ging and half to himself. "Couldn't have used this vial with the Lead Glassmith watching. Not when so many Glassmiths have become this jittery, ready to spot evil spirits wherever they look."

The liquid splashed through the hollow glass, but rather than settling at the bottom, it continued to swell until two identical waves crested inside the wheels. With a small shudder, the cart began to trundle forward.

Reishi hopped up beside Zhi Ging and started to shuffle about, moving crates around while the lantern floated above them.

"Try to get some rest before we reach Hok Woh. I don't know about you, but something about breaking multiple fundamental laws of physics always takes it out of me."

Zhi Ging stared at him in confusion. "Aren't you going to steer us? We're going to roll straight off the cliff at the next bend."

"No, we won't," Reishi said calmly, pulling a battered sun hat from one of the crates and dropping it over his face. Zhi Ging gaped at him. *Is he serious?* She stood up, legs shaking on the moving cart, ready to leap back to the safety of the path. She wasn't about to become the shortest-living Silhouette of all time. Besides, she'd already been over that edge once—she didn't plan on doing that ever again.

Zhi Ging stared in horror as the cart rolled closer and closer toward the cliff edge. She glanced down at Reishi, who, against all reason, had started to hum. The lantern spun above him, light flashing through the paper-cutting outline. Zhi Ging took a deep breath and prepared to jump, when, at the very last second, the cart turned to follow the curved path.

"Told you so," Reishi sang, without even lifting the hat from his face. Zhi Ging could feel the smugness radiating off him. She stuck her tongue out at him, not caring if he could see her through the straw hat.

They traveled in silence for a while, but she couldn't hold her curiosity in for long.

"How are you doing this? Was there some sort of water spirit trapped in the vial?"

"Nope."

Silence.

She racked her brain. "Then is it more jellyfish? Are there some steering from inside the wheel?"

"Nope."

"Would you even tell me if I guessed it right?" she asked, frustrated.

Reishi raised the brim of his hat, opened his mouth, then paused to consider it. "Nope," he admitted with a self-satisfied smile, and dropped the hat back down.

Zhi Ging rolled her eyes and pulled the stone out of her pocket. It was still warm to the touch, and when she held it up, she could make out hints of amber beneath its dark green surface.

The jade was surprisingly light as she tossed it from hand to hand. Although she knew dragons never flew below the cloud sea, Zhi Ging couldn't stop herself from scanning the horizon for the telltale flicker of their tails. She'd already been wrong about them not hunting in fog.

Her concentration slipped and she pitched the stone a little too high. It shot past her outstretched hand and landed on Reishi's stomach. He sat up in surprise, his hat falling to the floor of the cart. When he looked up, Zhi Ging screamed and scrambled backward.

Reishi's face had vanished, and a stranger was staring back at her.

CHAPTER 6

The person now sitting across from her looked no older than herself, and his saffron robes flapped loosely around his body. His eyebrows shot up and he patted his face, stroking a hairless chin that only moments ago had been covered by a short beard. He still looked like Reishi, sort of. Just a much, *much* younger Reishi.

"Urgh, Gertie is definitely diluting the Crease Cream," he grumbled. "It should have lasted until Wun-Wun at the very least. Right, guess we're going to pay her a visit after all."

The now-considerably-younger-looking Reishi hopped off the cart and pulled out another vial, this one filled with thick emerald smoke. Zhi Ging leaped down after him, brandishing the stone like a talisman.

"What's going on? Are you really Reishi, or are you some sort of shape-shifting spirit that's copied his face?"

"Just Reishi, I'm afraid."

"But . . . why aren't you old anymore?"

"Rude, I was midfifties at most." He smiled, shaking his head and pouring the vial into the wheels. "This is one part of being a Cyo B'Ahon that we don't tend to broadcast. We're immortal yes, but not because our bodies are frozen in time. Instead, we maintain immortality by *age-shifting*. We try not to do it outside of Hok Woh because, clearly"—he winked at her—"it can be pretty disconcerting for those around us."

Zhi Ging lowered the stone and folded her arms. Her head hurt. This was all too much for one day.

"How many more questions am I going to have by the time we reach Hok Woh?"

Reishi chuckled, holding the cart still while its smoke-filled wheels began to rock. "That's rich coming from you! Almost everything you've done since finding the stone has caused nothing but questions. Luckily, researching impossible riddles is something Cyo B'Ahon love to do. And besides, you're about to become a Silhouette, the next year of your life is guaranteed to be filled with a whole lot more questions than answers."

THEY REACHED ANOTHER CLIFF JUST BEFORE DUSK. This time, they were looking out over the actual sea. Zhi Ging had only ever heard descriptions of it from Aapau, and her eyes hungrily drank in the shifting patterns of light. *I hope Aapau gets to see this again before her Final Year ends.*

Bleached wooden houses dotted the shoreline beneath them, huddled together in the bay while sunset danced across the seafoam.

"Is that Hok Woh?"

"No, that's Wun-Wun. We can walk to Hok Woh from here though. I just need to pick up a few things from Gertie at the floating market first." His expression turned serious. "Now, whatever you do, make sure to keep your eyes down and don't talk to any of the stallkeepers."

"Why? Are they dangerous?" Zhi Ging gulped. *How scary does something have to be to scare an immortal Cyo B'Ahon?* she wondered.

"No. But they're extremely good at their jobs and I don't want to pay for all the tat they'll trick you into buying."

Zhi Ging rolled her eyes as Reishi cracked up at his own joke.

He tied the cart to a large tree, and they inched their way down the cliff's weather-beaten steps toward the shore. In the distance, Zhi Ging could see several small boats. Although the water was calm, one kept overturning and flipping its two passengers overboard. Shoals of puffy white fish would scatter each time the boat tipped over, only to rush forward once the pair clambered back on board.

Reishi tapped her on the shoulder and pointed at a glowing collection of lights. Zhi Ging peered through the haze and realized it was a market floating above the waves.

Stalls in every shade of twilight fought to catch her eye, their silk entrances fluttering in the breeze.

"I should have asked Aapau to take me below the cloud sea years ago," she whispered, gazing at them in amazement.

Reishi beamed and jumped down, skipping the last few steps to land with a soft thump on the white sand. Zhi Ging's lantern twisted away from him and began to drift around the side of the cliff.

"Wait, come back!" she yelped, trying to catch it between her fingers.

"Don't worry, it's heading toward Hok Woh's entrance." Reishi gave a bemused snort. "Just like any other Silhouette lantern. "We'll catch up with it later. Come on, the floating market never stays in the same spot for long."

They hurried toward the lights, and Zhi Ging realized the tents were actually connected by a mazelike series of sand pathways. The tide rose and fell in the deep trenches separating the paths. Just before they reached the market entrance, Reishi pulled her back.

"All right, we're looking for the most garish, over-the-top tent in this place. There'll be some stiff competition, but you'll know it when you see it. Now, try to keep up." With that, he vanished into the crowd.

ZHI GING HAD NEVER EXPERIENCED SO MUCH NOISE and color in one place. The air was filled with a nose-tickling mix of spices and bursts of melting sugar. Reishi darted along the pathways, clearly used to weaving among the jostling crowds. She trailed after him, determined not to let his saffron robes out of sight.

There was a sudden splash up ahead and cheers from the crowd. A stocky man carrying a barrel twice his size had misjudged a turn and fallen headfirst into the sea. The barrel sank beneath the surface, and the waves sparked with tangerine mist.

Those closest to him pulled the man out and slapped him on the back while he squeezed the now-orange water from his hair. Reishi called out and threw a pebble in his direction. Zhi Ging watched open-mouthed as the man caught it, then rubbed it over his clothes. Water streamed out between his fingers, leaving a perfectly dry trail behind the pebble. She tapped her own pocket. Could the jade stone do that too? Or was that greedy to expect it to do more after the stone had already saved her life? Zhi Ging turned to ask Reishi, but he had vanished. There was no sign of him anywhere. She spun around, trying to push down the panic rising inside her.

This is fine. I know which tent we're looking for. Find the tent; find Reishi. Easy.

Zhi Ging hurried along the main path, ignoring the stall owners who waved identical amulets at her, claiming they kept the Fui Gwai at bay. She turned a corner and came across a stand draped in black velvet. An ornate glass box containing a single piece of paper took up the center of the display. The paper floated around and occasionally slammed against the sides of the box, as if caught in an invisible breeze. Faint traces of purple calligraphy covered its surface, and Zhi Ging watched it, mesmerized. There was something strangely familiar about the way it moved.

The paper seemed to notice her and fluttered closer. It tapped against the glass and its surface rippled, fragments falling away to reveal a paper cutting of a dragon. The miniature creature bowed to Zhi Ging, its ornate tail swishing in excitement as she stepped forward.

"Don't even think about it. There's no way you could afford it," the stall owner grunted, dropping a territorial hand over the box. Beneath his fingers, the paper rippled again. The fragments floated back up, concealing the dragon and transforming it into a paper cutting of a starling.

Before she could reply, Zhi Ging was pushed roughly out of the way by someone checking the price of a cerulean salamander skin. She slipped back into the crowd, vaguely insulted but also excited to explore the rest of the market.

A few twists and turns later, she stumbled across the tent Reishi must have been talking about. Its huge hulking sculpture resembled a golden wave on the verge of crashing down and swallowing the smaller tents around it. When she tried to step inside, the entrance slipped sideways and pushed a drab little tent squatting in its shadows forward instead. Zhi Ging stopped and tried again, but it spun away each time. She glanced around, wondering if anyone else could see the roaming entrance. When she turned back, the smaller tent had scooted forward and nudged eagerly against her shoes.

"All right, all right. No need to be so pushy."

Her fingers closed around the stone in her pocket, and Zhi Ging's eyebrows furrowed in anticipation. Whatever was inside couldn't be any stranger than anything she'd already faced.

Could it?

She shook the thought loose and stepped forward, holding her breath as the gray tent rustled and draped over her.

CHAPTER 7

Towers of curiosities stretched up from the floor, and a mysterious buzzing sound filled the tent. It was just as well Reishi wasn't with her. There wouldn't have been space for them to stand side by side, even now that he was so much smaller, with his robes pooling around him.

Zhi Ging followed the humming through the warren of trinkets until she arrived at a cone-shaped beehive rising up from the center of the tent. She leaned forward to take a closer look at the bees, hardly able to believe her eyes. Their furry bodies were an iridescent emerald green. Nothing at all like the bees back in Fei Chui. She found herself wondering whether the Glassmiths would have been as suspicious of them as they'd been of her.

"Interested? They create the finest weather wax in the world."

Zhi Ging jumped and turned to face the oldest woman she had ever seen. Her face was hidden under a web of wrinkles, deep craggy lines that crinkled across her face with each word.

"What's weather wax?" Zhi Ging asked hoarsely, trying not to stare at the living crown of bees nestled in the woman's white hair.

The woman's eyes lit up. "Oh, my dear girl, weather wax is going to change your life. If you treat your clothes with it, you'll never need to worry about bad weather again. Even if it's pouring rain, you won't feel a thing. You're in luck too, I have one final discounted jar of Spring Sunshine left. April twenty-fifth, that one's always a bestseller."

There was a burst of familiar laughter, and Reishi appeared behind the old woman.

"Don't let Gertie fool you with that, Zhi Ging. Any regular beeswax will have the exact same effect—she'll just charge you triple the price. I warned you not to talk to the stall owners."

Gertie swatted him away good-naturedly; it was clear they were old friends.

"Hush, don't you pay him any mind. These are special, child. Their wax can absorb the exact temperature and conditions of the perfect spring day. All you need to do is keep the wax activated after you've spread it on your clothes, moving regularly so it doesn't resolidify."

Reishi interrupted again. "So, what you're saying is rub your arms in the cold or run around and, magically, you'll warm up. Wow, what a miracle!" he teased.

"But why are they green?" Zhi Ging asked, watching as a bee nuzzled against her hand. Gertie smiled and her eyes glinted with mischief.

"Well, if they weren't green we wouldn't be having this conversation right now, would we? Instead you'd probably be saying something incredibly boring like, 'Why do you keep bees in such a small enclosed space? What's wrong with you?' They're a good icebreaker and, more importantly, they make excellent thieves." Gertie brandished Zhi Ging's jade stone triumphantly, and a smug-looking bee buzzed past to rejoin the hive.

Zhi Ging yelped and lurched forward, surprised by how wrong it felt to see the stone in someone else's hand. Reishi had only gifted it to her a few hours ago, but a wave of protective fear flooded through her.

"Wait, no, you can't have that!"

"Don't worry. Gertie's just curious to see what people have hidden in their pockets. Which is why I always make sure to empty mine before I visit." Reishi laughed, spotting a bee sulking empty-handed at the edge of his own robe.

Gertie winked at them and pulled a thin metal pin from her hair. She tapped along the edge of the stone, whispering to herself. Suddenly, the metal hissed and rusted between her fingers. Zhi Ging took a half step forward, worried the stone had been damaged too. The woman turned sharply and snatched up Zhi Ging's left hand. She winced as the woman traced a finger over the faint gold lines still shining from her palm. What if Gertie also thought they were marks from summoning a spirit? She didn't even know how to explain them.

"So, you're the one Fei Chui chose to protect." Gertie took a step back to examine Zhi Ging, her eyes sparkling with curiosity. "Everyone beneath the cloud sea saw it, the entire mountain suddenly lit up in a white blaze. In all my years, and there's been a few, I've never seen anything as bright as that ribbon."

"What do you mean? The Glassmiths didn't protect me, Reishi and I had to use the ribbon to escape them."

Gertie's expression softened and she gently brushed Zhi Ging's hair. "A village is made up of much more than the people living in it, my dear girl. Sometimes, learning to understand and recognize what's truly exceptional takes more than a lifetime. Even if the current Glassmiths didn't see your worth, their ancestors could. They chose to protect you. Where else do you think that ribbon of light came from?" She pressed the stone back into Zhi Ging's hand and frowned when Zhi Ging bent her thumb to cover the golden swirls. "Why do I get the feeling you're trying to hide those?"

Zhi Ging flushed and slipped her hand into her pocket.

"I'm not sure what they are. I guess I'm just worried what people might think . . ." She trailed off, not sure how to finish. She was already different in Fei Chui, but at least that difference had been obvious only when there were dragon scales nearby. If the gold lines didn't fade

56

completely, they would be an immediate sign to anyone she ever met that there was something strange about her.

Gertie nodded, as if reading her thoughts.

"Right, let's get you a glove to help heal those sand burns. My gift to you." Gertie snapped her fingers and the bees sprang into action, pulling scraps of fabric out from the jumble piled around them. Zhi Ging stared in amazement as a discarded scarf inched its way back toward the heap, seemingly moving by itself. Gertie followed her gaze and chuckled.

"Order ants. Every stall owner's best friend. At least, the stall owners who know about them, and can afford them. So, just me really. They make sure everything's always returned to its rightful place. They're great against pickpockets too. An order ant will happily drag the item, even if someone's still wearing it, back to my tent. Reishi got them for me as a present, *back when he still knew how to respect his elders,*" she added, deliberately raising her voice. Reishi waved her complaint aside and meandered deeper into the tent.

"Here we go!" Gertie cried, shaking a long, tattered gray glove. She leaned forward and quickly plucked a hair from the top of Zhi Ging's head.

"Ouch! What was that for?" Zhi Ging rubbed the spot, then pressed her palm flat against her scalp, in case Gertie went for a second hair.

"It'll be worth it, I promise."

The old woman ran the strand of hair through the eye

of a needle and threaded it along the fraying seams of the glove. The fabric began to transform, shifting from gray to a warm sandy hue that matched Zhi Ging's arm perfectly.

"You're lucky, you know. I'm one of the only ones left who knows how to make these." Gertie patted the glove protectively before handing it over. "Make sure you're careful with it when you're in Hok Woh. Rough movements will tear the fabric and, intelligent as they are, none of the Cyo B'Ahon will know how to restitch this."

Zhi Ging nodded and slid the glove up to her elbow. It fit perfectly. Even she couldn't spot the thin line that separated the glove from her arm.

"This is incredible, thank you."

"Your hair remembers what your arm looked like before, so it'll help conceal the gold lines. Our memories are stored in our hair, you know. Millions of tiny moments saved on each strand. That's why you go gray when you age, you start to lose memories. They're still there of course, just fainter."

Zhi Ging stopped stroking the glove to look up at her, puzzled.

"I thought our ancestors lived on in our hair, protecting us? That's why everyone in Fei Chui's hair glows near dragons, it's their ancestors warning them danger's near." Zhi Ging ran a hand through her own black hair. "Aapau always used to say, 'No matter how big your life is, you're one of thousands that have come before you and, in time, you'll also need to protect the future.' She told me that's why our hair's at the top of our head—it's a reminder our ancestors should always be at the top of our thoughts," Zhi Ging's face scrunched up in confusion. Gertie raised an eyebrow and smiled.

"Who says one of us has to be wrong? In my experience, few things in life have only one purpose. The world's far too creative for that."

She ruffled Zhi Ging's hair, and a small card appeared between her fingers as she pulled away. There was a simple face painted on one side and two feet daubed in thick brushstrokes on the back.

"Next time you want to find the floating market, fold this in half. Like this." She bent the card so the smiling face was turned outward with its feet hidden underneath. Gertie tossed the card a few feet away. There was a slight pause, then the card shook, the ink spilling to the floor. The ink pooled, then solidified, lifting the card up on two small black legs. The card bent its new knees experimentally, then trotted over, leaving tiny ink-splash footprints behind it. There was a small, muffled cheer as it bumped against Gertie's shoe and she scooped it up.

"Wow! You are the most intelligent, talented person in the world," the inky face chirped. Zhi Ging burst out laughing. The voice was clearly Gertie's, just much higher pitched.

"Why, thank you." Gertie beamed, picking it up. She unfolded the card and handed it to Zhi Ging with a wink. "Whenever people arrive at my tent, it's usually for a favor, so I've built in an automatic compliment for each card. I might as well be in a good mood when they show up with their, usually ridiculous, requests."

"I need another jar of Crease Cream," Reishi interrupted, ambling back over with his arms filled with flasks and vials. Gertie tutted and waggled her eyebrows at Zhi Ging, as if to say, *See?*

"It definitely wore off faster this time. Have you swapped out any of the ingredients? I've told you I can't get caught accidentally ageshifting outside of Hok Woh. Especially now. You know the rumors spreading about Cyo B'Ahon in other provinces. I can't risk being . . ." He trailed off, seeming to suddenly remember Zhi Ging was also in the tent. He and Gertie exchanged a meaningful look and he mouthed, *Later.* Zhi Ging frowned at them; it didn't make any sense. *Surely Cyo B'Ahon are welcome everywhere?*

"What are you suggesting?" Gertie gasped theatrically, breaking the tension. "I've told you, it's all that research you Cyo B'Ahon do. It cancels out the Crease Cream. Your poor old brain needs so much storage space for facts that it's forced to steal the wrinkles from the rest of your body. I haven't put any more on since your last visit and look how perfectly aged I've stayed."

Reishi burst out laughing.

"Nice try, but don't forget I know you really *are* that old." He tapped her on the forehead with an empty jar, and she swatted him away. Gertie lifted the lid of a small pot buried under a large bag labeled *Dodo Feathers,* and the tent immediately brightened with the scent of marshmallows and lilac. She filled the jar and handed it back to Reishi.

"All right, let's check how strong this batch is, shall we?" He smeared a small amount across one cheek, and the skin beneath it caught and stretched. It drooped as his hand moved across his face and, within seconds, his features had aged over forty years.

"Much better. This should be enough to anchor my wrinkles in place for a few days. Where is Jack by the way? I was hoping to say hello. Has he finally gotten sick of you and run away?"

"Ha! More like he spotted you and decided to vanish before you guilted him into carrying everything back to the cart, again," Gertie shot back.

"That's no way to speak to a valued client."

"You're right, I'd never speak to a *valued* one like that."

Zhi Ging put a hand over her mouth and shook with silent laughter. The way Gertie spoke to Reishi was *very* different from the Lead Glassmith's over-the-top groveling.

"Never mind, my new Silhouette here can help carry these to the cart." He turned to Zhi Ging. "I've a few things to talk to Gertie about but I'll meet you back at the entrance in half an hour."

"Wait, what?" Zhi Ging blurted, looking incredulously at the teetering pile in his arms.

"Ignore him." Gertie laughed and patted her on the shoulder. "My bees will carry everything. Go. Explore the market." She clicked her fingers and the bees swarmed forward, each landing on a different item in Reishi's arms. Gertie shuffled after them and pulled a battered notebook from her pocket as she started tallying up the costs. The bee from earlier bumped against Zhi Ging's hand, a small ball of emerald weather wax clutched between its forelegs.

"Oh, sorry. I don't have any money," she said, wondering if it understood.

"Take it," Gertie called over her shoulder. "He feels bad for stealing your stone earlier."

"Thank you very much." Zhi Ging slipped the wax into her pocket, and the bee drifted off, buzzing happily to himself.

CHAPTER 8

Zhi Ging wandered through the market, letting the crowd jostle her down new paths. One stall offered miniature fortunes written on grains of rice, while another sold jewelry crafted from heat-sensitive sand. She watched as the stall owner hunched over candle flames to transform pellets of sand into clouded glass beads.

A cart filled with desserts trundled past, the sweet smell of sago pudding and brown sugar nin gou wafting over the crowds. Zhi Ging's stomach rumbled, and she followed after the treats. *Maybe I can swap some of the weather wax for a bowl.* The cart vanished around a corner, and Zhi Ging skidded to a stop, almost walking into her own face.

In front of her was a sprawling tent covered in mirrors. When others walked past, their reflections rippled and shifted. A sign pinned to the tent boasted that the glass in each mirror had been created to charm and confuse onlookers. A mirror with an ornate gold frame reflected the backs of people's heads, while another held on to different facial features, dropping them on the next person to glance over. Zhi Ging giggled and watched her eyes change color with each blink, their rich black replaced by a bright mustard yellow, then a hibiscus pink.

Others jostled past but she couldn't bear to leave before testing every mirror. She hurried over to the next one, but it didn't reflect anything. Instead, thick mercury smoke covered the surface. *Has it stopped working?*

She leaned closer, her hand drawn toward the hazy surface. Right before her fingers brushed against the glass, gray-eyed figures roared up, clawing furiously against the surface.

Thralls!

The twisted faces of those possessed by the Fui Gwai howled at her through the glass. Zhi Ging jerked away but tripped over her own feet, and she slipped, tumbling against a row of hanging mirrors. An arm grabbed her just before she crashed through the tent, and beneath the sharp jangling of smashing glass, Zhi Ging could hear angry yelling coming from inside.

"Run!" the person holding her arm shouted, pulling her into the crowd.

They wove between startled groups and raced along a twisting pathway until the arm pulled her sideways, hiding them behind a metal dumpling cart piled high with bamboo steamers.

When it felt like the coast was clear, Zhi Ging spun around and discovered that her rescuer was a boy around her age, maybe a year older. She was surprised to see that he had one blue and one green eye, both flecked with gold.

"Did that mirror permanently change our eye colors?" Zhi Ging asked, panicked. She twisted to check her reflection in the metal cart and found her natural eyes staring wildly back at her.

"Uh . . . no, that's just how my eyes always look . . . ," the boy said slowly. Zhi Ging turned back to him with an apologetic wince, embarrassed by how rude her reaction must have seemed. *Why did I assume everyone outside of Fei Chui also had brown eyes?* He quickly shook his head before she could explain. "Don't worry about it. Most people just stare when they first notice the color, no matter what province I'm in. So that was actually kinda refreshing." He stood up and offered her a hand. "I'm Jack Oltryds, by the way. First time at the floating market I'm guessing. Are you one of Reishi's new Silhouettes?"

"Yeah, I am." Zhi Ging beamed, the full force of what she was saying filling her with warm pride. "I'm the new Fei Chui Silhouette." *Not an orphan, not a post pipe scrubber. A Silhouette.*

"Congratulations! I hope—" A faded scrap of yellow paper flitted out of Jack's pocket and tapped impatiently against his forehead, cutting him off before unfolding. After a quick glance, he shoved it back into his coat.

"Sorry, Gertie's list won't leave me alone until I've ticked everything off, and the market's closing soon. I'm sure we'll bump into each other again, though." He gave her a quick, rueful wave and hurried off. She waved after him, unsure if he really meant it.

It was only after he vanished that Zhi Ging realized his eye colors had swapped sides after he read the note.

ZHI GING MEANDERED BACK BETWEEN THE TENTS, but she was distracted now. Part of her hoped to bump into Jack again just to check if his eye colors had switched back, but she also wanted to ask him more about how he knew Reishi. Was he Gertie's grandson or just another kid who hadn't been chosen as a Silhouette? Was he waiting to be retested in a year's time? She hadn't even had a chance to ask.

A stall owner leaned forward, shaking jars filled with miniature snow clouds, but Zhi Ging hurried on, Reishi's warning against speaking to stallkeepers echoing in her mind. She pushed through the crowd but froze when she spotted the metal dumpling cart from before. This wasn't right. Was she lost? She spun around in the opposite direction and hurried to find the main path. What would she do if Reishi left without her?

The stalls began to blur as Zhi Ging raced back down the path, frantically retracing her steps. Finally, she rounded a corner and saw a much older-looking Reishi pacing back and forth. He waved a torch frantically once he spotted her, and she hurried toward him, feeling a small flicker of disappointment when she realized he wasn't surrounded by a trail of Gertie's emerald bees.

"Sorry, I got completely lost, but—" She wheezed, struggling to catch her breath. "I bumped into Jack and he mentioned seeing me again soon. Is he waiting to take his Scout exam?"

"Unfortunately not. Gertie would never forgive me if I stole her prize apprentice." Reishi's eyes lit up, distracted by movement behind her. "Quick, turn around! Closing time is my favorite part of the market."

Zhi Ging turned and watched as stall owners started to trickle out from their tents. They expertly looped gold rope through their stall frames before securing it to their belts. Zhi Ging glanced up at Reishi in bafflement. *How is packing up his favorite part of the market?*

The stall owner closest to them glanced over.

"You'd want to step back a bit there, folks. The initial gust will knock that torch flame right out."

Reishi grabbed Zhi Ging's arm, and they retreated along the beach until the stall owner nodded, satisfied. She slipped a russet bell out from her sleeve and began to ring it. Within seconds, the chiming was echoed by identical bells throughout the market.

As one, the stall owners pulled on their ropes. Air billowed around the bay and sand soared over Reishi and Zhi

Ging in a shimmering arc, the tents shrinking down to the size of paper lanterns. The nearby stall owner scooped up her now-miniature tent and held it out toward Reishi. He dipped the torch beneath the tent, and it filled with a warm glowing light. Zhi Ging watched, mesmerized, as a line of stall owners gathered in front of Reishi and his torch.

"The prize of tent lighting goes to whoever spends the most at the market each night," Reishi whispered triumphantly. "And whenever I'm here, I always make sure that's me." He paused, a sudden guilty look flashing across his face. "Uh, maybe don't mention that to the Head of the Cyo B'Ahon when you meet her though."

Gertie and Jack approached, their tent now resembling a solid slab of gold. Jack wriggled his eyebrows at her and mouthed *Watch out,* before tipping his head to the side. Zhi Ging peered over his shoulder and spotted an extremely angry-looking man. He was holding a tent covered in miniature mirrors and ranting to everyone around him about damage. Zhi Ging felt her face flush red, and she took a few steps back so she was hidden behind Reishi. Jack winked as he and Gertie walked off with their illuminated tent, his shoulders shaking with silent laughter.

Once all the tents had been lit, there was another chorus of chiming bells, and the tents were released. They floated up and soon the sky was filled with glittering color. The stall owners were lifted after them, swaying gently from their ropes as the tents drifted across the night sky.

Reishi and Zhi Ging watched in silence until the tents were no larger than luminous dots, indistinguishable from the stars.

"I always like to stay a bit longer," Reishi murmured without looking down. "If you're lucky, you sometimes see one of them shooting back across the sky. Usually after they've realized they've left something behind or, even worse, someone's underpaid."

Eventually, he sighed contentedly and turned to Zhi Ging.

"Right, time to collect the other Silhouettes."

THEY PICKED THEIR WAY BACK TOWARD THE CLIFF steps, but rather than climbing up, Reishi continued around and led them along the shore toward a secluded pebble beach. There, illuminated by their own paper-cutting lanterns, was a cluster of ten other Silhouettes. They were whispering among themselves, and the crunch of pebbles beneath Reishi's feet made it difficult for Zhi Ging to hear their conversation. She squinted at their outlines, wondering which of Wengyuen's six provinces they were all from.

Gahyau floated in the middle of the Silhouette huddle, Zhi Ging's lantern perched above his bubble like an oversized crown.

"Welcome!" Reishi called out, twirling the torch to catch their attention. "I hope your journeys here were perfectly dull and uneventful."

"What is *she* doing here?" a familiar voice snarled, and

69

Zhi Ging felt her stomach drop. In all the chaos and excitement, she had completely forgotten that she wasn't the only Silhouette from Fei Chui.

There, pushing her way to the front of the Silhouettes, was a furious Iridill.

CHAPTER 9

Iridill jabbed a finger toward Zhi Ging, glaring at her while the other Silhouettes glanced between them in confusion.

"Were you really so desperate not to end up in the post pipe that you followed Reishi all the way here? I'm Fei Chui's Silhouette, not you!"

Zhi Ging felt her face flush red. This was not the start she had been hoping for.

"Miss Seoipin," Reishi cut in across them, his voice sharp and authoritative. "You are here because you received a Silhouette lantern. As did Miss Yeung." He pointed at the lantern above Gahyau. "This year, there will be a second Silhouette from Fei Chui. In the meantime, your continued presence in Hok Woh ahead of next month's challenge is at my discretion. Do you understand?"

Zhi Ging's stomach tightened. Aapau had never mentioned there would be challenges once she got in.

Iridill's face soured but she lowered her finger and took a step back.

"Yes, sir," she muttered, still glowering at Zhi Ging. The other Silhouettes shuffled uncomfortably, eyes darting between the two girls from Fei Chui. Gahyau bounced toward Zhi Ging and nudged her elbow, encouraging her to take her place with the others. She brushed sand from her sleeves, suddenly self-conscious at how worn her clothes looked compared to the others, with their gleaming shirts embroidered with gold thread, pearls, and silk. *Only children of district rulers could afford clothes like that. What if all the other Silhouettes were just like Iridill?*

"Right." Reishi continued, a more pleasant tone returning to his voice. "As I was about to say, I know you all traveled a long distance to be here tonight, so let's keep this short and get you settled into Hok Woh."

The Silhouettes shifted in excitement, and Zhi Ging realized with a start that while she had been exploring the market, they must have been waiting anxiously on the beach for Reishi. She glanced up at the moon high above them. Hadn't Reishi mentioned reaching Hok Woh by sunset? They must have been standing here for hours.

Reishi fumbled in his silk pouch and lifted out a smooth pebble. It was identical to the one he had thrown the drenched man in the market.

"This is a hydrophobic pebble. They can't stand water and have no problem ignoring every possible rule of physics just to stay dry. Completely useless for most things, but perfect for reaching Hok Woh. Watch." He skimmed the pebble out across the waves. Halfway through its first arc, the pebble twisted in the air. It curved sharply to the left and skipped six times before it came to a bouncing stop several feet from the shore. It hopped up and down, avoiding each breaking wave, and the gibbous moon's reflection shimmered beneath it. Reishi nodded at the group.

"Everyone ready? Let's go." He strode up to the shoreline and leaped forward, his feet never dipping below the surface as he mimicked the pebble's bounding pattern. Gahyau floated at his shoulder, easily keeping pace with the Silhouette Scout.

"Well, aren't you coming?" Reishi called back once he noticed that none of the Silhouettes had moved to follow, the sea wind pulling at his words. The water lapped gently against his shoes while he stood on the surface. Zhi Ging bit her lip, trying to remember Reishi's exact movements, but the pattern faded with each breaking wave. She hadn't realized they'd have to memorize his steps.

The others hesitated while Zhi Ging dipped a toe into the dark waves. It was *much* colder than stepping into the cloud sea.

"Aren't you going to help us?" she called to Reishi, splashing water halfheartedly in his direction. The crashing waves swallowed his reply, but Gahyau soared back toward the group. He herded their paper lanterns out over the sea, nudging them toward Reishi before tapping a tentacle against his own bubble. It burst and the yellow jellyfish landed in the waves with a soft splash. The water shone around Gahyau, and two of the other Silhouettes waded forward.

"Look!" the taller of the two boys cried out. "There's glass stepping stones just beneath the surface. That must be how we get across."

The boys clambered onto the illuminated step and gestured for the others to join them. Zhi Ging grimaced as Iridill barged past, the girl's bead-covered robes knocking against her. *Reishi should have just invited the Fui Gwai and dragon too. It couldn't get much worse than this.*

THERE WAS A SHORT ROUND OF APPLAUSE FROM Reishi when the group eventually reached him on the seventh stepping stone.

"There, that wasn't too hard now was it." His eyes twinkled, surveying the sodden group before him. Each of the Silhouettes had misjudged at least one of the stepping stones and had to be pulled back up by the others. *Well, by* most *of the others.* Zhi Ging glared at the back of Iridill's head, knowing each "accidental slip" from the Lead Glassmith's daughter had really been an attempt to push her into the sea.

"Wow, tough crowd," Reishi muttered when they just stared silently back at him. "Most Silhouette groups enjoy that little bonding experience."

Reishi crouched down and rolled up his sleeves, his hand catching on the moonlight before he pressed it against the glass step. A thin web of curling silver lines sprawled across his left palm. There was a faint rumbling, and the sea began to rise and spin around them while the lantern flames simultaneously winked out. Zhi Ging reached out in a daze to touch the waves, but her fingers brushed against glass instead.

They had sunk inside the hollow stepping stone.

She shivered and felt the other Silhouettes huddle closer. It was like a reverse post pipe. Dry and safe inside, with water ready to drown them the second they stepped outside.

The rumbling restarted and she looked up just in time to see a thick panel slide over their heads. The sea rippled over it, and in the new darkness, Reishi began to tap experimentally against the glass walls.

"Aha! Here we go," he cried. "I always forget it'll be a different height depending on how much Crease Cream I've used."

Zhi Ging hadn't heard any difference between the last two taps, but seconds later, she heard the unmistakable gurgle of rushing water. Panic washed through her. There was a crack in the glass. It was about to flood!

She could already see a bright light in the distance coming toward her. The Silhouette next to her yelped, and the hollow stepping stone filled with the sound of panicked hands trying to find the chip in the glass. But then, more small lights appeared. The space brightened and filled with puffs of sunlight-filled cloud.

Zhi Ging blinked and realized they were standing at

the top of a narrow spiral staircase. Rather than a single hollow pipe, there was a second outer wall of glass surrounding their pillar. She laughed in disbelief and ran a shaking hand along the inner wall. Whatever Reishi had just pressed had let the outer wall flood with seawater, allowing Gahyau in. What she had thought were floating clouds were actually glowing white jellyfish, all no larger than her palm.

"Incredible," Zhi Ging breathed. Even Iridill wasn't immune to the sight and the girl's pinched features softened in amazement. Gahyau bobbed through the space between the walls, gently nudging other jellyfish out of the way before coming to a stop in front of Reishi.

"All right, everyone, Gahyau will light our way down. Grab your lanterns and follow me." Reishi signaled to the yellow jellyfish, and they set off.

"I can't believe this is here," Zhi Ging whispered, recognizing the glass beneath her feet. It was the cheap, clouded glass apprentice Glassmiths would train with before their first outing to the glass terraces. The heat-sensitive sand used to create these steps didn't even need dragon lightning; a midday sunbeam was enough to melt it. Zhi Ging snorted. She would pay to see the Lead Glassmith's expression if he ever knew Reishi had allowed such poor-quality glass into Hok Woh. Then again, the glass wasn't exactly useless. Dotted with air pockets, the rough glass stopped the dripping Silhouettes from slipping down the stairs in their damp shoes.

Zhi Ging let the others squeeze past and trailed a hand along the glass. *This is even better than walking through the cloud sea.* Every sound was muffled and only patches of glimmering light interrupted the perfect stillness. She smiled and took a deep, steadying breath. The world beneath the cloud sea had been unimaginable to her a few days ago.

What would be waiting for her beneath the *actual* sea?

THE GROUP SQUELCHED DOWN THE WINDING STAIR-case and eventually reached a towering glass door. Zhi Ging could make out an intricate lock system sprawling across the full length of the double doors. It was clear no one who wasn't welcome in Hok Woh would be getting in. But who were the Cyo B'Ahon trying to keep out?

To the side of the door was a thin rope with hundreds of woven Pan Chang Knots tied to its surface. The rope coiled across the floor, with one end vanishing into a hole carved into the glass ceiling.

"Each one of these red knots has the name of a different town, city, or village in Wengyuen embroidered onto the center of its looping pattern," Reishi explained, pulling the rope toward the Silhouettes. "Find your hometown and tie your lantern to that knot."

The others rushed forward, eagerly searching the Pan Changs for their own province, and the red knots fluttered along the rope like a chain of interlaced butterflies. Reishi caught Zhi Ging's eye and gestured for her to wait.

"The ceiling will only accept Silhouette lanterns that belong in Hok Woh. Glass doesn't forget, it knows what to look for in the rice paper," he murmured, his voice almost too low for Zhi Ging to hear. "If the ceiling spots something different, that hole could snap shut, severing the rope."

"What happens to me if it does?" Zhi Ging felt her veins fill with icy seawater. Being shamed as a Silhouette fraud in front of Iridill wouldn't even be the worst of it. What if she was sent back to Fei Chui alone?

Reishi grimaced and shook his head. "Let's not worry about that yet. Hopefully your lantern can convince both a Silhouette Scout and Hok Woh's entrance."

Their eyes drifted toward the ceiling, and Zhi Ging winced. A curved sliver was visible at the edge of the hole, a glass panel ready to stop anything other than a Silhouette lantern from passing through.

"I really wish we'd checked that earlier."

She gingerly tucked her lantern under her arm and trudged toward Iridill, who was already tying her own lantern to Fei Chui's knot. Zhi Ging squeezed down beside her, loosening the cords to add her own lantern. The two paper lanterns bunched together under the Pan Chang Knot, and Zhi Ging held her breath, watching Iridill peer suspiciously at her lantern. Beside the others, it was noticeably frayed, the crumpled parchment standing out against the smooth scrolls around it.

Once all the Silhouettes were done, Reishi stepped

forward and tugged hard on the rope. It sprang up, lanterns bouncing from side to side as they shot toward the ceiling. The rope shook when Iridill's and Zhi Ging's lanterns fought to fit through the hole, the red Pan Chang straining against the weight of the second lantern. Reishi took a half step forward, but then the wooden frames creaked and bent together, and both lanterns vanished up through the space. Zhi Ging felt her shoulders relax, and she spotted a similar look of relief flicker across the Silhouette Scout's face.

Hok Woh had accepted her lantern.

A hatch on the doorframe slid open, and Gahyau squeezed through the thin tubes that made up the lock system. He pulled panels aside and flipped latches as he wound toward the center of the door, occasionally doubling back on himself to trigger a new number of glass tubes to shift and click into place.

Finally, the jellyfish reached the middle and pulled aside the thick bar that connected the two sides of the door. Reishi pressed a hand against the glass, whispered a quick thank-you to Gahyau, then turned to the group. They instinctively stood a little straighter, holding their collective breath. Zhi Ging could feel excitement coursing through her.

This is it. Everything Aapau and I have worked for.

"Welcome, Silhouettes, to Hok Woh." Reishi smiled, bowing his head. "Realm of the immortals."

CHAPTER 10

The doors swung open to reveal a vast, circular hall made entirely from glass. Wild, twisting shards soared up from the floor and wove together across the walls.

"You might recognize some of this." Reishi nodded at Zhi Ging and Iridill. "Everything in here was custom created for us by generations of Glassmiths. The last Lead Glassmith . . ." His voice washed over Zhi Ging as she spun around, willing herself not to blink. It was like they had stepped into a crystal nest.

Glowing white jellyfish floated between the walls and pulsed beneath the glass floor. Zhi Ging watched as a few drifted up toward the domed ceiling. The curved glass was decorated with a stained-glass pattern of cranes caught in flight. When the jellyfish sailed past, the birds' broad wings shimmered, and flashes of color glinted down on the Cyo B'Ahon hurrying across the hall. Zhi Ging gazed at the colors dancing across her arms, and the Silhouettes around her tapped the floor, mesmerized by the jellyfish darting beneath their feet.

". . . understood? Right, I'll let Ami, the Dohrnii, know you're here and she'll join us on the tour."

"Wait, the Dohr-what?" Zhi Ging blurted, dragging her eyes away from the jellyfish. Iridill snorted as Reishi turned toward her.

"As I just said, the Dohrnii is the Cyo B'Ahon who looks after Silhouettes during their first year. She's relatively new to Hok Woh herself, just over a hundred years since her own Silhouette year, so she'll understand how challenging some of you might find the next twelve months."

Iridill elbowed Zhi Ging hard and smirked down at her.

"He means you, NoGlow," she hissed.

Zhi Ging's cheeks flushed but she bit her tongue. Iridill could say whatever she wanted; there was nothing that could make her leave.

As long as the Head of the Cyo B'Ahon agreed with Reishi's invitation . . .

Reishi strode over to the wall and pulled a glass shard down. Water swirled out from the wall, and Gahyau was swept up in the current to land with a gentle splash in one of the basins that circled the hall. Reishi snapped the shard back and pulled a sheet of rice paper from his pouch. The Silhouettes leaned forward, trying to read his handwriting before he dropped it into the basin.

"Did anyone see—" a short-haired Silhouette began but was quickly shushed by Iridill. Gahyau pulled the rice paper closer and traced over the message. The dark ink absorbed into his tentacles, and he pushed through a panel at the bottom of the basin, squeezing himself back into the main wall. He grabbed the tentacles of the nearest jellyfish, and the black ink passed between them. *What just happened?* Zhi Ging glanced at the others, but they seemed just as confused as she was.

Reishi's message continued to move jellyfish-to-jellyfish across the wall and, at one point, beneath their feet before it reached a final jellyfish.

To Zhi Ging, it looked no different from the others, but this time the ink coiled up from its tentacles. She watched in amazement as Reishi's original message raced across its body. The jellyfish quivered and turned opaque before returning to its natural white glow, all traces of the inky message gone.

Zhi Ging spun back around to face Reishi. "What was that? What did Gahyau do?"

"That's how most Cyo B'Ahon keep in touch." Reishi tapped the bramble-like scar on his left palm, as if that was explanation enough.

"Marzi, Ami's jellyfish, will have shared my message with her. She'll be here any minute now."

On cue, the door to their left burst open and a willowy Cyo B'Ahon, currently aged around forty, swept into the hall. Her ivory robes billowed around her, and there was a bundle of soft black cloaks tucked under her arm.

"Welcome!" The Dohrnii beamed, eyes sparkling behind blue-tinted glasses as she offered each of them a cloak. "You have no idea just how thrilled I am to have you here."

Zhi Ging couldn't help but smile back. She knew the Dohrnii probably said the same thing every month to each new group of Silhouettes, but somehow, she felt like Ami was speaking directly to her.

The Silhouettes' red Pan Chang Knots from before had been pinned to the fronts of the cloaks, proudly proclaiming where each new Silhouette was from. Unlike the others, Zhi Ging's own cloak had a white knot, the same color as Ami's robes. The loops in the center were loose and hastily woven together. *She must have just tied it after spotting the second lantern.*

"Right, let me introduce myself properly. I'm Amigda Lin, but everyone calls me Ami. I'm *hoping* Reishi's already explained, but I'm Hok Woh's current Dohrnii. It's my job to look after all incoming Silhouettes and make sure you're all settled in. Oh, and I also look after the baby jellyfish in the Seoi Mou Pou and—oh dear, I'm rambling when you must all be so exhausted after that journey. More about the jellyfish later." She chuckled and adjusted her glasses, the blue light catching in Zhi Ging's eye. "Apologies, I just learned we're welcoming Hok Woh's first ever Second Silhouette, so my mind is racing through all the changes we'll need to make around the dorm. I want to make sure both of our Fei Chui Silhouettes feel equally at home." A few of the Silhouettes murmured to each other, and Zhi Ging looked down, a blush creeping up the back of her neck. She'd hoped to finally just fit in. Twelve years of being singled out had been more than enough.

"The most important thing to remember from today's tour is, any problem you have, no matter how big or small, please come to me and I'll do what I can to help."

Ami leaned toward the group and, in a stage whisper, added, "Reishi was the Silhouette Scout who found me one hundred and eleven years ago, so you can hide in my office any time you need a break from his terrible jokes."

"Outrageous." He snorted. "Not even five minutes in and you're already trying to turn them against me. What a betrayal."

Ami's laughter bounced around the hall. "Oh, I think your jokes will have done a good enough job of that on their own." She turned back to the group and pointed at the cloaks.

"All right everyone, pop those on and let's get going. The fabric will help dry the rest of your clothes. You'll be nice and toasty again by the time we reach the first stop of the tour."

The Silhouettes scrambled to wrap the cloaks around themselves and Zhi Ging sighed with relief when the cold damp immediately began to leave her body.

Reishi and Ami led the group along a winding corridor, their heads close together in hushed conversation. At one point, Ami glanced back and Zhi Ging was sure she looked right at her, a fierce curiosity in her eyes. Jellyfish darted past through the glass walls around them, completely uninterested in the new Silhouettes.

A girl at the front of the group yelped and froze, forcing everyone behind her to skid to a stop. One of the passing Cyo B'Ahon had suddenly ageshifted, her cloak ballooning around her like a giant jellyfish. The woman, who had looked in her thirties only moments before, now looked no older than eleven and was pointing excitedly at the white Pan Chang Knot on Zhi Ging's cloak.

"That's her! The Second Silhouette," she hissed, nudging the Cyo B'Ahon beside her. "I told you I hadn't been seeing things, there really were two lanterns tied together!" Reishi spun around, chuckling at the Silhouettes' shocked expressions.

"That reaction is exactly why I need to use Crease Cream whenever I'm shoreside." He gestured to Zhi Ging and lowered his voice. "What Gertie said earlier was true. Whenever Cyo B'Ahon are working on a complicated idea or theory, our brains pull lines and wrinkles from the rest of our body. After a certain stage, it pulls actual years to help work out a solution. That's how we ageshift and it's why I shrank down on the cart, I was trying to figure out how you held on to the air rails. As long as we keep thinking and challenging our minds, we're effectively immortal. Sometimes though, we *accidentally* ageshift—usually when we're shocked or excited. We can't help it any more than you can stop yourself jumping when something surprises you. When Cyo B'Ahon accidentally ageshift, they usually drop back down to the age they were when they first arrived in Hok Woh. It's their 'comfort blanket' age." He smiled at her. "Others are ageshifting now because they're excited to see Hok Woh's first ever Second Silhouette. News spreads quickly here, secrets are almost impossible to keep when everything is shared through jellyfish."

Zhi Ging's eyes darted between the Cyo B'Ahon streaming past them in the corridor. Every so often one would spot her behind Reishi, and their eyebrows would shoot up. Each time this happened, it was followed by a faint pop, and their cloaks would bloom around them, the fabric catching in the air as they shrank.

"It's also why anyone in Hok Woh who isn't a full Cyo B'Ahon is called a Silhouette," Reishi continued. "Sometimes, students can tower over ageshifted Cyo B'Ahon. The name Silhouette refers to your shadows falling over their desks while you observe their research."

"Sure," Zhi Ging croaked, eyes darting between the ballooning cloaks. "That makes perfect sense."

There was a polite cough, and they turned to see Ami standing in front of double doors carved from smoked glass. She pressed a hand against it, and flecks of silver caught in the light.

"If everyone's ready, I'd like to invite you into Hok

Woh's greatest treasure, the Seoi Mou Pou." Ami's eyes gleamed and her voice lowered to a reverential whisper as she looked at each of them one by one. "The next time some of you step into this chamber will be for your graduation ceremony in a year's time, when you become Cyo B'Ahon."

CHAPTER 11

Before Zhi Ging's eyes could adjust to the shimmering lights, there was a faint thud as another Silhouette bumped his head against the ceiling. He stopped to rub the spot, and Zhi Ging was surprised to find her own body swaying. It took her a second to realize they were standing at the top of a raised, narrow platform. She looked up and her nose almost brushed the ceiling.

"Ah, forgive me," Ami said, slipping in behind them. "I must have ageshifted last time I was in here and forgot to reset the platform height." She smiled apologetically and pulled on a discreet lever, lowering the platform away from the ceiling. It wobbled as the group sank down, and Zhi Ging had to reach out and steady herself against the silk ropes that stretched along the walkway.

"For anyone with a fear of heights, I'd actually recommend looking down," Reishi said when they came to a gentle stop a few minutes later. "For once, the view actually does a brilliant job of distracting you from your nerves." The Silhouettes leaned over the walkway, and Zhi Ging's eyes widened in wonder. Somehow, despite being deep below the sea, they were now standing above the sky. Thousands of constellations sparkled up from the floating darkness beneath them. Even from Fei Chui, she had never seen the stars this clearly.

"Each one of them is waiting to be matched with their very own Cyo B'Ahon," Ami whispered. "During your graduation ceremony, one will be paired with you and placed in your palm, connecting you to all other Cyo B'Ahon in Hok Woh."

"Wait, what do you mean?" What are they? Iridill asked, not tearing her eyes away from the hypnotic swirls of light.

"They're baby jellyfish. The silver lines they leave on your palm will shift into sentences each time your jellyfish receives a message. Without them, we could never share ideas or knowledge instantly across Hok Woh."

Zhi Ging blinked in surprise and crouched down to stare into the dark water.

She wasn't peering down on swirling galaxies. She was standing above thousands of miniature jellyfish.

The blooms drifted through the water and twisted like a starling murmuration of pure light.

"I think," Zhi Ging began, mesmerized by the glittering ribbons, "this might be the most incredible thing I've ever seen."

Ami beamed, obviously delighted with her reaction. She gave the Silhouettes a moment to look down into the Seoi Mou Pou, then cleared her throat, gesturing for the group to form a semicircle around her. The shimmering glow from the jellyfish danced across the Dohrnii's face as she spoke.

"For over one thousand years, Cyo B'Ahon have been the guardians of this nation. Our role is to maintain peace between the six provinces of Wengyuen and counsel rulers against decisions that could lead to war or plunge their province into chaos."

Zhi Ging glanced around, and while most of the other Silhouettes were nodding along to every word, Iridill was picking distractedly at her cloak.

"There are twelve skills needed to become a Cyo B'Ahon. Six to protect those you will watch over and six to achieve immortality. Each question you answered on your entrance exam was linked to one of these skills. Having a natural ability for one over the others is not enough. Without all twelve, you will never make it as a Cyo B'Ahon. Reishi, would you like to talk us through them?"

He nodded and stepped forward, the embroidered crane on his robe catching against the light.

"Let's begin with the skills needed to protect the provinces. To stop rulings that will hurt future generations, you must have a deep understanding of both the provinces and those living in them. This involves a natural aptitude in six areas: Climate, Calligraphy, Concealment, Flora,

Fauna, and Folklore. During your time here, you will be taught by Cyo B'Ahon who have dedicated their lives to each of these areas. Of course, to become a Cyo B'Ahon you must also prove yourself capable of immortality. This can only be achieved by combining the six skills essential for ageshifting: Perception, Prediction, Perseverance, Recall, Reasoning, and Rapport." Reishi paused, his expression growing serious as he surveyed the group.

"Each month, Silhouettes will take part in a challenge to test one of these twelve skills. Only those who pass will continue in their Silhouette year. The Scout exams are a good indication of who has potential to become a Cyo B'Ahon, but we can't risk anyone having just been lucky on the day."

Zhi Ging was surprised to spot worry flicker over Iridill's face. *What does she have to worry about? The Lead Glassmith will probably still throw her a weeklong welcome-back feast if she doesn't make it through* . . . Ami placed a hand on Reishi's shoulder and smiled down at the group.

"Thank you, I couldn't have explained it better myself. Now, are there any questions?" The others were silent, their expressions somber after Reishi's warning. Zhi Ging bit her lip and tentatively raised her hand.

"Yes, Zhi Ging! What is it?"

"What happens to anyone who doesn't pass a challenge?"

Behind her blue-tinted glasses, Ami's delicate eyebrows shot up, and the Silhouettes held their breath, waiting for her answer. Reishi chuckled and stepped forward, breaking the sudden tension that had filled the Seoi Mou Pou.

"Oh, we just send them home. Nothing dramatic, I'm afraid. It's just a bit disappointing for everyone involved."

Zhi Ging grimaced and looked down. It'd be more than a bit disappointing for her. Murrine would have told all the Glassmiths about her "spirit summoning" by now. What punishment would be waiting for her if she stepped back through the cloud sea?

"I've got a question," Iridill drawled, pointing a finger toward Ami. "What happened to your arm?" The Cyo B'Ahon blinked and pulled her sleeves back to reveal multiple silver welts.

"One of the risks of being Dohrnii and caring for baby jellyfish, I'm afraid. Just because I'm immortal doesn't mean tentacle stings don't leave a mark. But"—Ami flashed a smile at the group, her sleeve fluttering back down—"it's worth it to hold living starlight, don't you think?"

THE REST OF THE TOUR PASSED IN A BLUR, WITH THE Silhouettes shown countless classrooms, workshops, and laboratories. One room had been filled with hulking glass stalactites, dozens of Cyo B'Ahon gliding between them on rolling ladders, scratching complicated equations onto the dark glass. There had been gasps of delight, followed by immediate shushing, when a giant turtle swept past the thick glass wall that separated the library from the sea, its shadow gliding over rows of books.

Eventually, Ami stopped the group in front of a plain wooden door. It was the only door Zhi Ging had seen in Hok Woh not carved from glass.

"Final stop of the tour, everyone. Make sure you remember it; this is the entrance to your new dorms."

She slid the door back, and they stepped into a soft, warmly lit circular space. Sedate flames crackled from a sunken fireplace in the center of the room and filled the air with the heady scent of jasmine. Paper screen doors wrapped around the walls, and dappled light shone through them, shadows dancing across the common area as a few night-owl Silhouettes moved about inside their rooms. It was like the group had stepped inside a paper lantern.

Dozens of Silhouette lanterns had been strung up across the center of the dorm, each pinned in place by a gold clasp engraved with the Silhouette's hometown. Zhi Ging grimaced at the Fei Chui clasp. Her and Iridill's now slightly crumpled lanterns were pinched beneath it, their two paper-cutting outlines squeezed against one another. *Hopefully that isn't a sign we'll have to share a room too.*

Zhi Ging turned toward Reishi. "How many Silhouettes are in here?"

"At the moment, there's around ninety of you." Reishi nodded toward the domed ceiling. There were more doors above the lanterns, with wooden ladders connecting the platforms between each level. "We can fit just over one hundred and fifty in here, but recently there have been fewer towns and villages meeting with Silhouette Scouts like myself." A frown flickered briefly across his face before his smile returned. "Which, luckily for you, means there should be a few empty rooms on this level."

"Oh! In that case, is there any chance my room can be away from—" Her eyes darted toward Iridill nervously, and Reishi nodded, understanding immediately.

"Absolutely. Ami," he added, his voice rising, "there's a spare room here so you go ahead with the others and I'll get Zhi Ging settled in."

Ami nodded and led the rest of the new Silhouettes up one of the ladders.

"Thank you," Zhi Ging murmured, a weight lifting off her shoulders.

Reishi stopped in front of a dark screen door and nodded at the glowing paper screen beside it. "Why don't I introduce you to your new neighbor?"

Zhi Ging pulled at the sleeves of her cloak, suddenly anxious. Hopefully they were better than Iridill, whoever they were.

Reishi knocked on the door to her left. There was a pause, some muffled clattering, then the screen slid open to reveal a girl around Zhi Ging's age. Her black hair was pulled into a haphazard bun, and her round cheeks were covered in dark ink smudges, as if she'd fallen asleep while writing.

"Mynah, this is Zhi Ging from Fei Chui," Reishi said. She's going to take the room next to yours. "I'd like you to keep an eye on her until she's settled."

Zhi Ging stepped forward. "Nice to meet you, Mynah."

The girl blinked drowsily at Zhi Ging and waved, but didn't say anything. When she smiled, the black ink smeared across her cheeks flushed a soft buttery yellow.

Zhi Ging's eyes widened in surprise, but the marks had already faded back to black as Mynah quickly slid her door shut again.

Reishi gave Zhi Ging a reassuring smile. "I'm sure you'll get along, she's usually much chattier." He tapped her screen door. "Right, rest up and come by my lab after class tomorrow—it was the seventeenth one on Ami's tour. I want us to work on recapturing the air rails together."

Zhi Ging nodded uncertainly. She had lost track after the fifth lab. Was Reishi's the one that hung upside down from the ceiling or the one filled with thousands of different-sized gemstones?

Reishi looked at her quizzically, then bent down so he was level with her.

"Don't worry, no Silhouette really works out the pattern of Hok Woh's corridors before their second month. Until then, Gahyau will help you out. If you follow him, he'll bring you straight to my lab."

"Thanks, Reishi." She sagged with relief. "I feel like Hok Woh's at least three times bigger than Fei Chui."

"*I* don't even know my way around all of it." Reishi

95

laughed. "Each time a Silhouette becomes a full Cyo B'Ahon, we expand further out across the ocean floor. It's up to them how they want to design their new space."

He straightened up and gave her a quick nod before leaving.

Zhi Ging was still staring after him, when a hand shot out and grabbed the back of her cloak. She yelped and tumbled backward into Mynah's room, rough clay cylinders clattering around her. Every surface in the girl's room was covered in them.

"What do you think you're doing?" Zhi Ging cried.

Mynah flapped her arms frantically and pointed to a small hourglass perched beside a large clay cylinder. The last few grains trickled down in slow motion, and Zhi Ging jumped as Mynah cracked the cylinder in half and tipped the contents into her mouth. She coughed experimentally, then turned back to Zhi Ging with a large smile.

"Sorry about that, I didn't mean to pull your cloak so hard. You probably thought I was so rude earlier too, but hopefully you can tell why I didn't say anything!"

Zhi Ging leaped back, knocking more clay cylinders over. The voice coming out of Mynah's mouth was Reishi's.

CHAPTER 12

"How are you doing that?" Zhi Ging spluttered. Mynah tapped her throat and laughed in Reishi's deep voice.

"Oh, it's actually pretty easy. Have you heard of throwing clay?"

Zhi Ging nodded hesitantly.

"Well, I figured if you can throw your voice *and* throw pottery, there must be a way to combine the two. These little clay sculptures are voice boxes that help me mimic different Cyo B'Ahon. Have a look." She picked up a cylinder from her desk and tossed it over. It was lighter than Zhi Ging expected and had a name scratched into the base.

"But how do you make these? Don't people notice when you put clay around their throats?"

Mynah threw her head back and laughed. "Luckily, I don't need to sculpt on sleeping Cyo B'Ahon. My first few attempts weren't great, but I've gotten really good at guessing voice box measurements just by talking to people. I could probably even re-create yours now," she added with a modest shrug. Zhi Ging scrunched up her nose and self-consciously rubbed her throat.

"I kinda wish you hadn't told me that."

"Don't worry, I never mimic other Silhouettes, that's no fun. Making Cyo B'Ahon tutors say ridiculous things on the other hand . . ." She waggled her eyebrows at Zhi Ging, and they both smiled.

"What about your own voice? Where does that go when you're using one of these?" Zhi Ging asked.

"Technically, it is still my voice, I've just transformed it. All I do is take the biggest possible breath and scream into one of these until my voice is gone, trapped in the clay." She picked up another sculpture and twirled it between her fingers. "Screams work best because of their higher kinetic energy. They bounce around inside the clay and absorb the new shape. All I need to do then is leave the sculpture alone until the sand timer runs out. My voice will mold into the same tone and timbre of the voice box it's caught in." Mynah paused and tapped the sculpture against her cheek, the patch of ink flashing blue.

"The one glitch I can't seem to solve is that it only lasts until I take my first sip of water. For some reason drinks, or even soup, completely reset my voice."

Zhi Ging opened her mouth to ask another question but was interrupted by the sound of her own stomach rumbling.

"Speaking of soup . . ." Mynah giggled. "You must be starving, I bet you haven't had a decent meal in ages."

Zhi Ging laughed and poked her stomach as it gurgled in agreement. "How did you guess?"

"Ami always gets so excited showing new Silhouettes around and forgets to include the dining hall. Come on, let's get you a proper midnight feast!" She grabbed Zhi Ging's arm and pulled her out of the dorms.

THE DINING HALL WAS FILLED WITH CIRCULAR TA-bles that bloomed out of the floor like glass mushrooms. Although it was almost midnight, a few Silhouettes were still scattered around the tables, heads bent together as they compared homework scrolls between bowls of steaming noodles. Zhi Ging spotted the same crane from Reishi's robe carved into the far wall. It gazed down at them with a distinctly imperious expression, its curved neck and long beak casting shadows across the room. A large glass egg floated in a basin between its legs, and etched above it was the same phrase she'd spotted carved on walls throughout Hok Woh: *Hok Laap Gai Kwan.*

Zhi Ging mouthed the sentence, the unfamiliar words catching on her tongue.

"What does that mean? I kept seeing it on Ami's tour."

"Oh, that's the Cyo B'Ahon motto. It means 'A crane among the chickens.'" Mynah wrinkled her nose. "It's quite smug as mottos go. Think of Cyo B'Ahon as cranes and everyone else in Wengyuen as a chicken. Sure chickens have an okay life, but they never aim for greatness. They don't even know what they're missing and will never

99

experience what it's like to truly fly. Cranes are . . . higher up the pecking order," she finished, rolling her eyes at a joke Zhi Ging suspected Reishi had repeated to Silhouettes multiple times. It sounded even stranger to hear it coming from Mynah's mouth in his voice.

"Apparently the fire in our dorm is the last surviving flame from when the original Hok Woh was burned to the ground by jealous 'chickens' a century ago."

"Wait, why would anyone attack the Cyo B'Ahon?" Zhi Ging asked, her face scrunched up in confusion. Reishi had never mentioned an attack, but she knew Aapau wouldn't have encouraged her to become a Silhouette if she didn't think it was safe.

Mynah shrugged and looked away.

"Most of the Cyo B'Ahon who were around at the time don't like to talk about it. But I think it's telling that they rebuilt Hok Woh under the sea, where there's no risk of being destroyed by fire again." She coughed awkwardly and waved toward the center of the room. "Anyway, enough about that. Ami probably wouldn't want me telling you about the fire on your first day. Grab a seat and I'll get our food."

Zhi Ging wove between the tables, trying to find a spot where the crane wasn't looking directly at her. No matter which table she tried, its judgmental eyes seemed to follow her around the room. Did it know she hadn't finished the Scout exam? Eventually, she gave up and plonked down with her back to it at one of the smaller tables.

Mynah pottered over and put down a tray stacked with two empty soup bowls, a large teapot of boiling water, and eight intricate porcelain spoons. She placed one of the bowls in front of Zhi Ging with an expectant smile. A rough triangular stone rose up from the center of the bowl, its base fused to the blue-and-white patterned china.

"Take your pick." Mynah slid the spoons toward her, and Zhi Ging looked at the empty bowl in confusion.

"Um how do I . . . ? I mean, do you normally eat stones? Is that a thing in Hok Woh?"

"We're not quite that weird here." Mynah laughed and gestured at the spoons again.

"Erm, all right. I guess I'll go with"—Zhi Ging's hand hovered between two options, before settling on a sand-colored spoon decorated with curling clouds and thin green strokes—"this one."

"Ooh good choice. That's one of the best homei spoons." Mynah nodded enthusiastically, Reishi's voice booming around them.

She rolled up her sleeves, and Zhi Ging noticed her arms were also covered in ink splatters. Mynah filled both soup bowls with boiling water, until just the peaks of the stones were visible, then picked up a gold-speckled spoon with a wooden handle. She paused, checked that Zhi Ging was watching, then slammed her homei spoon down against the sharp tip of the stone.

The porcelain spoon shattered and fell into the boiling water. Shards sank below the surface and started to expand. Zhi Ging watched in astonishment as the fragments merged and transformed into a warm bowl of congee. The gold flecks rose to the surface and became a salted duck egg, while the wooden handle puffed up into a yau zaa gwai, the savory fried-dough stick Zhi Ging would get as a breakfast treat each birthday. Mynah sighed happily and breathed in the comforting smell.

"Cyo B'Ahon really have the best food in all of Wengyuen. I've been here for eight months now and the meals are still my favorite part of Hok Woh! Go on, your turn."

Zhi Ging brought her own spoon down through the rising steam. The clouds floated to the surface and, with a faint pop, expanded into wonton dumplings. The green lines became finely chopped spring onions and the bowl filled with thin yellow shrimp-roe noodles. Mynah giggled at Zhi Ging's wide-eyed expression, all traces of Reishi's voice vanishing as she slurped down her congee.

"Why do you still look so impressed? You saw what happened with my homei spoon!" Mynah's own voice was light and fast, the words spilling out over each other when she spoke.

"I just can't believe this exists. Back in Fei Chui, Aapau and I would spend hours—" Zhi Ging's face dropped as she suddenly remembered the argument they'd had on what had turned out to be the last time they'd wrap dumplings together. Had Aapau even heard her apology when the Lead Glassmith led her into the roaming pagoda for her Final Year?

"Hey, is everything all right?" Mynah asked softly, the patches on her cheeks turning blue as she scooted closer to place an arm around Zhi Ging.

"Yeah, I'm fine." Zhi Ging squeezed her eyes tight, trying to push the memory back down. She gave Mynah a tight smile, and her eyes flickered to the girl's blue cheeks.

"Do you mind me asking about . . ." Zhi Ging tapped her own cheeks and trailed off, unsure if she was being rude.

Mynah nodded, adjusting her bun before it came loose.

"I have a condition called vitiligo. Small pale patches started to appear on my arms and face a few years ago. They weren't painful, but more and more kept showing up. My great-aunt is the Head Matchmaker in Omophilli but, even with her connections across all six provinces, no one could work out what had caused them."

Zhi Ging subconsciously traced a finger across her left arm, wondering if her gold lines would still be visible under Gertie's glove.

"I spent a month in bed, bored out of my mind, while they tried to work it out. All I had for company that entire time was a small fish tank filled with mimic octopuses. They'd been gifted to my great-aunt years ago by Ami."

"Wait, the same Ami who just led the tour?"

"Course, Omophilli is one of the main cities that pays the Cyo B'Ahon tithe. I think Ami even used to collect it in person, but she suddenly stopped just before I was born. My great-aunt still brags about how she used to have dim sum with Hok Woh's Dohrnii. Ami's the only person she ever made an honorary member of the Matchmakers' Guild."

Zhi Ging stabbed a dumpling with her chopstick and frowned, not wanting to interrupt. *Are Ami's visits ending linked to the rumors Reishi mentioned in Gertie's tent? But what could any Cyo B'Ahon be afraid of?*

"Anyway," Mynah continued, "one day it finally clicked. If a mimic octopus could learn to change its colors then so could I. I'd clearly already done it once!" She lifted her congee bowl up and scooped the last of the meal into her mouth before grinning at Zhi Ging.

"I've got no interest in making my skin go back to how it was before though. Imagine being a Cyo B'Ahon who can ageshift *and* chromashift. I'm still learning how to control it, but soon I should be able to walk around bright pink or deep blue, any color I want to match my mood." She stretched out her arms, and the patches around her elbow flickered to a rich green.

Zhi Ging looked down at her own hand and wondered if Mynah had ever managed to turn her skin gold. Just as she was about to ask, there was a timid cough behind them.

"Mind if I join you?"

The two girls turned around, and Mynah beamed at the gangly boy hovering by their table.

"Pinderent! Since when did you ever have to ask? Of course, sit down. This is Zhi Ging, she's just joined us from Fah . . . Oh sorry, I can't remember the name now." Mynah squinted at Zhi Ging's white Pan Chang, but the knot had twisted against her cloak.

"No worries, unless you're interested in glasswork most people haven't heard of my village." Zhi Ging smiled and swiveled around to Pinderent. "I'm from Fei Chui."

"No way!" he breathed, his eyes brightening as he squeezed in beside her. "I'm from Geng Zun, my village is in the valley at the bottom of the jade mountain. My dad helps carve glass terraces for you guys. This is so great, most of the other Silhouettes are from huge cities and no one's even heard of Geng Zun—"

Mynah burst out laughing, delighted at his excitement.

"Zhi Ging, you should be incredibly honored right now. That's the most Pinderent's ever said in one go in the entire three months he's been here."

"That's just because you always talk over me." He flushed, waving his chopsticks at her before turning back to Zhi Ging. "Are you the only Silhouette this month? Apparently the Scouts didn't invite anyone the month before I joined."

"Oh no, there were a few of us. I'm not actually sure which provinces they're from, but . . ." Zhi Ging hesitated, worried they might react like the ageshifting Cyo B'Ahon in the corridors. She'd enjoyed not being different, even if it was just for one meal. "I was the second Silhouette picked from Fei Chui."

Mynah's mouth fell open and she turned to Pinderent, grabbing him by the shoulders.

"Are you going to be all right, Pinderent?" she asked with exaggerated concern. "Two whole people who have heard about your jade mountain. What if this is *too much* excitement for one day?"

Pinderent groaned and wriggled out of her grip. "Ignore Mynah, she loves to be overdramatic."

"Who me?" Mynah gasped, her cheeks flashing multiple colors. "I have absolutely no idea what you're talking about."

The three of them collapsed into giggles, but Zhi Ging stilled when she spotted Iridill coming into the dining hall. A few other Silhouettes from the tour trailed behind her, nodding at her every word.

"Is she the other one?" Pinderent asked, following her gaze. He stood up and waved warmly at Iridill. "Hey, Fei Chui!"

Iridill stopped, her eyes narrowing when she spotted Zhi Ging hunched behind him. She strode over to their table and glowered at Pinderent until he awkwardly sank back into his seat.

"Do I *know* you?"

"Uh, no." Pinderent's voice was little more than a squeak. "But I'm from Geng Zun and your friend mentioned you were also from Fei Chui, so I thought you'd like to join us."

Iridill sneered down at Zhi Ging. "Ew. NoGlow, are you telling people we're friends? That's so pathetic." She turned back to Mynah and Pinderent. "You'll soon learn it's not worth your time talking to NoGlow. Don't expect her to even make it past her first challenge."

Mynah stiffened and placed a hand on Zhi Ging's shoulder, the patches on her elbow turning a dark, stormy gray.

"I think we'll make our own decisions, *thanks.*"

"Whatever." Iridill scoffed and spun around, and the other Silhouettes scurried after her.

An awkward silence settled over them, and Zhi Ging could feel Pinderent staring at her in concern.

"Anyone else think we should feed that girl to Pou Pou?" Mynah asked in a stage whisper.

"Who?"

Pinderent pointed a chopstick toward the crane, and it was only when a nearby Silhouette pulled a rice paper message from his sleeve that Zhi Ging realized the egg floating in the basin was actually an exceptionally chubby jellyfish. It was easily five times larger than Gahyau.

"Since none of us have been matched with our own jellyfish, we all use Pou Pou when we want to message a Cyo B'Ahon. It's much faster than running around the corridors, trying to spot a tutor who may or may not have ageshifted. A Silhouette worked out a few years ago that Pou Pou prioritizes messages that come with a snack—"

"Bribe," Pinderent coughed.

"So now everyone offers him a treat each time they need to use him. That jellyfish honestly has the best life in all of Hok Woh." Mynah sighed, watching the Silhouette empty a whole bowl of grass jelly over Pou Pou's outstretched tentacles.

"If we *did* try to feed Iridill to him, he'd never pass a message on for us again. She'd be waaay too bitter," Zhi Ging said, deadpan.

Pinderent snorted and Mynah clapped her hands in delight, cheeks flashing yellow.

"Anyway, forget about her, you'll be fine with us," Pinderent said, pushing an open steamer of sau bao toward her. Zhi Ging bit into the warm pillowy bun, and sweet lotus paste coated the roof of her mouth with a rich, woody caramel. She took another bite while the sound of her new friends chatting washed over her. Zhi Ging smiled to herself. Maybe she'd finally found a place where being different didn't matter.

CHAPTER 13

"Wake up, we're going to be late for class." Mynah slammed Zhi Ging's door open, revealing the empty dorm behind her. She fumbled in her pocket and pulled out an extremely squashed bo lo bao, a trail of golden crumbs spilling out over the floor.

"I got this for you at breakfast, Pinderent's already gone ahead to save us a seat. You never want to sit front row for any tutor's lessons. They're big fans of *participation*."

Zhi Ging reached for the bun, and Mynah jerked back, taking a large bite.

"No way, you don't get this until we get you up. And the longer you take the more I'll eat!"

Zhi Ging groaned and stumbled out of bed to follow her friend.

"Wait! Don't forget your cloak, you have to wear that outside of the dorms."

"This one?" Zhi Ging murmured in a daze, lifting the soft black cloak Ami had given her.

"Yeah, hurry up. We have to wear them all year. How else would they tell us apart from ageshifted Cyo B'Ahon? The ones specializing in this skill will sit in on our lessons and they *always* grab the best seats."

"Fine, let's go!" Zhi Ging shrugged the cloak around her, and her jaw dropped when Mynah shoved the rest of the pineapple bun into her own mouth.

"Huh! U'm unly jukung," Mynah chuckled, her mouth full. She lifted her left hand from behind her back to wave a second, slightly less squished, bo lo bao. "Tuh-duh."

Zhi Ging rolled her eyes and laughed, snatching the second bun from Mynah before racing out toward the corridor.

"WHAT TOOK YOU SO LONG?" PINDERENT WHIS-pered as they squeezed past disgruntled Silhouettes and Cyo B'Ahon toward him in the central row. "I've had to fight people off for the last ten minutes. Pretty sure one of them was our ageshifted tutor from two months ago too."

"Sorry! We had a—"

Thunder rumbled around the classroom, and the crowd jumped, all hushed conversations coming to an abrupt stop. The main doors blew open, and a broad middle-aged man swept in. Zhi Ging leaned forward in amazement as a rainbow unfurled beneath his feet.

"Welcome all." The man's voice boomed around the classroom. "For those of you in your Silhouette year, my name is Wun Hong Choi, you may address me as Tutor Wun. Over the next month, I will share a glimpse into how Wengyuen's ever-changing climate can be swayed by Cyo B'Ahon. Those who choose to specialize with me after graduation will learn to bend and twist weather, leading villages out of drought and guiding storms away from harbors." He gestured to the back of the class, and the Silhouettes turned to face a wall of ceiling-high glass vats, each filled with a churning haze. "It may not be spirit magic, but combined centuries of Cyo B'Ahon research means we can now capture the worst of Wengyuen's weather before it erupts, sealing it within those vats and releasing it slowly, rather than allowing a storm to swallow a city whole." The Silhouettes in the back row shivered and leaned away from the murky glass.

Tutor Wun turned toward a broad glass stalactite that stretched down from the ceiling and began to sketch across its flat surface. "Let's begin your training with Nephology—the study of clouds. Can anyone tell me what each of these have in common?"

Zhi Ging glanced at Pinderent, but he shrugged. Mynah, meanwhile, was flipping frantically through a stack of library books, muttering to herself.

"No one?" Tutor Wun folded his arms and turned around. "Perhaps one of Reishi's latest Silhouettes? Let's see if any of you can crack it. Come on, it's very simple."

"Argh!" Zhi Ging screeched, leaping out of her seat.

She rubbed the angry red pinch mark on her arm and glared as Iridill's hand slithered back into the row behind her.

"Marvelous, good of you to volunteer, Miss . . ."

Zhi Ging looked up and realized the entire class was staring at her open-mouthed. She gulped and turned back to face the tutor.

"Yeung, sir. Yeung Zhi Ging."

"Well, Miss Yeung, why don't you come down to the front and share what you think the connection is."

The ageshifted Cyo B'Ahon murmured excitedly among themselves and stared at her with obvious interest. A few aged back up for a better look, snippets of conversation floating up between them.

"That's her, the Second Silhouette! Look, you can tell by the white Pan Chang Knot."

"Do you really think Sintou will let her stay?"

"I thought she'd look more . . . well, special."

Zhi Ging felt a prickling heat rising up the back of her neck and tried to ignore the hushed conversations spiraling around her. She glanced back helplessly at her friends, before inching out along the row. Mynah and Pinderent held their thumbs up and mouthed *good luck,* but she could tell they weren't too confident in her chances either.

Tutor Wun handed her the chalk and ushered her closer to the stalactite.

"Go on. What do you see?"

Zhi Ging peered at the sketches, willing the clouds to

reveal their secret. They began to blur and merge in front of her as she stared, unblinking, up at them.

"Awkward," someone coughed from the group to scattered laughter. Zhi Ging didn't need to turn around to know it was Iridill.

"I, uh—" She paused, watching the clouds fuse before her. *What did this remind her of?*

A memory of watching the cloud sea with Aapau flashed across her mind. They had spent a whole afternoon following clouds shifting between shapes. Zhi Ging turned back toward Tutor Wun, her heart beating.

"What they have in common is *everything*. It's all the same cloud! You've just drawn it at different stages of its floating cycle." She raced the chalk across the glass board, a thin ribbon of white lassoing the clouds together to show how they flowed into one another.

"Excellent!" Tutor Wun gestured for Zhi Ging to stay beside the board, and Iridill glowered from her seat, her arms crossed in frustration. "Miss Yeung is correct. Every cloud has almost unlimited shape potential, remember that. This"— he gestured, tapping one of the illustrations—"is the ideal shape for a cloud to carry rain, but the others . . ." He swung his chalk in a perfect circle around them. "Well, that's what we're going to focus on. I want you to work out what each of the other cloud shapes is best suited for carrying. Don't limit yourself to unoriginal options like lightning or hail, I want to see teams think inventively. To think like Cyo B'Ahon."

Tutor Wun pointed toward an ageshifted Cyo B'Ahon in the front row. "Gwong is currently working on a way to share warmth through snowstorms. *That* is what I'm looking for. I want options that can help the people of Wengyuen."

Zhi Ging glanced over at the tanned Cyo B'Ahon. *Would Gertie's weather wax be able to compete with warm storms?*

"You'll have four weeks to work on this project outside of your nightly homework and, ahead of the next Silhouette challenge, I'd like a demonstration from each pair. The Cyo B'Ahon in this room will help guide you through the trickier physics involved in Nephology. You can use Pou Pou, the dining-hall jellyfish, to send them questions anytime you want. Now, let's break you into groups."

Zhi Ging looked on in growing dismay as Tutor Wun paired up the other Silhouettes. She could see what was about to happen.

"Right." He clapped his hands together as the Cyo B'Ahon introduced themselves to the newly formed teams. "Is anyone not in a group? You can work with Miss Yeung here."

Slowly a single hand raised from the center of the row, and Zhi Ging's heart sank.

Iridill.

"NOGLOW, WE NEED TO TALK."

Zhi Ging groaned. She'd managed to avoid Iridill for the rest of Tutor Wun's lesson but had known the girl would pounce once class finished. Mynah and Pinderent stopped beside her, arms folding in unison as Iridill marched over.

"Just say the word," Mynah snarled, the patches on her cheek turning charcoal gray. Pinderent gulped anxiously and checked to see if Tutor Wun was still in earshot.

"It's all right," Zhi Ging murmured. "I might as well get this over with. What do you want, Iridill?"

"I have zero interest in working on this project with you—"

"Same," Zhi Ging said, cutting Iridill off.

"*Excuse* me?"

"We can work on it separately. You research in the library tonight and I'll do tomorrow. We'll swap handover notes each morning before class. There's no need to talk at all. That good with you?"

Iridill's mouth opened and shut several times in shock before she regained her usual sneer.

"Fine by me." She sniffed and flounced off.

Pinderent waited until Iridill vanished around the corner, then gave an impressed whistle.

"Zhi Ging, if you ever work out a way to fill a cloud with that level of boldness, I'll give you my entire stash of mochi for it."

"I think that might have been all of it." She laughed shakily. "I'm not sure I'll be as brave next time if she has her little group around her."

"Oh!" Pinderent yelped, his feet dancing in excitement.

"If you want to avoid Iridill, I can get you all the way out of Hok Woh for a few hours each week. All you have to do is join the greatest dragon boat team this side of Wun-Wun. We've been a Silhouette down since the last challenge. It was just me and Hiulam training with the Cyo B'Ahon last week."

"Not this again." Mynah laughed, rolling her eyes. "You try to recruit every new, unsuspecting Silhouette to join Team Bolei before they get a chance to see you race. Or should I say *sink*."

"Shhh, Mynah's just jealous she has to watch us from the stands."

"Don't believe a word he says, Zhi Ging! They haven't won a race the entire time I've been here."

"All right, all right!" Zhi Ging laughed, waving her hands between them as Pinderent and Mynah fought to outdo each other's dramatic gasps. "I'm in. Anything to get me as far from Iridill as possible."

CHAPTER 14

Zhi Ging arrived outside Reishi's lab twenty minutes later, out of breath from chasing Gahyau along the corridors.

"Don't tell me there are *more* Glassmiths after you?" Reishi snorted as she skidded to a stop in front of his door.

"Very . . . funny." Zhi Ging wheezed, rolling her eyes while, on the other side of the glass, a triumphant Gahyau waved two tentacles in racing victory.

Reishi chuckled and slid open the heavy lab door. Hundreds of interconnected glass tanks filled the space, spilling out across the floor and dangling from the ceiling. Zhi Ging twisted her head to follow one particularly haphazard tower of tanks and couldn't help but notice how it mirrored the towering jumbled piles in Gertie's tent. The only difference was that, here, all the mysteries were neatly stacked inside glass.

Each tank was home to a different breed of jellyfish. Some teleported between tanks, while others flashed multiple colors or turned their water to ice, then steam, and back again. In one particularly large tank, a single jellyfish repeatedly burst into thousands of miniature dazzling jellyfish before re-forming.

"It looks just like the fireworks back home!" Zhi Ging gasped.

"Good eye. This particular jellyfish was actually inspired by Fei Chui's spring festival. When I first became a Scout, I always arrived at the cloud sea just in time for those fireworks. He's still one of my favorite creations. Definitely more impressive than floating in a bubble," he added in a stage whisper. Zhi Ging laughed as Gahyau crossed his tentacles in outrage.

They worked their way through the lab, ducking under low-hanging pipes and stepping over miniature tanks, until they reached a desk piled high with scrolls. Although, to call it a desk didn't do it justice. Its surface was an intricate map of Wengyuen, which had been painstakingly traced in sand, then encased in glass. Reishi gestured toward a chair facing the desk.

"I've arranged a meeting with Sintou, the Head of the Cyo B'Ahon for you at the end of the week, unfortunately she wasn't free before then. Make sure to bring your lantern along. In the meantime, I thought we could keep things simple today and start with an introduction to air rails. Now, where did Gahyau get to?"

Zhi Ging glanced around as the jellyfish reappeared from behind one of the tanks with another Silhouette, who was carrying a stack of scrolls. When they lowered the scrolls, Zhi Ging beamed.

"Jack! What are you doing here?"

He waved as Gahyau bobbed forward, a bamboo steamer of lo mai gai and three cups of tea balanced above his bubble.

"Told you you'd see me again soon! What do you think of my Silhouette disguise?" Jack spun around in a black cloak, the red Pan Chang Knot fluttering against his shoulder. "Reishi stole this for me a few years ago and I've been able to sneak in and out of Hok Woh ever since."

"I think you'll find the term is 'borrowed,'" Reishi interrupted with an amused smile. "You're lucky the Cyo B'Ahon who owned it no longer needed their old cloak."

"But wait, how do you get past the glass entrance?"

"Oh, that part's easy." Jack's eyes glittered mischievously, and he nodded toward Gahyau.

Zhi Ging gasped, turning to shake her head at Reishi. "And I thought you hated breaking rules!"

"*Bending,* not breaking—there's a very important difference. The other Cyo B'Ahon know Jack works for me, they just don't know he occasionally hand delivers items to my lab. And besides, thanks to Gertie, I've known him far longer than most people I meet while shoreside. He's been helping with my air rail research."

"Helping?! I was the one doing all the most dangerous work!" Jack snorted. "Every few weeks, Reishi would load me up with new air rail–scanning equipment that he *promised* would finally work. I'd wave it around wildly while the floating market traveled between provinces, sometimes hanging on by just my ankle. After that, I'd have to risk the wrath of both Gertie *and* multiple Cyo B'Ahon by sneaking back into Hok Woh with the readings."

Reishi burst out laughing and pulled the scrolls from Jack's hands. "I'll admit Gertie's never happy when she's left to deal with customers alone, but 'wrath of the Cyo B'Ahon' is a little dramatic, don't you think?" He rolled his eyes and ageshifted down, tapping a scroll against Jack's red Pan Chang. "Once you're in this, none of them even recognize you. All they see is another Silhouette hurrying past."

"Can I keep the cloak even though someone's stolen my job now?" Jack glanced at Zhi Ging, his eyes switching between green and blue as he winked.

"Oh, if you want to keep working on the air rails . . ." she began, feeling her cheeks flush red. She hadn't realized she'd taken his place.

"Nah, they're all yours," he said, and then turned to side-eye Reishi. "Reishi somehow pays me even less than Gertie!"

"Remind me again, which one of us demanded you should be paid 'per air rail found'?" The Cyo B'Ahon chuckled, pushing the lo mai gai toward them both. "And yes, you can keep the cloak. We don't want to risk a 'wrath' next time you wander through Hok Woh's corridors."

"This food is worth the risk!" Jack laughed, handing the steamer over to Zhi Ging. She unwrapped the dried lotus leaf and blew on her fingers when steam sprang up. The leaf fell away to reveal a tightly packed parcel of glutinous rice filled with diced chicken and mushrooms, scallions, and a salted duck yolk. She breathed in deeply, savoring the rich, comforting smell, and took a bite. It tasted just like the ones Aapau made.

Reishi ageshifted back up to fifty, breaking off a piece of his own lo mai gai for Gahyau.

"I've been meaning to ask you Zhi Ging, how's your arm healing? Are the gold lines still there?"

She tugged the glove down carefully, remembering Gertie's warning about not tearing the fabric. Jack leaned forward, the color in his eyes flickering back and forth.

"Oh."

Her arm was completely blank, with no hint whatsoever of the swirling gold lines that had covered it a day earlier.

"Hmmm, maybe they only appear at high altitudes." Reishi frowned, drumming his desk in thought. Zhi Ging's eyes darted from her arm to his face in concern. Was he thinking of dragging her back to Fei Chui to check? The Glassmiths would still be looking for her, and if the Lead Glassmith really thought she was a spirit summoner, her punishment would be a lot worse than being squeezed into the post pipe.

"Why are you trying to find air rails anyway?" she

asked in an attempt to distract him before the thought could enter his mind. "What do they do? You never actually told me."

Reishi's face lit up. Behind him, Gahyau threw up two exasperated tentacles while Jack groaned and sank into a chair, obviously knowing they were in for a long monologue. Reishi ignored them and jumped up, tugging scrolls from between tanks. Zhi Ging winced as a large tank screeched forward and tipped dangerously toward him, but Jack quickly pushed it back in place with his foot.

"The air rails could change *everything*. I've been trying to work out a way to use them since before the first Hok Woh bur—" Reishi broke off and tried again. "Even before I invited Jack to help."

Zhi Ging's eyebrows furrowed in confusion. *He was going to say, before the first Hok Woh burned down,* she thought. *Why didn't he want to mention that? Is he keeping it from me or from Jack?*

"The sky is covered with thousands of overlapping air rails. You won't usually notice them, since you step through so many each day. But have you ever felt like there was a hair on your face and, when you tried to brush it away, you couldn't find it?" In his excitement, Reishi didn't wait for an answer. "Well, that's a snapped rail. Or when a baby is learning to walk and it looks like they've tripped over nothing, that's really them struggling against a low-lying rail."

Jack nudged her arm, pointing toward Gahyau. "The rails are how he floats around, his bubble runs along them."

"Exactly." Reishi nodded. "It's the same with the dragons in Fei Chui. Have you ever wondered how such large, wingless lizards can fly through the air?"

"Not really," Zhi Ging answered truthfully. "Most of us in Fei Chui were just focused on not being eaten by one."

Jack grinned. "Fair enough."

Reishi cleared his throat before continuing. "Well, a dragon's long, curling whiskers are constantly gauging the temperature while they're soaring through the air. At the same time, their talons are covered in microscopic temperature-control valves. They can adapt instantly, absorbing or releasing stored heat so that their talons are always at the exact same temperature as the air rails."

Jack spotted Zhi Ging's confused expression and pointed back toward Gahyau.

"It's probably easier to use Gahyau as the example. Air rails and bubbles are pretty similar. If you poked your finger through a bubble it would burst. But if you poked it with something the *exact* same temperature as its surface, it'd stay intact. If there was a way to get your body to the same temperature as an air rail, it'd be like holding on to a solid metal beam."

"That's exactly how it felt on the cliffside!" Zhi Ging gasped, squeezing her left hand.

"Right! But how?" Reishi began to pace. "Even if your fingers were, for one perfect second, the exact same temperature as the air rail, your next heartbeat should have fractionally thrown it off, snapping the air rail. Instead, under your hand, the air rail not only stayed solid but *became visible*."

"Whoa," Jack breathed.

Reishi began pacing and ageshifted back down. "I've spent decades trying to adapt the temperature valves in a dragon's talon, but the amount of energy needed to fuse that with a human foot?" He grimaced. "Well let's just say I don't think anyone cares too much about learning how to walk on air rails when they're a pile of ash."

"Hang on! You're not going to try any experiments like that on me are you?" Zhi Ging jumped back, her tea wobbling dangerously on the glass desk.

"No, not at all! All I want to do is learn how you did it in the first place. If we can re-create it and teach others, well then . . ." A dreamlike sheen washed over his face. "Then all Cyo B'Ahon could once again travel safely through every province."

Zhi Ging chewed on her lip, filled with uncertainty. "What if I can't do it again? What if it was a fluke?"

Gahyau floated forward to rest his bubble supportively against her hand. It felt like a slightly damp, but reassuring, cuddle.

Reishi waved a hand. "Try not to worry about that for now. Worst case, we can always re-create the original conditions. Jack and I will just push you off a cliff and see what happens." He chuckled.

"Oh, I know the perfect tent we could use to break your fall too! There's a mirror-covered one in the floating market that *loves* people crashing into it," Jack added, barely able to keep a straight face.

"Great." Zhi Ging snorted. "Glad I've got that to look forward to."

"I've spoken with Ami and she's agreed for you to spend time after class helping with my research. As long as you keep passing the Silhouette challenges, I'd like us to spend an hour each evening trying to solve both how you held on to the air rails and how you created that lantern. Sintou recently renewed my funding so we can run as many experiments as it takes. Of course, if it begins to impact your homework . . ."

"It won't, I promise!" She couldn't let that happen. Not when she had so much more to prove. The guaranteed break from Iridill every evening also didn't hurt.

"Perfect! And if Sintou re-allows tutor tours, we can of course look at taking evenings off from research."

"Tutor tours?" Jack asked, looking at Reishi in confusion. "What are they? Do you need me to help on those as well as the Silhouette challenges?"

Reishi shook his head. "Cyo B'Ahon tutors used to bring groups of Silhouettes out across the six provinces on research trips. It was a great way to show, in person, how decisions and ideas dreamed up in Hok Woh could have a real impact on others' lives. Unfortunately, Sintou banned the tours after—well, after the attack on the original Hok Woh."

Zhi Ging held her breath, hoping he would finally reveal more about the original Hok Woh, but Reishi stopped himself short.

"Ami has been trying to convince Sintou to reinstate the tours for years. You're very lucky to have her as your Dohrnii, Zhi Ging. All Silhouettes are." Reishi paused and smiled at Zhi Ging. "You know, your arrival might have been exactly the inspiration she needed. She was up early this morning, multiple scrolls tucked under her arm as she marched into Sintou's office. After I told her how you wouldn't accept anything less than an invite to Hok Woh—well, I've not seen her this excited in decades. She had so many questions about you after the welcome tour. You really impressed her."

Zhi Ging flushed, unused to the feeling of pride ballooning inside her. Apart from Aapau, no one in Fei Chui had ever paid her any attention. But now Cyo B'Ahon, some of the most important people in all of Wengyuen, were interested in her.

"Who knows, if Ami does manage to bring back the tours, dragon boat races might stop being the only time Silhouettes are allowed shoreside between challenges."

Zhi Ging glanced at the hourglass on his desk and yelped. She'd completely lost track of time.

"I'm so sorry, I need to go. Jack, it was really good to

see you again, but I'm meant to be at dragon boat training now. It's my tryout for Team Bolei."

Reishi's eyes widened in horror. "With Bucbou? Is she still the team captain?"

"I'm not su—"

"I used to race with her. Dragon on a mountain, falling off a cliff, that's nothing compared to how Bucbou deals with those who show up late for training. Run!"

CHAPTER 15

"What took you so long? The others have already gone shoreside to the boat." Pinderent hopped from foot to foot at the bottom of the stairs, his anxious expression reflected against the dark glass.

"Sorry, I got lost on my way back from Reishi's."

Zhi Ging hurried after him up the steps, wincing at the stitch in her side. Hopefully the sun had already set; she didn't need anyone else seeing just how red and out of breath she was.

"That's okay," Pinderent continued, hauling her up the last few steps. "I think we made it before Bucbou so we're—"

"Still late."

A woman with a shaved head stood scowling at them from the helm of a wooden boat, fingers curled around a long wooden paddle, gripping it like a sheathed sword. Four others were already seated in the boat, and Hiulam, the other Silhouette on the team, grimaced at them in sympathy.

"You can both stay after training and lower this boat back into the sixth stepping stone." Bucbou leaped up, her feet seeming to float in midair. It was only when her cloak rippled behind her that Zhi Ging realized the Cyo B'Ahon was standing on a dragon head sculpted from a single sheet of purified glass. It had to have come from Fei Chui! Only an experienced Glassmith could work glass until it was practically invisible.

"The only way a dragon boat team can win is if all eight crew members work in sync. How can that happen if our Silhouettes don't even arrive on time?"

Pinderent blushed and looked down, his ears burning red. Zhi Ging gulped and took a step forward.

"That was my fault. Pinderent invited me and then I couldn't find my way back to the main hall. He's only late because of me."

Bucbou turned toward Zhi Ging, her eyes narrowing in scrutiny when she spotted the white Pan Chang Knot.

"So, you're the Second Silhouette. I should warn you, I'm much more difficult to impress than Reishi. Have you ever used one of these?" She held up the wooden paddle, tutting when Zhi Ging shook her head. "Let's start you off as a Central Paddler. Based on your arm length, you wouldn't make a better Pacer than Pinderent. We'll then trial you as Steerer. I want to see how you handle obstacles blocking the boat's path. If you prove not to have any skill in either position, I'm sure you'll enjoy watching the race from the stands."

Bucbou nodded curtly, then pulled a whistle from her robes and blew three loud trills. She leaped back off the glass head and gestured for Pinderent and Zhi Ging to follow after her.

"All right, team. Thanks to this delayed start, we're going to begin tonight's training with some anticurrent drills."

Groans erupted across the boat.

"Right, Hiulam, I saw that eye-roll! Hand your paddle over. You're acting Drummer for the rest of tonight's training."

Pinderent held out a hand to steady Zhi Ging as she clambered over the dragon head, careful not to snap its delicate glass horns.

"Maybe I should have taken my chances with Iridill," she hissed. "Bucbou has to be the scariest Cyo B'Ahon here."

"Yeah, that's about as much of a warm welcome as you're ever going to get from her. But she's an incredible racer and I promise it'll be worth it once we start training." His eyes darted toward the Cyo B'Ahon, and he lowered his voice. "Especially since it's harder to hear her once our paddles are splashing against the waves."

"Silhouette, catch." Bucbou tossed a paddle toward

them, and Zhi Ging fumbled for it, the narrow handle slipping between her fingers. The Cyo B'Ahon closest to her shot out a hand and caught the edge of the flat blade before it tipped overboard.

"Thanks," Zhi Ging croaked, her eyes wide with relief as she recognized Gwong from that morning's lesson.

"No problem," he murmured. "Bucbou's punishment for anyone who drops a paddle is for them to swim a lap to shore and back. No one should ever have to do that on their first day of training."

Zhi Ging glanced out across the dark water and shuddered; without the lights from the floating market, she couldn't even see the shore. She clutched the paddle tightly and nodded at Gwong before picking her way toward the back of the dragon boat. With each step, she felt her heartbeat grow faster. Could everyone else tell how nervous she was? What if the Cyo B'Ahon on the team had been training for decades?

Hiulam cocked her head to one side as they stepped past one another.

"Hey, no need to look so serious!" she whispered, waving a hand in front of Zhi Ging's pale frown. "Honestly, if you don't capsize us in the next hour, you'll have done better than most Silhouettes who try out for Team Bolei."

Zhi Ging gave a shuddering laugh and loosened her grip on the paddle. "Thanks, you've got no idea how much I needed to hear that."

"No problem and, hey, you'll be sitting behind Gwong and Yuttou. They're the clumsiest ones on our team so Bucbou won't even notice if you make a mistake."

The two Cyo B'Ahon gasped in mock outrage, and Zhi Ging laughed as she squeezed in behind them.

"Good to have you on the team," Gwong shouted over the crashing waves. "And—"

"And even better to finally not have Hiulam babbling away behind us," Yuttou cut in over him, ageshifting down to give Zhi Ging a better view of the rest of the team. Hiulam shook her head at the betrayal.

"You know what Zhi Ging? Everyone would actually be really impressed if you used your paddle to flip these two overboard. And that's my professional opinion as longest-lasting Silhouette on Team Bolei."

Bucbou blew her whistle over Zhi Ging's laughter and Hiulam glanced toward the front of the boat.

"Right, I'd better get to the drum. Zhi Ging, as a Central Paddler all you need to do is remember three easy rules. One, always keep both hands on your paddle, otherwise a wave will snatch it away in seconds. Two, never try to change the boat's route. B'ei Gun, our Steerer"— Hiulam nodded toward a serious-looking Cyo B'Ahon standing at the back of the boat—"will use his oar to keep us on course. If you start pushing against his plan, it'll mess up your strokes *and* you'll ruin the rhythm the two Pacers up front have set. And three, the Drummer creates the dragon boat's heartbeat, so *obviously*, they're the most important of the eight crew members and should be given snacks after every training session."

Yuttou and Gwong immediately began to boo, and Hiulam laughed as she jumped out of reach of their waving paddles.

"No one's ever going to fall for that." Yuttou snorted. "And you're not even the real Drummer, that's Gu Sao's position."

"If we hadn't been a Cyo B'Ahon down tonight, Bucbou would have sent you straight back to the dorms for rolling your eyes. You're lucky Gu Sao's Scouting this week."

"Ah, it was worth a try!"

A shrill whistle cut through the air, and Hiulam grimaced when she saw Bucbou glowering at them in impatience.

"That is *not* the face of a happy Bucbou. Not that any of us have ever seen what that looks like." The boat rocked as Hiulam hurried toward the drum and Zhi Ging took a deep breath, trying to calm the nerves that had started to creep back in.

"All right, Second Silhouette," Bucbou roared over the rising waves, "let's see what you've got."

Icy spray doused Zhi Ging as the others plunged their paddles into the dark water and the dragon boat jerked forward, pushing away from the glass stepping stone. There was no backing out now.

CHAPTER 16

Almost an hour later, Zhi Ging heaved her paddle back out of the water and onto her lap. Her hair was damp with sea spray, and thick black strands clung to the sides of her reddened face.

Yuttou groaned and held out both hands, clenching them experimentally. "Hey, can anyone still feel their fingers after that last sprint?"

Zhi Ging shook her head, too exhausted to speak. Visions of racing lengthwise over cresting waves, paddles churning as Bucbou pushed them to go faster and farther each time, flooded her mind. Gwong leaned sideways and dunked his entire head beneath the waves before whipping it back, droplets splashing against the others. Zhi Ging blinked hard. *Is that steam rising around his neck?*

Bucbou, the only crew member not to look exhausted, leaped onto the glass dragon head and blew three final short blasts of her whistle, her eyes gleaming. "That's more like it! If we maintain that speed during the next race, Team Bolei might finally win an audience with Sintou."

There were a few feeble cheers from the Cyo B'Ahon, and Pinderent turned to give Zhi Ging a shaky thumbs-up.

"Now," Bucbou continued, "five final paddle arches, then we'll finish up with a tour of the racecourse." A whisper of a smile flickered across her face when she spotted Zhi Ging's exhausted expression. "It's tradition for each new Silhouette to see the course after they've passed their tryout. You'll never get to see it this clearly during a race, not with five other boats tearing through the water."

Zhi Ging's heart leaped as Yuttou nudged her in congratulations.

She had passed!

Somehow, between spluttering out seawater and repeatedly bumping her paddle against Gwong's, she had actually impressed Bucbou. She sighed in relief, her shoulders finally able to relax. It felt great knowing there was one more spot in Hok Woh where she'd be safe from Iridill. But it felt even better knowing it was a spot she had proved she deserved. Even if people asked questions about her lantern, no one could take this from her.

Zhi Ging's entire body creaked as she lifted the paddle horizontally over her head for the paddle arches. *There's no way it was this heavy at the start of training.* Keeping their arms and backs straight, the team bent forward, pressing their noses toward their knees before sitting back up. Zhi

Ging's arms shook under the paddle's weight, and she had to grit her teeth as Bucbou counted them down. Finally, the Cyo B'Ahon blew her whistle, and the paddles clattered down around her.

"Well done, all of you. I'm glad to see Team Bolei finally coming together. It's only taken four decades." She turned to face Zhi Ging. "If you pass all twelve of your challenges, you might just be invited to join permanently and represent the glass province alongside us."

"Wait, is all of Team Bolei from the glass province?" Zhi Ging asked excitedly.

"We didn't want to say until you'd made it through your first training session!" Yuttou beamed, tapping at a subtle row of glass beads embroidered around her collar. "Silhouettes can train with any team—"

"Whichever one needs new crew members," Gwong explained.

"—but after graduation you race with your province team, which for Team Bolei is anyone who grew up around the jade mountain."

The boat bounced as it skimmed over one of the glass stepping stones. Zhi Ging peered over the side and spotted a porcelain dragon head peering up at them beneath the sea surface, its snout covered in delicate blue brushstrokes. How had she missed that before? Were there more dragon boats inside the other stepping stones?

As if sensing her thoughts, Bucbou tapped her paddle against the next stepping stone, a flash of gold glinting up at them through the glass. "There are six boats in total, each with a different dragon head made from either paper, gold, silk, glass, porcelain, or carved lacquer. These dragon heads have been gifted to us by the current rulers of the six provinces and stand as symbols of our continued alliances across Wengyuen."

Zhi Ging turned back to the glass dragon head on their boat. It really had come from Fei Chui!

"Like the provinces themselves, each dragon boat has its own distinct advantages and disadvantages. A skilled team must prove themselves capable of success no matter which boat they race in. The Silhouettes we invite must discover the unique benefits, and overcome the limitations, of all six dragon boats. That, after all, is the true mark of a Cyo B'Ahon. Someone who can steer smoothly, undeterred by the chaos around them."

Bucbou paused and narrowed her eyes, tracing a hand across a thin crack beneath the dragon's glass horn.

"The last team to race with the glass dragon should have reported this. I'll have to get it replaced when I'm collecting the new paper dragon head. Let's not risk damaging it further during the racecourse tour."

She pressed her hand against Hok Woh's entrance stepping stone, and a small panel popped open, sending hundreds of white jellyfish streaming out toward them.

Each jellyfish hooked a tentacle over the side of the boat, then set off, pulling Team Bolei forward in a glowing white cloud. Without the loud splashing of paddles and

Hiulam's chaotic drumming, the only sound left was the water rustling like silk against the teak frame. Zhi Ging felt an unexpected pang of sadness watching the jellyfish bloom. Their flowing, luminous movement reminded her of how Aapau's hair would glimmer near dragon scales. If she did manage to pass all twelve Silhouette challenges, she wouldn't leave Hok Woh until after Aapau's Final Year was complete. After that, Aapau would be gone forever.

"These jellyfish mark the course border during the actual race," Yuttou whispered, nodding toward the jellyfish. "We want to stick to the center as much as possible. From there, they should look no different from starlight reflected in the water. If they ever look this big during a race, we've messed up badly."

"What happens if we row outside the border?"

B'ei Gun leaned forward, joining the discussion.

"We'll get time penalties if that happens before the last bend, but if we drift after the third and final bend . . ." He trailed off, the light reflecting up from the jellyfish giving his grimace a sinister gleam. "You'll work that out once you see it."

"It's not like the Fui Gwai has hordes of thralls waiting outside the course border." Yuttou rolled her eyes, unimpressed by his theatrics. "Anyway, no team has ever gotten close enough to it to be in actual danger."

"It?" Zhi Ging began, wondering why they were being so cryptic. "What is—?"

"There's still that blind spot," B'ei Gun interrupted.

"One last sea stack that blocks out the final curve to the finish line. No one watching from the stands would even know if a dragon boat drifted out into danger."

"Can you please stop trying to frighten every new Silhouette we get!" Yuttou groaned, throwing her arms in the air. Beneath them, the dragon boat veered smoothly to the right in a wide arch, marking the first bend in the course.

Gwong turned around and nudged Zhi Ging. "Steerers are known for being the team pessimists, but you can't really blame them. They have to spend the entire race worrying about the team crashing into another boat, hitting a sea stack, getting caught by a stealth wave, capsizing, or veering off course. B'ei Gun's right that it's dangerous, but Sintou would never have built Hok Woh this close to it if she thought there was any real danger."

"But what is *it*?" Zhi Ging demanded while B'ei Gun huffed behind them.

"You'll see in a few minutes," Pinderent called back, his relaxed smile doing more to reassure Zhi Ging than anything Gwong or Yuttou could say. If it didn't panic a worrier like Pinderent, surely it couldn't be that bad.

Whatever it was.

The second bend was filled with sea stacks, giant crumbling towers of moss-covered rock that loomed over them. The jellyfish were forced to slow down, carefully navigating the boat between the stone arches and pillars.

The team ducked as they passed under a particularly

low arch, and the popping sound of Cyo B'Ahon ageshifting down echoed around the stone pillars.

When they reached the third bend, almost all the jellyfish removed their tentacles and began to swim out into the darkness.

"Where are they goi—" The rest of Zhi Ging's question caught in her throat when she saw what was now illuminated in front of them. Their boat was floating a short distance away from the mouth of a deep circular canyon.

While the surface was calm, Zhi Ging could see currents roiling beneath it. Water plunged into its depths, dragging rivers of sand and large fragments of rock down with it.

"It's an underwater waterfall," Gwong explained excitedly. "The only waterfall beneath the ocean in all of Wengyuen. Even Sintou doesn't know what's at the bottom."

Trapped starlight fell in glittering constellations down the waterfall overhang and the jellyfish paled in comparison, their lights dim against the shimmering cascade.

"What would happen if we tried to paddle over that?" Zhi Ging asked in a hushed whisper, her voice barely audible over the rumble of the waterfall's currents. The gleaming water reminded her of molten glass, its slick, glossy movement luring in anyone unaware of just how dangerous it could be.

"I'm guessing nothing good," B'ei Gun muttered, never once taking his eyes off the waterfall. "*I* think it's the Fui

Gwai's lair." He waved down Yuttou's protests and jabbed a finger toward the dark heart of the waterfall. The roaring sound of waves thundering into the abyss seemed to grow louder as he continued. "Most provinces already believe the Fui Gwai was accidentally released by a Cyo B'Ahon in an experiment that went wrong. Are you seriously telling me you don't think it could have come from there?"

"That doesn't make sense." Yuttou shook her head. "The original Hok Woh was based in one of the higher mountains in the silk province. If, and it's a ridiculously big *if,* one of us really did release the Fui Gwai from the waterfall, why would we then build the new Hok Woh right beside its lair?"

B'ei Gun grumbled, clearly unconvinced, his eyes still fixed on the tumbling rapids.

Their boat curved in a wide arc, skirting around the rest of the underwater waterfall and past the final sea stack. Zhi Ging shook her head.

No, there can't be anything down there, she thought. *Reishi would have mentioned it to Aapau.*

She drummed her fingers against the boat, desperately trying to distract herself from another, more worrying, thought. Then again, she hadn't heard about the burning of Hok Woh until yesterday.

What else are the Cyo B'Ahon keeping secret?

CHAPTER 17

"Ah, Zhi Ging there you are." Reishi stood in front of his lab, back in the yellow ceremonial robes he had worn on the day of her Scout exam. "I'm glad you remembered your lantern. Sintou's been looking forward to seeing it in person."

Zhi Ging swallowed, wishing Gahyau could join them. She'd gotten used to seeing his reassuring bubble over the past week. What if the Head of the Cyo B'Ahon refused to accept two Silhouettes from Fei Chui?

Reishi glanced back at her as they hurried along the corridor.

"You haven't mentioned this visit to any of the other Silhouettes, have you?"

Zhi Ging shook her head firmly. A few of the others back in the dorm had given her strange looks while she'd struggled to unclip her lantern from Iridill's, but she'd hurried out before they'd had a chance to ask any questions.

"Good." Reishi fell silent, waiting for a pair of Cyo B'Ahon to pass. "I think it would be best if you didn't mention it to any of the Cyo B'Ahon on Team Bolei either."

"Why not?" Zhi Ging adjusted the lantern in her arms, peering up at him in confusion.

"Sintou is . . ." He hesitated, searching for the right word. "There was an attack on Hok Woh one hundred years ago. Some believe it was led by a Silhouette who failed their final challenge. It affected every Cyo B'Ahon, but Sintou most of all. She became very reclusive. I'm one of only five Cyo B'Ahon she still agrees to see regularly."

"But what does that have to do with Team Bolei?"

"Dragon boat racing is the only chance most other Cyo B'Ahon have to meet her. After winning, the team are invited to spend an hour in her office and, until the next race, their captain represents them at the weekly audience with her inner circle. Sintou controls the tithe we collect from across Wengyuen so this time with her can be invaluable. It's a chance for Cyo B'Ahon to pitch their current experiments and get more funding for their research. Which is why—" Reishi nodded at a group of Silhouettes filing out of the library, waiting until they had turned a corner before continuing. "Which is why some might not appreciate it if a Silhouette was able to meet with Sintou in her first week, when they'd spent decades trying to achieve the same thing."

"Why is she agreeing to meet with me?" Zhi Ging asked in a small voice.

"Because, until this month, the possibility of a Second Silhouette was something no Cyo B'Ahon could imagine. Sintou is the one who assigns exam scrolls to each Scout, careful to limit the number of Silhouettes that can be accepted each month. Even how she prepares the rice paper scrolls is a carefully guarded secret, I was only trusted with it after five hundred years as a Scout. As Head of the Cyo B'Ahon, she would also have given the Glassmiths strict instructions when rebuilding Hok Woh, detailing how the entrance should react to imitation lanterns. But it accepted yours. Of course she's curious to meet you."

"Does she know I didn't actually finish my Scout exam?"

"Yes, I've already spoken with Sintou about that, but she wants to hear from you before making a final decision. If you want her to let you stay, you need to convince her you deserve to be here just as much as any of the other Silhouettes."

Zhi Ging gulped. Making the dragon boat team probably wasn't enough.

They stopped in front of a smooth section of glass wall. Jellyfish bobbed past in the dark water, unfazed by their presence.

"Officially, there are no hidden doors anywhere in Hok Woh." Reishi paused, bent down, and hooked his finger into a chip at the base of the wall, sliding it back. "But, hopefully, you're about to learn Sintou has a secret soft spot for things that exist against the rules."

"YOU TOOK YOUR TIME."

Zhi Ging jumped, thrown by the woman's impatient tone. There, seated at a hexagonal table in front of them was Sintou, Head of the Cyo B'Ahon. Her gold robes fanned out across the floor, and a white flame crackled in the glass wall behind her, throwing her into shadow. Her face was lowered, eyes fixed on the six-pointed checkers board on the table.

"Come along, Reishi, it's your move. I've been waiting all week to see where you'll place the next marble."

"No, Sintou," he said gently, ushering Zhi Ging into the room. "You're meeting the Second Silhouette today, remember?"

The white flame shifted behind the Head of the Cyo B'Ahon, stretching across the glass to illuminate the room.

Sintou finally looked up and Zhi Ging's eyes widened in surprise.

The Head of the Cyo B'Ahon was old.

Not old like Reishi or Ami, but old like Aapau or even Gertie. *Why would anyone choose to be that age when they could ageshift?*

"Hmmm, come closer girl. I can't read your Pan Chang Knot."

"Oh! It says Fei Chui," Zhi Ging squeaked, her cloth shoes slipping against the floor as she hurried forward.

145

Up close, she could see Sintou's hands were covered in deep purple burns. She shivered, watching the skin pucker when the Head of the Cyo B'Ahon stretched up to examine the white knot. They looked so painful.

"So, you're the one everyone's been chattering about. My morning reports have been filled with little else. Tell me, why should I allow you to disrupt Hok Woh's longest-standing tradition? Will you also ask to become Dohrnii before graduation?"

"No! I—" Zhi Ging faltered, the argument she had spent all morning perfecting suddenly vanishing from her mind.

"Show her your lantern," Reishi urged, and Zhi Ging placed it on the table. The flame trapped behind the glass wall inched higher, and Reishi's handwriting caught in the light. Sintou peered at it closely, comparing the paper cutting carefully against Zhi Ging's profile before returning the lantern.

"How did you create this? I've heard Reishi's version which—courtesy of Gahyau—involved a dramatic reenactment, but I'd like to hear your side."

Zhi Ging swallowed, her throat dry. "I—I think it might have been something to do with the air rails? Or maybe, there was still some lightning around me after the dragon attack, it could have sparked the paper . . ." She trailed off, seeing Sintou pull a pair of scissors from her sleeve.

"May I?" The glass blades glinted against the lantern,

and Zhi Ging nodded. The Head of the Cyo B'Ahon cut a small sliver from the base and placed it into her empty teacup. She pulled multiple vials from her robes and emptied them over the parchment, but there was no reaction to any of them, colored liquids sliding off its surface like oil.

"I told you," Reishi whispered from the side, catching Sintou's surprised expression.

"It really is just simple parchment," she muttered, and dropped the cutting into Zhi Ging's unresisting hand.

"Please let me stay, I promise I'll work out how I—" The paper rustled in her palm, then shot up and merged back with the rest of the lantern. A tense silence stretched between the two Cyo B'Ahon, then Sintou placed the lantern back into Zhi Ging's hands. "That parchment was ordinary. You, despite appearances, are not. I'm curious to see what else you reveal during your time here."

"Does this mean she can stay as Second Silhouette?" Reishi asked, ageshifting down in excitement.

Sintou ignored him, her eyes never leaving Zhi Ging's as she pulled a thin scroll from her sleeve and unfolded it across the table.

"I believe, for Miss Yeung's own safety, that would be best. Bucbou brought this to me after she returned from Fei Chui with the new glass dragon head this morning."

Reishi turned pale, skimming through the note faster than Zhi Ging.

It was a warrant for her arrest, signed by the Lead Glassmith.

The final two lines blazed up from the page, the dark ink searing across her eyes.

WANTED

FOR CHARGES OF SPIRIT SUMMONING AND
ATTEMPTED ALLIANCE WITH THE FUI GWAI.
NO TRIAL TO BE OFFERED ON CAPTURE.

"But none of that's true!"

Sintou shook her head. "I'm afraid that doesn't matter, not when Bucbou spotted identical fliers far beyond the jade mountain. The next time you step foot in the glass province, you will be imprisoned. Hok Woh is your only home now."

"Are you sure I'll be safe here?" Zhi Ging asked, her heart pounding in her chest.

"No one from Fei Chui can seize you while you're under my protection, but how long you remain here is up to you." The trapped flame curled into a tight ball, and Sintou's shadow stretched over Zhi Ging. "The Cyo B'Ahon in Hok Woh may welcome a Second Silhouette, but I will never accept one who fails a challenge."

CHAPTER 18

"NoGlow! What did you do to my father?" The entire breakfast table jumped and turned to see Iridill marching toward them. Kaolin and Cing Yau, two porcelain province Silhouettes who had taken to shadowing Iridill everywhere, scowled at the group from over her shoulder.

"What are you talking about?" asked Zhi Ging.

Iridill hurled a crumpled letter toward her. "I bet you were hoping to catch me with it too. *That's* why you looked so surprised when you saw me on the beach last month. Good thing I left before you cast the curse!"

Zhi Ging flattened out the paper, her eyes widening as she read through the scrawled note. No wonder Bucbou had seen warrants everywhere.

"What? But . . . how?" she whispered to herself as Mynah plucked the letter out from her hand.

There was a short pause, then Mynah's cheek patches burst into a bright, vibrant pink.

"No way! Zhi Ging, I didn't know you could do that!" She cackled, an impressed glint in her eye.

"Wait, what happened?" Pinderent asked when Iridill snatched the letter back before he had a chance to read it.

"NoGlow cursed the entire village of Fei Chui. She climbed to the top of the jade mountain, *without* my father's permission—"

"He's the Lead Glassmith," Cing Yau added, smirking at the table while she tapped the glass bead recently tied to her Pan Chang. The second, unspoken, sentence radiated off her in Mynah and Pinderent's direction: *You picked the wrong Fei Chui Silhouette.*

"—and did . . ." Iridill flailed her arms, struggling to think of the right word in her rage. "Some sort of spirit summoning! Everyone's heads blazed white-hot, as if there was a dragon right above them, then every single strand of hair came loose and shot up toward the jade mountain. The curse even got the Glassmiths who had been searching for Reishi's stupid stone. You *balded* everyone, Zhi Ging!"

Zhi Ging stared open-mouthed at the furious girl, Gertie's comments swirling in her mind.

It wasn't a white ribbon after all; it really was thousands of Fei Chui ancestors leaping to protect me.

Her heart tightened in her chest.

Why did they care about me?

Mynah glanced between the two girls and coughed. "Iridill, serious question. Does this mean, right now, you should really look like this?" With her face carefully blank, Mynah slowly lifted a boiled egg up from the table.

"Arghhh," Iridill growled, snatching the egg from Mynah and hurling it to the ground. "I swear Zhi Ging, if you *dare* try anything like that with me, I'll make it the biggest regret of your life."

"I didn't do anything!" Zhi Ging protested, but Iridill had already stormed off, Kaolin and Cing Yau scurrying after her. She turned back to the group, dazed by the force of Iridill's fury.

"Should I still ask if she wants my final notes for our cloud project?"

There was a pause and then the table erupted into laughter.

"SO WHAT HAPPENS TOMORROW, YOU KNOW, AT the Silhouette challenge?" Zhi Ging whispered as Tutor Wun called another pair forward to talk through their project.

"I found out from Siwah that it's going to be the Fauna challenge," Pinderent murmured, nodding at a Silhouette two rows down struggling to stop a cloud escaping from its jar.

"But, apart from that, no one really knows," Mynah added. "They change the actual challenges each year to stop us pestering new Cyo B'Ahon for clues."

"Wait, won't we just get tested on all of this?" Zhi Ging

waved a hand over her scrolls. It had taken her two whole nights to memorize the formula for snowflake patterns. Mynah shook her head.

"You'd think so but, ever since the attack on Hok Woh, a lot of Cyo B'Ahon don't trust the Scouts' shoreside exam anymore. Just in case one of us guessed our answers, they like to retest our skills before assigning us to the next tutor. We've tried complaining to Ami about how unfair it is, but the Head of the Cyo B'Ahon won't budge. Her argument is we shouldn't waste the tutors' time—if we don't actually have a knack for their skill, tutors shouldn't have to wait until the end of the month to find out."

"Waste their time even though they're immortal?" Zhi Ging asked a little too loudly. She ducked low in her seat as Tutor Wun glanced across at them, thick brows drooping over his eyes at the disruption. She waited until he had turned back to the presenting group, then leaned closer to Pinderent. "But how does Siwah know it's definitely the Fauna challenge?"

"It's the only challenge she has left, she's been in Hok Woh for twelve months now."

"Yeah so you'll have Climate as your last challenge before graduation." Mynah nodded at Zhi Ging. "Your twelfth challenge is the only one you'll ever have studied for in advance. Make the most of the weeks leading up to it too. Siwah's nice, but most final-month Silhouettes only agree to tell you what challenge is coming up if you promise to trade some snacks or carry their scrolls for them." "A couple of mango puddings usually works," Pinderent added.

"Please, as if she's even going to make it past tomorrow." The group jumped at the interruption. Iridill was watching them closely, a lazy smirk spreading across her face as Kaolin and Cing Yau snorted in unison.

After screaming at them in the dining hall, Iridill had shown up late for class. For a moment, Zhi Ging had begun to think she'd get to present alone, but no such luck. Instead, they had stood side by side and woodenly demonstrated their suggestions for the eight cloud shapes. Compared to the others', theirs had been the least imaginative, but at least Zhi Ging's sand-carrying cloud for Glassmiths had gotten a faint nod from Gwong. She'd been secretly smug when Iridill hadn't thought of it, especially considering how often she reminded everyone her father was the Lead Glassmith.

"And, finally, we have Master K'Ah and Miss Niu."

Pinderent and Mynah scrambled up, cloud-filled jars clinking in their arms as they squeezed along the row to the front of the classroom.

"Why don't you leave us alone, Iridill?" Zhi Ging muttered. "You were clearly just listening in because you wanted to know about tomorrow too."

"Please, I'm obviously going to pass. I'm the Lead Glassmith's daughter."

"And that doesn't mean *anything* outside of Fei Chui. You're not going to get extra points from the Cyo B'Ahon just because—"

"Silence during the presentations," Tutor Wun snapped, and the two girls slumped down in their seats. Mynah raised an eyebrow from the front of the classroom and mouthed *You okay?* Zhi Ging nodded, and her friend turned back to the jars spread out across Tutor Wun's desk.

"For the first cloud, we thought its flat shape would make it perfect for carrying flowers. This would be much better for the perfumers in the silk province, who need to haul large baskets on their backs." Mynah removed the lid and gently shook the stratus cloud loose. She nodded toward Pinderent, and they each grabbed a cloud edge before swinging their arms up. It billowed above them and the room filled with thousands of fluttering jasmine petals.

"Outstanding! This is exactly the sort of innovation I was expecting from *all* groups."

Zhi Ging felt herself blush when Tutor Wun glanced toward her and Iridill. Maybe they should have worked together after all.

Her guilt grew with each new cloud Pinderent and Mynah revealed, all carefully crafted to suit a different province. In the front row, impressed Cyo B'Ahon nodded as Pinderent talked through a snow cloud that could simultaneously carry salt.

"So yeah, it means no matter how heavy the snow gets, carts should still be able to travel along roads, since the falling salt would grit the paths at the same time. We're hoping it'll help some of the higher mountain villages that can get stranded for months during the winter."

"Well done, both of you." Tutor Wun nudged the cloud dusting his desk with salt back into its jar. "If you continue to pass the rest of your Silhouette challenges, I do hope at least one of you will consider becoming a Climate-focused Cyo B'Ahon, like Gwong, in the future."

"We actually came up with an extra cloud, inspired by his warm storms, as a surprise for everyone," Pinderent murmured, his ears burning red from Tutor Wun's compliments.

"Gwong helped us with the physics for this one too," Mynah added, pulling a steaming jar from her cloak pocket.

She smiled at the crowd and unscrewed the lid. Large altocumulus clouds rose up to fill the ceiling. They bounced and wobbled against one another, then white orbs began to drop down over the class. Zhi Ging caught one of the falling orbs and was surprised by how warm it was. Had they created hot hailstones?

"Good catch!" Mynah shouted over the sound of falling orbs. "Enjoy it before it cools down."

Zhi Ging peered back down at the warm orb, finally recognizing what it was.

"No way," she breathed, breaking it in half to reveal a golden, liquid center. It wasn't a hailstone at all; it was a lau sah bao, Pinderent's favorite custard bun.

Tutor Wun roared with laughter, before ageshifting down in surprise when a bun bounced off his head.

Excitement rippled through the rest of the Silhouettes, and within seconds, they went from ducking the buns to clamoring after them. Hidden in the sudden bustle, Iridill shouldered past Zhi Ging, knocking the lau sah bao from her hands.

"Just you wait, NoGlow. You'll remember your place soon."

THAT NIGHT, ZHI GING STAGGERED BACK TO THE dorm, exhausted after another failed attempt to find the air rails with Reishi but relieved that it meant there hadn't been time to worry about tomorrow's challenge. She yawned and slid her bedroom door open. The yawn quickly turned into a shriek as her foot sank into freezing water.

Doors sprang open around her, and Silhouettes poured out to see what had happened. They huddled around Zhi Ging's door, and a hush fell over the group. Her entire bedroom had been flooded. The narrow bed sagged under the weight of a waterlogged mattress, and homework scrolls had been tossed into the dark water that now swirled around her ankles.

The glass wall at the back of her room had been covered in a vicious red dye. It dripped down the smooth surface, staining the water beneath it. Mynah squeezed Zhi Ging's arm and waded through the water to snatch a note stuck against the glass. Her eyes widened as she read it, and she hesitated before passing it to Zhi Ging. Scrawled across the sheet in thick red brushstrokes was a single sentence.

BETTER PRACTICE SCRUBBING BEFORE YOU'RE SENT BACK TO THE POST PIPE.

Zhi Ging shuddered and splashed back out to the main dorm. There, on the higher platform, Iridill smirked down at her, Kaolin and Cing Yau sneering over her shoulders. *This* must have been why Iridill was late for class. The girl gave a mocking wave, then vanished into her own room, the door snapping shut behind her.

Zhi Ging crumpled the note between her hands and flung it into the central fireplace, watching red smoke rise while it burned.

Tonight is not *going to be my last night at Hok Woh.*

CHAPTER 19

"Did you manage to sleep ok?" Mynah whispered as they followed the line of Silhouettes trudging up the steps toward the surface.

"Yeah, thanks again for making space in your room."

"You can stay with me for as long as it takes for your stuff to dry," Mynah insisted. "Urgh, I still can't believe Iridill!"

Zhi Ging smiled weakly at her friend. She hadn't even told Mynah the meaning behind that particular shade of red dye. It was the color poured into the post pipe to signal for a traveling healer, when the local one wasn't available. An extra little reminder from Iridill that Aapau wasn't around anymore.

They reached the top of the staircase, and Zhi Ging breathed in deeply, closing her eyes as salt air raced through her hair. After a month of living deep beneath the ocean and training on the dragon boats only at night, the feel of real sunlight on her skin was incredibly comforting.

"Hurry up," Kaolin muttered behind them. "The rest of us are stuck on the stairs until you get on the boat."

Zhi Ging's eyes opened and she turned to see a wooden junk, a three-mast sailing boat, floating beside them, its red bat-like sails flapping against the sea breeze. She took a step forward, and her face lit up. There, helping the Silhouettes on board, was Jack.

He spotted her and leaped down from the junk, a thick gold rope trailing behind him.

"Zhi Ging! How've you been? Looking forward to your first challenge?"

"Not really," she admitted, though she felt less nervous now that she'd seen him. "I didn't know you'd be here."

"Reishi got me this job a few months ago." Jack stood up proudly, puffing out his chest while his eyes flickered between green and blue. "I'm now the official Silhouette Skill Challenge Transporter."

"Catchy title," Zhi Ging chuckled, and he scratched the back of his neck sheepishly.

"Yeah, I'm still working on that. Anyway, let's get you two set up." He twisted the rope between his hands and tied two wide hoops along its length. Mynah grabbed one and lowered the hoop over herself.

"Thanks, Jack, these are so much better now that you've taken over." She turned to Zhi Ging, handing her the second hoop. "As the Dohrnii, Ami should be the one tying these for us, but she could never get the sizes right. There used to be a stampede every month to avoid the bottom hoop. That one would always be tiny." She paused, spotting Zhi Ging's puzzled expression, and demonstrated with her own hoop. "We're meant to sit in these, like swings, but the final hoop used to be so small you'd just barely squeeze both feet in. Whoever was stuck with that would have to stand and cling on to the rope above them. A few Silhouettes swore it was even worse than the actual challenges."

Zhi Ging grimaced, then glanced back toward the sailing boat in confusion. "Why aren't we traveling in the junk?"

"Where's the fun in that?" Jack laughed. "Officially, that's just for me to get here. By the way, if any of the Cyo B'Ahon—apart from Reishi—ask, I definitely *don't* know about the secret glass stepping stones and always use this junk to reach Hok Woh. You two better wait on it for now, I need a bit more space for the others," he added, glancing toward the Silhouettes still waiting inside the staircase. Zhi Ging and Mynah pulled themselves onto the side of the wooden junk and watched while he finished looping the rope into tight hoops.

"Hey, look at that." Mynah nudged Zhi Ging and nodded toward Iridill. The girl's entire demeanor had changed the second she spotted Jack. She even lowered her head, long hair falling over her face, when he tried to hand her a hoop.

"That's weird. I've never seen her react like that to

anyone," Zhi Ging muttered, squinting against the bright ocean light. Was Iridill blushing?

Iridill suddenly turned her head toward them, and the two girls flinched, falling backward into the junk.

"Good thing being subtle isn't one of the challenges," Zhi Ging wheezed, helping Mynah back up.

"Oh, I'd be long gone if it was." She laughed, the patches on her cheek flashing yellow and green. Jack leaped onto the junk behind them and clapped his hands together.

"All right, everyone, time for another Silhouette challenge, or for some of you, your *first* Silhouette challenge." He shot Zhi Ging an encouraging smile. "Ami and your future tutor are already waiting at this month's secret location and no," he sighed, holding up his hands, "I don't know what they have planned so there's no point badgering me on the way over."

"He definitely does," Mynah whispered to Zhi Ging. "But no one's been able to crack him yet!"

Jack pulled a large paper lantern decorated with feathers out from a crate and hooked the end of the gold rope through it. Zhi Ging copied the Silhouettes around her as they lifted their hoops to rest behind their knees. She spotted Pinderent at the other end of the boat, his hands gripped tight against the hoop.

We'll be okay, she mouthed, and he nodded, eyes wide with anticipation. Zhi Ging looked around, taking in the jumble of determined, serious, and anxious faces squeezed in around her. What was waiting for everyone back home if they failed? Was she the only one who didn't even have a home to go to?

There was a faint crackle as Jack lit the lantern and the Silhouettes held their collective breath.

Visions of what would happen if she failed began to race through Zhi Ging's mind. The warrant had said no trial, but what did that mean for her punishment? She shuddered, flashes of being left on the glass terraces as dragon food or being sealed into the post pipe filling her imagination.

Was she still under Sintou's protection during these challenges? What if they landed near the jade mountain and someone tried to arrest her in front of the other Silhouettes? Why hadn't she thought to ask Reishi about this during their last air rail session!?

Jack stepped into his own hoop and pushed the lantern skyward, leaving no more time for her to worry. The gold rope lifted behind it, and one by one, the Silhouettes floated up into the air.

THEY LANDED WITH A THUMP IN THE MIDDLE OF A lush forest. Bamboo towered over the Silhouettes, and strange animal cries echoed through the humid air.

"Does anyone know what the Fui Gwai sounds like?" Hiulam whispered, and the group huddled closer together. In front of them were multiple wooden crates, some no larger than the palms of their hands, while others rose above their shoulders. A number had been painted on the front of each locked crate.

Behind them, Jack set to work untying the hoops in the rope. Zhi Ging watched him and gulped, the unspoken message clear. There was no guarantee every Silhouette would be coming back to Hok Woh.

There was a faint rustle, and Ami stepped into the clearing with a stout-looking Cyo B'Ahon. His robes looked muddy and frayed beside her pristine white robes, but there was something inherently welcoming about his face.

"Well, you all look absolutely petrified," he said. "Who organized your last challenge?"

"Tutor Wun," Siwah squeaked from the back of the group.

The Cyo B'Ahon slapped his leg. "Ah, that explains it! I still have nightmares about taking his challenge six hundred years ago. Hopefully, most of you will find today less dire. My name is Ai'Deng Bou and those who pass this challenge will learn all about the fauna that thrive across Wengyuen. Anyone who chooses to specialize with me after their Silhouette year will learn to decipher roars and squawks, neutralize venoms, and, most importantly, discover how one might *nudge* evolution along without damaging a species or its habitat."

Gertie's emerald bees flashed across Zhi Ging's mind, and she smiled.

"Now," Ai'Deng Bou continued, shaking a bamboo cylinder packed with numbered sticks, "everyone pick a stick."

The Silhouettes inched forward and Zhi Ging could tell that, like her, each of them was hoping someone else would go first.

"Go on, these won't bite," Ai'Deng Bou encouraged, tipping the bamboo toward them. Before long, each Silhouette was considering the number carved into their chosen stick, unsure if they had just improved or ruined their chances of passing. Zhi Ging's eyes flickered from the *4* in her hand toward the clearing, trying to spot the matching crate.

Ai'Deng Bou caught her eye and smiled.

"I see some of you have already worked it out." He ambled toward the crates, and there was a muffled growl as he knocked against one of the numbered boxes. "Inside each of these is a chimera, animals that have been created by combining two or more different creatures. Some have been given new heightened abilities, while others can now pull power from their surroundings. Your task today is a simple one—"

Ami stepped forward, a delicate hourglass raised high above her head.

"Great, another timed challenge." Pinderent gulped, his own stick shaking in his hand.

"All you have to do is get your chimera back into its crate before the final grain reaches the bottom of the hourglass, which it will in exactly one hour." Ai'Deng Bou gestured toward them. "Quickly now, find your matching crate and make sure you don't blink as they're released. You'll only have one chance to identify your chimera among the others."

The Silhouettes scurried forward, trying to spot their crates. Zhi Ging stumbled to a stop in front of a large crate and crouched down, her hands held out in front of her. *Maybe I can catch it before it even gets past the clearing.*

Ai'Deng Bou's voice grew muffled, and Zhi Ging couldn't tell if it was because of her own heart pounding in her ears or the thump of footsteps racing to find matching numbers.

Without warning, the crates sprang open and there was a blur of feathers, scales, and fur as the chimeras leaped out, soaring over the Silhouettes.

CHAPTER 20

A flash of blue barreled into Zhi Ging's legs, knocking her over. She twisted her head to the side, and a giant salamander's tail smacked against her cheek. Its tail erupted into water, and she struggled to breathe as the wave cascaded over her. Zhi Ging rolled to the side, coughing up the brackish water.

All around her, Silhouettes were struggling to their feet, staring at the escaping chimeras in horror. Hiulam was frantically patting at a scorch mark on her sleeve, while Pinderent pressed his hands against his ears in pain. Only Mynah seemed unaffected, her cloak flapping behind her as she chased after what looked like a silver pangolin.

"Careful everyone," Ai'Deng Bou's voice warned above the chaos. "You'll have to think quickly when catching your chimera. Each creature will respond differently, and some may have predator DNA mixed into their design."

He glanced toward Ami's hourglass. "Fifty-nine minutes to go. Remember, your chimera must be back inside its cage before then to pass this challenge."

Zhi Ging's eyebrows furrowed in worry, but when she looked down, she spotted a glistening trail twisting through the grass. *I can track it!*

Zhi Ging squeezed the gray water from her cloak and raced after the salamander.

DAMP HAIR CLUNG TO HER FACE AS SHE CREPT deeper into the forest. The sweltering heat made running difficult, but Zhi Ging couldn't risk losing the trail. She didn't know how much time she had left, but loud cracks of crates slamming shut had begun to echo through the bamboo. At least six Silhouettes had already returned their chimeras.

The trail twisted sharply to the right, and she skidded to a stop in front of a steep drop. A dark river rumbled at the base of the gorge, and Zhi Ging winced. If she didn't catch the salamander before it crossed the river, she might never find it.

She wrapped an arm around a small boulder and began to ease herself down the steep surface. Suddenly, the rock began to shudder, and fur shot out across its surface. The crazed face of a macaque appeared between Zhi Ging's fingers, and she screamed, falling into the deep water.

The furious monkey leaped after her, hackles raised as

it landed with a heavy thud on the riverbank. Zhi Ging kicked away, desperately trying to reach the far shore before the macaque stepped into the water. Her right heel stung with each kick, but she didn't have time to check the injury.

"That one's mine, NoGlow." Iridill appeared at the top of the gorge drop and skidded toward them, pebbles splashing into the river.

"Have it!" Zhi Ging yelled back, her eyes never leaving the macaque's face as it plunged its paws into the water, yellow teeth snapping at her. Iridill crept behind the monkey and shrugged off her cloak, a determined look in her eyes.

Does she know it can turn to stone?

"No wait, that won't work!" Zhi Ging cried, but it was too late. Just as the macaque reached the deep center of the river, Iridill leaped forward, engulfing it inside her cloak. Her yell of triumph quickly turned to a scream as the macaque's paw shot out, seizing the Silhouette's hair before turning back to stone. The monkey's new weight dragged Iridill beneath the surface, and no matter how hard she thrashed, her hair remained caught within its stony grip.

Zhi Ging splashed back toward them, the pain in her ankle sending sparks through her vision. She dived down and tugged furiously at the macaque's paw, but it was calcified in place. Zhi Ging tore at Iridill's hair, strands snapping between her fingers as she tried to pull it loose.

"Don't you dare!" Iridill's eyes were wide with fear. "Touch my hair again and I'll—" Bubbles blurred the rest of her words, and she grabbed at Zhi Ging's hands, her left snatching Zhi Ging's right in panic.

"What are you doing! Let me help you." Zhi Ging jerked back, then stopped, staring at their crossed arms in sudden realization. *We've been trying to solve it the wrong way!*

She pulled the other girl deeper underwater, and their hands hit against the pebbles that made up the riverbed. Iridill tried to break loose, but Zhi Ging tightened her grip.

Her own lungs were starting to ache now, which meant Iridill couldn't have much time left. Zhi Ging pushed one set of crossed arms beneath the pebbles, sliding their linked hands under the stone macaque until it tipped into the hollow space between them. For a second, it looked like a small child being carried between its parents. Finally, Iridill understood Zhi Ging's plan. The two girls crouched low against the riverbed, then, as one, kicked up, lifting the heavy chimera between them.

Their heads broke through the river's surface, and they gasped for air, the stone macaque still balanced between their hands.

"We need to move carefully," Zhi Ging wheezed, treading the water. "If he slips now, you'll be dragged back down to the riverbed. We need to get your hair out of his paw."

"Yeah, I get that!" Iridill snapped, but there was more fear than anger in her voice.

They inched back toward the shore, keeping a close eye on the macaque in case it shifted back to its fur body. Why had Ai'Deng Bou even created it?

Once they could feel silt beneath their shoes again, the two Silhouettes relaxed. Iridill snatched her hands free from Zhi Ging's and wrapped her arms tight around the stone monkey. She staggered slightly under his full weight, her head tilting toward the paw still clamped around her hair.

"I could have had him back in the crate by now. It's your fault for luring him into the river."

"Are you serious? I was trying to get away from him. And anyway, I just saved you—you'd have drowned if I hadn't been here!"

"Whatever," Iridill snapped. "Just don't use this as an excuse when the crates shut without your chimera inside." She took a step back from Zhi Ging, her gaze hardening. "No one will ever believe you tried to save me anyway." Iridill spun around and raced back up the gorge, shrieking when fur began to sprout across the macaque's stone body.

ZHI GING TOOK A TENTATIVE STEP FORWARD AND tears sprang to her eyes, the pain in her ankle worse than ever. This couldn't be how her first challenge ended! She looked around frantically, but there was no sign of the salamander's trail anywhere. All she could see along the riverbank were Iridill's damp footprints racing away from her.

Zhi Ging snatched a handful of pebbles and flung them hard against the gorge wall. *It isn't fair!* The pebbles ricocheted against it and scattered between nearby boulders.

Plock.

What was that?

Plock. One of the pebbles bounced back into view and continued to hop in place. Zhi Ging blinked in surprise and quietly inched toward it. She had seen only one other pebble ever react like that. *It has to be hydrophobic, just like the pebble Reishi used to reveal the stepping stones.*

Zhi Ging crept closer and peered over the boulder. The salamander! It had wedged itself into a crevice and was snoring gently while the pebble bounced against it. Each time the pebble hit its tail, the salamander's skin would ripple and transform into a small pool of water, sending the hydrophobic pebble soaring back into the air. Zhi Ging caught the pebble when it leaped up again, worried the constant tapping would wake the salamander.

"How am I supposed to get you back into your crate?" she whispered, leaning forward.

The salamander's eyes flicked open. Claws scrabbled against stone in its attempt to escape, and its entire body became transparent before dissolving. Its new water shape sank down, spilling out between the boulders.

"Oh, no, you don't!" Zhi Ging shouted. She snatched Gertie's glove off and held the fabric under the falling water. The liquid salamander poured into the glove and Zhi Ging held her breath as the seams groaned under the weight, but the fabric held.

Just.

Water sloshed against the top of the glove as Zhi Ging staggered back toward the crates. She ran, bursting through the clearing as the waiting Silhouettes began to shout, gesturing wildly at the near-empty hourglass. There were only seconds left!

She hurtled toward the others, but her ankle finally gave out, and she crashed down into damp sand. Ai'Deng Bou took a half step forward, eyes wide with concern.

"No!" Zhi Ging yelped, watching the glove sail out of her hands. Every pair of eyes turned to follow its slow arc over the crates, the salamander solidifying in midair as the water spilled out.

"I can't fail now, I'm not going back to Fei Chui!" Zhi Ging cried, sand-covered hands reaching desperately for the chimera. Gold lines cascaded up her elbow, and air rails flared up around the salamander, slowing its fall. The sudden flash of light forced the others to shield their eyes, but Zhi Ging watched open-mouthed as the salamander's claws veered to the side, sliding along an air rail to drop straight into her open crate.

How had she done that?

The air rails winked out, and Ami spun around in astonishment, eyes widening at the gold on Zhi Ging's arm. Zhi Ging scrambled to pull her sleeves low, hiding the lines before anyone else noticed.

Behind the Dohrnii, Ai'Deng Bou leaped forward and snapped the lid shut. He glanced across at the now empty hourglass and blew a whistle.

"And that marks the end of the hour. Zhi Ging, you've passed the challenge."

The Silhouettes around her erupted into deafening cheers, Iridill's scowling face quickly hidden as the others raced forward to congratulate her.

CHAPTER 21

That night, unable to sleep, Zhi Ging grabbed a pair of scissors and crept out of Mynah's room. Her friend's patches flickered while she dreamed, and the colors had kept her awake for hours. Zhi Ging crinkled her nose. That wasn't fair. It wasn't really Mynah keeping her awake.

After the initial excitement of passing her first Silhouette challenge, Zhi Ging had begun to notice the faces missing from the group around her.

Siwah had failed her final challenge.

She shuddered, remembering Pinderent's and Mynah's expressions while Ami led the fourteen unsuccessful Silhouettes away. She could tell instantly this wasn't the first time they'd had friends leave without a chance to say goodbye.

"Siwah won't even remember us," Pinderent had sighed while Jack floated them back toward the junk, and Zhi Ging had wondered what he meant.

It was only that evening, back in the dorm, that she

174

learned the true sacrifice of failing a Silhouette challenge. While all belongings, including lesson scrolls, would be delivered back to their homes, none of the failed Silhouettes would ever remember their experience. Thanks to an elixir Ami would provide, they would have no memory of their time in Hok Woh once they woke up the next morning.

Sintou had banned Silhouettes from retaining memories after the first Hok Woh burned, concerned another failed Silhouette would lead a future attack or be persuaded to reveal Hok Woh's new location. A gold coin etched with two cranes would be their only proof of time spent in the Cyo B'Ahon's hidden realm. The coin would mean their family paid a smaller tithe, but it also disqualified those who had failed from ever taking a Scout's entrance exam again.

"I can't let that happen to me," Zhi Ging murmured, staring up at her Silhouette lantern. *If I'm forced to take the elixir, I won't even remember that the Lead Glassmith has a warrant out for me. I'll be arrested the second I step foot on the jade mountain.*

Zhi Ging tiptoed across to the fireplace in the center of the dorm, where the flames now burned low. They seemed to brighten and fade depending on the time of day. She peeled up one of the water-damaged scrolls she'd left to dry beside the fireplace and began to snip away. Soon papercutting animals were scattered around her, creatures from Fei Chui and that morning's chimeras re-created in miniature. Zhi Ging felt her shoulders loosen.

For some reason, she had always found paper cutting incredibly calming. Once she had finished, Zhi Ging swept the cuttings into the fire, but a single paper dragon soared over the flames, caught by a warm current of air.

She leaned back to watch it and felt something dig into her side. Zhi Ging shifted forward and pulled the jade stone out of her cloak pocket.

"When did you get there?" she whispered. The frantic rush to move anything salvageable out of her flooded room felt like a lifetime ago. The jade gleamed in the firelight, and she started to bat it absentmindedly between her hands, rolling it gently along the metal grate that circled the sunken fireplace.

After a while, Zhi Ging's eyelids began to droop. Suddenly, a memory of the dragon that had attacked her on Fei Chui's jade mountain, with its crackling lightning inches from her face, flashed across her mind. She flinched and hit the stone harder than she meant to, sending it skittering along the grate until it fell into the fireplace.

The flames froze.

Air became hazy with heat, and the fire stretched into thin threads of light. Panic ripped through Zhi Ging as they enveloped the stone and sank beneath the jade surface. *No no no, this can't be happening!*

The dorm plunged into darkness, and the fire that had burned for a hundred years, the last trace of the first Hok Woh, was snuffed out.

Seconds later, there wasn't even a hint of smoke, and

the silent fireplace felt ice-cold. Zhi Ging leaped forward, desperate to find even a fragment of an ember to restart the fire. Instead, there, curled beside the stone, was the paper dragon. It had fallen in just as the flames had warped, and while its tail had started to smolder, it was mostly intact.

Zhi Ging bent forward to pluck it out, her heart thumping. She couldn't leave any evidence of what had happened. *What if they kick me out? I need to relight the fire.* The thin paper tore in her shaking hands, and the paper dragon drifted back down, its fangs hitting against the stone.

There was a tense second of silence, then the stone shattered into a thousand pieces. A luminous cyclone roared out from its core and filled the room with blinding light. Zhi Ging screamed and whipped her hand back, the gold lines on her arm sparking and hissing as they absorbed the heat. She toppled backward but the blaze vanished as quickly as it had appeared, leaving her shaking in the dark.

In the muffled gloom, the only clue that anything had happened was a new lingering scent of white flower oil spreading across the dorm. *How did no one wake up after that light? Did I imagine it?*

Zhi Ging gradually became aware of a faint cheeping coming from the firepit. She crept closer and froze, convinced she must be hallucinating after all.

There, shaking itself free of ash, was a duckling. He ruffled his snowy feathers and looked up at her, his head tilted to one side. The duckling waddled to the edge of the pit and hopped up and down. The remnants of the jade stone—*eggshell,* a dazed, distant part of Zhi Ging's brain corrected—crumbled under its tiny, webbed feet and quickly became indistinguishable from the paper dragon ash.

"I was *not* expecting you," Zhi Ging whispered, lowering her hand toward the duckling. He hopped into her open hand, nuzzling his head against her thumb.

There was a dull thud behind her, and the dorm door slid open to reveal Iridill staring wide-eyed at the empty fireplace. A flickering candle dropped from the girl's hand and rolled toward Zhi Ging.

"Oh, NoGlow. You are going to be in *so* much trouble."

"Iridill, wait, I can explain—" Zhi Ging jumped to her feet and yelped as the duckling wriggled free. He chirped and waddled determinedly over to the candle. Before Zhi Ging could pull him back, the duckling opened his beak and swallowed the flame whole.

CHAPTER 22

Zhi Ging dropped to her knees and scooped up the duckling as Iridill sprinted from the dorm. The candlelight flickered while it traveled down the duckling's throat, blooming once it reached his stomach. His entire body started to glow, and Zhi Ging had to look away, the light leaving dazzling imprints in the darkness. When she turned back, color had swept through his feathers. His chest filled with rich violet, and copper feathers fanned out under his cheeks. A comet of white trailing out from his eye was all that remained of his original coloring.

The duckling inspected his new feathers, chirped happily to himself, then promptly fell asleep, clearly exhausted from his transformation. Zhi Ging held him closer, the glittering colors dancing across her face while he snored.

"What are you?" she whispered, staring at the streak of emerald feathers between his closed eyes. Footsteps echoed along the corridor, and she turned to see Ami, Reishi, and

Iridill staring at her. The Cyo B'Ahons' eyebrows shot up when they spotted the duckling in her hands.

"Zhi Ging," Ami said softly, trying not to wake the others in the dorm. "Come with us, please."

Zhi Ging gulped and stood up, placing a protective hand over the duckling. *I won't let them take him away.* The victorious glint in Iridill's eyes vanished when Reishi placed a hand on her shoulder.

"Thank you, Miss Seoipin, we'll take it from here. You can go back to your room."

Iridill frowned but it was obvious from his tone that it was an order.

Ami, Reishi, and Zhi Ging walked in silence down the jellyfish-filled corridors, the duckling's snuffling the only sound Zhi Ging could hear above her pounding heartbeat. They eventually arrived at Ami's office, and she ushered them in. Once the door shut behind them, Reishi turned to smile at Zhi Ging.

"You can breathe again. You're not in trouble."

"I'm not? But the fireplace!"

Reishi chuckled and Ami shook her head, amused.

"Do you honestly think we'd trust the only flame, the final fragment of the original Hok Woh, to a handful of Silhouettes?" Reishi asked. "Zhi Ging, someone has accidentally extinguished that fire at least once a year since we moved Hok Woh underwater. Although, no one has ever done it in such a unique way." His eyes flickered to the sleeping duckling. There was a faint click, and the room lit up, a familiar scent of jasmine and orchids wafting over them. Ami had pulled a small glass case, no larger than a jewelry box, out from her desk drawer. Nestled inside the glass was a dancing flame.

"I keep part of the flame here, in case of accidents like this." A strange expression flashed across her face as she opened the case. "It also helps me remember the original Hok Woh. Not that I could ever forget that night."

Reishi placed a concerned hand on her shoulder, and Ami's face flushed.

"Sorry about that." She smiled weakly at Zhi Ging and shook her head. "Why don't you both wait here while I relight the fireplace?" Before they could reply, Ami hurried from the room, the corridor filling with light as she stepped out with the caged flame.

"Is she all right?" Zhi Ging asked hesitantly, watching Ami's shadow stretch out against the glass. Reishi sighed and gestured for her to sit.

"Ami was the Cyo B'Ahon who first raised the alarm. In the darkness, she initially mistook the villagers' torches for the floating market but quickly realized what was happening. Although her warning saved countless Cyo B'Ahon, she still blames herself for Hok Woh burning."

Zhi Ging glanced over at Reishi, and he tilted his head away from her. For the first time since they'd met, she caught a glimpse of deep sadness hidden beneath his features.

"I'm sorry we made her remember the attack," Zhi Ging murmured guiltily, placing the sleeping duckling on the desk. Reishi stroked the black and white stripes wrapped around the duckling's wings, his familiar smile creaking back into place.

"Where did this little guy come from anyway? Did Ai'Deng Bou let you keep a chimera?"

"No . . . Reishi, I'm so sorry but your jade stone is gone. It shattered and the duckling hatched out of it." Zhi Ging raced on as Reishi's eyes widened in surprise. "I know you gave it to me as a present. I promise I wasn't trying to break it on purpose . . ."

He held up a hand, and Zhi Ging trailed off, watching him anxiously.

"In that case, it's time for my confession. It was never my stone to begin with, not really."

"What do you mean?" Zhi Ging couldn't stop the flash of irritation in her voice. She had nearly died because of that stone. Twice.

Reishi had the decency to look sheepish as he cleared his throat.

"I hadn't actually planned to visit Fei Chui, or any of the glass province, during my last Scouting trip. Wengyuen's far too large to cover even half a province in a month. That's why all the others who arrived with you are from the southern peninsula of the porcelain province." He shook his head, refocusing on his explanation. "But when I was crossing the Jyuging River I spotted that jade stone trundling along the riverbed. It was moving determinedly against the current, back toward the mountains. I decided to follow it and, five days later, we arrived beneath the cloud sea. At that point, I assumed it must belong to Aapau. She's the only person on the entire mountain skilled enough to train jade to return like that."

Zhi Ging smiled, pride for Aapau swelling inside her. Even a Cyo B'Ahon could see how special she was.

"However, once we passed through the cloud sea, the stone stopped moving. I went straight to Aapau, but she told me she had never seen it before in her life. I couldn't understand why it had led me to a village of Glassmiths." His gaze drifted back toward the snoring duckling, and his eyebrows knit together in confusion. "Maybe it was never trying to reach Aapau in the first place . . ."

"What do you mean?"

"Well, it disappeared immediately after I chose Iridill as the Silhouette. Then, an entire team of senior Glassmiths spent a full day searching for it, only for you to find it in some of the worst fog Fei Chui has ever seen. I think this duckling might have always belonged to you, Zhi Ging."

They stared in silence at the sleeping duckling, jumping when Ami reappeared in the doorframe.

"All done!" She beamed, the flame's glass case tucked under her arm. "Zhi Ging, why don't I put this away and walk you back to the dorm."

THEY PADDED ALONG THE EMPTY CORRIDORS, AND every so often, Zhi Ging could feel Ami glancing toward the duckling in her arms.

"Is it okay if I keep him?" Zhi Ging asked, then held her breath. If Reishi was right, and the duckling really had worked this hard to reach her, she couldn't lose him now.

"Oh, of course. If we didn't allow animals in Hok Woh, Ai'Deng Bou would never speak to any of us again. I actually wanted to talk to you about something else. I saw what happened at the end of your challenge . . ." The Cyo B'Ahon's gaze flickered toward the faint golden lines, and Zhi Ging winced. *I never should have left Mynah's room without my glove. What if Ami thinks I summoned a spirit to help me pass?*

"Do they appear often?" Ami pressed, her face furrowed in concern.

"No, they only started this month. Right before I came to Hok Woh." Zhi Ging shifted the duckling in her arms so Ami could see the gold running along her palm. "Do you know what they are?"

"I saw something similar on another girl once, long ago." Ami hesitated and placed a concerned hand on Zhi Ging's arm, the gold glinting between her fingers. "Be careful, Zhi Ging. These lines can only appear so many times before you—"

The duckling hiccupped in his sleep, and his body pulsed with light, revealing they had reached the dorm entrance.

Ami frowned, glancing at the light shining through Iridill's door, which was cracked open. The Silhouette's crouched shadow hovered just behind it, a dark blur against the paper screen. Iridill was clearly trying to listen in.

"Before I what?" Zhi Ging whispered. The Cyo B'Ahon shook her head, her expression hidden in the gloom.

"Please, for me, avoid doing anything that sparks those lines again."

"But I don't even know how I'm doing it," Zhi Ging croaked, watching Ami's outline melt back into the dark corridor. "How do I stop them?"

There was no reply.

Zhi Ging was left alone, her skin itching as she stared down at the strands coiled around her arm.

CHAPTER 23

The next morning, Zhi Ging woke up to the duckling's feathers tickling against her cheek. He had settled on her pillow overnight and was now looking expectantly at her.

"You hungry? Let's try to find you something in the dining hall." She scooped him up and became aware of angry voices floating out from the dorm.

She inched her screen door open and sighed with relief when she saw the fireplace crackling away. A cluster of Silhouettes had gathered around the central bulletin board, whispering heatedly among themselves. Zhi Ging lowered the duckling into the hood of her cloak and hurried toward them.

"What's going on?" A sudden wave of panic raced through her. "Have they changed the challenge results?"

"What? No, nothing like that." Pinderent shook his head.

"It's an absolute joke!" Mynah shouted, her cheeks

flashing orange and gray as she stabbed a finger against a new scroll pinned to the board. "They're delaying our Chau!"

The other Silhouettes muttered mutinously around her.

"Our what?" Zhi Ging whispered to Pinderent. She'd never heard that word before.

"It's our reward for passing. Chaus usually happen immediately after a challenge, when they whisk the twelfth-month Silhouettes back to Hok Woh for graduation. They don't want any of us sneaking into the Seoi Mou Pou to try to catch our friends' Cyo B'Ahon ceremonies, so they arrange the Chau for the same time."

"For Tutor Wun's Chau, we got to meet a group of professional rainbow dancers," Hiulam added. "They were like the ribbon dancers back in my province, but had these incredible lacquer poles that could catch wisps of rainbows, streaming the colors behind them while they danced."

"Exactly!" Mynah interrupted. "So, when Ami sent us back yesterday, we assumed it was just because of Siwah. She was the only twelfth-month Silhouette who took part in the Fauna challenge, which meant there was no rush to distract us with a Chau after she failed. But now"—she waved back toward the note—"it's been 'indefinitely delayed.' How is that fair?"

One of the taller Silhouettes jostled to the front of the group, a battered scroll clamped in his hands.

"I *told* you this was going to happen! We were lucky to even get a Chau last month."

"Wait, am I missing something?" Zhi Ging asked. "Why would they stop the Chaus?"

The Silhouette turned to face her, his features pinched.

"The Fui Gwai. *It's coming for us.*"

Mynah rolled her eyes, but Zhi Ging noticed some of the others didn't seem as skeptical.

"Come on, Mai Seon. You've been saying that pretty much since you got here."

"But am I wrong?" he snapped, stretching the scroll open between his hands. It was a map of Wengyuen. Mai Seon pressed it against the board and began to point at multiple gray markings daubed across the map.

"Each of these is the site of a Fui Gwai possession. They used to be scattered, happening at random, but look." He ran his finger along a cluster. "The attacks over the past month have started moving closer and closer to Hok Woh."

Zhi Ging shivered and saw Pinderent's face blanch.

"I still think it's a coincidence," Mynah muttered, but Hiulam shook her head.

"But that would explain why Ami looked so tense all through yesterday's challenge. Didn't anyone else notice? I was the second one back and she spent the entire time pacing around, her eyes fixed on the hourglass. Doesn't she normally at least chat with Silhouettes who've passed?"

"Exactly!" Mai Seon slapped his hand against the map. "What if she was worried because she *knew* the Fui Gwai was nearby? Or, if not the Fui Gwai itself, maybe some of its thralls searching for new victims for the spirit. After all, that forest was right *here.*" His finger tapped an empty space surrounded by gray markings, and the others stilled. Even Mynah started to look concerned, the vivid orange of her cheek patches fading to a pale cream.

"We need to ask someone. Maybe Ai'Deng Bou?" Zhi Ging said, her eyes meeting Mai Seon's. "If we're in danger, the Cyo B'Ahon have to let us know."

AI'DENG BOU'S CLASSROOM WAS HIDDEN DEEP INside a giant greenhouse. Zhi Ging gazed up, trying to spot the glass ceiling, but it was concealed behind layers of towering plants.

"We could have just done his challenge in here," she murmured to Pinderent. Around her, the other Silhouettes were carefully picking their way through gnarled tree roots and thick clumps of moss. When they finally spotted their new tutor, he was standing with his back to them, searching for something between the bushes. The Silhouettes shuffled forward and the Cyo B'Ahon turned with a start.

"Ah, there you all are!" He paused, his eyes flickering back to the bushes. "Any chance one of you spotted a sheep on your walk over? Gray wool, pink nose, *incredibly* smug face."

The Silhouettes shook their heads, and he sighed.

"Never mind, I'm sure he'll turn up soon. Oh, but if

he wanders past during class, make sure you don't touch his wool!"

"Why? Is he dangerous?" Zhi Ging asked, her hand leaping up protectively to the duckling snoozing in her hood.

"Not at all, I just, eh, got my calculations slightly wrong with him. I was attempting to weave different grains into sheep's DNA, so crops like wheat, barley, or corn could grow along their wool. I thought it'd be a great help for some of the more isolated villages." Ai'Deng Bou rubbed his nose. "Unfortunately, I forgot just how static wool can be when I started with corn. The second he brushed against the other sheep, their wool crackled with electricity and his coat doubled in size. He panicked and bolted through Hok Woh, leaving trails of fresh popcorn behind him. It took weeks for me to track him down and get him back to this greenhouse, but I think he might have escaped again."

Zhi Ging bit her lip, trying hard not to laugh. She could image Cyo B'Ahon ageshifting in shock as a blur of popcorn galloped past them in the corridors. Mynah was already shaking with silent giggles beside her.

"Anyway, let's get started." Ai'Deng Bou gestured toward the giant lily pads floating on a nearby pond. "Everyone pick a seat."

Zhi Ging and the others raced forward, each trying to claim the largest one.

"Come on, Pinderent, we can share." Zhi Ging laughed

as her friend stood dejectedly on the shore, staring out at all the filled lily pads. She leaned forward to paddle toward him, and the duckling leaped out from her hood. His small wings sent a flurry of water splashing over the others.

The Silhouettes shrieked in excitement, and Ai'Deng Bou ageshifted down in surprise. Their now ten-year-old tutor splashed into the pond, oversized robes billowing around him as he chased after the duckling. Ai'Deng Bou pulled a handful of sunflower seeds from his pouch, and the duckling immediately stopped, sniffing the air. He quacked in excitement and leaped into the Cyo B'Ahon's palm.

"Who does he belong to?" Ai'Deng Bou asked, tickling the duckling under his beak.

"Uh, me," Zhi Ging squeaked. The Cyo B'Ahon waded toward her and tipped the duckling, and the last of the sunflower seeds, onto her lily pad.

"What's his name?"

"Malo." The name tumbled unexpectedly out from her mouth, and the duckling ruffled his feathers, pleased with her choice.

"Malo, yes, that suits him." Ai'Deng Bou nodded. "You can keep bringing him to class as long as he doesn't interrupt."

Iridill rolled her eyes and turned toward Cing Yau.

"More special treatment for the precious 'Second Silhouette,'" she hissed in a stage whisper. Ai'Deng Bou turned to frown at her. Behind him, Mai Seon gestured at Zhi Ging, then pointed at the Cyo B'Ahon. *Ask him,* he mouthed. She took a deep breath and raised her hand.

"Can I ask you a question, sir?"

"Of course, and there's no need to be so formal in my lessons."

"Well, um, *some* of us were wondering if you could tell us about the Fui Gwai. Are the rumors true? Is the spirit really getting closer to Hok Woh? What would happen if it got past the glass entrance?"

Ai'Deng Bou's face darkened and he ageshifted back up to sixty. "I don't cover spirits in my lessons. I prefer to focus on the creatures that have natural homes in Wengyuen's lands, seas, and skies. No good can ever come from crossing paths with spirits, whether it's one of the ancient sand spirits or this new Fui Gwai."

"But the Fui Gwai's been around forever," Hiulam argued. "My grandmother nearly got caught by one of its thralls when she was my age."

Ai'Deng Bou shook his head.

"Your grandmother and I have very different ideas of 'forever.' I can assure you it has existed for no more than one hundred years—one hundred and ten at most. However, many in Hok Woh believe it's nothing more than a century-old excuse dreamed up by villagers fed up with paying a tithe to the Cyo B'Ahon. By claiming we had accidentally released an evil spirit, they could justify their . . . hostility toward us."

"I heard that rumor was actually started by an old Silhouette, furious after they were kicked out of Hok Woh for failing a challenge," Pinderent added.

Ai'Deng Bou's face flickered, as if he was actively trying to stop himself from ageshifting. After a long pause, he shook his head.

"Who can say? I personally believe the Fui Gwai is very real. Over the years, I've seen distant glimpses of too many thralls, those possessed by the spirit and forced to attack their own families, to believe it could be a simple rumor. But that's not what today's lesson—"

"What if more attacks happen? Will we get sent home?" Mynah interrupted.

The Cyo B'Ahon shook his head. "If anyone has any other questions about the Fui Gwai, please speak to Ami. As your Dohrnii, she can answer any questions you have that aren't related to my reading lists or homework deadlines."

"Can you at least tell us why our Chau was moved back? Please?" Mynah pushed, knowing this could be her last chance to ask.

"Ah, an *excellent* example of another question for the Dohrnii, Miss Niu."

Ai'Deng Bou waded across the pond toward his own lily pad and pulled a piece of chalk from behind his ear.

"Now, today we're going to focus on the chimeras you met during yesterday's challenge. In crate number one we had a pangolin mixed with . . ."

Zhi Ging let the rest of his lecture wash over her, an anxious finger tracing over the gold lines now safely re-hidden beneath Gertie's glove. Failing a challenge suddenly didn't feel like the only thing threatening her time in Hok Woh.

CHAPTER 24

"All right Team Bolei, time to grab your paddles!" Hiulam hollered across the dining hall. Bright green paddles were tucked under each of her arms, fanning out behind her like wooden wings. Malo chirped in surprise and tilted his head to the side, a stray noodle hanging forgotten in his beak.

"Don't worry, you're still the only duckling here." Zhi Ging laughed, scooping him into her hood. Pinderent waved at Hiulam as she waddled between the packed tables toward them.

"Why didn't you tell me you'd gone to the equipment room? I could have helped carry those," he said, pointing siu mai–topped chopsticks at the paddles.

"Well . . . ," Hiulam began, her eyes sparkling with mischief. "If you'd helped with these, I couldn't have asked you to carry the race cloaks up, could I?"

Pinderent groaned and shook his head. "Those always

stink after a month in the cupboard! Even Bucbou hasn't worked out a way to shake the smell of stale sea air. Eh, I don't know why *you're* laughing," he added, turning toward Zhi Ging with a grin. "You're going to help me carry all eight up the stairs!"

"Not a chance!" Hiulam shrieked, paddles clattering to the floor as she flung her arms up in outrage. "It's Zhi Ging's first race so she gets to release our boat from the stepping stone. Would you really deprive her of that?"

"Ugh, fine. But you're helping next time." He waved his chopsticks toward Zhi Ging and yelped in surprise when Malo popped out of her hood, gobbling the siu mai in one quick bite.

The Silhouettes around them burst out laughing, and the duckling ruffled his feathers, delighted by both the attention and his unexpected snack.

"You better not be full after that." Mynah snorted, cheeks flashing yellow. "I was hoping someone would share these with me during the race." She pulled a small pouch of sunflower seeds out from her cloak and waved it in front of Malo. The duckling leaped out of Zhi Ging's hood and onto the table, hopping up and down in excitement at the idea of more treats.

Behind him, Hiulam snatched up another paddle and tugged on Zhi Ging's sleeve.

"Come on," she whispered. "Let's go before Pinderent remembers you'd still have enough time to help carry the cloaks afterward! Releasing the boat's much faster than lowering it back after training."

CREW MEMBERS FROM EACH DRAGON BOAT TEAM spilled out of the glass staircase, and Zhi Ging gasped, gazing up in wonder. Six large bamboo stands towered above her, rising and falling with the waves. The floating structures were connected to the entrance by thin rope bridges, each daubed in glowing paint to match a different team's colors.

"People cheering for Team Bolei will sit in that stand," Gwong shouted over the crashing waves, pointing toward the one connected by a bright green rope. "And it looks like word's gotten out that we've got the Second Silhouette on our team!" he added with a chuckle. Zhi Ging gulped, eyeing the considerably larger crowd already squeezing into their stand.

"Keep an eye on the rope bridges after the second bend," Bucbou interrupted, stepping out from behind them. "If you see a bunch of Silhouettes and Cyo B'Ahon switching stands, it's usually a good sign of who they think will win the race, and who our main competition should be."

"Yeah, but you also don't want to look, in case everyone's running away from ours," B'ei Gun muttered.

"Hey, cheerful as ever!" Yuttou laughed, ruffling his hair. "Let's go, Zhi Ging. You need to get our boat for us." She pointed at the Cyo B'Ahon jumping between stepping stones, paddles lit up by their glowing race cloaks. Thin wooden platforms had been tied around each stepping stone, with some of the more eager racers already lined up along them.

"We competed with the sixth dragon last time, so we're restarting with the first one tonight. The one closest to shore."

"There's a small hollow in the center of the glass stepping stone," Hiulam whispered, when they reached the first stepping stone. "Press your thumb into it, then make sure to jump back onto the platform. The boats spring out quickly!"

"Got it," Zhi Ging said with an exaggerated grimace. She had no plans to come face-to-face with a dragon ever again, no matter what it was made of.

Her fingers quickly found the dip in the smooth glass, and she pushed down. The stepping stone rumbled beneath her, and Zhi Ging leaped back seconds before the dragon shot out like a firework. This dragon's head was an intricate paper origami mask with swirling calligraphy covering its cream surface. Zhi Ging's heart leaped and she glanced back toward the packed stand for Team Bolei. Between her parchment lantern and the cutting that had released Malo, racing with the paper dragon had to be a good sign!

The dragon boat finished its graceful arc through the air and crashed down in front of the team, glittering seawater raining down around them.

"Ugh, do you mind?" a Silhouette on Team Tsadeu snarled, flicking droplets from her red cloak. Zhi Ging's stomach dropped as she turned around.

Iridill.

"What?" The girl's eyes narrowed at Zhi Ging's shocked expression. "Let me guess, you thought you were the only new Silhouette invited to join a team? Hate to break it to you NoGlow, but you weren't special in Fei Chui and you aren't special here." She lowered her voice so the rest of Team Bolei couldn't hear. "I should be the one racing with the glass province Cyo B'Ahon, not you. You only got picked because you're the 'Second Silhouette'—whatever that even means—but you can't keep snatching what's mine. Once Team Bolei see me race, they'll realize what a real Fei Chui Silhouette can do and forget all about you."

"I bet Team Tsadeu only invited you so the waves would drown out your constant reminders of who your father is," Zhi Ging shot back, prerace nerves causing the words to tumble out before she could stop them.

Iridill's eyes narrowed in fury.

"How dare yo—Bleughhh!" She threw a hand over her nose, reeling away as Pinderent reached the stepping stone, the stench of stale seawater drifting up from the mountain of glowing cloaks in his arms. He glanced between their scrunched faces with a bemused expression, a clothespin stuck to his nose.

"I dold ou dey smeld!" He flung a green cloak over Zhi Ging's shoulders, and she grimaced. It smelled like she had just wrapped herself in a musty, dried-out puddle. Out of the corner of her eye, she saw Iridill shove her way down the platform, putting as much distance as she could between herself and Pinderent.

At least the stench had some benefits.

Farther along the stepping stones, more dragon boats began to appear from beneath the surface. The glass dragon, with its near-invisible head, erupted out by Team Syun Zi, while the porcelain dragon for Team Wong Gam dipped low in the water, its heavy white clay outlined in cobalt blue.

Zhi Ging rose onto her tiptoes, eager to see the other dragons, when a flash of golden silk caught her eye.

"Hey, what's that?" she asked, peering at the fabric-covered sedan rising out of the entrance stepping stone.

"That's Sintou's sedan! She hasn't been to a race since my first month," Hiulam squeaked in excitement.

"I don't get it," Zhi Ging whispered as Silhouettes on the other teams jostled for a glimpse of the sedan. "Why are they getting so excited? Only the Cyo B'Ahon from the winning team get to meet her, don't they?"

Hiulam tore her eyes away from the gold silk. "Apparently, and this is just a rumor, but I heard that if you're one of the Silhouettes on the winning team—"

Pinderent interrupted with a flurry of nonsensical words, the clothespin on his nose wiggling back and forth.

"What are you trying to say?" Zhi Ging asked with a laugh, unclipping it.

"Challenge immunity! If your dragon boat wins a race that Sintou's watched and the next Cyo B'Ahon tutor happens to have been on your team, rumor has it they automatically let you pass their Silhouette challenge."

"No way!" Zhi Ging could feel her heart racing.

"Yes, but consider how many Cyo B'Ahon there are in Hok Woh versus how many are currently tutors," B'ei Gun cut in across them, ageshifting down beside them. "Simple probability would argue that there may only be a single tutor across the six teams. The chances of that particular Cyo B'Ahon then also being present at the next Silhouette challenge are infinitely smaller."

"Ah come on, B'ei Gun." Gwong chuckled. "We want to motivate the Silhouettes before a race, not do whatever it is you're doing. You know Bucbou won immunity at least twice during her first year!"

"Yes, but she became a Cyo B'Ahon before the attack on Hok Woh."

A whistle cut over his grumbling, and all six teams fell silent. Back in the stalls, Cyo B'Ahon and Silhouettes alike leaned forward in their seats, hoping to catch a glimpse of their secretive leader through the silk.

"Thank you, everyone." A soft, low voice floated out through the sedan, the sea breeze draping each word around the watching crowds. "Tonight marks a special moment in Hok Woh history. It is the eleven hundredth dragon boat race since we rebuilt Hok Woh beneath the waves."

Polite applause echoed across the six stands, and the

Cyo B'Ahon ageshifted up and down in celebration, their cloaks blooming around them.

"As you all know, the dragon heads adorning tonight's boats have been gifted to us by rulers across Wengyuen's six provinces. In exchange for the monthly tithe they pay, we must continue our promise to support them, offering guidance in times of both conflict and peace. These six sculptures represent the main exports of each province: paper, gold, silk, glass, porcelain, and carved lacquer." Sintou cleared her throat before continuing. "I ask all those competing to show the utmost respect for the artisanship needed to create these dragon heads. Just as we must care for the citizens of the six provinces, so must we care for their creations."

Zhi Ging jumped as the water flared with light, hundreds of jellyfish rising to the surface to illuminate the dragon heads.

"With that said, I believe all six stands are now full and, on my signal, the race can begin."

A small flame flickered to life at the edge of the sedan and raced upward.

"Wait, was that the signal?" Zhi Ging yelped as the team bundled into their dragon boat.

"Just keep watching that flame!" Pinderent warned, leaning back to help her into the boat. The boat dipped under them, and the dragon's paper whiskers brushed against the sea surface.

"Careful!" Bucbou snapped, leaping up to wipe the

droplets away. "We only keep our agility advantage for as long as this stays dry. Once the waves soften the paper, it'll be almost impossible for B'ei Gun to steer. We need to be well ahead of the others before that happens."

"Sorry!" Zhi Ging and Pinderent said simultaneously. "We didn't—"

A thin, shrill whistling filled the air, and Zhi Ging spun around. *Where did the flame go?*

The sky filled with glittering light as the firework exploded, showering the bamboo stands with golden dust. The jellyfish surrounding the boats streamed forward, tentacles linking together to form the racecourse outline.

"Go! Go! Go!" Bucbou roared as the boats around them jerked to life. Zhi Ging tore her eyes away from the dying firework and spotted Iridill's team charging ahead, their carved lacquer dragon glowing like hot wax. Seawater crashed over the paper dragon, and Bucbou's instructions became muffled as Zhi Ging drove her paddle into the churning water.

If anyone was going to win immunity, it was her.

CHAPTER 25

"Hold on!" B'ei Gun yelled as they shot through a thin gap between the gold and porcelain dragons. Zhi Ging's paddle shook wildly in her hands, rattling against the wooden frame of Team Wong Gam's boat.

"We can't let them anywhere near us," Bucbou barked. "That porcelain makes it the heaviest boat in the race. One sideswipe from a wave and that's it, our paper dragon's no better than pulp."

Zhi Ging's eyes darted toward their origami dragon head, and her breath caught in her throat. Its horns and whiskers had already started to slump, sodden with seawater. Dark ink dripped down its beard, the strong calligraphy strokes softening on the paper. They hadn't even reached the first bend yet.

The team raced forward but Team Tsadeu's carved lacquer dragon stayed frustratingly out of reach. No matter how fast they paddled, they never pulled closer. Iridill's boat sliced through the sea, the Cyo B'Ahon sending a barrage of waves back to throw the other teams off course. Pinderent and Bucbou had no choice but to repeatedly swing their paddles up, batting away waves that threatened to crash over the paper dragon. Each time they did, Team Tsadeu tore farther ahead.

"On your right!" Yuttou shouted as they reached the first bend, jabbing a finger behind them. B'ei Gun pushed his oar sharply to the side, and the glass dragon roared past, Team Syun Zi's purple paddles obscured by the churning water. A wave crashed hard against Team Bolei's dragon boat, and Zhi Ging screamed as her left side plunged into the sea.

"Remember the drills," Bucbou roared. "We are *not* about to capsize! Right-side crew, grab your partner and HEAVE."

Zhi Ging felt Hiulam grasp her arm and wrench her back toward the right. Paddles hit against teak as all eight crew members flung their weight against the tilted edge of the boat.

"Next dragon incoming!" B'ei Gun cried. The gold dragon was seconds away, its metallic snout aimed toward their side. Another hit now would sink them.

"Everyone needs to *push*," Zhi Ging yelled, willing gravity to be on their side. The dragon boat lurched under them but refused to righten.

"Three seconds," B'ei Gun croaked, his voice cracking in alarm.

"Zhi Ging, grab my cloak!"

Without waiting, Hiulam flung herself over the raised side of the boat, her flailing hands snatching at the water beneath them. Zhi Ging caught the edge of her cloak just before it slipped overboard, but the force of Hiulam's dive pulled her forward, and Zhi Ging slammed hard against the side.

"What are you doing!?"

The dragon boat groaned, teak panels creaking, and tipped back to the right, landing hard against the water's surface. A wave surged out beneath it, forcing Team Si Cau's gold dragon back down the bend. Yuttou and Gwong leaped forward and pulled a drenched Hiulam out of the water.

"What were you thinking!?" Bucbou screamed. "What if the boat had landed on you!? Or Zhi Ging hadn't grabbed your cloak in time!?"

"But it didn't, and she did!" Hiulam cheered, still dazed from her headfirst plunge into the freezing water.

"Team Si Cau's coming back, guys," B'ei Gun warned, hopping anxiously from foot to foot.

"All right team!" Bucbou shook her paddle in the air. "Two bends to go and only two boats ahead of us. Let's show Sintou what we're made of. Central Paddlers, get us out of here!"

Zhi Ging roared along with the rest of the team, adrenaline coursing through her. Their arms whirred through the water, determined to catch the glass dragon before the second bend. A sudden wind whipped between them, and Zhi Ging's hair lashed across her face. Storm clouds churned above them, and heavy droplets turned the sea to sparkling chaos.

"Silk dragon's catching up!" B'ei Gun cried, eyes trained on Team Chi Hei speeding toward them. The air filled with the sound of rippling fabric, and Zhi Ging's mouth dropped open as the silk dragon head billowed outward. Its features vanished, transforming into a large silk kite that pulled the boat forward. The silk dragon roared past, the crew waving their blue paddles in the air. Zhi Ging felt her stomach twist with envy. How were they meant to beat that?

"Don't give up now!" Bucbou shouted as the team stalled. "That wind could die again at any second and even if it doesn't, Team Chi Hei will have to slow down once they reach the sea stacks in the second bend. Look at the stands if you don't trust me!"

Zhi Ging twisted toward the bamboo stands in the center of the course and realized Bucbou was right. Although a few Cyo B'Ahon were hurrying along the rope bridge into Team Chi Hei's blue stand, most were staying put. There were still far more supporters in their green stand.

The Drummer, Gu Sao, began a new beat, his urgent rhythm rallying the team. They charged after the silk dragon, eyes trained on the boat's tail as it darted under the towering sea arch that marked the start of the second bend.

"All arms tight to the boat," Yuttou shouted over the crashing waves. "Last thing we need now is a snapped paddle."

B'ei Gun narrowed his eyes in concentration, steering the team through the maze of stony sea stacks. Zhi Ging gulped, peering up at the craggy rocks rising out of the sea. *Never mind the paddles—one of those could snap our entire boat in half.*

The now sodden paper dragon head had begun to wilt, clumps dropping into the dark water, making it increasingly difficult to steer. Zhi Ging tucked her paddle closer and copied the tight, focused strokes of Gwong in front of her.

Suddenly, the rock surfaces lit up, filling the bend with blazing metallic light.

"Gold dragon coming up behind us!"

The Cyo B'Ahon on Team Si Cau had scooped dozens of the glowing jellyfish out of the water and placed them on the gold dragon head. Their shimmering light turned the golden surface into a blazing torch.

"Use that light, everyone!" Bucbou yelled. "We can avoid hidden rocks as long as we stay in front of them."

Zhi Ging and the others hunched low, slamming their paddles into water that now gleamed like liquid gold. Their boat wove between the jutting rocks, and the gold dragon soon fell behind, their steering slowed by the need to keep jellyfish balanced on its metal snout. B'ei Gun steered Team Bolei around the final towering sea stack, and Zhi Ging's mouth dropped open when she spotted the silk and glass dragons caught at the base of a stone pillar.

The glass dragon head had become tangled in the silk, a glass horn and several whiskers piercing through the fabric. Both teams were frantically trying to disentangle the material, their boats teetering dangerously beneath them. Zhi Ging shook her head in disbelief. If they'd outpaced the glass dragon earlier, it would have been them trapped in that silk now!

"I told you they wouldn't keep their advantage!" Bucbou cackled. "It's up to us to catch Team Tsadeu now. I refuse to let them win four races in a row!" She jabbed a finger toward the faint red glow on the horizon, and their paddles plunged back into the icy water.

THEY CAUGHT UP WITH THE CARVED LACQUER dragon as it sailed into the third and final bend. The boats' two drumbeats rose to a thunderous level, Gu Sao and the other Drummer determined to drown each other out. Pinderent and Bucbou faltered, struggling to match their strokes against the new discordant rhythms.

Zhi Ging peered past the sodden paper dragon head, and her heart leaped. Through thick sheets of rain, she could see the Pacers on Iridill's team also hesitating, thrown by the clashing drumbeats. This was their chance!

"Pacers!" she yelled, waving at them. "We need to block out the sound and just follow Gu Sao's hand movements."

Zhi Ging racked her brain, and her eyes landed on the drooping paper head.

"The paper dragon! It's too sodden to help with steering now anyway. Break off a bit and stuff it in your ears, then it won't matter how loud the other Drummer gets."

"You genius!" Pinderent gasped, leaping up to grab a large handful of the dragon's paper beard. He broke off a lump and threw the rest back to the crew members behind him.

"Zhi Ging, here!" Hiulam yelled, her voice even louder than normal now that she couldn't hear herself. She tossed the last of the dragon's beard toward Zhi Ging, and it landed with a squelch in her hands. The calligraphy danced across the paper, and the ink shimmered to a rich purple. A woman's face appeared across the flowing ink and, for a split second, smiled up at Zhi Ging. Her eyes widened in surprise, but the face vanished as Team Tsadeu's boat slammed against them, sending them veering sharply to the right.

"We need to keep away from that border!" Bucbou ordered, eyes trained on the underwater waterfall churning at the center of the bend. "We're about to reach the course blind spot. If they hit into us behind the sea stack, no one in the stands will see!"

The two boats were neck and neck as they raced around the bend, teak splintering as the dragon boats crashed against one another.

"Back off!" Hiulam screamed, waving her paddle wildly at Team Tsadeu. Iridill lunged forward and snatched the paddle from her hands. Hiulam screamed as the girl flung it past the jellyfish border toward the underwater waterfall. It floated for a second, then was snatched down by an invisible current, shattering into fragments as it was dragged past the rocky overhang into the waterfall's depths.

"Don't!" Zhi Ging shrieked as Hiulam leaped up, snarling at Iridill. "If you go overboard now, you'll get pulled into the underwater waterfall too." Her heart pounded in her chest; she couldn't tell if Hiulam could even hear her through the paper mush in her ears.

"You can't trust anyone in the blind spot, Silhouette or Cyo B'Ahon!" Bucbou growled. "Some will do anything to get an audience with Sintou, particularly if they're new Cyo B'Ahon like those on Team Tsadeu. They have more to prove with living relatives back home. Racing rules don't exist once we're in the blind spot." She bent low until her arms were level with the boat's side. "We're almost there. One final sprint and we'll be over the finish line!"

Green cloaks rippled as the crew copied Bucbou's stance, their noses pressed against their knees to help reduce air resistance. Heavy rain drummed against Zhi Ging's back, and her breath caught in her throat when she spotted Iridill's team smirking at them. *What were they planning?*

The paper dragon shot forward, and wood drummed against wood as Team Tsadeu tried to knock paddles out of their hands. B'ei Gun pushed his oar sharply to the right, forcing their boat out of reach but dangerously close to the border. The jellyfish illuminated the currents churning inches away from them, dragging starlight over the waterfall's edge. Bucbou's orders seemed to leach into the surging water, and all Zhi Ging could hear was the sound of her own breathing.

B'ei Gun pulled them back toward the center of the course, keeping pressure on the oar while they curved close around the final sea stack. Out of the corner of her eye, Zhi Ging could see the carved lacquer dragon's snout falling behind. They might actually win!

Zhi Ging heard a muffled noise that sounded like someone calling her name and turned to see Iridill scoop a clump of moss off the sea stack, piling it onto her paddle.

She could just make out the girl's next words. *"Nice try, NoGlow!"* The wad sailed through the air and landed on what was left of the paper dragon's head. Before Zhi Ging could blink, another splattered against her paddle handle, covering her hands in sand and moss.

The other two Silhouettes on Team Tsadeu exchanged a glance, then snatched at the sea stack. As one, they swung their paddles up, sending clumps of moss flying forward. There was a loud tearing sound, and the paper dragon head slumped, the added weight too much for its already waterlogged frame. It plummeted into the sea, and paper fragments tangled against the front paddles, pulling Pinderent and Bucbou down.

Zhi Ging jerked forward and grabbed on to the sea stack, rainwater rushing between her fingers.

"Use your paddles! We need to get this water out!" Bucbou howled, her voice barely audible over Yuttou's and Gwong's furious shouting, the front half of the boat sinking into the sea.

"Hold on, I have an idea!" Zhi Ging yelled, tightening her grip around the sea stack. She held her breath as the carved lacquer dragon sped toward them. There'd only be one chance to get this right.

Just before it reached them, Zhi Ging pitched her paddle forward, jamming its wooden blade deep into the dragon's snarling red mouth. The impact jerked her boat forward, but the paddle locked them in place.

"You ruined our dragon head, so it's only fair we use yours to win!" Zhi Ging roared, twisting the paddle sideways to trap the blade between the dragon's lacquer fangs.

Iridill and a Pacer tried to shake their boat loose, paddles churning the water, but all it did was push Team Bolei's boat forward, driving them out past the blind spot. Zhi Ging let go of the sea stack as the headless dragon boat righted itself and Pinderent looked up in surprise, his paddle no longer needed to push them through the water.

"Wait! Everyone stop!" the Steerer on Team Tsadeu cried, but it was too late.

The two boats shot past the finish line, but only one crossed it first, pushed forward by the other. There was a collective intake of breath, then the air around Zhi Ging exploded with applause.

CHAPTER 26

Mynah bundled through the crowd of celebrating Silhouettes and threw herself at Zhi Ging and Pinderent.

"That was incredible!" she screamed, hugging them tight. "You should have seen how many people were racing between the red and green stands once your boats vanished into the blind spot. I've never seen a race that close!"

Malo danced excitedly between their feet, waving an imaginary paddle between his wings. Zhi Ging laughed and bent to scoop him up, but Mynah gasped and grabbed her wrist.

"Whoa, are you okay?"

"What is that?" Pinderent asked, seeing what Mynah had just spotted. "Did a jellyfish sting you?"

Pinderent and Mynah were staring at her wide-eyed. Rain splashed against the thin gold tendrils that spiraled out from her palm in overlapping lines. She'd forgotten to put Gertie's glove back on after the race.

"Yeah, it must have," she murmured, trying to ignore her racing heartbeat. "I think I grabbed one when we nearly capsized."

She hated lying to them, but she couldn't tell them she had no clue what the marks were. Not when she hadn't had a chance to talk to Ami since the Cyo B'Ahon's warning.

Mynah frowned, her cheeks flashing a sallow cream.

"Well, you should get Wusi to look at it in the sick bay."

"That can wait!" A beaming Hiulam appeared behind them. "We're about to throw the biggest party any of the provinces have ever seen. This is Team Bolei's first win in forty years! Gwong's promised us the biggest tray of lau sah bao that'll fit through the dorm door."

Thunder boomed overhead and a few nearby Cyo B'Ahon ageshifted down in shock. The other teams were already vanishing back down the steps, holding their paddles above their heads to block the worst of the downpour.

"All remaining Silhouettes to me," Bucbou cried, herding the black cloaks trickling down from the stands. "Let's get you back into Hok Woh before this storm really hits."

Behind her, four Cyo B'Ahon hurried forward to lift Sintou's sedan, frowning at the dark droplets that bloomed over the silk.

"Wait, where's Malo?" Zhi Ging spun around, scanning between ankles for his colorful feathers. Lightning crackled across the sky, illuminating the glass stepping stones, and she spotted him waddling determinedly after the sedan. She called after him, but her shouts were swallowed by another roll of thunder. Static sparked across her cloak, and in the next flash of light, she watched openmouthed as Malo leaped up and vanished through the silk coverings.

ZHI GING RACED DOWN THE STAIRS, USING THE chaos of Silhouettes flinging off sodden race cloaks to slip down the corridor after the sedan. How was she going to get him out?

She hurried along the twisting glass walls, expecting at any second to hear the Head of the Cyo B'Ahon shouting about her feathery hitchhiker.

"Malo, get back here!" she hissed, pressing herself flat against the curved wall in case one of the sedan carriers noticed her. Zhi Ging peered around the bend and spotted his beak poking through the silk before vanishing back inside. He was going to be in so much trouble once she got him! Her annoyance vanished and another thought popped into her mind. *How much trouble will I be in for letting him escape?*

Zhi Ging quickened her pace and rounded the corner just in time to see the end of Sintou's embroidered robes vanish behind the sliding glass wall, a small Malo-shaped bump trailing beneath the gold fabric. She hurried back the way she'd come and waited for the four Cyo B'Ahon carrying the now empty sedan to leave, before sprinting back down the corridor.

She ran her hand along the base of the wall, trying to remember where Reishi had pressed.

"At least the Lead Glassmith's dragon door was easy to find," Zhi Ging muttered to herself.

She dragged her fingers along the length of the corridor and finally caught against a chipped ridge in the smooth glass—barely noticeable unless you knew where to look. A delicate crane was etched into the hollow, its face gazing out at her.

"Don't worry," she whispered to the bird. "I won't tell anyone else about this. I just need to get Malo back."

The glow of a passing jellyfish caught against the glass, and the crane seemed to ruffle its feathers in agreement. Zhi Ging smiled and hooked her finger into the hollow, sliding the fake wall aside.

"AH, I WONDERED WHO THIS LITTLE FELLOW BE-longed to." Sintou's thin white eyebrow rose up, vanishing into a furrowed forehead, when Zhi Ging stepped into the room. "Your duckling appears to believe I'm in possession of some secret sunflower seeds."

Malo hopped down from the Head of the Cyo B'Ahon's shoulder and waddled across the checkers board, careful not to knock any colored marbles from their spaces.

"I'm so sorry, I know I'm not supposed to be here without an invitation—"

"What's your name, Silhouette? You look familiar."

"It's Zhi Ging, ma'am." She held up her white Pan Chang Knot. "The Second Silhouette from Fei Chui?"

"No, that's not it." Sintou paused and slowly turned over Zhi Ging's hand to reveal the gold shining up from her palm. She brushed an arthritic finger across the lines.

"Ling Geng? I thought after you split the pa—"

"Oh no, I'm Zhi Ging. Yeung Zhi Ging." She bit her lip, immediately regretting her interruption. Had anyone ever spoken over the Head of the Cyo B'Ahon?

Sintou's eyes clouded over for a moment, and she released Zhi Ging's hand. The flame curled under the glass floor, and she tapped the checkers board.

"Join me for a game, Zhi Ging. Reports from your first tutor and the timings for your Fauna challenge were . . . underwhelming." The Head of the Cyo B'Ahon's eyes flickered to her white Pan Chang. "But one can tell a lot about someone from how they move across the board. Perhaps our game will reveal what makes you worthy of the title of Second Silhouette."

"I don't want to interrupt your game with Reishi," Zhi Ging mumbled, glancing at the complex pattern of green and white marbles peppered across the board. It hadn't changed since her first meeting with Sintou. Why hadn't Reishi come back for his turn?

"Nonsense. I can remember each marble's position. I'll reset the board when he finally tears himself away from his air rail research. Now, which point would you like to play as?"

Zhi Ging glanced down at the star-shaped board. Each point had been decorated with a famous landmark from one of the six provinces. The mother-of-pearl inlay closest to her had faded and chipped over time, but with its eight-tiered eaves, she would recognize Fei Chui's pagoda anywhere. Aapau was there now, spending her Final Year stuck inside that roaming tower.

"Ah, Fei Chui." Sintou nodded, following her gaze. "In that case, I'll play as its mirror, Omophilli." She slipped the white marbles back into a satin pouch and added purple ones to the point directly across from Zhi Ging's. Malo snuffled at the marbles before huffing in disappointment when they turned out not to be sunflower seeds.

"I'll offer you the same terms I grant all Cyo B'Ahon. For each marble you place in Omophilli's starting point, I will answer one question of your choosing. However, for each marble I place in Fei Chui's starting point, you must tell me a truth about how those from your province view Cyo B'Ahon. I fear the Scouts have become too worried about protecting my feelings, but I see the monthly decline in collected tithes." Sintou sighed deeply before placing the final purple marble on her point. "Shall we begin?"

"Yes," Zhi Ging squeaked, not quite believing what was happening. *Did Iridill's paddle hit me during the race?*

"Wonderful. As this is your fledgling game, you may make the first move."

The flame crackled behind the glass and surged up the wall, highlighting the gold on Zhi Ging's palm as she ran a hand over the board. Ten marbles meant ten questions. She might finally learn what the lines meant.

Zhi Ging took a deep breath and plucked a green marble from the second row, hopping it over the first toward the center of the board. Sintou nodded and flicked a purple marble forward. An intense silence crinkled the air between the Silhouette and the Cyo B'Ahon, twin frowns fixed on their faces as they raced pieces across the board.

For a while, Malo chirped enthusiastically for both sides, but he soon grew bored and hopped down to examine the fire. The trapped flame cascaded down to greet him beneath the glass, fanning out beneath his tail to give Malo a golden robe that rivaled Sintou's. He quacked in delight and strutted around Zhi Ging's chair, showing off his fiery new tail.

The sound of glass clicking against wood sped up, and Zhi Ging's eyes widened when the Head of the Cyo B'Ahon moved a marble sideways, inadvertently clearing the perfect path. Zhi Ging snatched up her own piece and hopped it over two green marbles and one purple to land neatly in the center of the Cyo B'Ahon's starting point. She beamed and looked up in time to see a flicker of surprise on Sintou's face.

"Well. If you and Reishi fail to discover more about the air rails, he can at least use your research sessions to improve his checkers skills. Now, what would you like to ask me?"

Zhi Ging could feel herself blush, both from the begrudging compliment and the question she was about to ask.

"Why do these keep appearing?" She held out her hand toward the Head of the Cyo B'Ahon, the golden spirals dancing in the firelight. "What are they?"

Sintou frowned and tapped a purple marble against the wooden board. Zhi Ging held her breath, hoping the Cyo B'Ahon wouldn't refuse to answer what was really two questions.

"I have seen similar lines before, centuries ago, on another girl not much older than you. Her name was Ling Geng. I don't know why they keep appearing, but I can tell you something about their legacy." Malo stared up at them, his feathers glinting in the firelight. "These lines first appeared in your family as a curse, but your mother shared them with you as protection."

Zhi Ging sat up straight, her heart racing.

"You know my mother? Is she still alive?" Aapau had never been able to answer that question. Zhi Ging ran a shaking hand through Malo's feathers. "Does this mean you know where I'm really from?"

"I never met her, but I know she would not want you

to let these lines go to waste. Do not call on them unless you are in danger."

Zhi Ging's eyes widened. *Ami shared a similar warning!*

"What do you mean 'go to waste'? I don't even know how I'm—"

The flame blazed and streamed across the floor toward the glass door. The winning Cyo B'Ahon from Team Bolei burst in. Their excited conversations floundered and stuttered to a halt when they spotted Zhi Ging at the checkers board. B'ei Gun inhaled sharply, his gaze landing on the shimmering lines on Zhi Ging's arm.

"Another time," the Head of the Cyo B'Ahon murmured, closing Zhi Ging's gold-lined palm before rising to greet the others. "Welcome, Team Bolei, and many congratulations on your long-awaited win."

Zhi Ging slipped past the hushed group, her neck prickling as B'ei Gun's eyes narrowed, his glare following her out of the room.

THAT EVENING, REISHI WAS DISTRACTED DURING their air rail research. He and Gahyau exchanged countless covert looks, the jellyfish's usual yellow fading to a sallow sheen each time Reishi shook his head.

"What's going on?" Zhi Ging finally asked, taking off a pair of moonlight-infused mittens that had well and truly failed to sense a single rail. She tossed them onto the growing pile of unsuccessful fabric on Reishi's desk.

He grimaced and gestured for her to have a seat.

"A message meant for another Scout was accidentally sent to Gahyau this afternoon. Your presence as Second Silhouette has caused some unexpected complications."

Zhi Ging felt panic crackle up her back.

"What do you mean?"

"Please don't misunderstand, most Cyo B'Ahon are thrilled you're here. They see it as a sign Sintou is finally ready to return things to how they were before the attack. Back to a more welcoming and open-minded version of Hok Woh. However . . ." His expression darkened. "Your arrival has added to the rumblings among a small, but powerful, group of Cyo B'Ahon. They've been demanding for decades that their hometowns be allowed a higher number of Silhouettes. Unfortunately, that now means they see your presence as a direct snub of their requests."

He sighed again, ageshifting down while he paced back and forth. "The message revealed some of them no longer support Sintou's position as Head of the Cyo B'Ahon. If she was removed, none of her rulings would be binding—including your continued protection against the Glassmith's warrant."

"But what can I do?" Zhi Ging asked, her heart pounding. "Sintou said I'm only protected as long as I'm a Silhouette. If you make me leave now . . ."

Gahyau floated toward her and pressed his bubble against her hand as Reishi continued.

"I'm not asking you to leave, but you have to keep

Gertie's glove on at all times, even during dragon boat training and challenges. There've been whispers for some time now that Sintou is looking to appoint her successor and, for this group, the timing of your arrival is suspicious. Time is meaningless to immortals. Whether you were appointed at the end of your Silhouette year or in a century's time wouldn't matter. They would still see it as a betrayal. The message warned your gold lines were proof of a secret deal with Sintou. If more Cyo B'Ahon spot them . . ." Reishi grimaced. Zhi Ging remembered the look on B'ei Gun's face, and her stomach tightened. She felt guilty for keeping her earlier conversation with Sintou from him, but she didn't want to give Reishi any more reason to worry.

"Before you met Sintou, I said you'd have to prove you were special in order to stay. I'm afraid it's more complicated than that. You need to appear special enough to be accepted as the Second Silhouette"—his eyes darted back toward the gold coiling along her arm—"but not so special that you become a threat to Hok Woh's more ambitious Cyo B'Ahon."

CHAPTER 27

For the next three weeks, Zhi Ging could barely focus in class. While the others clustered beneath the library dome to watch a pod of pink dolphins, taking notes as Ai'Deng Bou explained the hidden meaning behind each spin or tail flip, Zhi Ging stared impatiently at the rows of waiting bookshelves.

She had hoped to ask Ami more about the gold lines, but the Dohrnii had vanished, struggling to contain an infection that had ripped through the baby jellyfish in the Seoi Mou Pou. Reishi had checked through the scrolls in his own lab, but between them, they couldn't find any hint of what they were. Zhi Ging had spent every spare minute scouring the library for mentions of Ling Geng, the girl Sintou had mistaken her for, convinced their matching gold lines were the key to answering all her questions.

Her homework scrolls were often still empty by the time she collapsed into bed, and it was only thanks to Pinderent whispering answers in class that she had kept up with Ai'Deng Bou's lessons. She and Reishi continued to work on the air rails every evening, but they were still no closer to re-creating the solid beams from the cliffside. After multiple failed nights in the lab, even the sight of Gahyau pirouetting and tumbling in his bubble stopped cheering her up. Days ground to a slow trudge, and Zhi Ging found herself getting more frustrated with each book she slammed shut, still none the wiser.

The morning before their next challenge, Mynah bounded into the dining hall, waving a scroll in the air.

"It's finally happening! They've arranged a Chau for us. Pack your scarves and get ready for . . ." She grabbed Pinderent's chopsticks and drummed them against the side of the table. "An iceberg instrumental!"

"Oooh, I've heard about those." Pinderent beamed. "Groups of musicians travel the seas on giant icebergs, putting on concerts with instruments that have been carved from that same ice. I bet all the Cyo B'Ahon come along to this one."

"I guess that explains why we're only getting the Chau now," Zhi Ging said, stretching across the table to take the scroll from Mynah. "They had to wait until there was an iceberg nearby."

"Huh," Mai Seon scoffed. "That's what they want us to think. I bet they picked an iceberg because the Fui Gwai has never attacked anyone at sea."

"Oh, relax, Seon-Seon." Mynah laughed before turning to the group. "Listen, if any of you spot an evil spirit with unblinking, pupilless gray eyes tonight, please wait until *after* the concert to say anything. I don't want to miss a second of this Chau!"

Mai Seon frowned and jabbed his chopsticks into the last har gau. He waved the shrimp dumpling at her, shaking his head. "You shouldn't joke about things like that, Mynah. Once the Fui Gwai possesses you, that's it. You become one of its thralls forever. It takes your eyes for itself and you become nothing more than a puppet that brings it more victims." He took a deep breath, making sure he had the table's full attention. "What I want to know is when is the Fui Gwai going to stop growing its army and finally reveal *why* it's been collecting people from across Wengyuen. Spirits normally only turn on humans after they've been provoked or had something stolen from them. What if it plans to destroy the province of whoever upset it?"

An uncomfortable silence fell over the table, and even Mynah's cheeks faded to a pale gray. Zhi Ging shivered and stared down at the now-cold bowls of water around her, homei spoons clenched tight in her friends' hands. Would any of them even know if the Fui Gwai's revenge had already started back above the surface?

THE SILHOUETTES GASPED AS THEY STEPPED ONTO the iceberg, their breath clouding around them. Ice glistened beneath hundreds of lanterns, and masked musicians guided them through a tunnel toward the hollow heart of the iceberg. Zhi Ging pulled her cloak tight around her, suddenly wishing she had brought an extra pair of gloves.

Jack nudged her arm and handed over a steaming cup of jasmine tea.

"On the house," he whispered with a wink. A small cart piled high with teapots and treats trundled along behind him, violet liquid cresting in its glass wheels. Malo sat atop a bamboo steamer and chirped happily down at them.

"Thanks." Zhi Ging cupped the warm drink between her hands, grateful for its immediate effect on her chattering teeth.

"How are you doing?" Jack continued, his face softening in concern. "Are you feeling all right about the next challenge? You were so quiet on the way back from the last one. I'd been hoping to catch up but . . ." He hesitated. "I kinda got the feeling you weren't in the mood to talk."

Zhi Ging blew on the tea and looked up at his face.

"I don't think I realized how difficult it was going to be," she admitted. "Even though I didn't pa—" She caught herself in time and glanced at the Silhouettes walking along the tunnel in front of them. She couldn't believe she'd almost confessed she hadn't passed the original Silhouette entrance exam. Zhi Ging grimaced and frowned down into her cup.

She'd been late to the exam, starting long after the others. A flash of the Lead Glassmith guiding Aapau into the roaming pagoda while she ran toward them, voice raw from crying, flared across her mind.

"I thought the trickiest part was being picked as a Silhouette in the first place," Zhi Ging restarted, avoiding Jack's eye. "I didn't realize I'd have to keep proving myself once I got here. Why isn't the entrance exam enough?"

"Hmm." Jack gave a noncommittal shrug, his eyes darting to the Cyo B'Ahon at the front of the procession.

"Can I ask you something?" she whispered, placing her empty cup back onto the cart. Malo immediately hopped down and wrapped both wings around it, claiming it for himself.

"Sure, go for it."

"Why aren't you a Silhouette?" Zhi Ging rushed on, watching Jack's eyebrows rise in surprise. "I mean, you already know all about Hok Woh and Reishi clearly trusts you enough to bring us to and from challenges. You even sailed everyone over to the iceberg tonight in the junk and had a few Cyo B'Ahon come over to say hello."

"Yeah, turns out you really do become invisible once people don't expect to see you somewhere! Last time I was in my Silhouette disguise, I walked right past those same Cyo B'Ahon and none of them even noticed me. Don't tell Reishi though, I'm using the risk of being caught as my excuse for a raise!"

Zhi Ging grinned back at him, then lowered her voice. "I just feel like you're wasting your time watching from the outside. You know you only get three chances to impress a Silhouette Scout once you turn eleven. Next year's your last chance to take the test."

"I don't think I'm wasting my time." He stopped, looking at her in genuine confusion.

Zhi Ging stared at him open-mouthedly.

"How can you not? You have a chance to be immortal but you won't even try?" She shook her head. "I don't get it."

Jack sighed and pulled a homei spoon from the cart. He tapped it against a bowl filled with warm coconut milk, and the spoon's fragments landed on the surface as glassy beads of sago. Malo chirped in disappointment when Jack then grabbed two porcelain spoons and handed the spare one to Zhi Ging.

"I've known Reishi pretty much since I can remember. Gertie took me in when I was three, so I see him each time he's out traveling as a Scout. The floating market stops near most cities in Wengyuen so I've also met a lot of people whose kids have made it as successful Silhouettes. They're always incredibly proud but, also, sad. Once their kids become full Cyo B'Ahon, they never seem to leave Hok Woh again. They don't even visit their families." He tapped his spoon against Malo's snuffling beak. "I'll never understand that. I know you have the largest library in Wengyuen, but how could that compare to actually seeing the world?" He paused, a determined gleam entering his eyes. "I'd much rather work my way up through the floating market and end up with a tent of my own."

Jack offered Malo his final spoonful of sago and gave Zhi Ging a lopsided smile.

"And besides, Reishi's never invited me to take the exam. I'll take that as a sign he can tell I'd be a bad fit." He gave an unbothered shrug, then scratched the back of his neck. "You know, Gertie mentioned the woman who looked after you knew Reishi too."

"Yeah, Aapau. The Lead Glassmith would always try to throw massive feasts for Reishi, but he preferred her homemade egg tarts to anything they'd offer!" Zhi Ging smiled proudly at the memory.

"Really? Do you think she'd make some for me if the floating market ever stops near Fei Chui?"

Zhi Ging's face dropped. "She's not there anymore. She's in her Final Year. You know, everyone in Fei Chui thinks it's such an honor to let the village healer spend their last year in the roaming pagoda, traveling around Wengyuen as a thank-you for all the lives they've saved over the years, but . . ." Zhi Ging felt her grip tighten around the bowl. ". . . She would have been happy at home. *With me.* The Lead Glassmith didn't even give her a choice."

Jack was silent for a while, then refilled Zhi Ging's tea, gently tugging the cup from between Malo's wings.

"There might still be a way to see her." He glanced around and lowered his voice. "Reishi spent a few years trying to work out if Fei Chui's roaming pagoda moved along air rails. He once mentioned that whoever's inside it can control where it goes. It doesn't have to move in a random pattern. Maybe if I spot it from the floating market, I could get a message to Aapau, let her know you're here?"

Zhi Ging gasped, and her eyes lit up. "That would be incredible! You have no idea how much that would mean to me, Jack."

The Silhouettes in front of them shrieked, cutting off the rest of their conversation. The tunnel had opened up into a large amphitheater, and the twang and chime of tuning instruments filled the air.

The iceberg instrumental was about to begin.

CHAPTER 28

A plump woman hopped onstage and twirled a conductor's baton between her fingers.

"Welcome, everyone, my name is Syut Seng and I'm delighted to have you all joining us tonight! Now, has anyone here ever been to one of our iceberg instrumentals?"

The Silhouettes looked around sheepishly, but none of them raised their hands.

"Excellent!" she trilled as twelve instruments rose up from the ice around her. "These are always my favorite audiences. Hopefully we'll have a few more hands raised for my next question." She swung her baton and six musicians leaped onto the stage, raising the extra instruments. "Would anyone like to volunteer to join our merry band?"

Every hand in the room shot up, with some ageshifted Cyo B'Ahon waving both in the air. Malo hopped up and down beside Zhi Ging, his colorful feathers standing out like a beacon inside the white iceberg. Syut Seng caught her eye and nodded, beckoning her forward.

"Go on, make us proud!" Jack cried, his eyes switching between green and blue as he pushed her forward. Zhi Ging beamed and hurried toward the stage with the other chosen Silhouettes. She clambered up, and laughed when Mynah and Pinderent whooped, waving at her as they pushed their way to the front of the crowd. Malo tottered up after Zhi Ging and ruffled his feathers, clearly delighted to finally have his chance to shine.

Standing closer to the instruments, Zhi Ging could feel cold air pouring off them. A nearby musician grabbed an erhu and held it out to her.

"Oh, I don't know how to play that," Zhi Ging admitted self-consciously.

"Even better!" He laughed. "That means you're more likely to stumble across a combination of notes we'd be too scared to try." He spun the erhu in front of her, its two metal strings glinting against the hexagonal ice base.

"Seriously, we never match people to instruments they can already play," Syut Seng called back, handing Zhi Ging an icy bow. "That's what makes this fun, each concert is always completely different. And, since the instruments are carved from ice, the sound and volume will keep changing while they melt." She twanged one of the erhu's strings, before placing a triangle made from icicles in Malo's beak.

"Ready?"

Silence fell across the iceberg, and Syut Seng raised her

baton. The Cyo B'Ahon ageshifted down further, so no Silhouette's view was blocked, and their newly young faces gazed up at the stage, excitement fizzing around them.

"One, two. One, two, three, four!"

Sound soared up from the twelve instruments, the clear notes reminding Zhi Ging of the Lead Glassmith's dragon door with its clinking glass scales. The ice seemed to capture each bow movement and transform it into pure, clean melody. Music continued to swell around the iceberg, and soon Zhi Ging was twisting the erhu confidently between her hands while Malo pranced across the stage, his colorful feathers vanishing beneath a white flurry as he kicked up fresh snowflakes around him.

When the instruments were finally more water than ice, Syut Seng wove her way back through the dancing crowd and struck a large ice gong to mark the end of the show. The gong exploded and a wave of snow covered the cheering Cyo B'Ahon.

Zhi Ging looked around breathlessly at the others onstage, her cheeks warm from smiling. She and the other Silhouettes linked hands, and, as one, they leaped into the crowd, shrieking with laughter as they landed in the middle of Wengyuen's biggest snowball fight.

"I CAN SEE WHY MYNAH WAS SO MAD ABOUT OUR Chau being delayed now," Zhi Ging sighed, flopping down on a snowbank beside Pinderent. "That was the most fun I've ever had."

"It almost makes the challenges worth it, huh?"

Zhi Ging paused, surprised by the subdued tone in her friend's voice. "Hey, are you all right? What's wrong?"

Pinderent began to shake his head, then paused, glancing toward Mynah, who was in the line for Jack's snack cart at the other end of the amphitheater.

"I'm not like her, Zhi Ging. Mynah's never worried in the run-up to the Silhouette challenges but I . . ." His face crumpled and he turned away, scrunching snow between his gloves. "I don't know if I'll scrape through any more of them."

"Don't say that! And you're not 'scraping through.' You finished the Fauna challenge ages before me," Zhi Ging insisted, attempting to cheer him up.

Pinderent shook his head and sighed. "You don't get it. I've already used up all my luck. The challenges I knew I'd be safe for happened back-to-back. I have no idea how I'll get through the rest."

" 'No idea' doesn't mean you'll fail though. And besides, a Scout wouldn't have invited you to Hok Woh unless they thought you had a real chance."

He smiled weakly at her and sank back into the snow. "Yeah, I guess." He pinched the bridge of his nose and stared up at the iceberg's carved ceiling. "I just wish they'd give us some clues beforehand. There's no way to guess what the Concealment tutor has planned for tomorrow."

"What are you two chatting about?" Mynah called,

skipping back from Jack's cart, a plate stacked high with mochi in her hands. Malo waddled furiously behind her, weaving between her feet in the hope that one of the rice cakes would break free from the pile. "Never mind," she continued before either of them could answer. "You'll never guess what just happened! I was in the line and Iridill came over." She cackled at their grimaces and bit into a mochi before continuing. "No, wait for it, she came over and *wasn't* rude!" Mynah's eyes widened dramatically and her cheeks flashed green. "Instead, she asked if I could buy her a mango pudding. She was happy to let me keep the change too if I got it for her."

Zhi Ging shook her head in disbelief. "But that doesn't make any sense. Why would she do that?"

"No clue, but anyway that's why there's a double helping of mochi for us now."

Pinderent chewed thoughtfully on a peanut-filled rice cake and stared at the cart. "Didn't you two say Iridill acted weirdly before the last challenge too?"

"Yeah, when Jack was trying to hand her the rope, she almost seemed shy. Why?"

"Well"—Pinderent scratched his nose—"what if it has something to do with Jack? It seems like, both times, he's the one making her act differently."

Mynah's jaw dropped and the mochi in her hand tumbled to the snow, where it was immediately gobbled up by Malo.

"Wait. Do you think she *likes* him? Maybe that's why she keeps avoiding him."

"That doesn't seem right." Zhi Ging mulled. "She never got embarrassed around any of the apprentice Glassmiths back home, I can't imagine her acting like that just because she had a crush on someone."

"Well, either way, I think we've just found the perfect Iridill repellent! You watch, I bet as long as we hover near Jack before challenges and at Chaus, she'll never bother us again." Mynah tapped a new mochi against Pinderent's and laughed. "If you've cracked this, you deserve to be made a full Cyo B'Ahon immediately, no more challenges for you!"

Pinderent smiled back at her, but Zhi Ging winced, wondering if Mynah could see just how badly he wished that could happen.

BACK IN THE DORM, ZHI GING WAVED GOODNIGHT to the others and stumbled into her room, exhausted but happy. She flung her black cloak to the side and laughed as Malo immediately curled up in it, using the white Pan Chang Knot as a tiny pillow. She went to blow out her bedside candle and froze. There, on the center of her desk, was the ball of bright green weather wax Gertie's bee had gifted her. A creased note had been pinned beneath it.

Zhi Ging glanced behind her, then pulled the note loose. Written in dark purple ink was a simple instruction:

Use me at the next challenge.

Zhi Ging collapsed onto her bed, her heart thudding against her ribs.

Who could have left this for me? And how do they know it'll be useful in the next challenge?

Her mind raced as she sped through the possibilities.

Could it be a trick from Iridill? That didn't make any sense though; she knew just as much about the next challenge as Zhi Ging. If it *was* a trick, it could backfire easily if weather wax did turn out to be useful.

How about Reishi? Maybe it would look bad for him if Hok Woh's first ever Second Silhouette didn't even make it past her second challenge. *No, that doesn't sound like him.* He would never help her cheat, even if a failed challenge would end their air rail research. He could always rehire Jack.

Zhi Ging drummed her fingers against the side of the desk, frowning at the note. The purple ink was familiar. *Where have I seen that color before?*

Her breath caught in her throat when she realized.

Jack!

The wheels of his snack cart had been filled with the same violet liquid. It had to be him. He had been worried for her, asking how she felt about the next challenge. And, as Mynah had suggested last time, he probably *did* know the challenges in advance.

Zhi Ging stared at the note, her heart pounding. Why

had Jack decided to help her now? Did he know something about how difficult tomorrow would be?

Pinderent's worried face flashed across her mind, and Zhi Ging slipped the weather wax into her pocket. *This is what he was desperate for.* A small clue could be the difference between immortality and a year robbed of memories.

If she could get help, then she'd give it too. She would share the weather wax with Pinderent.

CHAPTER 29

Sunlight shone through the red sails of the junk, covering Zhi Ging in a crimson sheen as she climbed aboard for her second challenge. She glanced down at her tinted arms and shuddered. They looked just like the stained arms of a post pipe scrubber.

Jack ambled over to stand behind her, his eyes fixed on the rope between his hands.

"You ready for this?" he whispered.

Zhi Ging nodded and patted the small lump in her cloak, eyes flickering across the junk. Pinderent was standing beneath the main mast, his own fingers tapping anxiously against the half ball of weather wax hidden in his own pocket.

"Good luck, although I don't think you'll need it." Jack smiled at her, then slipped between the Silhouettes milling around the deck.

"All right everyone," he bellowed. "No new Silhouettes this month so let's keep our journey to the Concealment challenge nice and simple. Everyone grab a hoop and let's go!"

He lifted a lantern up, but unlike the last one, this had almost no decoration. In fact, Zhi Ging had to focus her eyes just to spot it against the junk's dark wood.

"Can you even see that?" she murmured, turning to Mynah—then yelped as she saw her friend's shoes rising past her. She'd forgotten to step into her own hoop. The Silhouettes around her lifted up, and Zhi Ging began to panic. Not even making it to the challenge had to be an automatic fail!

"Zhi Ging, on your left!" Pinderent's faint voice called out above her. She spun around and spotted the final hoop rising up from the deck. The gold rope drifted out over the sea, and Zhi Ging leaped after it.

Waves crashed beneath her, spraying up cold water, but her hands managed to grab the bottom of the hoop. She gritted her teeth and tried to pull herself up, but the rope was now slick with seawater. Her left hand lost its grip, and she tipped down toward the underwater waterfall. Zhi Ging's knuckles whitened around the hoop. If she fell now, the waterfall would swallow her whole.

Jack yelped in alarm and slid down the rope, swinging between the hoops to reach her. The Silhouettes' shouting had turned to screams, and even Iridill's face had gone pale. Zhi Ging shut her eyes, her entire body focused on the biting pain in her right hand. Each time Jack leaped between hoops, the rope would jolt, and she could feel her fingers slipping with every move. Something brushed against her left thumb, and Zhi Ging tensed. *An air rail!*

She tried to close her hand around it, but the faint prickling passed through her palm and vanished. No matter how she twisted her fingers, the air rail refused to rematerialize. The hoop shook above her, and suddenly hands grasped her arm. Zhi Ging looked up to see Jack pulling her back up beside him. Green and blue sparked across his irises, swapping sides with each blink. She swung her left arm up to snatch the side of the rope and, with his help, hauled herself safely into the swinging hoop.

They sat in silence for a while, trying to catch their breath. Eventually, Jack turned toward Zhi Ging and nudged her.

"Next time, if you want me to sit beside you, you can just ask."

AMI GREETED THE SILHOUETTES IN THE MIDDLE OF a vast desert. Thick, dense clouds covered the sky, and the sand beneath their feet was a dull gray. A solitary white starling floated high above them, its faint shadow dancing over the Silhouettes. Zhi Ging turned in a slow circle. The desert stretched for miles in every direction and the crumbled ruins of an abandoned shrine were all that was visible in the barren landscape. How was she meant to use the weather wax here?

"Are we still waiting for the Concealment tutor?" Mynah asked, glancing at the empty space around Ami.

"Not at all."

The group jumped as a new voice echoed around them, and a figure shimmered into view beside Ami. The Cyo B'Ahon was covered in strips of dappled gray fabric, the color blending perfectly with the sand around them. She leaned against a cane as she surveyed the group, and Zhi Ging's eyes widened when she spotted the woman's left leg. Below the knee was a metal limb, thousands of thin metal wires twisted together to form a crane's leg.

"My name is Yingzi. Those of you invited to train with me will learn a very different form of Concealment than that taught to previous Silhouettes. You see, my lessons used to center on spotting camouflage and disguise in others." The Cyo B'Ahon rapped the cane against her prosthetic, a metallic chime ringing across the desert. "But after Hok Woh burned, I realized it was more important to instruct Silhouettes on how to conceal their future identity as Cyo B'Ahon." Her eyes flickered to Mynah, an eyebrow raised at the blue patches on the girl's cheeks.

"Concealment is the simplest skill to assess, meaning my challenge is the shortest of the twelve. You have fifteen minutes to prove yourselves worthy of your place in Hok Woh."

Ami stepped forward and handed each Silhouette a small lit candle. Zhi Ging winced as the Dohrnii's sleeve slid back to reveal an arm covered in fresh jellyfish welts. The number of silver scars had grown since Ami had taken them on that first tour of Hok Woh. The infection in the

Seoi Mou Pou must have been worse than the Silhouettes realized. *No wonder none of us have seen her in weeks.*

Yingzi leaned back and, with a flourish, lifted a large gray tarp to reveal a hulking Komodo dragon. A thick leather muzzle rattled around its jaws, and its tongue flickered out toward the candles.

The Silhouettes took a collective step back as the Komodo dragon thrashed its tail against the metal cage. Zhi Ging glanced across at Pinderent in panic, and he grabbed her hand tight, the fear on his face mirroring hers. Yingzi placed her fingers against the cage bolt and considered the cowering Silhouettes.

"Passing is simple. I only have one requirement: *Become invisible.*"

CHAPTER 30

The cage door swung open, and the Komodo dragon thundered toward them. Silhouettes scattered out of its path, and Iridill screamed as its tongue shot out, barely missing her ankle. She shoved Pinderent out of her way, and he tumbled across the rough desert sand. His candle rolled out from his grip and was snuffed out.

Zhi Ging skidded to a stop and turned toward her friend, but Pinderent staggered up.

"Keep running!" he wheezed, clutching his side. "I'll be okay."

Some of the faster Silhouettes were already sprinting toward the shrine, and Zhi Ging raced after them, desperately hoping there would be enough hiding places left. The crumbling structure was no larger than the dorm common area, and years of sandstorms had already reduced one wall to rubble. *How is this Concealment?* It seemed all Yingzi was testing was which Silhouettes could run fastest.

There has to be more to it than this!

Behind her, she heard a thump and turned to see the Komodo dragon pin Mai Seon to the ground. He shook his candle wildly in front of the creature's face, but the flame had no impact. The Komodo dragon's tongue shot out between the slit in its muzzle and drool splattered down on the terrified boy. Yingzi rapped her cane against the metallic cage, and the Komodo dragon reluctantly stepped back, turning its attention to the remaining Silhouettes.

"Zhi Ging! Hurry up!" Mynah shrieked from the shrine. "You need to get off the sand and *hide.*" She whipped her head away and staggered forward. Heavy thumps of falling Silhouettes echoed behind her, and the sound of the creature's claws pounding through the sand drummed in time with her own racing heartbeat. Her lungs were burning by the time she reached the shrine, and terrified eyes stared back at Zhi Ging through the shadows.

There was no more space.

She lurched toward the collapsed wall and began to scramble up the rubble, trying to reach the upper eaves of the shrine. The candle flickered in her left hand, and she bent low, determined to protect it. Ami must have given these to them for a reason.

But how is it linked to Concealment?

In the distance, the Komodo dragon began to prowl toward the shrine, its tongue darting through the heavy muzzle. Zhi Ging pulled herself higher, and her entire body sagged with relief when she spotted an empty hollow between two stone slabs. All she had to do was hide there for the next ten minutes, and she'd pass. She rushed toward it but a hand shot out from the darkness, pushing her away.

"Not a chance, find your own spot," Iridill hissed. "And blow that out! Haven't you worked out candlelight's how it's tracking us?"

Pebbles clattered down the side of the shrine as Zhi Ging scrambled to regain her footing.

"What!" Her mouth dropped open as she stared at the flickering candle in shock. Surely Ami wouldn't make things harder for them?

Iridill inched out from her hiding place and scowled down at the others through what was left of the roof beams. "Everyone needs to blow their candles out *now*! If I can see the light from here, that stupid thing out there can too."

"But what if we need them?" Hiulam began.

"*No.* Kaolin, blow out the candles for anyone who refuses to listen. I'm not failing because of—"

"Wait, look!" Zhi Ging gasped, pointing back toward the gray sand.

Newly formed patches of glass glinted across the desert, spiraling out away from Ami and Yingzi.

What are they?

Thin sunlight broke through the clouds, and the Komodo dragon's head reared up, tongue lashing in excitement. Sand caught beneath the largest sunbeam began to shimmer, and the lizard lunged at the patch, grains of tacky, molten sand clinging to its muzzle. Zhi Ging's mouth dropped open. She'd seen sand like this before . . .

"Don't blow out the candles! We need them!"

"What?" Iridill looked ready to shove her off the shrine.

"No, Iridill, just listen! The Komodo dragon isn't tracking us by light, it's tracking us by *heat*."

"So? Same thing, the flames will still help it find us."

"But we can use the candles to hide ourselves! Don't you recognize that sand?"

Iridill was silent, frowning at her in confusion. *So much for being the Lead Glassmith's daughter.*

"It's heat-sensitive sand. The same sand apprentice Glassmiths use before they're allowed on the glass terraces. Hok Woh's entrance staircase is made from it, haven't you noticed? This sand doesn't need dragon lightning to turn to glass, all it needs is a small amount of heat. See those glassy patches in the sand? I bet each one of them is the exact spot a Silhouette dropped their candle. How many lit candles do we have left?" she asked, her heart racing.

There was a small pause while the others looked around, trying to spot the last flickering lights in the shrine.

"Only two," Mynah croaked. "We all started blowing them out."

"Mine went out while I was still running," another Silhouette whispered.

"We need to relight all of them." Zhi Ging could feel the nervousness ripple through the group.

"No way!" Iridill snapped. "That's such an obvious trick to lure the Komodo dragon toward us instead of you. Do you really think we'll fall for that?"

"You heard Yingzi, if we want to pass we have to make ourselves *invisible*," Zhi Ging said. "Glass is one of the worst conductors of heat, Iridill. Remember how cold the Glassmiths' workshop would get in winter? The Komodo dragon hunts by heat. If we can hide ourselves under a glass shield, it won't be able to sense us. *That's* how we become invisible."

"Look around, NoGlow. This shrine's been abandoned for centuries. Do you really expect there to be a glass shield lying around?"

She still isn't getting it!

"No, but we can make one."

The Silhouettes stared at her in silence, Mynah's cheeks flashing a concerned blue.

"If we combine our candle flames and turn a single patch of sand into glass, we can hide under it for the rest of the challenge. We'll need to work quickly though. Once we start relighting, the Komodo dragon will charge toward the heat." She looked down at the twenty faces obscured by the shadows. "But who wants to try anyway?"

Sand swirled across the shrine floor while Zhi Ging held her breath.

"See, NoGlow. None of us are stupid enough to—"

"Let's do it." Mynah stepped forward, relighting her candle against Hiulam's. The other Silhouettes peeled away from the shadows and began to shuffle back toward the entrance. Kaolin and Cing Yau hesitated, twisting the glass beads on their Pan Changs, then hurried after the Silhouettes leaving the shrine.

"Fine by me!" Iridill hissed from her hiding spot, pushing herself deeper into the hollow. "I'll enjoy being the only Silhouette left in the dorm tonight."

Zhi Ging shook her head and slid back down toward the others. There wasn't time to argue with Iridill.

The Silhouettes watched while Zhi Ging traced a large circle in the sand with her shoe, glancing over her shoulder every few seconds to check the Komodo dragon was still distracted by the sunbeam.

"This should be big enough for the shield. On the count of three, everyone who's already blown out their flame relight your candle and we'll lower them to the outline. Once the entire circle's glowing, everyone grab the fusing sand and swing it upward—you should be able to avoid burning yourself if you keep your hands in your sleeves. The air should help the molten glass solidify quickly and create a dome we can hide inside. Everyone ready?"

"I didn't like how many 'shoulds' you used in that sentence," Mynah murmured, passing her lit candle across Zhi Ging to another Silhouette.

"Don't worry, we *should* be fine," she whispered back, bouncing from foot to foot.

Mynah's cheek patches flashed yellow, and she snorted in disbelief.

"It's spotted us!" Cing Yau shouted, pointing over Hiulam's shoulders. The Komodo dragon's head had jerked up at the sudden bloom of candle flames and it was now hurtling toward them.

"Everyone, candles to the outline *now*!" Zhi Ging commanded.

The creature was moving faster than she'd expected. She tried not to think about what would happen if there wasn't enough time for the glass to solidify. If everyone failed, it would be because of her.

There were yelps of panic around her as several Silhouettes plunged their candles too deep into the sand, snuffing out the new flames. The eight remaining candles flickered against the surface, but the glass was spreading far too slowly.

"We just need a bit more heat," Zhi Ging urged as Silhouettes scrambled to relight their candles. "Even sunlight would—" She stopped, suddenly remembering the weather wax in her pocket. *This is what Jack's note must've meant!*

She shoved a hand into her pocket and pinched off a small chunk of weather wax, feeling strong sunlight spill between her fingers. The Komodo dragon sped up, its eyes now trained directly on her.

Zhi Ging leaped into the center of the circle and ran her hands across the surface, sand transforming to glass beneath her fingers. Time seemed to slow and the heavy thunder of the Komodo dragon's claws filled the air.

It still isn't enough!

"Copy what I'm doing," Zhi Ging cried, tearing what was left of the wax into pieces and throwing it to the Silhouettes. "Forget sleeves, the wax will protect your hands." Sunlight bloomed as they unleashed the emerald wax's full strength, and their hands raced over the sand, leaving trails of molten glass behind them.

Zhi Ging glanced up and saw the Komodo dragon was only seconds away.

"Everyone, grab hold and *swing*!"

She leaped out of the circle, and the fusing glass billowed up, rising into a dome between the Silhouettes. The Komodo dragon was magnified through it, its jaws straining against the leather muzzle.

Zhi Ging kept her arms lifted, warm glass draping around her to form a makeshift entrance.

"Get into the dome! I'll let the glass slide down once everyone's inside."

The Silhouettes streamed past her, squeezing themselves into the hollow. Zhi Ging grimaced, feeling the glass solidifying in her hands. The heat from the weather wax was already fading.

Suddenly, a dark shadow shot past, knocking Zhi

Ging away from the entrance. Iridill had darted from her hiding place, pushing her aside to reach the safety of the dome. The other Silhouettes roared in protest, and Zhi Ging scrambled back to her feet, glass seeping down over the entrance. Her eyes darted toward the advancing Komodo dragon, and she flung herself under the hardening dome.

The glass sealed behind her with a faint plink.

"Now what?" Hiulam whispered as the Komodo dragon paused.

"The glass should be keeping our body heat hidden," Zhi Ging said. "Without that, the Komodo dragon should mistake the dome for another boulder in the sand."

"That's still too many 'shoulds' for me," Mynah said with a wince.

They held their breath as the Komodo dragon slunk closer, clearly confused. Its tongue shot out twice in frustration, then it slithered away from the group. The Silhouettes peered after it, unable to believe their luck.

"We're invisible," Hiulam breathed in awe.

Their breath had begun to fog up the glass, when there was a faint tap against the surface. The group jumped and turned to see Yingzi smiling at them through the dome. Ami stood a little behind the Cyo B'Ahon tutor, a blurred group of failed Silhouettes beside her.

"Congratulations, your fifteen minutes are up. I look forward to seeing you in class tomorrow."

Zhi Ging spun around to hug her friends, shaking with relief. She'd never have forgiven herself if her idea hadn't worked. She turned to celebrate with the Silhouette beside her, then froze, her eyes darting back over the group. Mynah seemed to notice at the exact same moment, and they stared at each other in dismay, their stomachs dropping.

Pinderent wasn't in the dome with them.

CHAPTER 31

"Hurry up, your Chau's about to start. This story-teller never waits for his audience." Yingzi shepherded the Silhouettes toward a colorful yurt hidden between the sand dunes. Zhi Ging and Mynah hung back, hoping to catch a glimpse of Pinderent before he left. There had been a faint moment of hope when Yingzi had gathered two other successful groups, but he hadn't been among them. In the distance they could see Ami speaking to the failed Silhouettes. Her blue lenses glinted against the desert sand as she poured out a droplet of gray elixir for each of them.

"Come on," Jack murmured beside Zhi Ging. "It won't do any good to watch."

"Is that the memory elixir?" she asked, blinking back tears while the Dohrnii handed the spoon to Pinderent.

"Yeah." Jack sighed, rubbing his nose. "When he wakes up tomorrow, he'll have no memories of failing the challenge."

"But also no memories of us," Mynah muttered, wiping a hand across her eyes. Yingzi clicked her fingers at them from the yurt entrance, and Jack gently turned both girls away.

"It's not fair. I don't care if one bitter Silhouette years ago betrayed Hok Woh—Pinderent would never—"

Mynah elbowed her, glancing pointedly toward Yingzi. The Cyo B'Ahon's metallic leg gleamed against the desert sun. Had she known the Silhouette who'd led the attack on Hok Woh?

They filed into the yurt and picked their way over the large floor cushions to join the rest of the Silhouettes. Iridill scowled at them from the corner, Cing Yau and Kaolin crouched on the floor beside her—clearly still not forgiven for leaving the shrine with the others.

"Eh, you're welcome?" Mynah hissed at her. "You wouldn't have passed without Zhi Ging. Don't think we didn't notice you barging into the safety of our shield when you didn't even help!"

Before Iridill could respond, the lanterns dimmed, and the storyteller appeared from behind a hidden screen. His velvet gown shone in the faint light, and he sauntered toward a large scroll draped over the yurt's wooden beams. He pulled a peacock feather from behind his ear and dipped the tip into a lantern hanging from the ceiling.

"Welcome, little Silhouettes, and congratulations on the upcoming honor of learning from my great-great-great-aunt." He nodded toward Yingzi and her stern expression vanished momentarily behind a proud smile. "For to-day's story, I'll be sharing the incomparable, the singular, the extraordinary tale of Omophilli's Origin. Our world is split between humans and spirits and, like all Wengyuen's greatest stories, this is a tale of a time the two crossed paths." With a dramatic flourish, the story-teller reached up and tapped the top corner of the scroll with the now glowing feather. A thin flame leaped onto the paper and hovered expectantly, waiting for the story-teller to begin.

Zhi Ging glanced toward Mynah and smiled when she saw her friend sit up a little straighter, her cheeks flushing to the exact same shade as the flame. Having come from Omophilli, Mynah had probably heard this story multiple times, but it must be nice to have a Chau linking to her hometown.

The storyteller held the feather in front of his mouth, checked he had the tent's full attention, and began.

Once upon a time, a daughter was born to the Lord of Omophilli. With each year that passed, she grew more and more beautiful. The lord, caring more about his wealth than her happiness, declared that the man or woman who brought the rarest gift would have her hand in marriage. Suitors traveled from across the lands to present the lord with baskets laden with the finest silk, precious spices, and gold. However, his greed grew with each offering, and soon no gift was enough.

Zhi Ging gasped as the flame danced across the paper, cutting out characters and scenes while the storyteller spoke. When the flame reached the far side of the scroll, he flicked the peacock feather and the figures floated out across the tent. The Silhouettes watched transfixed as the story came to life above them. Zhi Ging reached up toward one of the paper cuttings, her own parchment lantern flashing across her mind. Had the storyteller summoned a spirit for this?

Years passed and stories of the daughter's beauty began to fade. However, one suitor refused to give up. He had spent years working in the lord's kitchens and had fallen in love with the daughter long ago. He traveled over mountains beset with dragons and braved the beasts lurking beneath the waves in his quest to find a worthy treasure.

Iridill shrieked, shoving Cing Yau in front of her, as a giant paper dragon roared toward them. Jack turned to Zhi Ging, laughing in amazement. She smiled shakily and ran a hand over Gertie's glove, trying to ignore her own pounding heartbeat. At least this dragon couldn't hurt her.

One night, in a desert at the end of the world, he stumbled across a palace spun from sand. As he watched, the sun rose above the horizon, and the palace

erupted into color. Light pierced the shifting sands and
transformed it to sparkling crystal. Jewellike fruits
draped down from the palace gates. The suitor took a
step forward but then gasped in dismay. As the sun's
heat continued to blaze, the palace dissolved and melted
back into molten glass. He ran forward, sifting through
the burning sand, but no trace of the palace remained.

The flame on the scroll flared up, and the paper palace crumbled to ash above their heads.

The suitor sat, waiting, in the desert for another twenty
nights. Finally, on the next full moon, the sand palace
reappeared. He held his breath, knowing he would have
mere seconds to pluck one of the hanging gems. As the
first tendrils of dawn brushed against the palace, he
darted forward, snatching a cherry-blossom ruby from the
gate. He hid the stone in his cloak pocket, away from the
rising sun. The triumphant suitor then began his journey
home while the rest of the palace melted behind him.

Mynah murmured and leaned forward, her uneasy frown telling Zhi Ging the story was about to turn. The storyteller paused, his own face becoming somber.

However, the palace belonged to a powerful sand spirit,
a S'Ah Gwai. Like all other spirits, it drew its elemental

magic from the realm around it. Through sand, the spirit could twist the world around it in the same way we shift reality in our dreams. When the fractured palace sank back without the blossom, the spirit roared, furious at the theft, and unleashed a vengeful sandstorm across the desert, searching for its stolen treasure.

"Gertie told me about this," Jack whispered, leaning toward Zhi Ging. "Apparently the sandstorm lasted for years and wiped out an entire city, engulfing it under miles of gray sand."

She shifted nervously and tucked her feet up onto the wide cushion.

The suitor, unaware of the S'Ah Gwai's anger, arrived back in Omophilli. He presented the sparkling jewel to the lord, warning him to never let sunlight fall upon the blossom. The lord was overjoyed and immediately began preparations for the marriage.

Confetti and paper hearts burst out from the scroll and covered the giggling Silhouettes. Mynah shook confetti loose from her hair and began to scrunch it up, throwing it at Iridill's back. Zhi Ging grinned, imagining how much Malo would have loved trying to catch the confetti in his beak. Maybe she could ask Ami if he could come along to her next challenge, rather than having Gahyau babysit.

The suitor and his bride soon had a daughter of their own, and all was well in Omophilli. But one day, the young girl heard a faint whisper, like sand rushing through an hourglass. She followed the sound until she found a velvet box hidden inside her grandfather's desk. The girl opened it and there, shining up at her, was the most beautiful flower she had ever seen. Mistaking it for spun sugar, the girl swallowed it whole.

Jack turned to Mynah and Zhi Ging, his eyes comically wide.

Dun dun duuun, he mouthed. They snorted but quickly fell silent when Yingzi glared at them, her finger on her lips.

The girl went in search of her grandfather and the hope of more treats. She stepped into the garden, glancing up as a pair of starlings flew past. An unearthly scream echoed across the grounds, chilling the midday sun. Her parents raced toward her as she fell, clutching at her left eye. The little girl slept for fifteen days, metallic lines flickering over her eyelid and across her face.

Zhi Ging stopped brushing confetti from her cloak and stared up at the floating paper cuttings, transfixed.

Metallic lines.

The fiery lines crackling across the girl's face mirrored the coiling movements of her own gold lines. *Are they marks from a spirit after all? Sintou* did *say the lines appeared in my family from a curse.*

When she finally awoke, her parents cried out in horror. The girl's eye, while healed, had been irrevocably changed. Her left iris had fragmented, splintering like glass into a dome of iridescent color.

The flame crackled across the paper, and Zhi Ging snuck a glance at Jack. *Did the girl's eyes switch colors between sentences too? No Silhouette from any of the other provinces has eyes like his . . .*

After piercing through the girl's eye, the stolen sand had streamed back to the spirit's realm. However, by eating the spirited glass, her body had absorbed some of the S'Ah Gwai's magic. The girl became gifted with the ability to alter reality simply by creating paper cuttings. Every whim of her imagination would become real, the cutting materializing the moment she shook it free from the paper. The lord built a wall around Omophilli, claiming fears of jealous rivals taking the little girl from her family. However, until his death, the lord used the girl's paper-cutting powers for himself, demanding she snip away at reality, creating extraordinary instruments and impossible weapons to bring him immeasurable wealth. And so Omophilli grew into the largest city above the seas.

The storyteller twirled his feather in the air, and what was left of the scroll crumbled to dust. He struck a dramatic pose and bowed, beaming as the Silhouettes whooped and stomped their feet.

"He's much better than the floating market story-tellers," Jack shouted over the applause. After indulging in multiple bows, the storyteller looked up and spotted Zhi Ging's white Pan Chang.

"It's you!" His eyes widened and he darted between the cushions to reach her. "So, you're the Second Silhou-ette. I heard you've caused quite a stir in Hok Woh." He pulled a new peacock feather out from his sleeve and crouched down until they were eye to eye. "Truth be told, you've caused quite a stir in every town and village that still welcomes Silhouette Scouts. How would you like to entrust me with your story? There are people across the six provinces who'd pay handsomely to hear about the first ever Second Silhouette. I'd make sure you got a fair share of the profits too."

"I, uh—" Zhi Ging glanced around nervously. "I don't know."

He gestured toward a bundle of scrolls at the back of the tent. "All I would need is an hour of your time. You can talk me through everything that happened and I'll pluck out the lines I like, tracing the story along an empty scroll." He leaned closer, his voice dropping to a whisper. "My secret is I mix the quill water with firework powder. It dries clear on the scroll but the flame dances beautifully

265

along it. That's how I get such clear paper cuttings each time. Although, if anyone asks, please tell them I've trapped and trained a miniature fire spirit. It's taken me years to get that rumor to stick," he added with a wink, smoothing down the wrinkles along his gown.

"Maybe? I'd need to check with the Scout who found me. Can I think about it?"

Behind them, Ami slipped back into the yurt, a now empty elixir bottle clutched discreetly between her hands. Before the entrance flap could close, a strange, guttural roar whipped through the air, cutting over every conversation. The Dohrnii went pale and the bottle slipped between her fingers, glass shattering at her feet. "Thralls!" Yingzi leaped up, rapping her cane against her metallic leg. "Silhouettes, to me. These are not creatures we can conceal from."

CHAPTER 32

The excitement from their Chau vanished as Silhouettes scrambled to find a rope hoop before the thralls closed in. Zhi Ging's knuckles whitened around her own hoop when she spotted a figure slithering toward them from a nearby dune. Mottled skin stretched tight across its pinched features and matted hair hung in clumps down its hunched back. It turned its gaze toward Zhi Ging, and she flinched under its stare. The thrall's eyes were like pools of mercury, pupils and irises smothered beneath a thick film of gray haze. It was almost impossible to imagine this had been an ordinary person before the Fui Gwai's possession.

The gray-eyed thrall threw back its head, and that same hollow growl filled the air. The sound echoed around them, and the sand shifted, surging toward the group as more thralls emerged from beneath the desert surface.

"We need to leave now!" Jack yelped, his fingers

trembling as he relit the lantern. Ami and Yingzi leaped into the lowest hoop as the Silhouettes rose into the air, the horrified storyteller pinned between them.

"Watch out!" Zhi Ging screamed, the sudden weight of three adults sending the rope veering toward a dune filled with snarling faces. Jack urged the lantern higher, but the closest thralls leaped up, snatching Yingzi's cane from her hand. She ageshifted down in shock, a stream of curses erupting over the unblinking gray-eyed faces.

"Yingzi, stop!" Ami urged, pointing at distant thralls who had turned their heads toward the Cyo B'Ahon's screaming. "We're supposed to protect the Silhouettes from thralls, not draw more toward them. There could be more still hidden under the sand."

An uneasy silence rippled along the hoops, and despite Ami's reassuring presence, the Silhouettes, and even Jack, couldn't stop themselves from frantically pointing out each new thrall that shimmered into view along the dunes. A few of the gray-eyed faces tried to follow the rope's shadow as it raced across the sand, but they fell back at the desert's border, sinking beneath the sand. Zhi Ging shuddered. *If we hadn't heard that first roar, the Fui Gwai could have turned us to thralls by now.*

THE FLOATING LANTERN CONTINUED TO SOAR across Wengyuen, and soon the red sails of the junk reappeared on the horizon. Zhi Ging peered up at the empty hoops dotted between the Silhouettes and felt her stomach tighten with guilt.

"Hey, what's wrong?" Jack asked in concern, sliding down the rope toward her hoop. "The thralls weren't able to keep up, it'll be safe once we get you back to Hok Woh," he added, misreading her grimace.

"It's not that." She clenched her hands around the hoop, fingers still stained green from the weather wax. "I really appreciate you telling me to bring the weather wax but I . . ." Zhi Ging glanced up to check that the other Silhouettes couldn't hear her over the sea breeze. "Pinderent wanted to pass just as badly as I did. It's not fair if I get help just because I'm the Second Silhouette. That makes me no different from Iridill getting special treatment in Fei Chui just because she's the Lead Glassmith's daughter," she whispered urgently. "I didn't mean to use the air rails in the first challenge to pass, but having the weather wax this time felt like cheating."

Jack's eyes widened in shock, but he quickly shook his head. "You deserved to pass just as much as anyone else. You were the one who realized the sand was heat sensitive."

"But I still got the weather wax clue before the challenge. It isn't fair to the others."

Jack pressed a finger to his lips, shushing her, and glanced down at the two Cyo B'Ahon beneath them.

"I don't have time to explain, but there's something

you need to know." He lowered his voice. "Iridill's the one who doesn't deserve to be here. More than half the Silhouettes from the past few years didn't. *Especially* the ones from the bigger cities."

"What are you talking about?" she asked.

Jack flushed and turned his head away from her. "You know the way you said you thought I could pass the entrance exam? Well, I have. More than once." He paused. "People have been paying me to take it for their children. People like the Lead Glassmith."

"What?" Zhi Ging gasped, the wind knocking the sound from her voice. She turned her head toward Iridill, and her eyes narrowed in understanding.

That's why she acts so strangely around Jack. It's not a crush. Iridill's just worried he'll reveal her cheating secret.

"I know it's bad but, I figured if others really did have Cyo B'Ahon potential, Reishi would find them the next year anyway. It wouldn't matter if they had to wait an extra year while the person I helped got invited."

"Did you help Pinderent?" Zhi Ging asked, her voice cold.

"No! I'd never even heard of the village he's from. My, eh, contracts are only ever for the children of wealthy rulers. Their parents would lock the exam scrolls away 'for safety' before a Scout checked them and I'd sneak in overnight to rewrite anything they got wrong. I'm usually only hired after someone's failed their first two exams. By then, their parents are desperate to get them into Hok Woh and will pay a *lot* for my, uh, help." Jack's neck flushed as he continued. "Please don't tell Gertie or Reishi, they'd never forgive me. But, even with Reishi paying me to bring Silhouettes to and from challenges, it'd have taken a lifetime before I could afford my own tent at the floating market. I only ever planned to help others take the entrance exam for a few years."

Zhi Ging shook her head and looked back along the rope, wondering who else had had "help" with their entrance exam.

"I think you should go back to your own hoop, Jack."

His face crumpled but he hesitated before pulling himself up the rope. "There's one more thing. The weather wax? It wasn't me. I have no idea who told you to bring it."

She blinked but refused to face him, her mouth setting in a stubborn frown, and he sighed before hauling himself back toward the lantern. It was only after he left that Zhi Ging let her face scrunch in confusion.

If it wasn't Jack, who helped me pass the challenge?

"—AND DID YOU SEE HOW RIDICULOUS HE LOOKED, flailing across the sand with that weird glowing pocket? I *knew* he was never going to make it!"

Zhi Ging and Mynah froze at the dorm entrance, catching Iridill miming a bumbling fall.

"Who are you talking about?" Mynah snapped.

The girl jumped, not realizing they had been in earshot, but quickly regained her composure. The circle of Silhouettes around Iridill murmured and shuffled their feet.

"Who else? That gangly loser, Pinderent. Honestly, how did he even pass his first challenge? He never should have made it this far."

"Take that back!" Mynah began, but Zhi Ging barreled past her and shoved Iridill hard on the shoulder. The girl stumbled for real this time, eyes widening in surprise.

"You're the one who shouldn't be here, Iridill. I know your secret!" she snarled, glaring up at her old enemy.

Iridill's eyes narrowed, and she sneered down at Zhi Ging. "Oh, really? Do you seriously want to talk about secrets?" She grabbed Zhi Ging's shoulder and twisted her around to face the wide-eyed Silhouettes.

"Everyone here thinks NoGlow is so special, but no one even wanted her in Fei Chui. You should have seen her on the day of the entrance exam. She showed up late and spent the entire time *crying*."

Zhi Ging wrenched herself loose and spun to face Iridill. "Shut *up*, Iridill. We both know why I was upset that day. The Lead Glassmith deliberately got Reishi to set the exam on the same day he sent Aapau away in the roaming pagoda. The last day I would ever get to spend with her."

Angry tears blurred her vision, but Zhi Ging refused to wipe them away. She took a deliberate step toward Iridill, and the girl flinched backward in surprise.

"I *knew* the Lead Glassmith would try to make the

exam easier for his precious daughter, but making me choose between saying goodbye to Aapau and starting the exam on time . . ." Zhi Ging shook her head as images of Aapau shooing her from the pagoda, urging her not to miss Reishi's exam, filled her mind. "I will *never* forgive either of you for that."

Mynah stepped forward and placed a cautious hand on Zhi Ging's shoulder. "Zhi Ging, maybe we should go," she said gently.

"No!" Zhi Ging snapped, pulling away from her friend. She jabbed a finger toward Iridill. "But that wasn't all, was it? Your father knew that wasn't enough to make sure you were picked, so he *paid* to have your mistakes changed. How dare you say Pinderent didn't deserve his place here."

Iridill went pale and pushed Zhi Ging out of her way, trying to escape to her bedroom.

"You can't prove that NoGlow!"

"Oh yeah? Show everyone your lantern. I bet we'll see your handwriting mysteriously shifts more than once."

Iridill's features pinched together, furious red blotches burning across her cheeks. Behind her, Kaolin and Cing Yau flushed, eyes darting toward their own Silhouette lanterns.

"Why are you getting upset? Pinderent was never cut out to be a Cyo B'Ahon," Iridill snarled. "Even his cloak turned on him during that challenge. Didn't you see? Seconds into the challenge it started to glow, making him a beacon for that Komodo dragon."

The blood drained from Zhi Ging's face as she replayed the beginning of their challenge. She, Iridill, and Pinderent had run in the same direction, Iridill had pushed him, and then . . .

Cold realization rushed over her. Pinderent's weather wax must have activated when he hit the sand. With heat radiating from his pocket, he would have immediately become the Komodo dragon's main target. If she hadn't shared the weather wax with him . . .

It's my fault Pinderent failed.

Zhi Ging breathed in sharply, the guilt threatening to crush her. She howled and launched herself at the smirking Iridill, knocking her back against a screen door, the thin paper tearing around them. They fell through and Iridill shrieked.

"Miss Yeung, my office! Immediately."

Zhi Ging turned around, her arms shaking. Reishi and Ami were staring down at her, a horrified cluster of new Silhouettes behind them.

CHAPTER 33

The next morning, Zhi Ging waited until the others had rushed out for breakfast before tiptoeing out of her room. Malo waddled out behind her, anxious to catch up with their friends, but she shook her head and scooped him into her hood.

"Sorry, but we've got to eat here now. Reishi made that part of my detention."

A faint yellow glow appeared along the corridor, and Gahyau floated into the dorm, a bowl balanced above his bubble.

"Thanks," Zhi Ging murmured, lifting a gray homei spoon from the bowl. "Is Reishi still mad at me?"

Gahyau wrung his tentacles together, his glow fading to a sallow half-light. The jellyfish rolled his bubble backward and gave her a glum wave, before vanishing back down the corridor. In the silence, Malo lifted the spoon with his beak and cracked it over the bowl's stone. He chirped in frustration when the bowl filled with plain congee, without even a sprinkling of white pepper or diced spring onions.

"Well, I guess I have my answer." Zhi Ging sighed, stroking his feathers.

How had it all gone so wrong?

After she'd been marched into Reishi's office, the Scout had turned away from her, disappointment radiating off him. Each time she tried to explain what had happened, he would shake his head, raising his hand for silence. It took a while for her to realize he was reading messages from other Cyo B'Ahon on his palm.

Verdicts from other Cyo B'Ahon.

The thought still made her wince. In the end, it was only one vote, sent jellyfish-to-jellyfish, that had saved her from expulsion. Zhi Ging couldn't bring herself to wonder which way Reishi himself had voted. While Yingzi had begrudgingly agreed for her to attend lessons, Zhi Ging's next month in Hok Woh would be restricted. She was now banned from dragon boat training, her meals were to happen in the dorm, air rail research had been replaced by nightly detention, and she was to be excluded from the next Chau.

Zhi Ging pushed the bland congee aside and gathered fresh scrolls from her room. She'd have to face Iridill again at some point. Maybe a lesson on Concealment was the best place for it.

A GROUP OF SILHOUETTES HAD ALREADY GATH- ered outside Yingzi's workshop, eager to catch a glimpse of the room before class began. They fell silent as Malo bounced toward them, and Zhi Ging's heart sank when she spotted the new glass beads glinting on their Pan Changs. They were identical to the ones Iridill had gifted Kaolin and Cing Yau months ago. What had she missed at breakfast?

"Iridill's still in the sick bay with Wusi. You shouldn't be here, NoGlow," Cinnabar, one of the Pacers from Team Tsadeu, said coldly. Malo looked between the Silhouettes, confused by the sudden hostility.

"I didn't mean to—"

"Zhi Ging! There you are, we went back to the dorms to find you." Mynah waved as she and Hiulam hurried toward the group. Zhi Ging felt relief wash over her when she spotted her friends' bead-free Pan Changs.

"Sorry," Hiulam added, her voice dropping to a murmur as she glanced at the other Silhouettes' Pan Changs. "We were hoping to catch you before you bumped into this bunch."

"What happened? I know I shouldn't have pushed her, but I had no idea Iridill was so popular."

"She's not." Mynah lowered her voice conspiratorially. "But I bet if we checked the handwriting on each of their Silhouette lanterns, we'd find at least one thing they all have in common with Iridill . . ."

A new Silhouette beside Cinnabar pushed tentatively against Yingzi's door and tumbled forward, a giant silk screen collapsing over him. Zhi Ging jumped and stepped

277

forward, staring at the new corridor path suddenly twisting out in front of them.

"Someone falls for that every year. Did you really expect my workshop to be so easy to find?"

Yingzi peered down at them from a small hatch in the glass ceiling. The silk-covered Silhouette spun wildly, trying to work out where her voice was coming from.

"You have much to learn about Concealment." A rope ladder unfurled from the ceiling as their tutor vanished back into the gloom above them. "Someone help him out of that silk screen." Her voice echoed down the corridor. "I don't want the fabric to tear."

ZHI GING CLAMBERED THROUGH THE HATCH AND blinked hard. Yingzi's workshop was empty. The Silhouettes who had climbed up before her seemed to be standing in the middle of the ocean, the glass free from the usual dapples and reflections that marked the border between Hok Woh and the sea. Only the sudden twist of a passing bale of sea turtles gave any clue of where the workshop ended.

"Where are we even supposed to sit? There aren't any desks in here," Zhi Ging whispered to Mynah, while Malo tentatively stretched his wings wide, trying to find the edge of the room.

"Do you always trust your eyes that quickly?" Yingzi shimmered into view behind them and snapped the hatch door shut. The tutor pulled a jade hairpin from her bun and held it out for the group to see. Zhi Ging felt her stomach twist, suddenly remembering the glass hairpin Aapau had gifted her for her twelfth birthday. She'd only had it for two months before it was destroyed in the dragon attack.

The top of Yingzi's pin was decorated with a white dome of shooting stars, their delicate tails connecting them to the jade.

"This is a DandelEyeOn. It reveals all forms of optical concealment. You should never feel safe in a room until you've used one. Particularly if you're shoreside."

Without warning, Yingzi hurled the hairpin upward, and the jade tip embedded itself into the invisible ceiling. Before Zhi Ging could blink, the shooting stars erupted down, covering the room in soft pearly fuzz. She laughed as Malo chirped in surprise, his feathers suddenly back to the snowy white from before he swallowed the candle flame.

"No way," Mynah hissed, grabbing her arm. The room wasn't empty after all. Not even close. The DandelEyeOn fuzz had revealed rows of glass desks and ten previously camouflaged Cyo B'Ahon. Yingzi gestured for the shocked Silhouettes to take their seats and plucked the hairpin out of the ceiling.

"Human eyes should never be trusted. Unlike spirits, who can see the true edges of reality, we often don't even experience the same reality as the person next to us. The skill of Concealment requires much more than the ability to fade into any background. It's about concealing a chosen truth from others, whether that's your location, your intention, or, increasingly important for Cyo B'Ahon, your identity." Her eyes flickered across to Mynah, whose cheeks were flashing blue and green beneath the thin layer of DandelEyeOn fuzz.

"I remember you from the challenge. I *never* remember Silhouettes before they finish their month with me. How do you expect to master Concealment when you constantly erupt with color?"

Mynah's shoulders drooped and her patches faded to beige. There was a muffled laugh, and Zhi Ging felt the wave of embarrassment rolling off her friend. Yingzi was the tutor Mynah had hoped to specialize with after graduation.

"Mynah can already conceal her voice!" Zhi Ging blurted out, leaning closer to her friend. "You should see the voice boxes she's sculpted. She can transform her voice into anyone's." *Even yours,* she wanted to add, but stopped herself. She didn't want to get Mynah into trouble.

Yingzi raised an eyebrow.

"So, you're the Silhouette behind those. I've heard the other tutors complain about the voice boxes, but none of them could work out who was creating them." She gave Mynah a second, more evaluating, look. "Perhaps we can find a way for your patches to help, rather than hinder, concealment. If you pass your final challenge, we may be able to train them to change texture as well as color. You could conceal your face with another's features without the need for a mask."

"Yes! That would be amazing," Mynah agreed eagerly.

"Let's save that excitement for after graduation, hmm?" Yingzi turned back to the group. "I've demonstrated how a DandelEyeOn can reveal optical illusions, but let's talk through other forms of concealment. Take the Fui Gwai, for example. Although the spirit can present itself as human, its eyes will always remain a solid gray. It conceals itself by filling the eyes of its victims with gray smoke. How are we then to differentiate the Fui Gwai from one of its possessed thralls? That will be the focus for today's class. Ah, no, Zhi Ging, not you." The Cyo B'Ahon stepped forward as the other Silhouettes scrambled to pull out fresh scrolls and ink. Yingzi placed the jade hairpin down on Zhi Ging's desk with a sharp click.

"I have a task for you before you participate in my lessons." Yingzi brushed fuzz from her metallic leg and pulled a small tweezer from a slot behind her knee. "I need you to reattach each white star to its correct place on the DandelEyeOn. Think of it as an extension of your detention."

Zhi Ging took the tweezers and grimaced, her eyes scanning the workshop. The DandelEyeOn must have released thousands of stars.

Behind Yingzi, Kaolin smirked as Cing Yau collected a handful of fuzz and blew it toward Zhi Ging. She glared at them but quietly got up and began to collect the stars from her own desk. She wasn't going to let Iridill's side-kicks be the reason for a second month of detention.

"Don't worry," Mynah whispered, once Yingzi had turned back to the rest of the class. "I can share my notes with you tonight. You'll catch up in no time."

"Thanks." Zhi Ging forced herself to smile. "But I might need to borrow your notes a few more times than that." The two girls peered out over the thick carpet of white fuzz, individual stars still cascading down from Yingzi's bun as she spoke. Zhi Ging glanced across at Mynah and knew the same thought had crept into her friend's mind.

She'd be lucky if she collected them all before the next challenge.

CHAPTER 34

Zhi Ging trudged toward the sick bay, Malo trailing behind her.

"You don't need to keep coming along, you know. *You* didn't do anything wrong."

The duckling ruffled his feathers and marched determinedly after her. Zhi Ging smiled, secretly grateful he'd chosen to keep her company through these detentions.

Wusi and Reishi broke off their hushed conversation when she slipped through the door. Apart from them, the circular wing was empty, and Zhi Ging breathed a quiet sigh of relief that Iridill had been allowed to leave the sick bay and return to the dorms soon after Zhi Ging's first detention.

"Today's scrolls are over there," Reishi said with a curt nod, pointing toward the piles scattered across each of the sick bay's beds.

"Be careful when you're transcribing the measurements," Wusi fussed, running a protective hand over the crumbling parchment. "Some of these scrolls are the only records we have on how to treat particular ailments. If the elixir dosage is off by even a milliliter, it could have serious consequences for the next patient who needs it."

"Don't worry, Malo will make sure I don't make any mistakes." The duckling hopped onto a nearby bed, sniffed the scrolls for hidden sunflower seeds, then flapped his wings at the Cyo B'Ahon.

Reishi nodded at Wusi, then left the room without another word. Despite herself, Zhi Ging felt her chest tighten. For the past three weeks, she had reported to a different room in Hok Woh each night, hoping that this would be the detention Reishi finally forgave her, but he never even said hello. Once he'd shared a few brief instructions with the supervising Cyo B'Ahon, Reishi acted as if she weren't even there. Apparently now he wouldn't even stay for her full detention.

Wusi waited for Reishi's footsteps to fade away, then pulled a yellow scarf out from one of the medicine jars.

"Fresh scrolls and ink are in the cabinet on your left. If you need me at any point, Heisiu, my jellyfish, is in that basin over there. You can reach me through him," she instructed, tapping her left palm.

"Wait, aren't you staying for my detention?"

"Absolutely not," Wusi scoffed. "I haven't missed a single dragon boat race in the three hundred years I've been Hok Woh's healer. I have to be in the stands in case one of the teams capsizes." Wusi wrapped the scarf tight around her. "And besides, Team Wong Gam needs all the support it can get from other gold province Cyo B'Ahon. Our racers are having a terrible decade."

"Any chance you know who Team Bolei picked as their new Central Paddler?" Zhi Ging asked in a quiet voice. They would have had to replace her, at least temporarily. But what if Bucbou decided her replacement was better?

Wusi hesitated at the door, then sighed, bustling Zhi Ging past the scroll-covered beds toward the far side of the room. The sick bay wing was the highest point in all of Hok Woh, and dappled moonlight filtered down through the waves above them.

"See that?" Wusi pointed at a strange shadow floating in the distance. "That's one of the bamboo stands the others will watch the race from. You can see the dragon boats twist between the first and second bend right above here. Depending on the level of wave churn, you can occasionally even glimpse the last stretch of the race. If—" She ageshifted down until she was eye to eye with Zhi Ging. "If, and only *if,* you promise to stay late and finish copying each of those scrolls, you can start your detention thirty minutes late and watch the race from here first."

"Oh, thank you! I won't leave until they're done." Malo hopped up and down beside her in agreement.

Wusi nodded and ageshifted back up.

"And don't worry about Reishi. Just keep showing up

to your detentions on time and things will get back to normal. Forgiveness takes time, but he has plenty of that as a Cyo B'Ahon."

"What if he doesn't forgive me before my next challenge? I might not even be in Hok Woh by the time that happens." Zhi Ging sighed, her breath fogging up the glass wall. "I feel like he's just getting more disappointed in me. I accidentally dropped one of Tutor Wun's cloud containers during last night's detention and I'm still nowhere near finished collecting the pieces for Yingzi's DandelEyeOn."

"I wouldn't be too sure about that." Wusi smiled reassuringly, her eyes flicking back toward the bamboo stand. "After all, Reishi's the one who assigns where you go. Quite a coincidence that, for tonight's detention, he picked the only spot in all of Hok Woh where you'd be able to watch the race."

Zhi Ging looked up at the healer, a smile creaking across her face for the first time in weeks. Maybe Reishi hadn't given up on her after all.

"HERE THEY COME!"

Zhi Ging and Malo stood on their tiptoes, nose and beak pressed against the glass as the dragon boats roared toward them. From the sick bay, it was impossible to see the ornate dragon heads, but they could follow the teams through their colored paddles. Team Bolei would be racing with the carved lacquer dragon this time, and Zhi Ging felt a pang of guilt for Hiulam. With Pinderent gone and her stuck in detention, Hiulam would be the only Silhouette racing tonight. Both of their places had been taken by stand-in Cyo B'Ahon; none of the new Silhouettes had wanted to try out after hearing Zhi Ging was part of Team Bolei.

The sick bay entrance suddenly flew open, and Zhi Ging jumped. Had Reishi come back to check on her?

Her breath caught in her throat when she realized someone was being rushed into the wing, carried between Reishi and another Cyo B'Ahon. The man howled in pain, and the others struggled to hold on as he ageshifted frantically, his body flickering to a different height with each step. Zhi Ging crouched down behind one of the empty beds and pulled Malo close. The duckling sensed her sudden unease and wrapped his wings around her arm in a tight hug.

"Hoi Leung, get Wusi and Ami," Reishi grunted to the other Cyo B'Ahon as he heaved the person onto the bed closest to the door. "Let them know there's been another Scout attack."

Another?! Who else has been hurt? Zhi Ging held her breath as Hoi Leung rushed past their hiding spot, the Cyo B'Ahon's hands shaking as she tossed two notes into Heisiu's basin. The healer's jellyfish raced his tentacles over the thin rice paper, then shot through a pipe and vanished into the main wall.

Within minutes, Ami burst into the sick bay, followed closely by a windswept Wusi.

"What happened?" Wusi barked, dropping to check the Scout's pulse.

"Baak Lok was attacked," Hoi Leung croaked. "He was Scouting for potential new Silhouettes in the silk province and was ambushed by villagers outside of Heung Zun." She carefully lifted Baak Lok's yellow robes to reveal the hilt of a dagger. "The woman who plunged this into his side claimed her son never returned from his Silhouette year. She left the blade in, as a warning Cyo B'Ahon were no longer welcome in the area."

Wusi placed her palm against Baak Lok's feverish forehead, her own face gray. She grimaced and leaped up, then began pulling jars of medicinal herbs and salves from the cabinets around them.

"I'm sorry, we can't take the blade out until we know if it's been poisoned. If there's venom in it—"

The rest of her sentence was cut off by Baak Lok's pained groans, the sound reverberating off the glass.

Reishi shook his head, his features gaunt. "This is why we need the air rails," he muttered to himself. "Until all Cyo B'Ahon can travel on them and bypass hostile areas, we'll never be safe shoreside."

Zhi Ging hugged Malo tighter, unable to drown out the injured Scout's wailing. If she hadn't wasted three weeks in detention, could she and Reishi have prevented this attack?

"Ami," Reishi murmured, crouching beside the Scout. "If he was attacked because another failed Silhouette never returned home, I don't think it's just a rumor anymore. We need to consider that the Fui Gwai is targeting them."

Ami shook her head, eyes narrowing behind her blue-tinted glasses. "It was Heung Zun, Reishi. I'd already removed that village from the Scouting route, it's not a safe area for Cyo B'Ahon. Those villagers are some of the most superstitious in Wengyuen, every single one of them blames us for the Fui Gwai's appearance. I wouldn't be surprised if the failed Silhouette actually just ran away from home. Haven't you noticed claims of missing Silhouettes only ever come from the smaller villages? Children from the larger towns and cities always make it back."

Zhi Ging flinched as Wusi leaned across her bed for a jar filled with dried ginseng roots. The healer froze, eyes widening in shock when she spotted the Silhouette and duckling crouched beneath her. Wusi glanced back at the other Cyo B'Ahon, her face flickering as she fought to stop herself from ageshifting down.

"I think," the healer began, gritting her teeth in an effort to still her shifting features, "we should all agree no one in this room speaks to any of the Silhouettes about this."

"Well of course," Ami began, but Wusi cut over her, eyes never leaving Zhi Ging.

"The last thing we need is Silhouettes panicking and trying to leave Hok Woh. That's the only way they could actually put the dorm in danger. The memory elixir offered after challenges completely obliterates a Silhouette's time in Hok Woh, they don't even remember their journey to the stepping stones. The Fui Gwai could never use one of them to find us. But, if it caught a spooked Silhouette who still had their memories . . ."

Malo shuddered in Zhi Ging's arm, hiding his face against her cloak.

I promise, Zhi Ging mouthed. Wusi's face stopped flickering, and she nodded quickly before snatching the jar of ginseng from its shelf.

"You should all get back to the dragon boat race. Find out if you were seen. If we're lucky, all eyes will have been on the teams rounding the second bend, but all it'd take is for one Silhouette to have spotted Baak Lok for panic to engulf the dorm. Fire's not the only thing that can destroy Hok Woh."

CHAPTER 35

Although Zhi Ging kept her promise, whispers of Baak Lok's attack soon trickled through Hok Woh, and the corridors filled with a contagious anxiety. The story grew and twisted with each retelling, and soon Silhouettes were whispering about an entire valley filled with Fui Gwai thralls who had lured Baak Lok into an ambush. Ami began to run nightly dorm checks, and Zhi Ging wasn't the only Silhouette who spotted concern flickering across her face whenever she thought they weren't watching.

One evening, after a detention spent helping Ai'Deng Bou shear his growing herd of popcorn sheep, Zhi Ging returned to the dorm to find Iridill, Kaolin, and Cing Yau blocking her path.

She sighed. "What do you want?"

"Want?" Iridill asked, an oil-slick smile spreading across her face. "We don't *want* anything. We're just here to make sure you see the new additions on the bulletin board."

Zhi Ging's stomach tightened in dread as Kaolin and Cing Yau stepped aside to reveal a bulletin board covered in identical flyers. Malo chirped in confusion, recognizing the portrait painted on each page.

It was Zhi Ging's arrest warrant.

"We've been busy while you were at detention," Iridill continued, twisting the glass beads on her red Pan Chang. "It took some time, but we've managed to leave one of these on every single library chair too. Now all of Hok Woh will know the truth about their precious Second Silhouette." She sneered down at Zhi Ging. "You accused me of cheating my way here, but you're worse. You're nothing more than a spirit summoner, there was never anything special about you."

"No!" Zhi Ging cried. "It's not true. You weren't even there when the dragon attacked me."

"Then how did you know to bring that weird green wax to Yingzi's challenge? Someone or *something* is still helping you."

"Just admit you've made a deal with the Fui Gwai," Cing Yau snarled. "What was it, you get to become a Cyo B'Ahon and the spirit gets to turn the rest of us into thralls?"

"No! I would neve— I don't even know who told me to bring the weather wax."

Iridill snorted and crossed her arms, smirking as bedroom doors cracked open behind her.

"Sure, that's believable. Why don't we let the other

Silhouettes make up their own minds, see which of Fei Chui's Silhouettes they trust—the Lead Glassmith's daughter or the unwanted Yeung."

She snapped her fingers and marched off, Kaolin and Cing Yau leaving a trail of warrants behind them. Zhi Ging stood frozen, the twisting panic in her stomach threatening to spill over.

Hok Woh was meant to be the one place she was safe from the warrant.

Mynah came out of her room and tossed a crumpled warrant after them.

"Don't worry, Zhi Ging. No one's going to believe that nonsense . . ." She trailed off as one of the new Silhouettes walked past, his eyes narrowing in suspicion.

"I need to get out of here," Zhi Ging croaked, clutching the Pan Chang on her cloak. Cyo B'Ahon had stopped staring at her white knot weeks ago, but it now felt like a beacon, reminding everyone she was different.

"But where are you going to go? Unless Iridill was lying, these warrants are going to be everywhere now."

"I know somewhere," Zhi Ging muttered, lifting Malo into her hood. "There's one place in Hok Woh even most Cyo B'Ahon won't find me."

"ZHI GING, I DON'T BELIEVE YOU'VE BEEN INVITED to continue our game of checkers."

Blinking hard at Sintou's blurred outline, Zhi Ging was temporarily blinded by the white flame that had roared up beneath the glass, greeting Malo like an old friend. The fire trailed after the duckling as he immediately began to snuffle around in search of sunflower seeds.

"If this is about your detention, I won't get involved." Sintou winced, attempting to unclench her arthritic fingers.

"Why don't you just ageshift down so it's not painful?" Zhi Ging blurted before she could stop herself. She felt a strange burst of annoyance, watching the Head of the Cyo B'Ahon massage her wizened hands. If Aapau had been able to ageshift, she never would have reached her Final Year and been sent away in the roaming pagoda. There never would have been a warrant, or even the threat of the post pipe, if Aapau was still in Fei Chui.

Sintou paused, then rolled up her sleeves, revealing the purple burn marks that stretched up past her elbows.

"Because of these." The fire dimmed beneath the glass, bathing Sintou in a pale, flickering light. "That flame comes from the burning remains of the original Hok Woh. It's responsible for these scars, but I'm responsible for our realm burning. The fire beneath us spread because of my arrogance. I was so sure Cyo B'Ahon were universally revered that I refused to acknowledge support had begun to waver across the six provinces. My failure to see the truth meant Silhouettes and Cyo B'Ahon alike died."

Malo shivered and squeezed himself between Zhi Ging's shoes. She bent down and stroked the top of his head, never taking her eyes off the Head of the Cyo B'Ahon.

"How could I ageshift, and free myself from these scars, when others touched by the fire cannot? Take Yingzi, your current tutor. No matter how far she ageshifts, she will never recover her lost leg. Ageshifting may remove wrinkles, but it cannot remove wounds."

Zhi Ging shuddered and glanced down at the fire beneath their feet. *Is that glass definitely strong enough to keep it trapped?*

"This is my penance," the Cyo B'Ahon continued, her eyes trained on the flames. "I keep it here as a constant reminder of Hok Woh's need for humility. We may be immune to aging, but we are no less vulnerable to the other dangers most mortals fear. How can we offer guidance and judgment to the six provinces if we see ourselves as above their citizens? There are certain Cyo B'Ahon who could benefit from this daily reminder," Sintou added, her voice dropping to a dry croak.

A cacophony of falling glass echoed around the room, and they spun around to see Malo perched on the checkers board, the now empty marble pouch still clamped in his beak.

"You already knew those weren't sunflower seeds!" Zhi Ging cried in frustration, dropping to snatch at the marbles spinning across the floor. The fire streamed beneath the glass around her, blazing tendrils pointing at the ones she missed.

"Thanks," she muttered, stretching her hand toward a

marble caught against the foot of the checkers table. The fire crackled, transforming itself into her blazing silhouette. Zhi Ging jerked back, her heart thumping hard. *No, not my silhouette.* The fire had reflected another face up at her. The same woman who had appeared on the calligraphy-stained paper during her dragon boat race.

Zhi Ging blinked hard, trying to shake the image of the glowing woman now dancing in front of Sintou's face.

"You've gone as white as a sheet. Take my seat," the Cyo B'Ahon urged.

Sintou pulled a small jar from her pouch, and the bracing scent of white flower oil filled the air, wrapping Zhi Ging in a calming veil of perfume. *It smells just like Aapau's.* She took a deep breath and rested her head against the checkers board, the pearl inlay of Fei Chui's roaming pagoda blurring between her eyes. She blinked and the pagoda refocused, stilling on the board. *Something about it isn't right.*

Zhi Ging straightened up and traced a finger across the scuffed mother-of-pearl. The eight tiers of the roaming pagoda were still there, but the familiar stained glass that should have formed one half of the tower was nowhere to be seen.

"That's the Omophilli tower," Sintou said softly, rotating the six-pointed board until Fei Chui's roaming pagoda brushed under Zhi Ging's fingers.

"Were they built by the same person?" Zhi Ging murmured. She spun the board back and forth, hypnotized by how, together, the two pearl inlays created one solid structure.

Sintou hobbled over to the other seat, then lifted Malo off the cushion and onto her lap.

"There was only ever meant to be one."

Zhi Ging looked up, a heavy silence falling between them.

"Before Fei Chui created the post pipe, glasswork orders from the furthest provinces would take months to arrive. The Lead Glassmith at the time had heard whispers of an Omophillian gifted with the ability to create any structure you could dream of, for a price."

Zhi Ging tensed, scared to even blink in case the movement distracted the Head of the Cyo B'Ahon. *It has to be the same girl from the storyteller's tale!*

"He gathered Fei Chui's collective wealth and commissioned a roaming pagoda not bound by the rules of physics. It was to be used exclusively by Glassmiths to travel across Wengyuen, collecting orders and delivering glassworks. The pagoda would serve as a new landmark, displaying Fei Chui's importance in the sixth, and most isolated, province. Payment was sent in advance, as such a complicated structure would take considerable time to cut from paper. However, while traveling to collect the pagoda, the Lead Glassmith was ambushed by bandits."

Zhi Ging shivered, imagining sinister faces looming out from the mists of the cloud sea. *Is this why the Lead*

Glassmith never leaves Fei Chui? Did another one never make it back?

"Did he survive?" she asked in a hoarse whisper, scared to hear Sintou's answer. The Head of the Cyo B'Ahon paused and placed Malo onto the checkers board.

"That depends on what you mean. While his body did recover, the man who arrived at Omophilli weeks later was unrecognizable from the confident, adventurous Lead Glassmith who had set off from Fei Chui. Memories of the attack festered within him and, rather than a pagoda that would grant Glassmiths the freedom to explore, he now demanded a tower that would protect them from everything outside of Fei Chui."

Sintou tapped a marble against the faded inlay and let it spin across the board, teetering between spaces until it reached Zhi Ging's starting point.

"However, his delayed arrival meant the original roaming pagoda was already complete, the paper cutting ready to be shaken free from its scroll. The Lead Glassmith roared and ranted, demanding the cutting be altered to suit his new requirements. Eventually, it was agreed the Omophillian would make one final amendment to the cutting, granting protection from all dangers, including death, to those inside the pagoda."

Zhi Ging winced, knowing how horrible it felt to be screamed at by a Lead Glassmith.

"However, no one had stopped to consider whether

there were limits to the Omophillian's paper-cutting pow-ers. While it had only been three decades, many had for-gotten she was not born with that gift. Unknown to all, the creation of the pagoda paper cutting had drained all but the final drop of the woman's power. When she added to the complex pattern, the last of her gift crackled through the scissors and into the scroll. The paper pagoda erupted out and split in two. The force of the rupture snuffed out every lantern within the city walls, and Omophilli was plunged into darkness. In the moonlight, the two half tow-ers spun before the Lead Glassmith. One retained the abil-ity to move, while a protective shield fused through the other. He was forced to flee in the roaming pagoda that night, such was the fury of those no longer able to profit from the woman's extinguished power. He had no choice but to forfeit the second tower, a sacrifice to prevent war between the provinces, and that half tower quickly became Omophilli's main landmark."

"But what about her? Was she hurt when she lost her power?"

Sintou blinked, then raised an appreciative eyebrow, smiling thoughtfully at Zhi Ging. "You know, in all the centuries I've been sharing this piece of Wengyuen his-tory, not one Cyo B'Ahon has ever asked that as their first question."

"Oh." Zhi Ging could feel heat rising up her neck.

"No, Zhi Ging," Sintou said soothingly, reading her

troubled expression perfectly. "I'm impressed. Most immediately asked about the protective tower, eager to know if we could claim it for ourselves, especially after Hok Woh burned. But you, you cared more about another's safety than your own. I can see why Reishi chose to invite you as the Second Silhouette."

Zhi Ging flushed, relief rushing through her. She hadn't realized just how much she'd needed to hear that. Especially with Reishi no longer talking to her.

"And no, the power left her body with no more pain than a static shock because she had released it willingly."

The fire flared behind Sintou, blinding Zhi Ging for the second time.

"Ah, Reishi must be on his way." The Head of the Cyo B'Ahon leaned forward and began to place green and white marbles across the six-pointed checkers board. She chuckled at the solitary green marble that had made it over to her starting point.

"He'll have to try much harder if he still plans to talk me out of my decision to Revert."

"What does 'Revert' mean?"

The Head of the Cyo B'Ahon smoothed down her golden sleeves and peered closely at Zhi Ging.

"It means, Zhi Ging, that I'm ready to die."

CHAPTER 36

"What do you mean die?!" Mynah shrieked, spilling ink across her half-finished homework scrolls.

"Shhhhh!" Zhi Ging leaped forward, clamping a hand over her friend's mouth. Nearby Silhouettes glanced up, and she waved awkwardly with her free hand.

"Sorry, she's just very excited about Yingzi's question about camouflage dyes."

"Buh wud do yuh mean?" Mynah asked in a muffled whisper against Zhi Ging's palm, her cheeks flashing purple and pink as she struggled to wriggle free.

"I'll tell you, if you *promise* not to shout again," Zhi Ging hissed, glancing around the library. Most of the other Silhouettes had turned back toward their own scrolls, but a few were clearly still listening in.

"Why don't I help you find that book for question three," Zhi Ging said in a stage whisper, hurrying Mynah down one of the winding bookshelf aisles until they reached the far wall. The outer glass here bubbled out to create incredible domed views of the sea. A shoal of fish soared past on the other side, dusting the two Silhouettes in glittering light.

"That's what it means to Revert," Zhi Ging murmured, wringing an ink-soaked scroll between her hands. "Apparently, some Cyo B'Ahon get tired of immortality and deliberately ageshift past the safe point. If you ageshift down past four, you reach a point where you 'Revert' and *forget* you're even a Cyo B'Ahon."

"Why would Sintou ever want to do that?" Mynah asked. "And what happens after she forgets? Does she just keep ageshifting down to zero and disappear?"

"No, you stop ageshifting and get placed in a haven." Zhi Ging scrunched up her nose, trying to remember exactly how Sintou had described it. "They're safe homes scattered across Wengyuen, run by people the Scouts trust. Reverted Cyo B'Ahon are raised with no memory of their time in Hok Woh. They just live out a normal life then die."

"But why would you put yourself through all twelve Silhouette challenges only to give it up a few decades, or centuries, later?"

"That's what I can't work out," Zhi Ging murmured.

"And why now? Everyone knows Hok Woh's the only place the Fui Gwai hasn't managed to find. If Sintou does Revert, she could get turned into one of its thralls before she even has a chance to grow old!"

"Maybe she knows someth—"

"Zhi Ging, there you are! I've been looking everywhere for you."

They jumped and turned to see Ami outlined against the aisle entrance. Marzi, her jellyfish, raced beneath the glass floor and gestured for Zhi Ging to follow after the Dohrnii.

Mynah's cheeks flashed white and she pulled a book off the closest shelf, humming loudly to give her friend some privacy in case she was about to get another telling-off. Zhi Ging gave her a grateful half wave, then hurried after Ami, chasing the Dohrnii down a new aisle.

"There's been a last-minute change to tonight's detention. You were meant to help me scrub the Seoi Mou Pou tank, but Reishi wants you to report to his lab instead." Ami sighed, annoyance flashing across her usually calm face. "He's decided to replace tonight's detention with an air rail session. As a 'break.'" The Cyo B'Ahon frowned and shook her head. "I can tell you've learned your lesson . . ."

Zhi Ging blushed, Iridill's horrified face as they crashed through the screen door flashing across her mind.

". . . but he's still refusing to let you join the next Chau. As Dohrnii, it should really be my decision whether you take part, but Reishi refuses to listen. He says he must set an example, show that not even the Second Silhouette is above the rules."

"That's okay, really. I'm fine with coming straight back to Hok Woh afterward," Zhi Ging said, before quickly adding, "If I pass, of course."

"Hmm, well I'll keep trying. I do think it would be a shame for you not to experience this Chau."

"Thanks, Ami, I really appreciate it."

The Cyo B'Ahon smiled and ageshifted down until they were the same height.

"You know, sometimes you really remind me of myself at your age. At least, the first time I was your age." She laughed lightly. "I'm not sure if Reishi ever told you, but I never knew my birth parents either. I remember what it was like to be underestimated, but I can see so much potential in you. I also know how important it can be to find a home, so I'm rooting for you at every challenge. A little more than I strictly should as Dohrnii."

Zhi Ging's eyes widened. *Was it Ami who left the weather wax clue?*

She opened her mouth to ask, but footsteps echoed along the corridor behind them, and the Dohrnii quickly ageshifted back up.

Ami winked at Zhi Ging, her blue lenses catching in the light, before sliding open the door to Reishi's lab.

ZHI GING LANDED WITH A THUD AGAINST THE floor cushions. Around her, jellyfish spun in their tanks, re-creating her latest drop from the makeshift platform.

"Let's try again," Reishi sighed, bending down to help her up. "I think I almost saw a flash of gold that time."

"I don't think this is working," Zhi Ging grumbled, rubbing a faint bruise on her knee. "Are we even sure there are air rails this far below the sea?"

"Definitely. Wherever there's air you can find air rails." He paused and scratched his chin. "Well, 'find' might be a little optimistic at the moment, but I promise they are all around us."

"Can we at least use some of the equipment you've been working on? I've tried keeping my eyes shut, holding Malo in my hand—" The duckling huffed and kicked the small pile of sunflower seeds in front of him. He had *not* enjoyed pretending to be the jade stone again.

"We've even tried pouring clouds Tutor Wun collected from Fei Chui over me. Re-creating the cliff edge clearly isn't working."

"As I've said, all you need to do is follow Gahyau. He's floating along the rails you need."

"Well, maybe I can't do it anymore," Zhi Ging snapped, her frustration at the past month finally bubbling over. Even though Reishi was once again talking to her, there was a new, uncomfortable barrier between them. "And I know I never should have pushed Iridill, but why am I the only one being punished? She's been horrible since she got here, but no one cared when she flooded my room!"

"Iridill is . . ." Reishi paused, watching Gahyau roll

between them. "Consider heat-sensitive sand. All it needs is the slightest pressure to be sculpted into whatever shape a Glassmith wants. Hate and heat are not so different here. Iridill's behavior has been shaped and polished over twelve years by her father's mistrust of those beneath the cloud sea. How she treats others now is a reflection, almost a magnifying glass, of the Lead Glassmith's private prejudices. However, all glass can be remolded, as long as the right form of heat is applied."

Zhi Ging frowned and ran a hand over the scattered sunflower seeds, a new thought curdling through her mind.

"But how is his mistrust of everyone beneath the cloud sea any different from Cyo B'Ahons' mistrust for people shoreside? What happens if we actually find the air rails?" Zhi Ging scooped Malo up and clambered off the cushions. "You never even considered sharing the rails with the rest of Wengyuen. What if Pinderent or one of the other Silhouettes got caught by the Fui Gwai on their way home? Why should the air rails only be used by Cyo B'Ahon?"

"Zhi Ging, you don't understand. We need the air rails to protect ourselves *from* everyone else. Certain villages still blame us for the arrival of the Fui Gwai. Each time someone is attacked by one of its thralls, they see it as our fault."

She threw her hands up in exasperation. "But that'll just make everything worse! We're already in a hidden realm under the sea but you want us to be even *more* separate? Even if the Cyo B'Ahon didn't actually release the

Fui Gwai, can't you see how that looks? Rather than help-ing the provinces, Cyo B'Ahon want to ignore thrall at-tacks and just pretend they aren't happening."

Reishi's stare grew distant and a strange expression flickered across his face.

"You don't know what non-Cyo B'Ahon are capa-ble of."

"That's not fair," Zhi Ging said.

"Cyo B'Ahon—*friends*—were killed in front of me. You didn't see the anger in their eyes when they attacked Hok Woh." Reishi's voice was soft and low. He rubbed his temples and Gahyau floated up to rest on his shoulder. "We were punished for being too entangled in their lives. Before the fire, province leaders would confer with Cyo B'Ahon on every decision. We were more than guard-ians, we were actively involved in their rulings. Until they turned against us."

"Why don't we stop the Fui Gwai?" Zhi Ging pushed. "If we caught the spirit, we wouldn't even need the air rails. Everyone would trust Cyo B'Ahon again. Anyway, you're not hated everywhere, look how excited the Lead Glassmith was when you arrived at Fei Chui!"

Reishi snorted and shook his head. "That's because he never travels below the cloud sea. He hasn't heard the new rumors spreading about us." He laughed bitterly. "No, the Lead Glassmith just sees us as his most valuable patrons. As long as we keep commissioning the roaming pagoda to collect Reverted Cyo—"

"Wait, what?" Did he just . . .

"Forget I said that."

"Wait, please. Just tell me how you contact the pagoda." *Could this be a way to see Aapau again? Will she come into Hok Woh to collect Reverted Cyo B'Ahon in person?*

"No Cyo B'Ahon should ever Revert. The last one to make that choice was my closest friend, we argued for years before he went ahead with the permanent ageshift." Reishi turned to pull a scroll from between two tanks, determined to end the conversation.

"Even if Sintou hasn't decided to Revert yet, could you send a message to Aapau?"

Reishi spun back, ageshifting down in surprise. "How do you know about Sintou?" Gahyau bounced down to land on his newly lowered shoulder.

Zhi Ging opened her mouth, but nothing came out.

"It doesn't matter, she's not going to do it—much to the disappointment of *someone*," he added darkly.

"But why did she want to?"

"A better question would be *who* talked her into it. The idea appeared out of nowhere around a decade ago. I warned her staying at her current age would impact her decision-making. It'd be healthier to ageshift at least once a year, to keep her mind sharp."

"Was it another Cyo B'Ahon?" Zhi Ging asked in a whisper.

Reishi hesitated, his frown deepening the furrowed lines between his eyes. "Possibly. I had thought it was just an overly ambitious Cyo B'Ahon—someone who felt they were more deserving of her title. But"—he glanced at Zhi Ging—"if even a Silhouette can wander into her office, there's nothing to stop someone else, or some*thing* else, from doing the same. Hok Woh may not be as secure as we thought." Reishi peered at the Cyo B'Ahon shadows passing on the other side of the glass wall.

"The Fui Gwai could already be here."

CHAPTER 37

Five days later, the Silhouettes once again floated up from the red junk, a sparkling lantern leading them to their Perception challenge. Zhi Ging tightened her grip around the gold hoop as they lifted up. The small hope of seeing Aapau still felt as fragile as an air rail; even saying it out loud seemed too risky. At the same time, she felt guilty whenever she thought about Aapau arriving at Hok Woh. Hoping for the roaming pagoda also meant hoping a Cyo B'Ahon had decided to die.

"Hey! I know where we're going," Mynah shrieked, pulling Zhi Ging out of her thoughts. The Silhouette swung in her hoop and beamed down at her friend. "That's Omophilli! Ooh, if we have time before the Chau I can introduce you to my great-aunt and—" Her face fell and she scratched the back of her head sheepishly. "Sorry, I forgot Reishi was still being really strict about that. Omophilli's not that great anyway, you're not missing anything."

"You know you're a terrible liar, Mynah." Zhi Ging laughed. "Each time you try, your cheek patches flash white."

Mynah patted her face and groaned. "Ugh, I thought I'd worked out how to stop that!"

"Never mind. You can tell me about the Chau when you get back tonight. I'm sure my detention scrubbing tanks will be just as exciting," Zhi Ging said, rolling her eyes.

"Hey Jack, we're drifting away from the city," Mynah called up. "You need to steer the lantern back to the right."

Zhi Ging glanced down before he could turn toward them. They hadn't spoken on the junk, and she still wasn't sure if she'd forgiven him for helping other Silhouettes cheat. *But you've also gotten help. You just don't know who from . . .* a quiet voice in her mind whispered.

"Don't worry about the lantern, it's bringing us to the right spot. Your challenge is happening just outside the city walls." Jack pointed at a thick bank of cumulus clouds floating toward them. "The sky above Omophilli isn't suited for travel, even birds won't fly over it. Watch those."

Zhi Ging peeked up and her mouth dropped as the clouds split in half, separating around the city.

"How did you never notice that?" she whispered, whacking Mynah's foot.

"Don't blame me until you've visited Omophilli properly," her friend laughed back. "There's no place like it.

Most people never even have time to look *around* the entire city, never mind up. But it's fine, I'll have plenty of time for cloud watching once I'm back as a full Cyo B'Ahon."

The lantern floated down beside a large geometric structure, and the Silhouettes finally let go of their hoops. Zhi Ging groaned and stretched her legs. This was easily the farthest they'd traveled for any challenge.

"Welcome, everyone." Ami glided toward them, smoothing down her white cloak. "As today's challenge is focused on my specialty skill, Perception, I'm here as both Dohrnii and your future tutor. Cyo B'Ahon never wish for luck, so I wish all of you the best of skill."

Ami glanced toward the structure's looming metallic entrance and clapped her hands together. "Today's challenge is a staggered individual one. You'll each enter the maze five minutes apart; if you catch the Silhouette in front of you, they'll fail their challenge."

She paused as nervous whispers erupted among the group.

"Please wait here until I call your name. First up, we have Miss Niu."

Mynah turned and gave Zhi Ging a quick hug, blue cheek patches giving away her nerves.

"See you back at the dorm." A soft yellow crept back across her patches. "Just two more challenges and then you'll have to call me Miss Niu: Cyo B'Ahon Extraordinaire! Maybe I'll even sign my old Silhouette cloak for you."

Zhi Ging laughed and hugged her friend back tight. "I can't wait!"

AMI CONTINUED TO CALL NAMES EVERY FIVE MIN-utes, and the group around Zhi Ging slowly dwindled. A burst of frustration hit her when she looked at the cluster of mostly unfamiliar faces around her. The month of detention meant she'd barely spoken to any of the new Silhouettes. Though she doubted they'd ever want to speak to her after that first impression . . .

Soon, she and Iridill were the only Silhouettes waiting to step into the metal structure.

"Miss Seoipin, you're next."

Iridill sauntered past her, then stopped, a slow smirk spreading across her face.

"Ouch, Zhi Ging! Are you summoning fire spirits now?" she shrieked, rubbing her arm while Ami frowned over at them.

Zhi Ging's mouth dropped open as she stared at the empty space between them. "I didn't summon anything! I never have."

"Even if you pass all twelve challenges, I'll make sure no one ever believes you did it without help," Iridill hissed, before darting past Ami to start her challenge.

Zhi Ging was still replaying Iridill's threat, when Ami's voice drifted over her.

"Miss Yeung? Zhi Ging, it's time for your challenge."

The entrance slid open, and she yelped. Five other Zhi Gings were staring back at her. Ami shimmered into view behind the figures and smiled at her shocked expression.

"To prove your skill of Perception, all you need to do is make it through the mirror maze. You'll need inward and outward Perception, a clear idea of how others truly see you." Ami pointed toward the top of the mirrors, her movements out of sync across the five reflections. "The name engraved there is that of the person whose Perception you need to understand. Only one reflection will show what they really think of you. The correct reflection will slide open to reveal the next set of mirrors in the maze but, if you choose the wrong one, the glass will shatter and your challenge comes to an end. The final few hexagons will reflect the person in question. These will be able to speak and answer questions, but you need to be very certain before you make each choice."

Ami pulled a slim hourglass from her robes and handed it to Zhi Ging. "Since you're the final Silhouette, there's no chance of anyone catching you. To make things fair, you need to make your way through the maze before this runs out. You can begin."

Zhi Ging spun back toward the glass. There, carved across the first set of mirrors, was a single name: Bucbou. While all five Zhi Gings had a similar frazzled look and windswept hair, only the reflection directly in front of her had seawater dripping from her cloak.

Bucbou has never seen me outside of training. Of course she'd imagine me as constantly soaked!

"Oh! I think I get it." She stepped into the hexagon, fingers stretching toward the drenched reflection. "How many hexagons are—"

A faint hiss echoed through the structure, and the door slid shut behind her, cutting her off from Ami. Zhi Ging gulped as light flickered at the base of the mirrors. At least she wouldn't be walking through the maze in darkness.

She pressed her palm against the glass, and her sodden reflection smiled, pulling the mirror aside to reveal the next hexagon. Behind her, the other reflections winked out, their mirrors transforming into rich green sheets of sea glass. Zhi Ging shuffled forward, unsettled by the thick silence that pressed in around her. It was like she'd gone back in time. Back to that last morning in Fei Chui, sneaking through the Glassmiths' workshop before dawn.

The name carved across the next set of mirrors was Jack. The six options lit up, and she squinted, waiting for her eyes to adjust.

"Well," she murmured, turning back toward the glass she'd just stepped through. "I know it can't be you. That would just bring me back to the start." The reflection stared impassively at her, offering no clues. Zhi Ging turned back to examine the other five. They all looked fairly alike, although some were slightly taller and one had a truly terrible haircut.

"It better not be you," she muttered, while the reflection

tried to fix its braid. "But how does Jack see *me*?" Zhi Ging inched closer, examining the next two mirrors. One was roughly the right height but refused to smile, and the other, when she peered closer, looked like it had decided to combine her features with Reishi's.

"Oh, I'm going to be so mad at him if it's you!" She snorted and, for a brief moment, forgot all about their argument. The next reflection looked exactly like her but was crouched in the corner of its mirror, staring listlessly down at the ground. That didn't seem quite right.

Zhi Ging turned to the last mirror and let out a small gasp. This reflection glowed, her smiling face illuminated by lantern light. Blue and green halos flared around her, their circles overlapping to create a rich jade. *Is this how the whole world looks through Jack's eyes?*

Zhi Ging reached toward the mirror, hesitated, then tapped a finger lightly against the surface. The reflection beamed, its reaction identical to the smile she'd worn while watching the floating market soar away. She paused before stepping into the next hexagon. It would have been nice to spend more time with Jack's old perception of her. It probably looked quite different now that they weren't talking.

Zhi Ging continued through the mirror maze, solving Mynah, Hiulam, Wusi, and Ai'Deng Bou's hexagons in no time at all. She faltered only when she reached Reishi's hexagon, flinching at the violent reflection snarling at her from the left. *Please don't let it be this one.*

Another reflection blinked at her, golden air rails

surrounding its body each time it closed its eyes. Did he only see her as a way to find the air rails? She turned to peer at the next reflection and stopped. This Zhi Ging flickered, ageshifting up and down between the ages of one and twelve. While the younger selves looked downcast, the oldest reflection had a new confidence about her, eyes filled with a fierce determination.

Is that really how I used to look when he visited Aapau? Zhi Ging wondered, as the reflection flashed back down to a lonely-looking six-year-old. This mirror seemed to make the most sense. Reishi had known her far longer than any of the others in the mirror maze, so of course his perception of her would have more layers. She crouched down, palm inches from the glass, and paused. The mirror had failed to seal properly after the last Silhouette and was already cracked open! Malo appeared in the hood of her once-again twelve-year-old reflection and flapped a wing urgently, signaling for her to peer through the gap. There were two voices coming from the next hexagon, and for a second, Zhi Ging wondered if it was Mynah using a clay voice box. As her eyes adjusted, she realized it was Iridill pleading with reflections of the Lead Glassmith. The Silhouette was hunched on the maze floor, shaking hands twisting through her long black hair.

"I could have passed on my own. Why didn't you let me try before hiring Jack?"

Cold laughter from five of the six reflections cut through the air. "Reishi would never have chosen you as

Silhouette without my intervention," one of the reflections barked. "Don't confuse yourself with your brother, there's *nothing* exceptional about you."

"Poor Favrile, he'll never be Lead Glassmith after those dragon burns. Four years on and he's still as bald as the night that lightning hit him," another reflection sniffed, dabbing his eyes while the other five glared at him.

"But I could take his place!" Iridill pleaded. "Just because the Lead Glassmith's usually the first son doesn't mean I couldn't do it. We don't need to hand the title over to another Glassmith." She stood up, hand clenched around her red Pan Chang. "If I come back as a Cyo B'Ahon, the others will have to accept me as the next Lead Glassmith."

The first reflection peered down his nose at his daughter, lip curling at the sight of her damp eyes. "You could never be a worthy replacement for your brother."

"You're the one who sent him away when his hair didn't grow back!" Iridill roared, rushing toward the glass. Her hands slammed hard against the surface, but rather than shattering, the mirror slid back to reveal the next hexagon.

It was the right reflection.

Zhi Ging sat in silence for a moment, her own heart thumping hard. Aapau had told her a few years ago that Iridill's brother was leaving Fei Chui, but she'd never known his own father had ordered it.

She caught her frown reflected in front of her and ran a hand along her own braid. In the Lead Glassmith's eyes, no hair would have been as bad as non-glowing hair. Without that halo of light, no Glassmith would ever work with you on the terraces. Not when it meant you'd both have less warning against a dragon attack. *No wonder Iridill panicked when I tried to tear her hair during that first challenge.*

Iridill had always teased her about how close she was with Aapau, but what if she'd been jealous? Aapau had never made Zhi Ging feel unwanted, despite her non-glowing hair, but the Lead Glassmith would have raised Iridill to believe acceptance was conditional, something given only to those who fit his idea of what was right.

How would that have felt for Iridill, seeing Zhi Ging wandering around Fei Chui with Aapau while her only brother had been banished beneath the cloud sea?

She glanced down at the hourglass clenched in her palm and scrambled up. Less than a fifth of the sand was left. Zhi Ging tapped against her ageshifting reflection and rushed into the next hexagon, head down as insults echoed over her. She flicked the nose of the same Lead Glassmith Iridill had chosen and stepped through as the glass once again slid open.

The base of the six mirrors flickered in the new hexagon, then dimmed, plunging her into darkness.

"Hello?" she called out, careful not to touch any of the glass. "Ami, I think one of the hexagons has stopped working." Zhi Ging strained her ears for a reply. Could the Dohrnii even hear her?

A faint glow appeared in the center of one of the mirrors, features twisting into view as it moved toward her.

Arms reached toward her through the glass, and Zhi Ging yelped, jumping backward.

"You!"

It was the same woman who had appeared in the flame in Sintou's office. The very same face that had seeped across the calligraphy on the paper dragon's sodden head.

"Why do you keep appearing everywhere?" Zhi Ging's voice cracked and she took another step back, until there was no space left between herself and the glass behind her. Would it count as failing if she was trying to escape?

The figure pressed both palms against the glass, and her fingers stretched out across the mirrors, interlocking behind Zhi Ging. Hundreds of gray-eyed thralls appeared behind her gleaming fingers, and Zhi Ging froze. *Is this the Fui Gwai?!*

Fear clawed at her throat, but when Zhi Ging tried to scream, all that came out was a dry rasp. She swung the hourglass in front of her, and the woman's features crackled. Just as quickly as she'd appeared, the apparition vanished, taking the thralls with her. Zhi Ging blinked hard in the sudden darkness, struggling to understand the final expression that had flickered across the woman's face. It had almost been *upset.*

The mirror to her left slammed open, and Zhi Ging jerked back, half expecting an attack of vicious thralls. Instead, it was Jack looking at her in concern.

"I heard you shouting, have you been stuck in here for long?"

Unable to find her words, Zhi Ging shook her head.

"Hey, look!" He pointed down at her hourglass before calling over his shoulder. "Ami, she's passed, there's still a few grains left."

Relief flooded through Zhi Ging, and she hurried out, then collapsed down onto the soft grass. She was never going to look in another mirror again!

The Dohrnii hurried forward, blue lenses glinting against the hourglass.

"I'm so sorry, Zhi Ging, that was my fault. A few of the other Silhouettes mentioned that hexagon seemed faulty, but I thought it would at least last until the end of your challenge. The Omophilli Matchmakers built it for me and I made sure to give them very clear instructions. I'll speak to them after today's Chau to find out what happened. Such a shame too." The Dohrnii shook her head. "I was hoping you'd all get to see how highly I think of you. A small bonus for making it through the mirror maze." She pointed toward the top of the mirrors, and Zhi Ging finally saw the name etched across the glass.

Ami.

Jack picked up the sparkling lantern, and Ami held out a hand, tapping her fingers against its surface.

"What do you say, Master Oltryds? I believe Zhi Ging has more than earned her place at the Perception Chau. I'd feel so bad if she had to miss out. I've planned a feast for everyone as well as a private tour of the city's spinning pagoda."

Zhi Ging sat up, disappointment curdling through the relief of passing another challenge. *I didn't know* that *was the Chau!* If she'd known there was a chance to see the other half of the paper-cutting pagoda, she'd have begged Reishi to double her detention instead. "Apart from those in the Matchmakers' Guild, no one has been allowed inside the pagoda since its creation. It'll be a truly incredible experience, both for the Silhouettes and an ancient Cyo B'Ahon like me." Ami glanced at Zhi Ging and smiled. "We're lucky Mynah's great-aunt is still Head of the Matchmakers. I couldn't have arranged this without her. What do you think, Jack—surely Zhi Ging shouldn't be the only one to miss out. This is the first challenge we've had all year where every Silhouette has passed."

Jack shifted uncomfortably and dropped his gaze.

"I'm really sorry, Ami, but I've already given Reishi my word. He made me promise that once Zhi Ging finished her challenge I'd bring her straight back for her final detention."

For one hopeful moment, Zhi Ging thought Ami would overrule him, but the Cyo B'Ahon simply sighed and shook her head.

"Of course, and I'm sure Zhi Ging won't take it personally." Jack flushed and his eyes darted toward her in worry. "Who knows," Ami continued, adjusting her glasses, "perhaps once Reishi's mood has improved I can arrange a second trip. It really is a shame for you to miss this Chau."

CHAPTER 38

Jack and Zhi Ging shared a single large hoop as they floated up from the mirror maze.

"I really am sorry you know. Not just about you missing out on the Chau but also because of, you know, the exams I've been taking." Jack peered at her from the corner of his eye.

Zhi Ging sighed.

"I know you didn't mean to hurt anyone, but what if there were others out there like me? What if someone had been relying on becoming Silhouette as their only way out of a terrible life. You stole their chance to escape when you took those entrance exams."

Jack winced and his eyes flashed frantically between green and blue. "You're right, I hadn't even thought about that. I'm really, *really* sorry. I was just so impatient to get my own tent." He flushed and turned away from Zhi Ging. "I don't know if you noticed, but not a single Silhouette ever has eyes that flicker like mine. Even traveling around with the floating market I've never seen anyone who looks like me."

Zhi Ging felt a sudden pang of sympathy. That was exactly how she'd felt in Fei Chui without glowing hair.

"Anyway, one day one of the stall owners mentioned a village high up in the silk province where everyone had eyes like mine. I begged Gertie to bring the floating market there next, but she refused. Apparently, that village doesn't allow any outsiders near—you can't even get to it on foot, they cut the rope bridges years ago. The only way to reach it now would be with a floating tent. If I had my own, the others would have to listen to me. Only tent owners get to choose where the market stops across the six provinces." He exhaled and his eyes stopped changing colors for a moment. "But I've decided to give the money back. A few more years of waiting won't kill me. There's only six Silhouettes left who I helped cheat. If I admit everything to Reishi, maybe he can go back to their villages and host another Silhouette entrance exam."

"Thanks, Jack, but . . ." Zhi Ging hesitated, Iridill's crouched shape in the maze flashing across her mind. "Maybe the ones who are still here do have at least *some* Cyo B'Ahon potential. Otherwise, they wouldn't have made it past their first challenge."

Jack stared down at the treetops shrinking beneath them, mulling the thought over.

"That's true. Then how should I explain it to Reishi?"

"I'm not sure yet, but we can try to think of something together. We've got the whole journey back, after all."

They sat in silence for a few minutes, then Jack nudged her gently on the shoulder.

"You see that path leading out of Omophilli?"

"Yeah?" Zhi Ging peered down, trying to work out what was special about the sand-covered path.

"Last time, when the floating market was passing by, I spotted a green stone trundling out of the city all by itself. I've kept an eye out for another one ever since."

"Wait—when did that happen, do you remember?"

What if it was the same stone Reishi followed? The stone that turned out to be Malo's shell.

"Oh easy, it was the last day of Omophilli's paper-cutting festival. That would have been the eighth of August."

"That's my birthday . . ." Zhi Ging peered back as Omophilli vanished behind them, sunset catching against the city walls. "How long," she began hesitantly, "do you think it would have taken a stone like that to reach one of the other provinces? The glass province, for example."

"Hmmm. It wasn't moving that quickly, I think it'd need at least two months—and that's only if it worked out a way to travel uphill."

Two months. That's exactly when Reishi spotted it at the province border!

"Whoa! What are you doing?" Jack yelped as Zhi Ging spun the hoop back to face the city.

"I think Reishi was right, Malo was always meant to

find me. Someone back in Omophilli sent him to me, as a birthday present." She frowned, red-tinted sunlight washing over them. "But who?"

"Maybe you need to bring him back to Omophilli to find out."

"How? Even though Ami's offered to take me, I don't know when that'll happen, if it ever does. What if I fail the next challenge first? If I have to take that memory elixir, I'll forget everything and stumble straight into someone who's seen the Lead Glassmith's warrant."

"Do you really think I'd let that happen?" Jack asked, his eyes wide. "You should have heard how much Gertie talked about you after you met, and this is someone who's rarely impressed! If you ever fail a challenge, you don't need to worry about the warrant. You could live with us in the floating market. I'll tell you everything you've forgotten, and we can use the Crease Cream to disguise you, say you're Gertie's cousin or something. Only if you want to, of course," he added quickly, his cheeks turning bright red.

"Are you serious? That would be incredible." Relief bubbled through Zhi Ging, and she realized with a start that it was the first time since Aapau had left that she felt completely safe. She turned to hug Jack, but the sudden movement spun their hoop in a circle, and they had to grip each other tightly as it twirled through the air.

"Tell you what," Jack continued, once they'd finished laughing, "the floating market is landing near Hok Woh in three nights' time. Your detention's over by then, so why don't you sneak out and I'll throw you your very own feast? Whatever the Silhouettes get tonight in Omophilli, I'll find a better version at the market stalls. I promise!" He leaned back and fumbled in his pocket before pulling out a miniature paint pot and a crumpled piece of paper.

Jack let a small amount of green ink pool on the scrap, then pressed Zhi Ging's right thumb into it. He winked, then kicked his foot up, dabbing her inky thumb against his shoe. Zhi Ging looked down and realized his entire right shoe was covered in vibrant patches of dye. In contrast, his left shoe had only one faint mark. Jack folded the paper back up, the puddle of ink tucked safely in its center, and pressed it into Zhi Ging's free hand.

"Once you get onto the stepping stones, wipe the rest of this ink over the tips of your shoes. You'll automatically start walking in my direction. It's much faster than using Gertie's card, and mine doesn't have a little face that'll squeak sales promotions at you every few minutes."

"I can't wait. Can I bring Malo too?"

Jack gasped theatrically. "Of course! I already have another bag of sunflower seeds waiting for him. He's the one I really want to hang out with anyway, you just happen to be his pet."

Zhi Ging snorted but her smile faded when she saw the junk rising toward them. She sighed, steeling herself for an evening of mindlessly scrubbing tanks.

One last detention, then life in Hok Woh would finally get back to normal.

CHAPTER 39

Zhi Ging pulled the last jellyfish tank toward her and stretched, cracking her neck from side to side. Malo chirped in sympathy and mimicked her movements.

"Hey," she whispered to Gahyau, "remember when I left Fei Chui to *escape* an eternity of scrubbing glass?"

The yellow jellyfish waggled his tentacles in encouragement and rolled into the final tank to help. His bubble squeaked as it rubbed against the glass, and Reishi looked up from his writing.

"Gahyau, I've told you Zhi Ging has to clean those on her own."

At that moment, a disheveled Ami burst into his lab, her normally pristine cloak covered in dirt.

"Reishi!" she howled, her voice raw and cracked. "Why isn't Gahyau in the walls, I've been trying to reach you. There's been another attack. I tried to stop it but . . ." Her voice dropped to a hoarse whisper. "The Fui Gwai. It's taken the Silhouettes."

Zhi Ging felt the blood drain from her face.

Reishi stumbled backward, ageshifting down as he steadied himself against one of the larger tanks.

"How many?" he demanded, his face ashen.

"All of them." Ami shook her head, tears filling her eyes. "I don't know how it happened, we were leaving the Chau and suddenly . . ." She shuddered and hugged her cloak tight around herself. "The spirit was there, an army of gray-eyed thralls behind it. I tried to stop it but—"

"I have to find them," Reishi croaked, calling Gahyau toward him. "I'm not losing more Silhouettes."

Zhi Ging felt fear crackle down her spine. Had the Fui Gwai already turned her friends into thralls? No one had ever worked out a way to reverse its possession.

"Let me help!" she said.

"No, it's not safe."

"There's one more thing," Ami whispered, pressing a shaking hand onto Zhi Ging's shoulder. "The Fui Gwai captured *successful* Silhouettes."

Reishi understood what this meant before Zhi Ging did. "None of them would have been given the memory elixir."

Zhi Ging's breath caught in her throat.

The Fui Gwai will know how to get into Hok Woh now. No Cyo B'Ahon is safe.

"Marzi sent a warning to all the other jellyfish," Ami

continued. "Only Gahyau was unaccounted for in the walls. The others are already hiding in the catacombs. Silhouettes aren't trusted with their location until after graduation, so we should be safe there if the Fui Gwai appears."

Reishi's eyes flickered between Zhi Ging and Ami. "Ami, take Zhi Ging to the catacombs. I'm going after the other Silhouettes." He hesitated and drummed his fingers against the crane embroidered across his chest. "If I'm not back by tomorrow morning, I want you to take her out of Hok Woh. I can't be responsible for more Silhouettes losing their—"

"I know," Ami whispered softly, a look of understanding passing between them.

Zhi Ging looked up at Reishi, desperately regretting how often they'd argued over the last month. "I'm sorry," she said, her voice breaking as Reishi turned toward her.

"You have nothing to be sorry about," he said sternly, and Zhi Ging could feel the protective force behind his words. "You were right, we should have tried to stop the spirit long ago, not waited until it attacked some of our own." Reishi took a step toward the door but paused. The Cyo B'Ahon frowned, then lifted Malo into Zhi Ging's arms.

"Keep her safe while I'm gone."

The duckling shook his feathers, the amber plume around his neck fanning out like a lion's mane.

Reishi nodded grimly at them, then darted from the room, Gahyau soaring after him.

"Come on," Ami urged, pushing Zhi Ging toward the door. "I don't know how much time we have."

THEIR FOOTSTEPS ECHOED DOWN THE EMPTY COR-ridors, and Zhi Ging had to race to keep up with the Dohrnii's anxious steps. Ami led her down an impossible number of twists and bends until they reached a large glass carving of a crane in flight. She pressed her hand against its beak, and its wings folded to reveal a hidden staircase. Zhi Ging gaped and stared back at the carving-filled corridor. *Is there a secret passageway behind each of them?*

They hurried down the steps, and Zhi Ging shivered when they emerged into the sudden cold of Hok Woh's catacombs. The glass corridor stretching out ahead of them was completely dark, with no jellyfish glowing in the walls. Zhi Ging hugged Malo close and took a tentative step forward, her foot vanishing into the deep shadows that lapped against the bottom of the stairwell.

"Quickly now," Ami whispered, pulling Zhi Ging along. Her voice became muffled and distant, swallowed by the thick darkness. "There's a hollow at the end of this tunnel where you can hide. No matter what sounds you hear, don't move from that space."

"Are you leaving me here by myself?" Zhi Ging squeaked, her words scrambling over each other in panic.

"I can't hear any of the other Cyo B'Ahon. Are they hiding in another tunnel?"

"I need to secure the main entrance once Reishi leaves." Ami's cloak rippled as she bent down beside Zhi Ging. "Wait here, I promise I'll be back soon."

She gripped Zhi Ging's arm in reassurance, but there was a nervous tremor in her fingers. Zhi Ging nodded mutely, relieved Ami couldn't see the fear in her face. Malo gave a feeble chirp, and the Cyo B'Ahon darted away from them, her footsteps obscured by the darkness.

TIME SEEMED TO STRETCH AROUND ZHI GING, AND the sound of her own ragged breathing filled the tunnel. *What if Ami doesn't come back?* Her heart drummed in her chest, and she sank to her knees. Would she even know if the Fui Gwai was stalking toward her right now, ready to turn her into a thrall?

She pressed a hand against the glass behind her, shuddering as the cold bled through her fingers. The water in the wall shifted, and she spun around, hoping to spot the familiar glow of a Cyo B'Ahon jellyfish, but there was nothing but darkness. Malo snuffled against her ankles, and there was a faint plink a few seconds later as his beak hit the far wall.

"Wait, come back! I'll never find you if you wander off in here." Zhi Ging scrambled after the noise, desperate not to lose him. She swept her arms out blindly until they brushed against his feathers. "Now's not the time to look for more sunflower seeds, okay?" she murmured, burying her head into his warm feathers. The duckling hiccupped and his body flared with light. Zhi Ging winced, spots dancing in front of her eyes. Before she could speak, Malo hiccupped again and the tunnel blazed into view. Zhi Ging clamped a hand over her mouth, desperate to stop the scream rising through her body.

There, submerged inside the tunnel's water-filled walls, were hundreds of lifeless, shadowy faces. Malo tumbled from her arms, still hiccupping wildly, and landed with a loud thud on the floor. The figures turned their heads toward the sound, and their eyes snapped opened in unison. Gray, pupilless eyes focused on Zhi Ging, and as one, the figures began to slam their fists against the wall. She yelped, stumbling backward as cracks spread across the inner glass, briny water oozing into the tunnel. *Fui Gwai thralls!*

The thralls snarled as bursts of light continued to spark across Malo's feathers and thin, needlelike tentacles shot out from their mouths. The duckling flapped his wings in panic and tugged on Zhi Ging's cloak. She grabbed him and began to sprint back toward the staircase, the gray-eyed faces twisting behind the hollow walls to follow her as she ran.

A panel shattered behind her, and a deafening roar filled the darkness as the water trapped between the glass walls surged out. Icy waves clawed against her legs, trying to drag her under. Zhi Ging flung herself up the steps, her feet slipping against the smooth glass. She shot through the crane door, but a hand clasped around her wrist as she tried to slam it shut. Zhi Ging jerked wildly but the hand dragged her steadily back toward the darkness. She howled and flung her free arm up, trying to grip the crane's neck. Her head twisted toward her captor, and in an instant, all thoughts vanished.

The gray-eyed figure clutching her arm was Pinderent.

CHAPTER 40

Jagged shards of glass floated above the rising water as Pinderent pulled Zhi Ging back down the tunnel. She choked and spluttered when the water reached her chin, but he showed no sign of stopping. Pinderent's face sank beneath its dark surface, his gray eyes shining up at her as Malo tugged frantically at her cloak, his entire body glowing as he struggled to keep her afloat.

"What's the meaning of this?" Ami's voice bellowed behind them. Zhi Ging felt a wave of relief rush through her.

Ami's back! Everything's going to be okay.

"She's no good to me if she drowns, you idiot," Ami snapped, tossing her glasses aside. Zhi Ging screamed in horror. Without her blue-tinted lenses, Ami's eyes were completely different. They were solid gray with thick, jagged seams of mercury seeping out from the pupil.

"Twelve years," Ami snarled. "Twelve years I've been looking for this girl and you almost *drown* her?" She pressed a finger against one of her jellyfish welts, and Pinderent's body jerked up, dragging Zhi Ging back toward the shallow water lapping against the staircase. More gray-eyed thralls appeared behind him, rising from the depths to form a barrier behind Zhi Ging. She whimpered, finally recognizing other faces around her.

They were all failed Silhouettes.

"Your mother thought she was so clever, spiriting you away from the pagoda all those years ago, but she should have known better than to try to cheat me. *I'm* the one who convinced her to create you. She never even realized I wasn't a real Matchmaker."

Zhi Ging staggered backward, hitting against Pinderent's cold body.

"What do you mean *created*?" she croaked, unable to take her eyes off the gray seeping out of Ami's pupils. "Why are you doing this? Are you working for the Fui Gwai?"

"Oh, you foolish, *foolish* girl. I *am* the Fui Gwai. Look around you." Ami flung her arms in a wide, sweeping circle over the thralls. "I've been collecting the unworthy from across Wengyuen for the past hundred years. None of the province rulers cared about possessions happening in distant villages. They never noticed how many thralls I had collected over the decades." Her jaw twitched. "I won't need these Silhouettes much longer though. Not now that I've convinced Sintou to Revert. Let's see the others scramble to defend Hok Woh without their precious ruler.

Once I take control of this realm, Wengyuen will finally learn how powerful a Cyo B'Ahon can be."

"But why do you need me?" Zhi Ging asked, her voice a hoarse whisper.

"I don't *need* anyone," Ami growled, her eyes flashing with a metallic glint. "That power was never yours to keep. Why couldn't you have failed your first challenge like you were supposed to? Do you have any idea how infuriating it's been, watching you scrape through each month? After you were banned from my Chau, I had to make sure you didn't make it back to Hok Woh at all. But you couldn't even stay quietly locked in the maze while the hourglass ran out, could you? At least your mother *intentionally* ruined my plan."

Zhi Ging's stomach tightened.

"But I thought you left me the weather wax, I thought you wanted to help me."

"Why would I ever help you?" Ami's face twisted in disgust as she snarled. "You should have been mine after that second challenge, when I summoned thralls to the storytelling Chau. But then that waste-of-a-welt thrall howled too early, spoiling what should have been a stealth attack." The Dohrnii's eyes narrowed and she stared hungrily at Zhi Ging. "No matter. Once I've drained your power I can finally connect the two halves of the pagoda and become truly immortal. Not this pathetic ageshifting version of immortality other Cyo B'Ahon are willing to accept."

"What power?"

Ami glanced at Zhi Ging's arms. Realization dawned on her, and she gripped her left arm reflexively. *The gold lines.*

Ami sneered at the shock on her face.

"You had spirit magic flowing in your veins, and you never even realized. Instead, you let it spill out uncontrolled, squandering some to create a pathetic Silhouette lantern from scraps and cheat your way through that first challenge. Thanks to me, you have more power than your mother, but it's still limited and you've been *wasting* it. No more. What's left of it is mine!"

Zhi Ging's mind flashed back to the first time the gold lines appeared. She had told herself she could do anything the Glassmiths could, and seconds later, for the first time in her life, her hair had glowed. The salamander-filled glove at Ai'Deng Bou's challenge had twisted in the air, defying physics seconds after she screamed she wouldn't fail. *Is that all it takes to release the power? I just have to say it out loud?*

"You can't have it!" she shouted. "Let me go and release the thralls!" Zhi Ging deflated as Ami began to laugh, the gray-eyed faces mirroring her amusement.

"Pathetic. You don't even know how to summon it. Let's have no more interruptions on the way back to Omophilli. You've already wasted enough of my time."

Pinderent gripped Zhi Ging's braid and pulled her head up toward Ami. Malo launched himself at Pinderent, but the thrall kicked him away easily. The duckling splashed into the water with a pained quack, and his left wing hung limply by his side.

"No!" Zhi Ging screamed, pushing against Pinderent with all her strength. Ami stepped over Malo, pulling a bottle of memory elixir from her cloak.

"I'll never understand why your mother wasted what must have been almost the last of her power creating *that,* the Matchmakers will never release her from the pagoda now. What protection was a duckling meant to be against me?"

Zhi Ging's eyes jerked down toward Malo, the realization knocking the breath from her lungs. Her mother had been the one to send Malo. Her mother was still alive!

Ami tipped the liquid into her palm, and it fell out in glistening beads. *No, not beads, something much worse.*

Zhi Ging thrashed against Pinderent's grip, cold fear slicing down her spine. They were miniature jellyfish from the Seoi Mou Pou, the starlight-filled room Ami had shown them on their first day.

"I did tell you once there were perks to being the Dohrnii." Ami smirked, stroking one of the gray jellyfish with her fingertip. "Most people only need to swallow one of these to fall under my control. Actually, I really should thank your friend Jack. He made my life a *lot* easier when he started taking the entrance exam for others. Each month he would unwittingly deliver guaranteed thralls straight to me."

"You have to let them go!"

"Enough," Ami hissed, her fingers curling around the jellyfish. Pinderent's other hand clenched around Zhi

Ging's jaw and yanked it open, forcing her to stop talking. "Did you ever stop to wonder *why* you're all called Silhouettes? Compared to us, you are nothing. Flat, unformed, as useless as every other mortal in Wengyuen. Now, let's see if you can mimic an actual silhouette, *seen but not heard*."

She plucked two jellyfish from her palm and glided toward Zhi Ging.

"One to remove your memories and another"—Ami brushed the jellyfish's tentacles against her arm, leaving a fresh welt—"to transform you into my final thrall. Don't worry, I won't keep you for long. Once the spirit magic's mine, I'll let you go. What's left of you at least."

Zhi Ging flailed against Pinderent's grip, but it was no use. She squeezed her eyes shut, tears racing down her face, and reached a desperate hand out toward Malo. It was her fault he'd been hurt.

Ami lowered the first jellyfish into Zhi Ging's mouth, and she jerked in pain, tentacles stinging as they coiled around her tongue. Toxic spasms shot through her as the tentacles stretched up, filling her mind with gray static.

Zhi Ging could feel her memories begin to leach away, familiar faces blurring into dull outlines. Soon there was nothing left but faint shadows of her time before Hok Woh. Her head lolled to the side, and she spotted a boy holding on to her braid.

Who is that?

He released his grip and her body crumpled forward, sinking beneath the icy black water. Zhi Ging's consciousness began to slip away, when the air above her flared. Noise flooded back into her world, and Zhi Ging became aware of heat bubbling through the dark waves. She broke through the water's surface with a ragged breath, the newly scorched air scalding her mouth. The jellyfish leaped out, its gray body boiling as it dove into the water. Ami stared at her in disbelief, the second jellyfish evaporating into waxy steam in her hand. Malo was blazing above them, a reverse silhouette formed of pure light. His wings and tail were wrapped in flames and fanned out around him like a fiery peacock.

No. The realization roared through Zhi Ging's body. *Like a phoenix.*

CHAPTER 41

Malo's wings crackled and lit the tunnel with gleaming light. He soared up, twisting his head from side to side, searching for the gray jellyfish. The air filled with thick steam when he dove beneath the surface, his fiery body transforming the dark water into a river of gold. He erupted out behind Zhi Ging, the escaping jellyfish clenched in his beak. Ami screamed and took a step forward, but he snapped it in half. The jellyfish's poison splattered against the water like burning oil, and Zhi Ging's memories were released. They billowed across the tunnel, hazy figures flickering through the steam as they raced back toward her.

Zhi Ging stumbled when she heard Aapau's voice echo around them. She looked up and saw the old healer speaking to an eight-year-old version of herself. The two figures were quickly replaced by another memory, moments from Fei Chui tumbling over one another with each flap of Malo's wings.

Suddenly a new image appeared, muffled and fainter than the rest. A woman with her back to Zhi Ging was frantically snipping small cuts into a folded piece of paper. She shook it open and the shape rippled out, transforming into a life-sized dragon.

"Get my daughter out of here," the woman urged the paper dragon. "Take her as far from Omophilli as you can. Hide her somewhere the Guild have no power."

The woman turned and Zhi Ging gasped, her eyes filling with tears.

It had been her mother all along. That was the face that had stared at her from the paper dragon head, the flame, and the mirror maze.

The realization sent shock waves through Zhi Ging. Her mother hadn't been summoning thralls in Ami's hexagon—by having them appear beneath the Cyo B'Ahon's name, she had been trying to warn her that Ami was the one controlling them! Her outstretched hands had been shielding Zhi Ging from the thralls, not trying to trap her.

She watched as her mother scrawled instructions across the paper dragon's talons, and her eyes flicked across the woman's arms. They were streaked with overlapping lines of gold, identical to her own.

Ami lied. The lines had never been something to be afraid of. They connected her to her family.

The Cyo B'Ahon snarled and stalked toward Zhi Ging, pushing Pinderent in front of her like a shield. His pupilless gray eyes narrowed, and his mouth opened in a wide grimace, the jellyfish wrapped around his tongue shooting tentacles forward. Zhi Ging felt her stomach twist. She'd never forgive Ami for what she'd done to her friend.

Malo swooped down and flapped his wings protectively in front of Zhi Ging. Flames roared out between his feathers, and Ami jerked back, smacking at a scorch mark on her sleeve.

"Do you really think that's enough to stop me?" She raised an eyebrow at the phoenix before turning to Zhi Ging. "Even if you get past a few thralls, the tunnel is filled with countless others. And, unlike you"—Ami tossed Pinderent aside, his body sinking into the dark water— "I don't care what happens to them."

Black ripples washed over her friend's face, and Zhi Ging lunged forward, struggling to make out his eyes. What if Ami had reversed his thrall possession? Pinderent could be about to drown! She jerked halfway through her leap and twisted up to see her cloak caught in Malo's talons.

"We can't leave him there!"

The phoenix shook his feathers and soared over the Cyo B'Ahon, then dropped Zhi Ging at the base of the stairs. He twisted in a tight circle, sending a wall of flames behind him, blocking Ami's path.

"I just told you I don't care about them," the Cyo B'Ahon sneered. She clamped her fingers against welts on both arms, summoning the linked jellyfish, and their thralls lurched forward. Zhi Ging scrambled backward, unable to look away from the possessed horde. She spotted

Mai Seon and Siwah advancing toward the flames. She felt a burst of bitter relief when she saw Pinderent rising back out of the water, his eyes still gray. This had to be why so many villages struggled against thralls. Those possessed still looked like family and friends. How could anyone fight them?

There was a shrill hiss as the first thrall stopped inches from the fire, and Ami howled, clutching at a welt that had begun to boil. The jellyfish leaped from the thrall's mouth, and the gray that had filled his eyes seeped down his face in thick waxy tendrils.

Zhi Ging gasped and tried to reach a hand toward him, but Malo screeched and tugged against her cloak, dragging her up the stairs. Ami roared and dug her fingers hard against the other welts, sending the thralls leaping through the flames. Pinderent's hand clamped around Zhi Ging's left wrist, dragging her from the steps. She tipped backward and flailed against the glass walls, her breath catching in her throat.

Suddenly, his grasp slipped and he fell backward, crashing through the thralls clambering up behind him. Two sand-colored scraps of fabric withered and turned gray in his hand. *Gertie's glove!* It had come loose, freeing her from his grip.

Zhi Ging sprinted up the rest of the stairs, darting through the door and slamming her hand hard against the crane's beak to seal it shut behind her. *That should buy a bit of ti—*

The glass shattered behind her, fragments flying across the floor as thralls poured through the crane's broken wings. Zhi Ging screamed and raced after Malo back along winding corridors toward the main entrance. Her cloth shoes skidded across the polished glass, and she smacked hard against the door. Malo flew in an anxious circle above her as she struggled to wrench it open. If she was caught now, it'd be so much worse than being spotted at the Lead Glassmith's door.

The floor shook as the thralls thundered into the circular hall, spilling out from every corridor, their unblinking gray eyes trained on her. Zhi Ging spun around, desperately looking for another way out. Could Sintou and the other Cyo B'Ahon hear this from the catacombs? What if Ami had already turned them into thralls too?

She slammed a fist against the glass and the double doors finally cracked open. Zhi Ging forced herself through the gap, before sprinting toward the staircase out of Hok Woh. Malo swooped low, fanning his tail across the steps behind her. They melted under the fiery heat, and the closest thralls howled as the stairs transformed into a river of molten glass. The phoenix unfolded his wings, and jagged barbs of glass fused together, stretching across the staircase to form a barricade against the thralls below.

"When did you learn to do that!?" Zhi Ging wheezed as Malo landed on her shoulder. His flames tickled harmlessly against her cheek.

Ami's voice growled below the entwined glass. "You really have no idea who you're dealing with." Her hand snaked up between the barbs and snapped a glass stalactite free. The Cyo B'Ahon twisted it expertly in her palm and stabbed the side of the briar-like barrier. A deep crack spread across the glass surface, and shards fractured to reveal Ami's snarling face.

Zhi Ging yelped and raced up the rest of the steps, then flung herself out of the hollow stepping stone. A heavy fog had smothered the sea, and she wasted precious seconds trying to spot the coastline through the thick haze. A wave crashed over the glass edge, icy seawater knocking her to her knees before thundering down the staircase. Zhi Ging twisted in time to see the fog swallow what was left of the swell.

Waves would know the way to shore no matter how heavy the fog got. She just had to follow them!

Cold laughter echoed up through the hollow glass, and Zhi Ging realized with a jolt that the rushing water had done nothing to stop Ami. The Cyo B'Ahon's face glistened with gray droplets, her mercury eyes never leaving Zhi Ging. She ageshifted rapidly, contorting her body to squeeze between what was left of the glass barricade, the stalactite clutched between her knuckles like a dagger.

Malo's wings blazed in warning, and he tugged on Zhi Ging's sleeves, desperate to pull them to safety. She leaped blindly into the fog and landed hard against the edge of the next stepping stone. The impact knocked the breath from her lungs, and her fingers scrambled to grip the slick glass. Malo had soared ahead, searing through the fog, and Zhi Ging glimpsed the village of Wun-Wun through the haze.

"Help!" Her voice cracked as another wave washed over her, the dark water pulling her down. The phoenix sped back, his tail hissing against the surface like a blazing comet. Malo grabbed Zhi Ging's hood between his talons and pulled her up, his wings crackling with heat. The water beneath them bubbled and evaporated around the hollow stepping stone.

Zhi Ging scrambled to her feet and turned back toward Wun-Wun and safety. The village had already begun to vanish back behind the thick fog. She hurried to the edge of the stepping stone, bent her knees, then hesitated. Malo pushed against her back, urging her to jump, but Zhi Ging shook her head and pulled him into a hug. She couldn't risk Ami turning everyone in Wun-Wun into thralls just to find her.

No. I have to stop Ami now.

Zhi Ging crouched down, staring hard at her reflection on the glass stepping stone, and an idea began to form.

CHAPTER 42

The muffled sound of water against wood rippled through the fog, and Zhi Ging flinched. Her arms had already begun to shake, but she'd hoped to be much farther ahead before Ami found them.

"Nice try, Zhi Ging," the Cyo B'Ahon's disembodied voice echoed behind her. "But you seem to have forgotten you're just a Silhouette. Any Cyo B'Ahon could have seen through your pathetic escape plan. Did you really think I wouldn't notice the silk dragon boat missing from its stepping stone?" Her voice turned bitter as her own dragon boat crept forward, searching for Zhi Ging's. "How *dare* you waste more of my time? Just give up. All I have to do is track you through the fog. It's easy to disrupt the mist, but impossible to smooth it back after you've sailed through."

Zhi Ging felt Malo shudder under her arm, and she winced as the silk fluttered up, sending swirls of fog billowing around them. She couldn't let Ami spot them yet.

She gave him a quick reassuring squeeze, worried to even whisper when Ami was this close. Malo's eyes were wide with panic, but he seemed to understand.

They glided forward across the water's surface, Zhi Ging desperately trying to calm the heartbeat thundering in her ears. The last thing she needed now was to miss the warning splash of Ami's boat creeping closer. The dark water swirled beneath her, rising as new waves hit against the current. What was causing that?

Zhi Ging twisted around and swallowed a scream. The snout of the porcelain dragon had reared up out of the heavy fog, inches away from her. Ami was still a blurred shadow at the back of the boat, but Zhi Ging could feel the Cyo B'Ahon's eyes snap toward her.

"There you are," Ami hissed, the glass stalactite still clenched in her fist. "Didn't you learn anything from your race? The silk dragon is useless without a strong wind."

"Just release the thralls," Zhi Ging whimpered, her voice barely audible through the fog. "Please, I'll come to Omophilli with you if you do. I'll even try to give you my power."

"Are you attempting to make a deal?" Ami cackled, leaping into the center of her boat. "Why would I ever settle for anything less than everything I'm owed? Oh, let me guess"—she sneered, spotting Zhi Ging's shadow inching backward—"you still think you can escape. Well, your attempts to stall me won't work, I—Zhi Ging, look at me when I'm speaking to you!"

Zhi Ging ignored Ami, her eyes trained on the now churning currents around them. *Almost there.*

The Cyo B'Ahon roared, clambering onto the porcelain dragon head as it picked up speed, racing toward Zhi Ging's retreating outline.

"I hold your life in my hands and you dare ignore me? You're more of a fool than your mother!" The Cyo B'Ahon's eyes widened, and she gazed in shock as Zhi Ging finally came into focus.

The Silhouette was floating above the water's surface, both hands raised up into the fog.

There was no dragon boat in sight.

"Where's the silk dragon boat?" Ami hissed, color draining from her face. Her foot slipped as the porcelain dragon jerked forward sharply, caught by a new current.

Zhi Ging met her gaze, grim determination etched across her face. "I never took the boat. All I needed was *this*."

The air above Zhi Ging erupted into flames, billowing fabric ablaze in a halo of light. Malo appeared from his hiding place beneath the silk, his outstretched wings burning through what had been the dragon head. Stray threads glittered down over Zhi Ging, transforming her into a silhouette of gleaming golden lines. Her right arm was wrapped tight around the phoenix's body, while her left held on to the silk that had carefully concealed his glow.

"The boat's still back in its stepping stone. If you'd

looked closer, you'd have seen that all I took was the silk dragon head."

"So what," Ami snarled. "You can't stay floating forever! Whereas I have all the time in the—" Ami's snarl twisted into a scream as the porcelain dragon spun wildly beneath her. Malo's tail fanned out behind Zhi Ging, fog evaporating to reveal the dark water around them.

They were at the edge of the underwater waterfall.

Wood splintered along the length of Ami's boat, and the oar shook wildly, unable to handle the force of the roiling currents. The heavy porcelain head tipped toward the thundering rapids, and Ami howled, kicking against the churning water. The Cyo B'Ahon ageshifted rapidly, and Zhi Ging's stomach twisted when Ami flickered back to twelve. They really did look alike at that age.

Zhi Ging urged Malo forward, and she reached a hand down toward the Cyo B'Ahon. She had only ever wanted to scare Ami into surrendering; she hadn't planned for her to actually drown. Her fingers grazed against the water's surface, and Zhi Ging gasped as the current jerked her roughly toward the overhang. The current was even stronger than she had realized. There might be only seconds left before Ami was dragged into the heart of the underwater waterfall, leaving her friends trapped as thralls forever.

"How do I reverse the possession?" Zhi Ging screamed as the porcelain head shattered, white fragments vanishing into the tumbling rapids. "You said yourself you don't need the Silhouettes anymore! Tell us how to release the thralls. If you do, maybe Sintou will forgive you."

Ami's eye darkened and she ageshifted back up, flinging the jagged stalactite into the waterfall.

"And why would I do that? Caring too much about non-Cyo B'Ahon is the reason Sintou isn't fit to be Head of Hok Woh. The six provinces should be ruled with fear, not respect. They're useless as anything other than thralls, just as you're useless without—"

Zhi Ging yelped as Ami leaped up, using the last of the porcelain to push herself out of the water. The Cyo B'Ahon's hands snatched at her cloak, and Zhi Ging jerked down toward the underwater waterfall. Malo screeched above them and beat his fiery wings against Ami's bare arms, but she didn't seem to notice.

"Let them stay thralls," she hissed before releasing Zhi Ging.

Ami dropped back toward the surface, Zhi Ging's white Pan Chang Knot clutched tight between her hands. She smirked up at them, no trace of fear on her face as a wave crashed over her, pulling her body under. The Cyo B'Ahon's white robes became indistinguishable from the churning sea foam, and she vanished into the depths of the waterfall.

Zhi Ging stared down at the thundering water in shock, a shaking hand on the torn patch on her cloak. Malo flared above her, light pressing through the ocean surface into its depths, but there was no sign of the Cyo B'Ahon.

"I'll find a way to free them," Zhi Ging whispered, her promise swallowed by the currents. The fog crept back across the water's surface, and soon the underwater waterfall once again vanished from sight.

Hidden, but still dangerous.

CHAPTER 43

Sintou and Zhi Ging stood in the center of the hall, watching Cyo B'Ahon stream past in pairs, carrying stretchers filled with former Silhouettes between them. Gray eyes stared blankly up at the domed ceiling, the thralls no longer able to walk or even stand.

"There must be almost a hundred of them," Zhi Ging whispered, watching the unending rush of Silhouettes being ferried toward the sick bay. Several of the tutors had ageshifted down in horror when they first stepped into the tunnel, coming face-to-face with students they had failed decades earlier.

"Something isn't right," Sintou muttered, her eyes narrowing as more Cyo B'Ahon hurried back toward the tunnel, empty stretchers rattling between their arms. "Possessions are complex and varied, but one central rule governs them all; they only last as long as the possessor is alive."

"Does this mean Ami survived the underwater water-fall?" Zhi Ging's hand shot toward her hood, fingers brushing anxiously against Malo's feathers. His feathers had lost their fiery length when they slid down the melted steps back toward Hok Woh. The last thing Malo had done before collapsing was flare one final time, the strength of the light drawing the Cyo B'Ahon back out of the real catacombs.

"Not necessarily." Sintou paused, lowering her voice. "The level of possession, not to mention the sheer complexity of concealing thralls across Wengyuen . . ."

Zhi Ging tensed, an uncomfortable realization prickling down her neck. She finished the Cyo B'Ahon's sentence. "Ami might not have been working alone."

"Exactly. Although, we would also be fools to underestimate her again. We can't dismiss the idea that this was the work of a particularly single-minded Cyo B'Ahon. We've trapped Marzi, her jellyfish, in an opaque tank just in case he tries to spy on us through the walls."

They stepped aside for a pair of ashen-faced Cyo B'Ahon carrying a Silhouette between them. Under his black cloak, the Silhouette's clothes were strangely dated, the embroidery style not seen for at least eighty years. Zhi Ging shuddered as they passed. Had he been trapped as a thrall all that time? "What's going to happen to the Silhouettes in the sick bay?"

"I suspect Wusi will try a number of elixirs. Possessions

can be extremely difficult to end, with some fighting against each new cure until they're finally lifted by the original possessor. Unfortunately, I don't think it'll be as simple as removing the jellyfish from their mouths—although that will be the first step tonight."

Malo hiccupped in his sleep, a burst of light flaring out from Zhi Ging's hood.

"Phoenix fire!" she cried, her heart racing. "One of the thrall's eyes lost their gray when he came right up to the flame. Maybe if Malo could transform again . . ." She trailed off as Sintou lifted him out of her hood.

"So that's why the fire in my office took such a shine to him," Sintou murmured, stroking his feathers in amazement. Malo snuffled in his sleep and brushed his cheek against her palm. "The fire used to burn down the original Hok Woh was also phoenix fire."

Zhi Ging felt her jaw drop open in shock.

"Hoi Leung," Sintou called, gesturing at a Cyo B'Ahon with an empty stretcher tucked under her arm. "Bring six of the gray-eyed Silhouettes to my office. I want to see if the fire can help remove their possession, even if only temporarily."

The Cyo B'Ahon nodded and ageshifted down, hurrying toward the others emerging from the corridor with filled stretchers. Zhi Ging itched to follow them, desperate to know if the fire could help her friends.

"Sintou, do you have a moment?" Yingzi shimmered

into view beside them, a long scroll trailing along the floor behind her. "We've accounted for at least seventy failed Silhouettes from Wengyuen's more isolated villages. Ami knew what she was doing. A lot of these areas aren't even included on Scout routes anymore—the same routes she, as Dohrnii, would have updated. Their families never even had a chance to tell us their children were missing." The Cyo B'Ahon's metallic leg tapped against the floor. "There's something else. The Silhouettes who just completed my Concealment lessons still haven't been found. No one knows what happened to them after the Omophilli challenge."

Zhi Ging froze.

Mynah!

Where had Ami hidden her newest thralls? They could be anywhere across the six provinces.

"Reishi and Gahyau left to look for them," Zhi Ging interrupted. "He left as soon as Ami told him about the attack . . ." She trailed off as Sintou and Yingzi exchanged a panicked look.

"He may have walked straight into a trap," Yingzi hissed, ageshifting down in alarm. "If he took Gahyau with him, there's no way for us to reach him."

Sintou frowned, her eyebrows vanishing beneath the heavy folds of her forehead. "I never should have allowed Gahyau to join him on Scouting trips, even hidden inside that silk pouch. Why didn't I ever consider what would happen if his only link to Hok Woh was trapped too?"

"Why would you?" Yingzi murmured. "Who, apart from another Cyo B'Ahon, would have planned for a jellyfish capture?"

Sintou glanced toward Zhi Ging, and her frown deepened.

"Excuse us a moment, Yingzi." The Head of the Cyo B'Ahon led Zhi Ging toward Hok Woh's entrance and crouched down, knees clicking until they were eye to eye.

"I promised you would be under Cyo B'Ahon protection during your time in Hok Woh but I've failed you. Let me send a message to Aapau, she can collect you in the roaming pagoda. You can't be the only Silhouette in the dorms. I've already told all Scouts to halt their exams until we've found a way to lift the possession. No other family in Wengyuen should entrust us with their child until we do. For your own safety, I think it's best for you to stay away from Hok Woh until we know more about what Ami had planned."

Zhi Ging looked up at Sintou's expectant expression and grimaced, struggling to understand her own hesitation. *Isn't this what I wanted? A chance to see Aapau again?*

Her stomach tightened as Pinderent was whisked past, his unblinking eyes staring at her without recognition. Because of her, there was now no way to question Ami about the possessions.

"Let me try to find Reishi," she hurried on before Sintou could protest. "I can't help the Silhouettes if I stay here, or if I join Aapau, but maybe I can at least help

Reishi. I don't know what sort of trap Ami might have set, but if he's being held by her newest thralls maybe, with Malo's help, I can help him escape *and* burn away their possession. Even if phoenix fire only lifts it for a bit, I could use that time to bring the missing Silhouettes back to Hok Woh's sick bay."

Sintou considered her, concern twitching at the center of her cheek. "Aapau's roaming pagoda really would be much safer. Ami chose to spend twelve years searching for you because you're a descendant of Ling Geng, the girl cursed with the ability to create reality from paper cuttings. If others realize who you are, Ami won't be the only one who tries to take your power. Your mother wanted to keep you from her fate, a lifetime trapped in the Omophilli pagoda—"

"But you're just asking me to stay in the Fei Chui half instead! They're the same tower, you said so yourself."

Sintou closed her eyes, lost in thought. "I really have failed you all. I've spent the decades since Hok Woh burned keeping myself separate. Despite Reishi's encouragement, I refused to get to know Cyo B'Ahon outside my inner circle. So now, I have no idea who I can trust in Hok Woh." She glanced back toward the hall and lowered her voice. "Any one of the Cyo B'Ahon now helping to carry Silhouettes could have colluded with Ami. This is far more responsibility than anyone your age should ever be asked to shoulder, but I'm afraid you're the only one I can trust to find Reishi and the Silhouettes." The Head of the Cyo B'Ahon placed her hand into the nearby basin. "But I won't send you alone. Even the Second Silhouette can use some help."

The water behind the glass walls rippled, and a colossal jellyfish waded toward them. Zhi Ging's mouth dropped open. It was Pou Pou, the jellyfish Silhouettes fed snacks to in the dining hall. *Has he been Sintou's all along?*

The Head of the Cyo B'Ahon chuckled at her shocked expression and raised a palm, silver scars dancing between her purple burns. "No Silhouette ever seems to wonder who Pou Pou belongs to. I must admit, it's quite nice to hear the constant chatter of the dining hall through him. The rumors you Silhouettes dream up are always particularly entertaining."

Pou Pou waved his tentacles at Zhi Ging and pointed toward a glass panel beside the entrance. She pulled it down in a daze, watching the jellyfish squeeze through and float out toward them in a bubble twice the size of her head.

"Gahyau may have been the first jellyfish to learn that particular trick," Sintou said with a proud smile, "but Pou Pou is an exceptionally good mimic."

The Head of the Cyo B'Ahon lowered Malo back into Zhi Ging's hood and placed a hand on her shoulder.

"You need to be careful out there; Pou Pou and Malo can only protect you so much. If Ami was working with someone, whether shoreside or here in Hok Woh, you can be sure they are just as dangerous as her. If, for any reason, you need help, you can always use the post pipe."

Zhi Ging jerked back, convinced she must have misheard. "What does the post pipe have to do with anything?"

"There are a number of jellyfish hidden inside it. They're used by Scouts to send messages back to Hok Woh. Those jellyfish can also help Scouts who suddenly find themselves in danger." She grimaced. "Unfortunately, I can tell you with certainty they can be relied upon in a fight. If you find yourself in a similar situation, Pou Pou will soar toward the closest post pipe hatch and release the others. I hope you won't need them."

"Can you . . ." Zhi Ging stopped, trying to steady her voice. "Can you send a message to Aapau anyway? I need you to warn her that she might not be safe in the roaming pagoda anymore. If Ami did survive, she might try to find another way to connect the two halves."

"Of course. If she wants, I can place her in one of our havens. One of our most trusted allies will be arriving nearby in two days' time. Aapau would be safe with her, she's taken incredible care of the last Cyo B'Ahon who Reverted."

"Thank you," Zhi Ging croaked, turning toward the melted staircase. Someone had stacked upside-down tanks along the slope, creating new temporary steps.

"Best of skill, Second Silhouette. You'd better leave

while the Cyo B'Ahon are still distracted with the stretchers." Sintou gripped Zhi Ging's hands tight between her own, dropping a new golden Pan Chang Knot into her palm. "There's a hollow glass bead woven into the center of this knot. If you need to pass through areas that aren't as welcoming of Cyo B'Ahon, Pou Pou can squeeze himself into the hollow. Keep him hidden and yourself safe."

Zhi Ging gulped and forced herself to smile at the Cyo B'Ahon as she stepped through the door.

"Next time I'm here, I'll have Reishi and the Silhouettes with me," she promised, hoping her words sounded more believable to Sintou's ears than they did to her own. The Head of the Cyo B'Ahon bowed, and Hok Woh's glass entrance closed between them.

EARLY SUNLIGHT HAD BURNED THROUGH THE FOG by the time Zhi Ging clambered back out of the entrance stepping stone. Pou Pou floated above her shoulder, and against the rippling waves, their shadows looked identical to Reishi's and Gahyau's.

Zhi Ging smiled down at the likeness, the new gold Pan Chang shimmering against her cloak. If a Scout could find multiple Silhouettes, maybe a Silhouette could find a single Scout.

In the distance, the village of Wun-Wun had begun to wake. Figures appeared from the wooden houses, unaware of just how close they had come to becoming thralls.

Zhi Ging turned to check on Malo, who was still snoring in her hood.

"Let's find Reishi, then find you the biggest bag of sunflower seeds in all of Wengyuen."

The phoenix snuffled in his sleep and rolled over, purple chest feathers catching against the light. Zhi Ging took a deep breath and leaped between the stepping stones, her own silhouette illuminated against the dawn as she raced toward the shore.

AUTHOR'S NOTE

Throughout this book, I've hidden little plot and personality clues in people's names that curious readers can uncover by sifting through ~~poor~~ creatively phonetic spelling and decrypting Irish-tinged Cantonese. Now that you've finished reading, it's only fair for me to share some of these clues. Others will stay a mystery until the next book.

FEI CHUI

All Glassmiths are named after styles of glass art or famous glassmakers.

Aapau—Cantonese: Granny (阿婆).

Favrile—A type of iridescent art glass developed by Louis Comfort Tiffany.

Fei Chui—Cantonese: Jade (翡翠).

Iridill—Pressed glass that has an iridescent surface added to it. Also known as Poor Man's Tiffany.

Murrine—A type of glass art where the colorful pattern/image is only revealed when the glass (usually in a rod) in sliced into cross-sections.

Yeung Zhi Ging—Cantonese: Bauhinia flower (洋紫荊).

This is the flower found on the Hong Kong flag. The character for Yeung (洋) also means foreign. In Cantonese, your surname comes before your first name. Depending on which province they're from, this will also be the case for certain Silhouettes and Cyo B'Ahon.

FLOATING MARKET/SHORESIDE

Jack Oltryds—Distorted spelling: Jack of All Trades.

HOK WOH AND CYO B'AHON

Ai'Deng Bou—Distorted Cantonese homage to David Attenborough (艾登堡).

Amigda Lin—Distorted spelling: Amygdalin.

A chemical compound found in bitter almonds. Absorbing amygdalin can lead to cyanide poisoning.

Baak Lok—Cantonese: Talent scout (伯樂).

B'ei Gun—Cantonese: Pessimistic (悲觀).

Bucbou—Cantonese: Waterfall (瀑布).

Cing Yau—Coming from the porcelain province, she's named after the Cantonese word for "celadon" (青釉), a classic style of ceramic glaze. However, because Cantonese is *brilliant* for homophones, her name could also be misheard as "pale weasel" (青鼬).

Cyo B'Ahon—When I'm in Hong Kong, most people call me by my Cantonese name (舒雲 / Syu Wun). My cousin once asked to see how my Irish name was written, and her pronunciation of it was just so incredibly creative that, to me, my name suddenly sounded like two distinct words in a secret code. I held on to that pronunciation for over twenty years, trying to find something equally bizarre and surreal to assign it to.

Since moving to the UK, I've met *many* people who seem to prefer my cousin's pronunciation!

Dragon Boat Teams—Each of the teams is named after the main export of their province:

1. Syun Zi—Cantonese: Writing Paper (宣紙).

2. Tsadeu—Cantonese: Carved Lacquer (漆雕).

3. Wong Gam—Cantonese: Gold (黃金).

4. Si Cau—Cantonese: Silk Cloth (絲綢).

5. Chi Hei—Cantonese: Porcelain (瓷器).

6. Bolei—Cantonese: Glass (玻璃).

Dohrnii—A (real!) species of biologically immortal jellyfish.

Fui Gwai—Cantonese: Gray spirit (灰鬼).

Gahyau—Cantonese: A term of encouragement (加油).

Gu Sao—Cantonese: Drummer (鼓手).

Gwong—Cantonese: Light (光).

Heisiu—Cantonese: To laugh (嬉笑).

There's a reason why he's the jellyfish of Wusi, the Cyo B'Ahon healer . . . laughter is the best medicine (sorry to anyone who just eye-rolled).

Hok Woh—Cantonese: Crane's nest (鶴窩).

The Cyo B'Ahon motto, Hok Laap Gai Kwan (鶴立雞群), is a genuine idiom. It really does mean "a crane in a flock of chickens." It really is VERY smug.

K'Ah Pinderent—Distorted spelling: Carpenter ant.

These ants can be infected by a fungus that takes over and controls the ant's movements. Look up ophiocordyceps unilateralis; it's terrifying.

Kaolin—Also coming from the porcelain province, he's named after the soft white clay used to create porcelain.

Mai Seon—Cantonese: Superstition (迷信).

Malo—Cantonese: Agate (瑪瑙).

Agate is a rock filled with colorful crystals, like a geode. In my head his name also reminds me of the "mallow" in "marshmallow," another snack I'm sure he'd love. For anyone curious about Malo's colorful feathers, he's based on a Mandarin duck.

Marzi—Shortened version of Marzipan.

Marzipan is made from almonds. As is cyanide (See *Ami*).

Mynah—Distorted spelling: Myna.

Incredible mimic birds.

Pou Pou—Cantonese: Bubbles (泡泡).

Reishi—A type of mushroom people used to believe could grant immortality.

Seoi Mou Pou—Cantonese: Jellyfish nursery (水母圃).

This is actually a terrible pun combining two separate words and I hope I'll be forgiven: (Seoi Mou—水母) Jellyfish and (Miu Pou—苗圃) Plant nursery.

Sintou—Cantonese: Peaches of immortality (仙桃).

This idea comes from Chinese mythology. Peaches symbolize immortality in art and are often given as a gift symbolizing a long and healthy life.

Syut Seng—Cantonese: Snow sound (雪聲).

Wun Hong Choi—Cantonese: Cloud iridescence (雲虹彩).

When the sun or moon is in just the right position, it can spark an optical illusion that fills a cloud with rainbow light. Look up *cloud iridescence* for some amazing photos of this.

Yingzi—Cantonese: Shadow (影子).

ACKNOWLEDGMENTS

Unlike most debut authors, I had a massive advantage going into my initial querying. Years watching from the other side meant I already knew Gemma Cooper was the greatest champion of an agent anyone could hope for! Gemma, thank you for taking a massive chance on me and helping to detangle Zhi Ging's world so it actually made sense (and for not batting an eye when I added a floating jellyfish to my first rewrite). Thank you for seeing what Zhi Ging's story could be before I ever did and, most importantly, for not throwing away your laptop when I sent over my millionth terrible title suggestion!

Thank you to all the team at Hachette Children's Books, in particular my incredible editors Nazima Abdillahi and Rachel Wade. I'm forever in awe of how you both seemed to magically teleport into my mind and immediately *get* Zhi Ging's story. The enthusiasm and time you put into every single email, meeting, and manuscript note has brought so much extra wonder to this book. Thank you also to the entire rights team, who went above and beyond to help get this book out there and achieved so much before it was ever even published.

Thank you to everyone at Delacorte Press, especially the brilliant Kelsey Horton. You have such a stellar editorial eye for spotting where to up the excitement and draw the reader in closer. Thank you also for having an almost magical ability of sending me exciting, week-making news just as I need it. I also need to say a huge thank you to Nichole Cousins: your enthusiasm and passion for Zhi Ging's story mean the world to me.

Thank you to my extraordinary cover illustrators, Yuzhen Cai and Vivienne To. The UK and US covers absolutely took my breath away. The days I first saw them will forever be some of the best I've had in publishing. I hope my writing lives up to the magic you've both captured in your artwork. To my art directors at both Hachette and Delacorte: These covers wouldn't have been possible without your seriously cinematic direction. Thank you for finding me my dream illustrators.

Thank you to Helen Scanlon, my oldest friend and the only non-McDermott I trusted to read an early version of this story. Thank you for lugging a two-hundred-plus-page printout to and from your office for weeks and *thank you* for having the bravery and honesty to tell me which parts you didn't like (none of them made it into the final book, so the world's missing out on you as an editor!). We have near-identical taste in books, and you are responsible for introducing me to almost all of my favorite authors. After my family, you were the first person I called after I got my book deal. I wouldn't be the reader, or writer, I am without you.

Thank you to Bridget Cullen, Helen's mother, who kept a cupboard stocked with crisps for me for over a decade and made me cry when she mailed me a handmade blanket made up of fifty-five individually crocheted patches to celebrate my book deal with Hachette. The center Irish patch is my favorite!

I never would have even attempted writing this book without the early support of two teachers: Ms. Monaghan at St. Mary's & St. Gerard's National School and Ms. Goodbody at Holy Child Killiney. I wish all teachers prioritized fiction reading and creative writing as much as you both did. Thank you for helping me discover that there can be just as much enjoyment in writing as there is in reading.

Thank you to Aisling Chambers: You and Taylor Swift have the joint honor of being my constant soundtrack through every version of this book. Your thirty-minute voice notes are proof that you are, and forever will be, a better storyteller than me. The glasswork in this book wouldn't exist if you hadn't indulged me in my repeat trips to Casa Lis while we were in Salamanca. I can't wait until we finally live on the same continent again—to think we once thought Wicklow to Dublin was bad!

Thank you to Emma Wray and Kate Griffiths, truly the world's greatest hypewomen and all-around enablers.

Thank you, thank you, thank you for being the most generous, supportive friends anyone could ask for. From sitting with me in an empty Hampstead Heath in honor of my lockdown-thirtieth to organizing not one but *two* surprise parties to celebrate my book deals, you two are the reason for all my best London memories.

Thank you to my cousin 鄭欣欣 for bringing me to all the best themed cafes in Hong Kong each summer and for single-handedly organizing the perfect trip around Taiwan. The cloud sea beneath Fei Chui only came about because of our visit to Jiufen.

Thank you to James Knight: I know you weren't expecting a slanket-wearing, deadline-racing rewrite gremlin when you asked me to move in. Without you taking on as much as you did over the last year, I couldn't have vanished into Zhi Ging's world as often as I did. Thank you. You are my favorite.

To my parents: thank you for raising a reader. Every single one of the 80,000 words in this book have their roots in the countless stories, both Cantonese and English, you shared with me growing up. Dad, thank you for always encouraging my writing, from surprising me with a professionally bound version of my Write-a-Book story when I was twelve to listening to my ideas while walking up that hill in Terracina. The reason Zhi Ging's story is my debut book is because of you—you were the one who told me she was my best idea. Mum, any creativity I have comes from you. All my favorite moments in this book pale in comparison to the actual childhood I got to enjoy in Hong Kong because of you. And thank you for letting me bring your own childhood into this book; Malo only exists because of stories you shared about your own noodle-eating pet duckling.

Thank you to Ciara: I hope you don't mind that I've hoarded so many half-remembered facts from your actually impressive degree in human genetics and transformed them into popcorn sheep and temperature control valves on dragons' talons. This is probably the only fiction book you'll agree to read all year, so thank you! P.S.—sorry I stole your Cantonese name for a character, then made her fail her final Silhouette challenge.

Blathnaid, this book is for you. From sketching out a squiggly world map together in Enniskerry to spamming you with screenshots over lockdown, you are the one I instinctively share every new idea with. Thank you for being my biggest cheerleader every step of the way and enduring multiple voice notes, especially when most of them involve extensive side tangents and nonsensical thinking out loud. Finally, thank you for being the very first person in the entire world to pre-order this book, *eight months* before it was even published! . . . I hope you don't want your money back.

ABOUT THE AUTHOR

SIOBHAN MCDERMOTT was born in Hong Kong and grew up on a steady stream of stories filled with Chinese legends and Irish folklore. She now lives in the UK and continues to order dim sum in Cantonese tinged with a distinctly Irish lilt. *Paper Dragons: The Fight for the Hidden Realm* is her debut novel and was inspired by moments across her life: from childhood ferry trips between Lantau Island and Hong Kong, to traveling around Taiwan, Italy, and Spain.

Helen Scanlon

3/24